i

Signals from a Lampless Beacon:

Their Burdens Lifted

Paul Traywick

iUniverse, Inc.
New York Bloomington

Signals from a Lampless Beacon:
Their Burdens Lifted

Copyright © 2010 Paul Traywick

This is a work of fiction. All of the characters, names, incidents,
organizations, and dialogue in this novel are either the products
of the author's imagination or are used fictitiously.

iUniverse books may be ordered through booksellers or by contacting:

iUniverse
1663 Liberty Drive
Bloomington, IN 47403
www.iuniverse.com
1-800-Authors (1-800-288-4677)

Because of the dynamic nature of the Internet, any Web addresses or
links contained in this book may have changed since publication and
may no longer be valid. The views expressed in this work are solely those
of the author and do not necessarily reflect the views of the publisher,
and the publisher hereby disclaims any responsibility for them.

ISBN: 978-1-4502-2466-6 (pbk)
ISBN: 978-1-4502-2467-3 (ebk)

Printed in the United States of America

iUniverse rev. date: 05/20/2010

"…Now *it is* high time to awake out of sleep…. The night is far spent, the day is at hand…."

Letter from the Apostle Paul to the Church in Rome: From Chapter XIII (AV)

To Eliza, Charles, David, and with particular gratitude to Benjamin

I

"I am the gloaming shadow—widowed—the unconsoled,
The Aquitaine Prince with his tower in ruin.
My one star has died; my star-fretted lute
Wears the sorrow-dark sun for funeral-blacks."

> Gérard de Nerval: "*El Desdichado,*" ll. 1-4 (tr. PT)

"O World, I cannot get thee close enough...!"

"Long have I known a glory in it all
But never knew I this."

> Edna St. Vincent Millay: "God's World," ll. 1; 8,9

"...There hath passed away a glory from the earth.

"Shades of the prison-house begin to close
 Upon the growing Boy,

But he beholds the light, and whence it flows,
    He sees in it his joy...."

    W. Wordsworth: *Ode on Intimations of Immortality from
    Recollections of Early Childhood,* ll. 18; 66-69

B LACKWATER, GLIDING IN limpid quiet, before joining with Clear
Creek, then both together with Shellcastle River, really an elongate bay
running inland, all of them ambling toward the Ocean, all dodging
among incursions of tidal creeks near where the watershed first becomes
brackish and estuarial, sinks down and allows the others, poised above, to
float like oil, not mixing with them.

    Parker Jones had been the one to proclaim the unmingling of Blackwater,
not haughty, but like the craft that plied streaming surfaces softly and aluff,
after Woody Paget as a man, tragically dead from violence done himself, had
been buried in the cemetery just furlongs away, among the generations of his
family. He formulated this idea after he had heard that Paget as a young boy
had nearly lost his own life in that water, breasting current and depth to save
the life of his younger brother.

    Parker had in mind those ancients who left wintry Dodona to fight before
Troy, along with the race who tilled the banks of Titaressos—Titaressos that
flowed not into but out over the "silver whirls" of Peneios, not mixing but
floating above, since Peneios broke away and flowed from Styx. For one shore
of Blackwater seemed the region of the dead.

    Parker alluded to epic legend. He thought he did, anyway. Even though
when he had mentioned it he felt himself tremble—"a rabbit crossing his
grave"—and uncertainty whether it might not be physically true. But Miss
Izora, she of Sybelline renown, when she heard of it, gave this dissenting
opinion: "Mister Parker may yet turn out to be the better of Miss Alina's
husbands"—for she had become inexplicably but deeply fond of Bob
Barrington—"and he may be right in what he says. But he may not be. There
is a lot to learn about water. Everybody has seen it come down from Heaven.
But nobody has seen it go back up, at least not knowing it for what it was.
Could be the rain that comes from highest Heaven is the rain that goes
deepest down into the river."

However all that may have been, years after Parker Jones had met death
himself, Josh Jones, his son, having just the night before narrowly avoided
joining the dead on the bank of the shadowy stream where they were supposed
to dwell, now that the ball was over, now that the guests were gone, climbed
the outside stair to his rooms in the Carriage House. He had taken his own

things away, because he hadn't wanted the Belles of Tuesday and Wednesday to have access to them; it would have been like their having access to part of himself. Some young men of his age would have welcomed that access, would have taken care to leave exposed every kind of thing to tell about themselves in particular ways. Now Josh was bringing his burden back again, packed in two canvas duffles. Now, the Belles were gone; of them, One probably forever.

Edward Strikestraw had rescued him on Blackwater, near the end of the deer-shoot. Wasn't that supposed to make him guardian over the remainder of the life he had preserved? Later, Josh had said to him: "I owe you my life." And a little while after that: "My girl? She's my life…now that I have one still." But at the hunt-breakfast, Edward had taken her from him. He had made her fall in love with himself; he had given Josh his life, then taken it back again.

Beginning after midnight on that morning, over curried eggs, Virginia ham, Champagne, Josh had begun to think he noticed something—something between the other two that had abraded his heart. But through what mode of sense? For he had seen nothing in particular, nor heard anything at all. Then, when Mary had asked to be taken back to Clear Creek where she was billeted with the other girls, and as they were going down the steps from Woodleigh, leaving the party in reduced progress at two o'clock, they had spoken. *She* had spoken. She had introduced herself, then Josh, she reminding Edward of their meeting in childhood. They spoke together briefly and casually. But you could tell that something was going on beneath the surfaces. Including the surface of the pier mirror in which their eyes had first met, of which Josh knew nothing. And as well, for, if he had, he would have made it crack from side to side. Yes, smashed it right before its owners and their guests. And to smithereens—whatever smithereens were. For that would have destroyed the dangerous world lurking behind the scrim of reflection. His father would surely have confirmed that, since he had known more than most about other worlds. Anyway, it hadn't had to happen.

Josh and Mary spoke very little on the dark, bumpy road back to Clear Creek. Neither even considered making idle observations, usual things to say—"small talk." Each knew it would be forced. Each knew that it would seem to the other forced, hollow, or desperate. Besides, Josh was beginning to grieve; Mary, to exult. Neither thing is good to talk about, except in your loudest, wildest voice, and to empty sky. Finally, when they arrived, with Josh already fearing the worst, then came worse than the worst:

"Thank you, Josh. I've had a lovely evening."

"Me too."

"Under the circumstances, I imagine."

"Yes. Under the circumstances."

"Does your side hurt much?" But the wound sustained at the end of the deer-shoot didn't hurt at all; at least, it didn't emerge as specifically painful from the whole anguished fabric of Josh's consciousness of himself. "Well, then, I'll see you in Augusta tomorrow night. I'm looking forward to it."

"Tonight."

"What?"

"It's nearly three o'clock."

"Oh, yes. Tonight. Of course."

Several minutes seemed to pass. Josh thought he could hear Blackwater sliding by, just beyond where the forest sprang up. He knew there were traces of his blood mingled somewhere in its currents. He heard it well up in its viscous, amber streamings—no, without light not amber, but like braids of pitch—swelling, swirling, stumbling tangled among its own tumult, hold, halt momentarily, in the emptiness of night.

It came. The kiss. Mary stood on tiptoe and kissed him, sweetly upon the right cheek. "Goodbye, Josh."

Now Josh was returning to the Carriage House, where he had lived since his sixteenth birthday. This building, one room deep, was, strictly speaking, not a dependency to Clear Creek; it was evidently older than the great House. And it could not have been a carriage house at all, for there was no place in it where a carriage might be kept. One could have been driven through the elliptically arched passageway that ran through the center of the ground floor, brick-paved, stuccoed, and without feature from its west to it east openings. But that was all.

This passageway separated the two rooms at grade level, each of them opening separately into the back garden. The second floor ran right across, and this storey contained Josh's rooms. Here, well after sunup, after the ball was over, after the guests were gone, Josh put down his duffles and went to bed without unpacking or undressing.

On the night table was a note from Yukoneta Browne, his Mother's housemaid. It was weighted by a kind of satiny, pink-embroidered pouch full of little objects of varying size, shape, consistency, and scent:

Mr. Josh,

Unless you have changed a lot of your habits, I don't think these things are yours. Those *girls* must have left them. I found them when I was trying to fumigate your rooms for you. Please give them to Miss Alina.

Happy Thanks G., Y. [The paper had run out.]

Stung by the kiss, lost in the Goodbye, Josh thought it best to put out the light, obliterate whatever could be put away by darkness. Little though there could be.

On Thanksgiving morning, Alina Ashfield Jones Barrington, Bob Barrington, Josh Jones and his Aunt Lavinia and Uncle Laurence all went to Church. They would have gone as willingly to the Post Office, if it had been open, to sit in a circle upon the floor and play solitaire, would have done anything, in fact, to get away from the houses they lived in, and been confined to, almost, by the festivities and guests, a few of whom had been really very difficult to dislodge. All breathed deeply, as of fresh air, on their ways there and back.

Josh had seemed a little gloomy early on Wednesday afternoon, leaving for Augusta to attend the ball, to escort "his girl." But he had returned next day at breakfast time apparently greatly cheered. Lavinia was pretty sure she knew the reason for the gloom but was puzzled by the cheerfulness. Nobody else thought about it. Not then.

Church was not an idle destination or brief escape for the Strikestraws of New Brunswick. Mainly, of course, because the Head of Household, Thomas, was also Parish Rector. Besides, the celebration at home was still to come. Edward awoke in the third bed he had slept in over four days. But he was not disoriented for a riven moment. No, he was locked onto the glidepath to his goal and believed he would never be diverted.

Not disoriented, but quite late. He dressed hurriedly, and he judged that he was sufficiently clean-shaven for the time being.

Once at the church, he climbed to the so-called choir loft, where Rhodë Harmon sat alone waiting for the service to begin. There was a minor disturbance on account of the effusiveness of their mutual greetings. Then the building was filled with the grand, buoyant measures of, "Come, Ye Thankful People, Come…," and the spirit of the day and season was unloosed; the strains in echo would confer a nearly sacramental imprint upon the traditional gourmanding that lay ahead.

Rhodë was gradually becoming undone. The 'done' part of the word mercifully did not occur to her. But the service must not last one minute too long. The successor bird to Turkey Number One, placed by Thomas himself at four o'clock that morning, had been introduced into the oven. At a time she considered critical, a nephew of Rhodë's was to come into the house, anoint the turkey with a glass of plum brandy someone had sent Thomas from Alsace after the War, and adjust the setting on the stove. The child might have made any of multiple missteps. But the focus of obsession is specific, and Rhodë had driven herself into anxious certainty that the nephew was going to leave the oven door ajar.

She always went down to Communion last. As the only Black communicant, she had thought that fitting. She said, as they were returning from the rail, "Mr. Edward, can you drive me home? Right now?" That she was willing to leave before the thanksgiving and benediction was a measure of her anxiousness. Some did that, at that time, but never she.

On the way to Front Street, she said: "I hope you had a pleasant visit down in South Carolina, Mr. Edward. Your cousin Virginia and her husband are coming, *all the way from Laurinburg!* Your grandfather thinks they may not bring the children." In an abstracted way, Edward was trying to see the connection, when he realized there wasn't any. Rhodë went on: "Mrs. Lucas is invited, and Billy—they call him William now—Did you know he was engaged? So she'll probably come, too. Did you know he was on the police force? But next year he is going off to an academy to be trained in something special. That means poor Sergeant Arnon will probably be on duty all the time. As it is, he's always on duty for all the Christian holidays. But this is not a Christian holiday, is it? Just because we observe it in Church…."

"I think it's a God-fearing man's holiday," Edward said as they turned into the driveway. Just in time.

"Thank you! Lord, how proud your blessèd grandmother would be of you!"

Blessèd?

Rhodë then sprang from the car, leaving the door open, and ran up the stair and into the kitchen, where she found the oven door closed tight, and all else well. Edward, entering the kitchen a little behind, asked: "Is everything running on schedule?"

"Everything is on *schedule*. It's a question of whether there'll be enough to feed everybody!"

"But you've told me who's expected. There seems to me to be far more than enough for that."

"No, I never finished telling you."

They heard another car enter the driveway and run all the way to the back of the house. They thought it would be Thomas, but it was Alenda Lucas. She was, in her small way, a patroness of the crafts, if not of the arts, and she possessed the largest of the privately owned collections of Old Jugtown pottery. She had brought with her the most precious pieces, filled with what she was able to find still of colored leaves, with unsheaved oats, wheat, and barley stuck in among them, a few heads of the wild garlic. These had set small grains like polished garnet.

"I hope these will fit in with anything else you've planned, Rhodë," Alenda said, as all three made trips up and down the back steps carrying the arrangements, water spilling from the sturdy vessels out onto their rare glazes, making them slippery and hard to keep hold on. Exotically angled sticks, some with two or three leaves, others bare, spread exuberantly, threatening the bearers' eyes, the women's hair-arrangements.

"Oh, these are beautiful, Miss Alenda. All I've done is put some stems of chrysanthemums into those Chinese vases. That's what Miss Grace used to do." But she immediately regretted implying even so remote a comparison between the two ladies. It was a thing she had meant to avoid entirely.

Now Thomas did arrive. Rhodë looked at the others, glancing up toward Heaven. For Thomas on Thanksgiving Day or Christmas Day almost always brought home from Church varying numbers of people who he had discovered were going to be either alone, or just in two's or three's for the feast. He had brought no one, however. He came up into the kitchen and said: "Rhodë, don't you know the Simmonses, who take care of Mr. Blanding?"

Rhodë had brought both *dindons aux pruneaux* to heel, and was now cutting biscuits, a familiar thing, rote and rhythmic, soothing to body and mind. "I do, Father, and both of them are very nice people. Emily and I belong to the same Sisterhood. She was *grammateus* the year I was *basileus*." Thomas found this information curious, but left it.

"Good. Mr. Blanding came to Church. They'll be bringing him on here."

"Merciful Savior!"

"What?"

"'Bringing him—'; not having to help him walk, not in a wheelchair; he's not already…?"

"Bringing him in his car, Rhodë. He is not permitted a driver's license."

"Thank Goodness! Nothing's happened to him?"

"Not that I know of—why?"

"Oh! I just wondered why he was at Church."

"Actually, I did, too. But we don't need particular reasons for coming to Church."

"No, Sir; we don't."

"And one or two other people we weren't expecting will be here, too.
I could have said so!

"I know there's enough provender. We always see to that. But I thought you could use a little extra help."

"I can, Father, if it's help that helps."

"I know what you mean. Anyway, that's why I asked the Simmonses."

"Oh, it will be a great help to have *them*. Will it be all right if Emily and I work in here—by ourselves? Joe could mix your drinks and pass them around, maybe with the cheese straws and my shrimp puffs? That would relieve me of that."

"A good arrangement. Joe is Mr. Simmons? We're not having crab puffs, too?"

"Oh, yes, Sir, and the crab puffs."

"Another thing: With all these people here, there's no need for you to wait at table. Just put everything on the sideboard, and we'll serve ourselves buffet-style."

"Now, Father, with all that help we can do it properly. Miss Grace…."

"Not everybody here will be particularly proper. This other way will be best." Rhodë thought momentarily of praying to Miss Grace about it. What, after all, was the Communion of Saints supposed to be for? "You always go to your sister's, don't you? Well, then. This year you can be a little early. Take plenty of everything with you, and send plenty with the Simmonses, when they leave. They might enjoy a bottle of wine, too. They can spend Thanksgiving afternoon better than by watching over Mr. Blanding." Rhodë couldn't quite free herself from the notion that Duzey Blanding, the brilliant and occasionally eminently presentable Town Drunk, was going to be carried in on a litter. But suddenly she thought she smelt burning plums.

Alenda, who was adjusting sticks and branches, and Edward watched all this exchange through the open door to the back porch. Edward said: "Set-piece: 'The nervous housekeeper.'"

"And, poor thing, 'Embattled stand-in Châtelaine.'"

Word trickled back to the kitchen that Virginia and Tuggs Whiteacre had arrived. Then their children, who had of course come with them—*all the way from Laurinburg!*—trickled back to the kitchen. The eldest, whose name was also Grace, after her departed great-aunt, had grown up. She said: "Let me give you a kiss, Rhodë. Happy Thanksgiving! Can I help with anything? I can't cook, really, but if you tell me just what to do, I'll do it." The younger brothers, too, greeted Rhodë politely but warmly. They went off then upon the lid-lifting sort of reconnaissance that hungry little boys pursue.

"Rhodë," Alenda said a little anxiously, coming halfway into the kitchen, "when you reach a stopping-place, please come and tell me whether you think the pots look all right where I've put them."

"I can come with you right now, Miss Alenda." Rhodë felt this unsureness was not much like Alenda Lucas. It wasn't.

Edward had set out toward the front of the house. In the breakfast room, he kissed his young cousin Grace, who had been given the task of arranging relishes for the sideboard. He found her to have become a charming young girl. She held him in Ivy-League awe. "How do you think the relish tray looks?"

"Looks like it was done by a professional caterer. Except…why not put a little more of the red stuff there in the center? It'll pick it up a bit."

"I thought so, too. I didn't know how much to put, because I don't know what it is."

"Doesn't it say on the jar?"

"It does, but I can't read it. The jar's been reused, and so has the label."

"Did you taste it?"

"I was afraid to. It seems a little too red."

"Shall I give it a try?" And he took a teaspoonful. Though not quite a full one. "It's delicious. Put more."

"Good, because it really does look festive."

In the entryway, Edward greeted those guests who were coming in the front door. That all of them were not gauged the solemn intimacy of the occasion.

But he was making his way to the old pier glass.

There appeared through the wrought iron gates at the end of the front walk Alenda's great silver Jaguar, William at the wheel. His mother had come in his car because she was transporting the jugs of sloshing water. Doors were heard opening and closing. William held the gates apart for his Aunt Bena (who usually spent Thanksgiving with other kin in Edenton), Miss Mary Lou Taliaferro, now very old and halt, and another lady and three men whom Edward did not recognize. These old folk had had a merry time squeezing into one car, even if it was a grand one. They were Thomas's gleanings from the Church service. Rhodë was spared knowledge of their arrival. For a while. William's bride-to-be, Martha Trimble, whom everybody knew, everybody loved (but not as William loved her—He was no better off than Edward was becoming), pulled up behind the others. She had driven herself in her new roadster, an engagement-present from Alenda.

Now Edward had reached the big mirror in the hall. *If she saw me in this, as I wish I could see her, she might think I cut a pretty good figure.* Then, Tuggs Whiteacre loomed in the background, exuding virility and idiocy—a soft, comforting combination, and a staple of Southern society at that time. Thomas could not understand what his niece saw in him, at least not at first. But he observed carefully, and eventually he realized that Virginia treated him as a pet. Thomas began to do likewise, and then the two men got along very well together.

However, this somewhat hulking image had to be got out of the way. After a while, Tuggs sauntered off, leaving room for the reflection—for a memory of the reflection—that Edward wanted to summon forth.

Now, as everyone knows, there are many loves, but, as Edward's own folk-psychology had already suggested to himself, one of these loves is joined with beauty. In the presence of this beauty, and under its enchantment, the lover may lose the sense of physiologic process, time, all change—so close will he have come to godlikeness and to dwelling outside the hours. The only thing that surprises him then is that The Many have not got to their knees.

Looked at from another's point of view, however, "All the world loves a lover." But that's about it.

As at Woodleigh, Edward took hold, firm hold, of the frame and stared into the depths of the mirror, even though the glass and backing were dusky and bluish with age. And then he closed his eyes, and in his mind's eye saw the gliding shadow, seeming to come to him, to smile upon him, a sumptuous form in black, overrippled with candlelit folds streaming all along the lovely topography, amber hair—But wasn't it quite dark?—falling in easy oscillations, luminous, numinous eyes, perfection of everything else, and of the whole.

Crazy. That was it. He was crazy as a March hare! Or as a bat. Beside himself, in the sense of the Ancients: Literally beside, that is, outside, ecstatic.

Fires had been laid in all the fireplaces, and Edward was supposed to be lighting them. The doors would be left open to the grey outside—trees, houses, the town's few grand and numerous modest monuments. And though there fell no burning leaf and no bird called, just thereabout, in the haze a cluster of dry leaves might appear, the color of gourd, or the fluting note of one white blossom of the *Camellia sasanqua*.

But this grey outside italicized the warmth of being within. Heightening of this agreeable effect was sought by old ladies gazing out through windows, or by men outside, kicking about in the peppery-smelling leaves of the pecan tree, lying heaped where they had fallen. The men smoked or held beakers—whiskey in, usually; occasionally, tobacco-spittle out (Thomas had warned that not every guest would be entirely proper).

Alenda besought Rhodë once more to look at her arrangements. "All the flower shop had right now," she said, indicating some very dark-red carnations and small tiger lilies, which she had added, along with rose-hips, ochre or scarlet or crimson. "I thought if the leaves were going to seem like so ghostly flames, then we might at least have a few vigorous embers for them to spring from?" Rhodë gave unqualified approval. She wondered again at Alenda, irresolute. What could be going on? Rhodë thought she might know. Miss Alenda, Miss Grace, and the Canon had all been great friends together, but Miss Grace had been gone for eighteen years now.

Eating and drinking had acquired momentum. Amazing how little time it took to consume a feast that had begun with the roasting of Turkey Number One, nearly twelve hours before! The helpers were almost ready to leave. The Simmonses were going to drive Rhodë on to her family. Then they were going to, as some say, "cut loose." They trusted, of course, that Duzey would be well looked-after. He was *their* responsibility. However, Reverend Strikestraw could do it if anybody could. "And," the Canon said, "the two of you just kick off your shoes and take it easy. Someone will bring him home." Bliss! For much as they loved their charge, devotedly as they rendered him their duty, it would be Heavenly Rest to be completely rid of him—even of the thought of him—for a couple of hours.

They couldn't drink the bottle of wine, because they were strict Baptists. So they did, anyway. And it was doubly refreshing for being perceived as impermissable, to these two nearly blameless souls.

Most of Thomas's fellow seminarians had long since stopped thinking; that's to say, thinking about the religion they professed, and had got down to serious parochial work. Diocesan work, in the case of one classmate, the Rt. Reverend James Somers, for years now Bishop of East Carolina. "You know, you could have been bishop, Tommy," he had said to Thomas during one of their conferences. They had had conferences far oftener than was usual between a bishop and one of his priests, because Thomas's teachings had started to develop along what could be called "original" lines; both clerics and most people in New Brunswick realized this fully. "Coming out of seminary, you certainly got the plum."

"Yes, and 'The Plum,' if by that you mean the parish across the river, nearly put me into an early grave." And he had returned, with the Bishop's collusion and assistance, to be Rector of the Parish in which he had grown up. Later, he was made a canon. "Besides, I would not have wished to be bishop. Being a priest is bad enough."

"Do you want to be defrocked?"

"No. It's too late. It would cause embarrassment, and it would accomplish nothing."

Bishop Somers had let it go at that. He trusted his old friend to be cautious, if creative.

Thomas had found few people to take issue with his surprise-promulgations. Disappointingly few, in fact. New Brunswick was a community in which for some reason nobody seemed interested in discrediting anybody else—at least, not outside the Court House, and it was in Bolivia. Thus, nobody had even questioned the important but spurious Parable of the Two Lamps. There had been only two repercussions, and that itself is far too strong a word.

First, Miss Bena decided to see whether the Presbyterian clergyman's wife had heard of the little-known passage. But this lady wasn't really interested in Scripture. She wasn't interested in much of anything just then, except in the program of rejuvenation that she had recently undertaken in partnership with a fisher-lad from Kure Beach.

Second, Miss Mary Lou had a Bible with a concordance. She had searched under "Two," under "Lamp(s)," "Steward," and even under "Bid/bade," this word having occurred so regularly, but when she found nothing applicable to the remarkable story she had heard from the pulpit, she simply concluded that the concordance wasn't very exhaustive.

Thomas had begun to enjoy greatly the company (not dependably easy to come by) of Duzey Blanding, who was convinced of nothing, open to anything, and astute when conscious.

For almost half an hour, Alenda had been skulking either just within or just outside the front door. In mortification, she realized she must have appeared to some to be playing the hostess. In fact, she had merely been seeking to get into the dining room without being seen. And finally it occurred to her that all she had to do was go first into the breakfast room. So she strode without betraying self-consciousness straight down the hallway, as if doing so were completely reasonable, as in fact it was. Did peals of laughter tumble out of the library, following her? She really was quite unaccustomed to feeling uncertain. She went into the breakfast room and from there to the dining room, which had been cleared and put back to rights. Under the windows, an old cellaret rested on its rickety stand. Alenda lifted the lid to disclose a stash of not regularly used liquors. She rummaged among the contents until she found gin and vermouth. She took them back into the breakfast room and set them out on the table for consideration.

She realized she needed to consult Edward. The recipe for martinis was not going to be revealed through meditation. Just as she had begun to wonder at herself for having to ask so much advice in the course of that one day, Edward walked in. "Oh, Edward! Just the man I need." Edward very much liked the idea of being needed by Alenda.

"I'm having these in order to prepare myself for an announcement I'm going to make."

"But nearly everyone has left." He began rolling up his sleeves and lifted the bottle of gin, but, even before beginning to unscrew the cap, began at once to hold forth. "Anyway, martini-drinking started in England during the War. Somebody added one part Italian vermouth—It must have been 'Cin-Cin-Cinzano'—to the gin, and they called this 'Gin and It,' for "Italian.""

"Good God!"

"I know. That's what we said when we heard about it."

"And they probably drank it without ice."

"Brits! I'm sure they must have. That hadn't occurred to us. That really is incredible—as a friend of mine puts it, 'It's so incredible, it's hard to believe.'" Edward was in an exalted state; he had been, for close to forty-eight hours. And now he was taking it out upon poor Alenda, who herself had something she must take out upon somebody.

He liked knowing something he could talk to her about. He liked the prospect of drinking a martini with her. She had a magenta blossom in her hair. "So, finally the Americans realized the proportion of vermouth ought to be decreased, to make way for more gin. And, naturally, that the whole thing should be chilled—they would have known that from the start. Come to say, to get the name, somebody must have switched to Martini and Rossi. The vermouth."

"Work while you explain. Make it an illustrated lecture." Edward began to, as he put it, "build" a pitcher of martinis.

"Cutting down on the vermouth got to be a fetish. Mr. Churchill said you should just glance briefly across the room at the bottle, while you were stirring. And I saw a woman in a movie—Lee Remick, or somebody like that. No, because there's nobody like Lee Remick. So it has to have been she. Anyway, she just dipped the glass stirring-rod into the vermouth, then into a vat of iced gin." The drinks were ready.

Edward poured them "straight up," and the two agreed that one part vermouth to five parts gin was palatable and probably salutary, and that any garnish would be superfluous.

"Edward...may I ask...are you particularly excited about anything?"

"I think I may be. Why?"

"Never mind; pour us another. Because I am, too. There's my announcement to prepare for." Edward was about to speak, but Alenda cut him off: "I know. Nearly everyone has left. But—and remember this—not every announcement is meant to be made generally." Alenda's black hair, the bright flower, the window behind her, the mists darkening beyond while the light inside grew softer and stronger—all these were producing strange chemistry within a young man who was nearly broken by passion to start with, and then had drunk two martinis.

"Come along, then, Edward," she said as she rose; "I may need some assistance."

"In childhood," Duzey was saying, while Alenda and Edward were "building" and drinking their martinis, "I lived in either one or the other of two worlds." He and Thomas had sat down in the library before a redolent wood fire, platoons of flame marching hastily and undirected among the blackening char.

"I expect one was real, and the other imaginary?"

"Generally, Canon, yes. But there was a great deal of each mixed into the other. One was space, and I in it; the other was a land of image and adventure...and I in it.

"I remember seeing beyond the nursery, through the window, the sky. They say I can't, but I do. Clouds, but space beyond them.

"Later I found, even inside, space beyond space. Past a curtain or a door. –To find that I could move past, too. Past no matter what, so long as into a place farther. Up: Trees; down, into caverns."

There came a loud crackling sound. An incandescing bit of firewood leapt from the fireplace. It described a graceful arc, glowing out, dark by the time it fell onto the carpet. Thomas was sure it landed upon the very spot where a silver phial with a bud of *'Déprez à fleurs jaunes'* and beads of mercury-minded water had fallen, some twenty years before.

"Ought I to get that up, Canon?"

"No, no, thank you, Duzey. Don't bother. It has gone out."

"Yet, early man must have needed to feel bounded, given his myths. Come to that, late man may need to feel so, too. It's unnerving to think of space and time running along without any end."

"It's so. I had forced myself to accept there must be a final wall. I couldn't hold fast, though. I imagined there were openings in it, as well, somewhere, somewhat like windows or doors.

"We had an engraving of a garden-space at Caserta: It showed a tall semicircular hedge, pierced by a series of window-like openings, round-arched. Then more space. The artist had taken few pains with what lay beyond."

"And we take such pains with what lies beyond what we are able, even scarcely, to see."

"Cosmologists and astronomers feel it their duty, I believe."

"I'd bet more of them than know it are seeking for a world beyond this."

"Probably so. However, once they've discerned anything, to them it automatically becomes part of this world."

"So long as they limit themselves to telescopes, electromagnetic receivers of one or another kind, particle-trapping vats of water, computation, and so forth. Rather like rushing through a gallery to 'see' as many famous pictures as possible, instead of being stopped dead by the just-imaginable beauty of the right Rubens. For instance."

"Rubenses are part of this world."

"Partly they are part.

"But, now, talking of openings from space into farther, or other, space, what are we to make of these 'black holes'?"

"There's something beyond them, too, don't you imagine?"

"Well, but they're black."

"No, Canon, I don't think they really are. This analogy is badly flawed, but we can start from it: Cut a hole in a sheet of paper, take it into a dark room. You don't see anything through the hole, but it isn't black.

"At least one respected theoretician thinks that, in order to understand all about them, about the expanding of our universe and the space it comprises… about the completion of its destiny, we will have to evolve further."

"Then we mustn't wait up."

"No, Canon. We mustn't.

"I did think, also, that Somebody must be furnishing that always-to-come space. That, I thought, was guaranteed by Necessity."

"That Lady and her counterpart, Impossibility, are a rough pair; two dames who could go bear-hunting with a switch."

A sound, not startling or very loud, of shattering glass came to them from far down the back hallway.

"Should I go and see what has happened?"

"In the absence of screams or the sound of running, I don't think so. If we're needed, I'm sure we'll be called upon. Do, though, have another little swallow of Cognac." And he poured one out. "And please, go on with your story."

"I've told it. I believe; haven't I? All except my doubts about my mind. I was afraid it was dangerously singular. I wouldn't, at the time, under any circumstances have confessed what I thought. However, my mind is efficient—during business hours, that is. I found that out later on." For, at the time of The Tragedy, Duzey had been studying at the premier school of engineering in the Country, if not the World, and, like an August mosquito late at night, bouncing her way along the ceiling, he was always at or just below the top of his class.

"You haven't told me about your childhood life of image and adventure."

"Oh! Of course. Before I became a man—or, in order to become a man—I had first to entertain then to put away childish things, as the saying goes. A world of my own, from which I thought I had driven everything that wasn't imaginary, although, unless I came 'trailing clouds of glory,' nothing could have been truly fictional. What would I have counterfeited it from but scraps of experience?

"But I thought it was imagined. I needed it to be. It mustn't be real; I think I was trying to hold reality at bay. But there was something else.

"The realm was Paradisal, wonderful. And I in it, wonderful. I wished for something, and it was to hand; I wanted things to occur in a way and at a time, and it was so. Eventually, I decreed that this was due to a faculty, not outside, but within myself. From bedtime stories I knew about wishes coming true, of possessing of the power to make them come true. I gave myself this power.

"But where is the glory in slaying a dragon if all you need to do is wish him to drop dead?

"After that, there was ash in the sky. All slipped a notch. I decided that the fulfillment of wish was due to my bravery in warfare, my wisdom in giving law. Then, the ash precipitated and fell like rain and all the colors ran. It was over, as I think I had all along known it would be, and that is why I had from the outset made sure the whole thing be imaginary. There was the sense, then already, that it would have to be yielded."

"You had, then, the choice of Adam and Eve."

"Sir?"

"Their choice was not between good and evil, surely."

"I thought it was. And now, ours."

"Oh, I think that is a self-repressive notion. One honored by time, of course. But their choice was between delicious, perpetual boredom, on the one hand, and discovery, if at cost, on the other."

"It's a pity, though, that deliciousness in perpetuity isn't possible apart from weariness of it."

"I wonder whether that is a pity."

"I wonder. One day I laid it aside. The magical faculty." Duzey got up to poke at the fire, and while on his feet stepped out into the hallway to see whether he could determine the cause of the crash they had heard minutes before. But all seemed well. "It wasn't real magic. Magic isn't real. If you're human, you have to accomplish whatever you accomplish as a human being. Otherwise, it's unfair, and it doesn't count."

The fire quickened.

Alenda and Edward came into the room, and she said: "Thomas, it has been a wonderful day. That is why I've stayed so long; Edward is marvelous company and has shown me how to make martinis. But now I must go. Duzey, please sit down." He looked about to, anyway.

"I'll walk you out to William's car."

"No, Edward. You keep Mr. Blanding company, and your Grandfather can see me out." Thomas rose obediently.

When they had reached the car, Alenda said: "Thomas, you *are* aware, aren't you, that I'm in love with you?"

All Thomas could manage to stammer out was, "You can't be; I'm not your type."

The Bishop usually visited Christ Church for Confirmation sometime in the spring. So the congregation were indeed surprised, on the First Sunday of Advent, the Sunday after Thanksgiving Day, when it most often falls, to see him enter the church with Thomas. For this meant that the Bishop would conduct the service, and not the Rector, who would assist him.

But all became clear when the Head of the Diocese climbed into the pulpit and announced: "I publish the Banns of Marriage between Thomas Grantly Strikestraw, of this parish, and Eleanor Alenda Thornwall Lucas, also of this parish. If any of you know cause, or just impediment, why these two persons should not be joined together in holy Matrimony, ye are to declare it. This is the first time of asking."

Josh Jones awoke on the morning of the sixth of December without any slightest thought that it was St. Nicholas's Day. Parker Jones had introduced to Clear Creek the tradition of observing this Feast. Thereafter, the observance was never omitted. It was not discontinued after Parker's death, because it served Alina and Josh as a memorial. They never said a word about it; not even to each other. They let it give clandestine life to remembrance, allowing it to move about undiscovered. As life from remembrance forever moves about us all, an undiscovered and undraining sea.

Instead Josh sensed himself gripped by a pestilence he didn't recognize. He sorted over it in his mind, trying to think what it might be. The first thing he could tell was that he felt unsettled and unwell. Then, entirely to his surprise, it occurred to him that he wanted a drink.

Me, the abstemious! For while away at school, Josh, who never smoked and at that time didn't drink, had maintained the requisite reputation for delinquency by telling his roommate—and swearing him to secrecy, to ensure the rapid diffusion of the confidence—that he had been caught smoking by the hall proctor so many times that now he had to go to the infirmary every week for a test to show he had not smoked again, or he would be "shipped"; moreover, that he came not from one but from two long lines of hopeless alcoholics, and that the doctor had told him that one drink, just one single drink, would put him over the edge.

Was that lie coming true? Even so, he got up, and pulling on a dressing gown of light cotton, woven, for some reason, to look like the grey woolen stuff of Navy blankets, and finely edged in black silk cording, went into his sitting room. There he poured a Scotch-and-soda. Tentatively, he began to drink it and was shocked to realize that his impulse had not misled him. He felt better right away. He drank more. He shaved, ran his brushes through his hair. He drank still more, and felt then even better.

This is disgusting! Yet, if it is going to give me some relief, I may as well make the most of it. So he sat down and sipped from the tumbler, feeling relief, awe, and horror, strangely brewed together.

Upstairs in the Carriage House, on its eastern side, the one facing away from Clear Creek's back garden and across a broad field in tilth, was an outside stair of stuccoed masonry, with a delicately forged iron balustrade. Alina had had it copied from the photograph of a house in Annapolis. From here, through a doorway that had begun as an east window, you entered the sitting room. You could tell it was the sitting room, because there was a chair in it. The bedroom, likewise, could be identified by virtue of its containing a bed. But that, as we occasionally hear it put, was about it.

Josh set his glass upon the walnut desk table that he had been persuaded to let be brought in; he followed in thought his gaze as it meandered about the familiar, entrusted interior, of the security of which he had years before made himself custodian—scoured pine floors, dado of wide planks of cypress wood, stripped of paint or grime. And the walls: Plastered lath—if there were much of the old wooden lath left intact within them after all the years. They and the ceiling had been scrubbed with wire brushes, with the use of a wide array of solvents. Thus there were revealed stucco patches the color of blue marl, blushes of some of the pigments that had been at different periods applied as wall-paint. There were networks of fissuring, some filled-in long ago, now sombre branchings, others newly repaired, these with plaster gleaming white as snow, in places even glittering with bits of silicate. All the scouring had been done some years before with a view to fresh coats of paint.

However, Josh had returned from school in time to put a stop to the homogenation of all these features. To him, their appearance just then was as gratifying as any other treatment he could think of might make them. That was before he had developed his passion for Tiepolo, but even so….

For these two rooms had been his father's studio. As a boy, he had watched Parker at work, often painting-out overcharged brushes directly onto the walls, and he knew now that some of the color held stubbornly by the old mineral compositions originated from this possibly slovenly habit. Magenta, a peculiar golden orange, a clear red—hues unknown to the paint-making industry of the Nineteenth Century, or of that before.

All this resulted in what Josh considered—with his father's eye, he suspected—a surface, after many years of intermittent and otherwise disunited decoration, a work completed by chance, and now at rest in its fullness.

Code. Everyone had heard of color-coding, and these were finished directives that Josh had set himself to decipher over a very long spell, not doubting that the network of cracking connected all the visual elements and formed a great map, as though in fresco. Today, he would study it. He had long since found situated upon it a lot of places—ones either that only he knew, or that only he and his father had known. Today, he would find his own situation upon it, and then follow where the pathway led. For he felt displaced now—or about to be—and knew he must move ahead.

Noise on the stair outside, then came a knock at the door. It was his mother, holding a globe of mistletoe greater than any he had seen among the branches of the winter oak. "Tommy cut some for Lavinia and Rennie. She sent this over to us." She stood on tiptoe to kiss Josh. He held his breath for this. "I know you don't want clutter up here, Darling, but it *is* getting to be the Yuletide. May I hang this in the New Window for you?" From the base of the cluster there streamed a horsetail of ribbons—red, green, white, and gold, and violet.

"Of course, Mother," Josh said letting out his breath as he backed away a little, as though to find perspective upon the mistletoe and her hanging it; "Thank you, and send word to Tommy, and I'll say something about it when I see him." He got, he supposed safely, across the room and stood between his mother and his glass, not yet empty, while she fixed the ornament to the embrasure of the "New Window," tall and of slender proportion, arched round at the top, broken by delicate bars that rose straight before branching and crossing and meeting each other in self-assured geometry. It was the other of two additions she had made to the building, when she had first decided to "take the shambles in hand."

"It looks terrifically festive; my spirits are lifted already," Josh called out.

I see they have been. "I hope they didn't need lifting such a very great deal." And she betrayed her unspoken thoughts by adding, a little too soon: "There is some mail for you. Connie has left it on the dining table." Then she went away. And Josh remembered that he hadn't left a shoe outside his door for St. Nicholas to fill.

He saw his mother out onto the stoop, and down the stair. As he was about to go back inside, happening to look down, he saw not a shoe, but a pair, new, in a style and finish he had admired. Both were stuffed full of candy canes.

It was around this time that Josh was oppressed by five dreams. The first three of them came during three consecutive nights. There was some discontinuity that involved the last two, and it was not until after the fifth that he recognized in them a series. But he was still unable to determine what they meant.

In the first of these, Josh had seen and felt himself deeply angered, more violently angered than in waking he had ever been, consumed almost by fury. But against what or whom he could not tell, and he thought also that the object had not been specified in the dream.

The second was characterized by sexual voraciousness. It amounted, in the dream, to madness. Again, the impulse was consuming to a degree that he had otherwise never known. Not in other dreams. Not in imagining. Not in fact. But the dream had not involved Mary Mountainstream, his lost love, so that he was spared at least the worst possible pain.

In the third dream, Josh finally saw himself as calm, but sorrowful to a depth his experience had not prepared him to see, foresee, or understand. He felt himself close to death from sorrow. But, as before, the reason for the sorrow was hidden from him. And Edward Strikestraw was nowhere to be seen, anywhere in that churning world.

It was on the morning after this third that his mother had come in with the mistletoe. And it was her gentleness, and sweetness, and bountifulness that had staved off another vision that night, Josh was later sure. On that morning, he had said to her: "I can't remember whether mistletoe is a parasite or a saprophyte, but Uncle Laurence will know. I wish Father were here to see this."

Alina did not answer right away, but she was not this time awash in a gully of tears through which she would have to smile. "I wish he were here, too. But, if he were, then what on earth would I do with Bob?"

Josh's fourth dream came and went, and he could retrieve no part of it. After he had dreamt the fifth, and had awakened, he knew, somehow, that the cycle was over. And he knew this in spite of there having been nothing final or complementary about the content of the vision. To the contrary, it was a dream of going forth. In this last, he stood at the end of a hallway, before a door, and was about to leave a house. But he did not know what house it was. He did not want to leave it; he did not want to go wherever it was he was bound for. But he had to go there—no way out of it could be found. Standing about, watching him, were people who were, he knew, the ones who were sending him away, and they knew that he realized this. But acknowledgement was betrayed on neither side.

Josh awoke. Just at first, he knew who the other people were. He tried to feel hatred for them, but could not. He tried to feel sorrow that he and they were parting, but he could not find them for the purpose. He wondered whether he pitied them—Because they must stay behind?—but he thought Probably not. Then they, and all material things that went to form the *tableau vivant* of that dream, sublimed, that is, went directly, without melting and undergoing the deformity of liquefaction, from the solid into the vaporous state, and from that they were diluted by a draft from the open window into nothing at all.

And then, seeing low, pale morning light streaming into his rooms, particularly through the tall arched window hung with mistletoe trailing bright-colored ribbons, he became aware that he had already forgotten who these people had been. "Had been," because they were gone out of his life, and he would never again see or know them. Never again dream of them. So he closed the window, which he always kept open while he slept, no matter the season or weather.

But what had happened in the fourth dream? He tried, with effort slackening daily, to remember—off and on, until, a week after Christmas, the Year flowed away into the night, as Peneios flows from Styx, as Blackwater, after nearly drowning him, had borne a stoppered bottle, bobbing crazily, with a folded note inside, away into late-autumn mist and evening darkness. The fourth dream, likewise, was finally filched away completely, stopped in the memory.

The mail Alina said had been left upon the dining table consisted of a stack of Holiday greeting cards, and a letter from Mary. It had been long in coming, and Josh would be long in opening it. He knew, he thought, approximately what it would say.

II

"There are the sources and extremities of dark earth and misty Tartarus, of the undraining sea and the starry heaven, all in order, dismal and dank...."

Hesiod: *Theogony,* 806-8; (tr. M.L. West)

ALINA AND BOB were having breakfast in the kitchen.
Parker and she had planned the New Kitchen to replace the last of the old kitchen houses, which had kept burning to the ground. Outside, the new construction was finished like the Carriage House, which it connected, through a doorway into Parker's former office at one end, with the great House, through the original butler's pantry at the other. Inside, the space was full of severely purist shapes and materials, but the brick floor, laid in herringbone pattern, ground and polished to a glass-like finish, hard indeed, but familiar and warm in its appearance, declared the room as somehow in part of antique framing.

Alina had stirred at her coffee—though it had no additives that needed to be emulsified, suspended, or dissolved—until Bob was sure it must be stone-cold. He said then: "I told you I'd try to talk to him about drinking, if an opportunity presented itself. Yesterday morning, I had my chance. And 'chance' is the word, because when people overdrink, whatever makes them do it in the first place usually is of more force than anyone's opinion or advice."

"What happened?"

"I was sitting here, just as now, looking over the *Times*. Josh came downstairs. He was dressed. It was clear to me that he had gone to sleep without undressing and changing into his nightclothes. He looked rather… He looked like Hell."

"Was he drunk?"

"No. That's what was wrong with him. He wasn't; he had a hangover. So I said: 'Good morning, Josh. Got a hangover?'"

"You shouldn't have made fun of him in that way; it will just make him withdraw from us about it. The drinking."

"I wasn't making fun of him. I was just calling a shot. He said: 'Good morning, Bob. Yes, I have.' I told him that he ought to have a drink.

"He looked at his watch then, and he said: 'Wouldn't that make me an alcoholic?' I told him that whether he was such a thing or not wasn't the point. That one way or other, he ought to feel better.

"I prepared a Scotch-and-soda. He took a few sips, and then said: 'I've tried this before. But this time, I think it may make me spit up.' I told him to drink some more. And I kept on urging him until I saw little beads of sweat pop out on his forehead. And then I could see him relax. And all of a sudden he…even his clothes looked better."

"Ought you to have done that?"

"I thought so at the time, and I do, still. Yes."

"You didn't think the first one would lead right into others?"

"I was fairly sure it would. But I wanted to create a window, so to speak, both of lucidity and of receptiveness. And I succeeded. Here is how it went: I asked him whether he had any interest in telling me why he was drinking. Not 'drinking so much;' just 'drinking.' All this time I was pouring a drink for myself."

"Is that why you fell asleep before lunch?"

"I didn't drink all of it, but yes, that's why. I thought drinking along with him might get us onto the same page of the Prayer Book."

"I wonder whether you're not cleverer than we thought?"

"It's a possibility I've begun to consider."

"But, did you get anywhere with him?"

"You judge. His answer was: 'Everybody drinks.' I said: 'Everybody but you. And now you do.' By that time, Josh as we know him was beginning slowly both to emerge and to slip away—He was getting exuberantly cheerful. I asked him point blank if he thought he had lost Mary."

"Bob! I can hardly believe the cruelty you allowed into it!"

"It's what I thought we were talking about. And you think it as well."

"What did the poor boy say?"

"Right off, he said: 'I hope not.' I said I hoped not, too."

"Is that all? I mean, was there nothing more?"

"A little more. The exchange between us seemed to have wound down; I looked over the paper a bit longer. Then all of a sudden—and he seemed oddly lighthearted—he stood up and said: '…But I'm afraid so.' Then he took his glass and went out into the garden. I watched him through the Thousand Panes. He looked up at the sky; there was sunshine on his face. Both kinds of sunshine. Then he sat down on the grass by the lily pool, in front of the sundial. He leaned back against it…."

"Then?"

"Then the sundial fell over."

It was by strange coïncidence that Josh had leaned against the sundial and toppled it, right at this moment, because he had already begun to feel that time and weather themselves were coming apart. For, lo, just as soon as the old stones had fallen all about him, and as he had sat forward upon the cork-colored grass, then a cloud overcame the bright sunshine, and all was grey and sad. Yet Josh felt suddenly, thinking about Bob's question just before, that Mary loved him. She must. She had not at all long ago said so, and behaved so. Could that all be changed, just by her meeting another man, even if he were one she had thought as a child she was in love with?

Hadn't Mary and Josh both been overwhelmed by love for each other? Hadn't they both said so, to that as well? He to her, but she no less ardently to him? No, such a thing as that must persist. You couldn't snuff it out like a candle-flame. He was joyful, joyful with love that went forth from himself and came back to him.

Then the sun had come out again. Against the blazing, blasting wintertide world everywhere around, though, Josh looked at it all in another way. His joy flew away, as he really believed Mary had flown. The joyousness of the appearing sun might as well have set.

A cat's paw, a small one, raked the surface of the lily pool. Josh looked up at the sky. He didn't know what time it was. He tried to read from the face of his wristwatch, but it told nothing. He had been through all this before: Away at St. Columba's, mostly, but sometimes, too, when at home. He would be trying to keep hold upon his hopes, expectations…it had taken such effort! He had lost his hold so often, fallen back into the suppression that had been dogging him on and off for years. He thought it had started some while after his father's death. But it had begun before that.

And he remembered that it had not visited him again since he had first met Mary Mountainstream, grown up. Not until now. He had neither learned nor formed for it any name. But it was an old, familiar companion. Not very good company, but easy to entertain. Oh, it took constant attention, of course, but a low degree of it. Or, was it that it required his complete indifference? For indifference was all there was, when this fell visitor appeared. So he bowed his head to it now and welcomed it, and with relief, because now he could rest from the killing striving after happiness, to generate it, sustain it.

"What would Meta say, I wonder?" Edward asked, careless of the reply, in the surfeit of his happiness.

"Meta would not entertain an opinion." Mary said. They were having a picnic lunch among the folds of the gentle mountains west of Roanoke. It was cold in the forest, halfway between Thanksgiving and Christmas. The sun shone from the greatest angle it had been able to achieve, but everybody could tell it was losing ground, day by day.

"I love you."

"I can't believe it, but I know you do."

"I still love Josh." Mary sat, with her knees drawn up, her arms around them, upon the scant warmth of a great outcropping of smooth rock, a formation less common here than lower in the chain of Eastern Mountains. Edward lay beside her, stretched out in full contact with the stone, to claim more of the warmth, to be able to look up at the sky and tell it how explosive he felt—detonated and explosive—and to be able to look up at Mary whenever he wanted to, and for as long.

"I hope you do."

"That is not quite what I expected you to say."

"But I know you have loved him. I know there must be good reasons for that, and that they have probably not changed."

Mary said nothing. She looked across the small valley before them; she wondered what they would be like as each other's mates, after the romp downhill, the longer, harder climb upward again. A bidding bell would eventually toll "across the valley of their dreams." They could not remain on this height; physical law would force them to seek states of lower energy. *Well, so long as we do it together.* "No, they haven't changed. I wonder when they will?"

"You may lose awareness of them. But they won't. Won't change."

"Are you trying to throw me back? I mean, after taking my measure."

"I haven't had time to take your measure. And I haven't tagged you."

Mary was puzzled. She thought for a while, and then said: "I think…I think I can respect your way of…well, your way. But it's not exactly what I wanted to hear, or seem to need to hear. Not just now, I mean, when I've left so much of myself behind, and left it so abruptly." Silence ensued. Then: "Possibly, so selfishly."

"But we've just established that you still have—probably always will have—your...all your...love. For Josh."

"Yes. But I won't be expressing it in the hundred ways I'd thought I would be."

"I see that it's a break. Never without regret."

"I made it willingly; with all my heart. You know so."

"I guess the difference is that I have given up nothing."

"And I've left Josh with nothing."

"Not if you still love him." A wind blew through the valley. A declivity in the rock formed a small pool. Beside it grew a seedling, too young to declare to the observer—to the ordinary observer—what tree it would become. The wind bent it briefly. Then it recovered; stood straight again. "But if you can't express your love, anymore, to any great degree, nor very often, then he will have been turned away. And he will feel that."

"Of course he will."

"And he will feel pushed aside, and substituted-for." The wind blew on through the valley and left it, quiet, behind.

"You couldn't summon up a little jealously, I don't suppose?" She looked down, shyly. She was very, very beautiful, nearly to the point of its being painful to look at her. Josh was jealous of the very sunlight and of the shadow that fell across her.

"I've been struggling against it ever since you left the Ashfields' hunt breakfast with Josh. The enemy—I mean jealousy, not Josh—has been bringing up reïnforcements steadily. But I can't afford to be afraid of them."

"You're saying all the right things...exactly the right ones...about my feelings for Josh. You're not putting it on...?"

Edward stopped looking at Mary through half-closed eyes, abandoned the warmth in the rock and sat up, ceased repeating his message to the sky. "Don't ever accuse—or suspect—me of that, or of anything like it." Mary was startled by the peremptoriness in his voice. But it softened right away; he would have liked to caress her with his words, too. "I began by saying I expected you to continue—well, not to continue being in love with him—to continue to love him, though."

"I'd rather have you true, than too good to be true." Edward saw that she was smiling. He was glad of it. For, needless to say, he loved her. "After all," and here a fine edge of bitterness sounded, no more than a leaf of brass, hammered to a flat note within a windchime, the music persisting, "you've given back his life."

"I had a hand in it, but only because, literally, I approached the place where he was drowning with some perspective, instead of being dropped into the middle of a commotion that was standing in the way of rational...."

"But I heard it took more than reason."

"Not much more. I did have to shout curses at people I didn't know, in order to get them out of the way. I acted on my assessment, which could have turned out to be wrong. I took out the thole-pin, the oar came free; Josh's boat practically righted herself." Here Edward left off.

"Still, you gave him back his life."

"It sounds as though you have come to me out of gratitude for that."

"That's absurd." She was tearful; Edward wished in passing that he were dead.

"Maybe you're trying to have me share some of your guilt. And that's fair enough."

"My guilt?"

"Well, I guess I've assumed you feel guilty for leaving Josh, when maybe you only feel pain. But there has to be some dispensation for loving and wounding at the same time."

"Do people ever tell you you're strange?"

"Constantly."

"What do you think I ought to do, Stranger?"

"I don't know. Certainly I don't, if I'm a stranger, and beside the point. But, Mary, I know I don't want to complete my life, unless with you."

"You will never be a stranger to me. And I'll stay at your side as long as we live. I just don't know where to situate Josh in it all."

"I think, wait, and you'll see. 'Blow on the coals of the heart, and we'll see.'"

"I know; 'We'll see, we'll see.'"

" But, while we wait to see: Look across to that little draw." Mary looked. "Come before me; watch where I'm pointing." He took her into his arms.

"What am I supposed to be looking for?"

"Do you see that little strip of white?"

"A waterfall!"

"From where we are, you can't see where it ends."

"In summertime, I imagine it can't be seen from here at all, with all the trees in leaf."

"Is that how it is with mountain streams?"

Thomas had taken off his wedding ring and put it away, and he was on his way to Alenda's house to tell her he had done so.

"I put it in a drawer in my desk that I reserve for things I shall probably never look at again."

"What a relief! You certainly know how to make a trembling bride feel secure." This exchange took place late in December, after Mary Mountainstream's letter had arrived at Clear Creek. "I hope you didn't find some remnant of the past that has alarmed you." For something preoccupied him.

"I did come across something from the past, and it was something I had forgotten."

"But it was not alarming?"

"No. Still, it was a thing that turns out to be part of a remarkable coïncidence. I want you to read this letter." And he held out an envelope of pale blue paper with fine diagonal striations. The handwriting was imposing, but not particularly legible.

"Is this something you found in the relegation-drawer?"

"No, it's not. It has just come in the mail."

So Alenda took out the letter and read it; and this is what it said:

Woodleigh House
Friday

My Dear Canon Strikestraw,

I am writing so that you will know what a blessing, as well as a pleasure, it was for us to have your grandson here just before Thanksgiving. I say "blessing," because, in the course of a deer shoot in honor of my niece and her fiancé, there was a boating accident. My nephew—strictly speaking, my husband's nephew, Josh Jones—came, I think extremely close to losing his life. But Edward was able to rescue him. Laurence and I haven't any children, and Alina—Josh's mother and my sister-in-law—hasn't any other ones. So Josh is doubly and trebly precious to all of us; our gratitude to your Edward will be unending.

Besides his heroism, he was the complete gentleman of a guest; his behavior toward everyone was so perfectly suited. As an example: He addressed the Colored couple who help us so much, with everything, really, as "Tommy," but "Mrs. Araby." —So sensitive, in these days of interracial unhappiness. And he left them a little something in an envelope, over which he had written, "With thanks for a wonderfully comfortable stay." And it was signed.

You probably remember the mother's admonition to us when we left for a house party: "Don't forget to give the maid a dollar." And the traditional rejoinder was, "If they have a maid." And the rejoinder to *that* was, "And if you have a dollar"! Edward has brought a wonderful transformation, very much of today, to these old customs of hospitality. You must be terribly proud of him.

My husband quickly grew to be very fond of Edward—they had long talks, covering just about everything, I should think. Laurence seems very eager to meet you, as well—Edward told him such a lot about you. He really is a most devoted grandson.

So we hope very earnestly that you will find time to come and stay with us, for a long weekend *at least*. Perhaps after your retirement, which Edward says is imminent. Not that there is very much here to do, or see. But it would be a happiness for us, especially in our relative isolation, to be able to look forward to a visit from you—and at *any* time (except in July or August, if you value your health!).

Meanwhile, we all wish you a joyful Holiday Season!

Sincerely yours,
Lavinia Cloudsley Ashfield (Mrs. Laurence Ashfield)

Alenda replaced the letter and handed it back. "That is lovely! Did you know about Edward's saving the life of the other young man?"

"Yes, I did; he said something about it. But he was preoccupied with another matter."

"You needn't tell me so! Remember, I spent Thanksgivng afternoon with him."

"Rhodë said he mentioned the young lady's name to her seventeen times. And they couldn't have been together by themselves for more than a total of around an hour-and-a-half over the whole weekend."

"Why do you suppose she counted?"

"Apparently, her experience in matters like this has led her to think the density with respect to time has prognostic value."

"And did she consider the time adequately crowded with references?"

"'Saturated.' And that is exactly the word she used, somewhat to my surprise. Her very words. I mean, word."

"Do you think he will bring her here at Christmastime?"

"It's all been worked out. They are going to spend Christmas with her people; New Year's, here, with me." Thomas gradually lifted his gaze to where the wall meets the ceiling. "Or do you think I ought to have said, '…here, with us'?"

"Either is perfectly all right with me. But it does raise a question."

"Yes. When are we to marry? It is your decision, of course. That is an inviolable tradition, I believe; Grace could tell us, if she were here. It depends only upon when you are ready to have me."

"I'm ready now, in that case, or at any time after now. But I realize we must go through some motions. For example, how long do you have to wait between asking the banns?"

"I don't think it is particularly a matter of Canon Law. I was brought up to think A month."

"Anything suits me. In that connection, I wasn't brought up at all. And I am in no hurry, now that you have accepted my proposal…."

"Alenda! An entirely ridiculous thing for you to say, and not at all how it happened."

"…but it does bear on your invitation from the Ashfields. Because I don't see that you can go before your retirement. And I should think the knot will have been tied by then, or shortly after."

"Well, I have not decided whether to go at all, for that matter."

"But, oh, yes, you *have* decided. And you have decided to go. And I know it."

Hamstrung again! How much I wish I could say "God damn it," as often as I liked. Without seeming unprofessional.

"Furthermore, I know that your having me read that letter has something to do with it, and that you have more to say on the entire subject."

And so they walked back up to Front Street and strolled decorously up and down the esplanade and talked. They talked about a lot of things, and about a lot of people: About Grace, William Lucas (Alenda's first husband), William, her son, and his and Martha Trimble's wedding plans; their own plans for life together after marriage—whenever they might decide to have it take place. They both felt they had Grace's blessing, they knew they had their offspring's, and Alenda was for some reason not too much concerned about the blessing (or not) of the husband to whom she had been untimely married, from whom untimely widowed.

Darkness came on, with the year bringing so many things to a close, in some instances shuttering them away forever; in others, laying the foundations for so much else that the days of the New Year would construct. They walked up to the Cape Fear Café, on Next Street, and sat down to have a plain dinner—shrimp cocktail and roast beef, always served on Sundays, from early afternoon through early evening. They did not want to part. Besides, conspicuously absent from the roll of persons they had discussed during their stroll was Robert.

They had spoken together about Robert before. They had spoken about him nearly countless times. There was no longer any doubt in anybody's mind about what his rôle in the War had been. Everyone was agreed that there ought never to have been any question. That if entrusting security to anyone might have been necessary, then it would have been first and foremost to Robert Strikestraw. But Thomas had said nothing, nor to Alenda nor to anybody else—not ever—about the child Anne had borne before she had met his son. For by this time, who would care? Until today.

He told Alenda now, however. And then he told her about his journey through brambles and brakes of pain and doubt and fear to Virginia, to interrogate Bunny. *Bunny Kubilsek!* After that, he told her about what he had come upon that morning, when he opened the "drawer of relegation:" The sealed envelope with "Edward" written across it that held the names of Anne's child's natural father and adoptive parents. And a notation that the child was probably, but not certainly (at any rate, in Thomas' view), a girl.

"I never knew—I don't know now—what moved me to extort this meaningless information from that wretched, dying man. But I did it. I was driven to do it. And then, when I had learned them, the names could as well have been fictional ones, out of a book I had never read. It has occurred to me, off and on, that this might still very easily be the case.

"But it is not the case. Because, although it did not register with me when Edward told me about his visit to the wilds of South Carolina, it did when I read Mrs. Ashfield's letter. The names of the adoptive parents were Mr. and Mrs. Parker Jones, of New York City—Parker and Alina Jones. This boy whom Edward happened to rescue—Jones—and his mother—Alina, and clearly at some point, if no longer, Alina Jones! They are *fratres uterini.*"

Abruptly, then, Thomas directed the subject of their conversation back to that of their marriage. He redirected it without room for demur. Anyway, it was a subject which both basked and reveled in, whether in speaking with each other or with their other friends and family, or simply when musing.

But Alenda could converse and cogitate at the same time, and she quickly realized that what her husband-to-be had told her was that Josh Jones and Edward had the same mother, Anne, Robert's young bride, who had left him a widower, himself lost not many months afterward. It was astonishing, to be sure. But there seemed nothing to be done about the discovery.

Alenda was certain, however, that Thomas would go to visit the Ashfields at "Woodleigh House," whatever Woodleigh House was. And if it should prove to be a retirement home somewhere, or even an insane asylum, or a tuberculosis sanitarium, then no matter; Alenda was going, too.

Winter's spectacle in the Southland involves a ruse used by the character Lucifer, who poses in borrowed robes throughout the First Act as Photolestes, his just-elder angel twin, and, wherever he can, in this costume, veils the growing light.

The thieving tilt of the Earth rids the oak of just so many leaves as allow the holy mistletoe to flourish in perfectly blended day and night, its berry becoming lustrous, fattened with seed-bearing pulp. This is one of the oscillations constituting the Great Reciprocity of things, as we may observe them one by one. The Back-and-forthness that Parker Jones had taught his son to watch for. Both father and son came to see in it something vaster than Newton's simple proposition: That every action is associated with an "equal and opposite" reaction, a thing we are taught in our early years and never question after that, for the most part, thinking of it, perhaps, as confirmed by the examples set to accompany the precept. Parker and Josh had speculated together about this a good deal: Whether there were two forces counteracting, rebounding, or whether there were an acting force exerting itself against some realm at rest. They decided that one of the two must be taking place, and, lying at the threshold of death, Parker had told Little John which one it was.

The poles slip, one wheeling up into sunshine as the other declines. The deer run. The wild ivy twines with the native holly, suckering about some sturdy stump not spared by a doomed woodman, unknowing, like us all, of his doom. Squirrels place acorns; birds, their brightest feathers upon this altar to Unconquered Sun. The toad, the precious jewel from its head. Another creature, the riven, lucent lantern-like thing the locust wears for a while as his skeleton. But all this happens in the First Act. Offstage. For an instance, deep in the wooded coastal plain of Onslow County, toward Hawes Point. Cold and gloom try to conceal the victory of the Day, assured before it is known.

Thomas had more to think over than he had let on to his bride, for he knew another name. As is common in alternatives, only one of the two possible resolutions allowed for a change of mind, or of heart. He spent a couple of days to himself. And Alenda had the good judgment to leave him to himself. But soon, he was on his way to visit her again. Mainly because he loved her, and did not want to be outside her presence; not because he had decided what to do.

III

"'Count stars. Think of the quietest thing. Like snow. I'm sorry you didn't get to see any. But now snow is falling through the stars—.'"

Truman Capote: from "One Christmas"

"...There comes a holier calm,..."

E. H. Sears: (the Hymn "St. Agnes," l. 14)

*H*OW *MEAGER THE remaining blood of my line is,* Laurence Ashfield said to himself. It was Christmas Eve, and on Christmas Eve you thought atavic thoughts like that. His nephew, Josh. He would protract the kindred, though not the name.

His mother, the redoubtable Miss Allie, had been as skeptical about mere names as anybody: "'What's in a name?' indeed! There are plenty of people named 'Ashfield' to whom your father wouldn't give the time of day!" All the while believing herself more forebearing. Magnanimously, she would usually add: "Now, connect that name to a *place*, and you may have reliable information."

Mother and son had been in unspoken agreement. A lot of people considered themselves distinguished by their names. More of them ought to work at distinguishing what names they had, though, Laurence thought, and would pass along. He was grateful to his fathers for their accumulations, good and goods—material, deeds, principles—things they had, or had done or taught, that had made his own life better than it would otherwise have been. Nevertheless, he was interested more in where he was going than in where he had come from. At any rate, what he had inherited and what had accrued to it he could leave to Josh, whose problem the question of succession would then become. To be entirely content himself, he had only to ratify a small dodge in the descending pathway of his family, and that to a nephew whom he loved, liked, and approved.

Laurence was already dressed for Midnight Mass—still hours away—in flannels, blazer, and a sumptuous necktie from Sulka. Lavinia had made him open this one present at the hour of sunset.

No rollicking festivity was going to jostle the old house about, not this season, though it had known so many others, of which some had been nearly seismic. This year, only the five of them—they would exchange gifts, have dinner together at four o'clock. *We three of this five, the blood of my line, will keep the feast...then who will come along behind us? It would be interesting to know.* Laurence found this not a distressing but a challenging thing to think about. He liked looking forward. He thought of Parker Jones, for a too-short while his brother-in-law, who had found in life nothing to fear, and found nothing to fear at the coming of his death. They had been great friends. He hoped he was like Parker, and he believed he might be, up to a point.

All of a sudden—he was standing in the East Room—he thought the fire fell dark in the chimneypiece, first flickering sickly, then dying down and going out. And was that a stain lying upon the cold hearth? The thought that it might be congealed blood crossed Laurence's mind. *Well, this is getting positively Dickensian, and necromantic.*

He left the room. He ventured out into the kitchen house, where he found Lavinia grappling with what looked to him like a bunch of red celery. "Is that rhubarb?"

"Yes. I suddenly felt a longing for it." Laurence looked stupefied. Lavinia looked up. "Oh, you *do* look handsome and dashing!" He feared it could only be the necktie. "Mary Alice and I are baking two rhubarb-and-cranberry tarts, one for them and the other for us."

"Good Gracious! There will be other things, too, won't there?"

"Of course there'll be; it's Christmas! By the way, soon you'd better go back inside. Josh is coming over with presents." And, sure enough, as Laurence entered the back hallway he heard three great crashes of the doorknocker.

Doorknockers! There's something Dickensian and necromantic about them, too, I think I remember. Before opening the door, Laurence glanced into the East Room in order to reassure himself about the fire, which he saw to be blazing brightly.

Laurence opened the door to Josh. They greeted each other, and there was a toppling transfer of Christmas packages. Then Lavinia came in; she too was dressed for Church, but over her costume she wore a chef's apron, too long, so redoubled at the waist, the red strings crossed behind and tied in front. She simply could not be made to look inelegant, each man thought. She was carrying a small tray with a goblet on it, half full of spirit. "Merry Christmas, Josh!" she said as she kissed him, and then led them across the hallway, "I want you to do the honors." On the hearthrug in the West Room, resting upon an extra pair of firedogs, lay a great bole of last year's oak, garnished with holly and yaupon, both heavy with red berries, and a large sprig of mistletoe, with its pale fruit, translucent, the color of ivory. There were juniper and pine, clusters of leaves of the liveoak, trails of ivy.

Josh took the goblet, and, squinting through it at his aunt and uncle, asked: "What besides all this could any upstanding Druid priest ask for?" And he poured half the liquor onto the Yule log. But then abruptly he cocked his head back, brought the glass to his lips, and drained it. This had not happened before. Lavinia and Laurence exchanged fleeting, slightly troubled glances.

"Oh, Josh! Do you think half a measure will make it work?"

"Don't take your superstitions too seriously, Darling," Laurence hurried to interject. "Any amount at all will bring us good fortune. Besides, how do you think the Sectarians get through the year?"

So they all cried *Wes hal*, hoping they were pronouncing it correctly, or if not, at least closely enough for geniuses of hearth and forest to comprehend. All of them drank tots of brandy from glasses that were fine, but not heirlooms, which then they hurled as hard as each one could into the fireplace. They applauded when the glasses smashed, when afterward the flames ferreted out unseen faults within the shards, splintering them again and again.

Then Laurence asked whether there weren't left over "any of those fire-crystals." And soon, like little children, they were kneeling, watching in wonderment as the red and orange flames soon took origin in green and blue, curling upward to dissipate in flickerings of violet and magenta. All the while, no one else knocked at the door.

When the crystals had been used up and the fire had returned to its usual coloring, Lavinia stood and asked: "Have you had supper yet, Josh?"

"No, Ma'am."

"Would you like anything?"

"Nothing to eat, thank you. I'd like a drink, though. Since it's the Holidays." He turned to Laurence. "Shall I make us some?"

"I'll join you," Laurence said. "It's getting to be about that time."

"Aunt Lavinia?"

"Too early for me, given how late we'll be up and about. And I have to finish the rhubarb tarts. Tommy is coming up to fetch theirs, and I think then we'll exchange a few presents." And she went off toward the kitchen house.

"Shall I give you a hand? Or can you find everything?" Laurence asked of Josh.

"Sit tight, Uncle Laurence, and leave it to me."

Laurence watched the Yule log while he waited. He had continued to kneel, looking into the fire where they had been sprinkling the crystals. *Like scattering-barley, before the offering of a sacrifice?* As he stood, there was a popping sound, and a final variant flame arose. In it, Laurence was sure he saw the face of Marley, the handkerchief tied holding the jaw well up, the mouth closed. All of this had vanished before Laurence could get to his feet. He took his place in a chair beside the hearth. *At least the handkerchief held; I don't think I could have handled a dire prophecy, not right now. Maybe a little drink will do me good.* Laurence thought back over the times he had told himself this, and he was not encouraged.

Josh returned with two whiskies-and-soda, his own several shades darker than the one he offered his uncle. The Yule Log had begun to burn nicely. That took care of worries about its "catching up." Immediately, though, you had to think about its burning too fast, for it must last all night, and the next morning's fire be kindled from it, if good luck were to make a home at Woodleigh House for another year.

"Do you like rhubarb?" Josh waited for a moment before answering, because he loathed it.

"They serve it in restaurants sometimes." That didn't seem quite adequate. "And they eat it in the North a good deal, I believe."

"Well, it has certainly always been a rarity around here. Will you excuse me for a minute? I'll go out and see whether it's giving your Aunt any special problem. Why not put something on the record player?" And he went out.

Josh considered his aunt and uncle to possess a very satisfactory sound-system. For people of their generation. Lavinia had insisted that its components be placed out of sight; soon, though, carols rang out, but—lightly…ones that were familiar and bidding. Josh turned out some of the table lamps. The Christmas tree, unchallenged, cast its powerfully transformative glow from little clear and colored lights, reflected from every hue of blown and molded glass, the ornaments all thin as paper.

Midwinter was not deep at Woodleigh, nor did frosty winds make moan. Nevertheless, all was now wrapped in the unflawed mantle, woven over centuries by numberless hands and voices, just to invest this Season. Josh thought he had finally learned better than to strive for it. You couldn't, deliberately, snare out of nowhere what was supposed to overtake you from outside yourself, stealthily, at first only half-recognized. Yet for years he had been trying to find his way once more into the folds of this cloak of Christmas. And now, sitting at fireside in his uncle's house, they seemed to fall and ripple and billow all about him.

While she and Laurence were alone in the kitchen, Lavinia said: "I have never, before this, known Josh to ask for a drink."

"No, he is clearly not indifferent to it, the way he has always seemed up to now. Not that I think he's drinking too much. I don't think he'd had anything before he got here, do you?"

"Certainly, he didn't seem to me to have had. And I *am* glad to see him a little…merrier."

"I wish I could be sure you should be glad."

The two tarts looked rather homely. Lavinia did not consider that the strips of pastry crisscrossed over the filling held promise of a festive enough presentation. So she removed them carefully, gathered them into a ball, and started over. She was aiming for something…a step beyond the usual. It had not registered with her that she had it already. She set to work on an elaborate filigree.

Laurence went back to Josh; when he reached the door, glancing in, he saw that the boy had settled far down into his chair, with his legs stretched straight out before him, ankles crossed. His hands were folded upon his flanks—that wound, at least, had healed completely and quickly. His eyes were closed. The glass on the table beside him was empty, except for hollow remnants of ice cubes.

Now. Was this sleep? Sleep, facilitated by alcohol? Or was it the rêverie Laurence was himself ready to fall into, under the summoning influence of the olden song and Christmas light. He walked softly across to his nephew, took up the glass, and went quietly out. And in the dining room he refilled the beaker then took it back and replaced it. To seem to withhold would be to entice—that much he knew; so he hoped the converse would stand. Both his own and Lavinia's families had produced kinfolk who drank too much. Lavinia had evidently been irrecoverably wounded by some consequence of that excessive drinking, but she had never spoken frankly about it.

Then Laurence sat down in his chair across from Josh. Both these chairs were a great deal more comfortable than the ones that took their places when the family were keeping state. (The hunt-breakfast, for an instance.) He picked up a loosely gathered collection of printed leaves that had started out as a paper-bound book. But before he had found his place, he noticed that Josh had opened his eyes, and was smiling dreamingly.

These were the things going on at Woodleigh just about when, in Savannah's old city, a man, a young man named Andy, opened the door and entered a barroom. "I have come to the right place," he said as he looked around the room. There were plenty of people to hear him say this, but none of them was listening. Andy went to the bar and bought a drink. He took it to one of the very few empty tables in the vast room, once a cotton warehouse. Tables closer to the trough, the musicians, and the roaring fire in the great hearth were already filled.

Since it was Christmas Eve, the musicians were playing bouncy versions of popular songs of the season.

The walls were of warm brick, and in them you could see sockets that had held the joists of a storey above. If you looked upward, now, you saw only shadowy space filled with cigarette smoke, blurred linearity of rafters, with colored lights woven all around and about them.

Andy looked back on this evening often in later years, and whenever he did he remembered windows of leaded, numberless octagonal panes interwoven with lozenge-shaped ones. Just as in a picture book from his childhood: The workshop, the elves tightening a few joints, adding afterthoughts of bright paintwork, while Santa Claus paced impatiently.

The windows in the big barroom were in fact plain sashes, with wooden muntins, six-over-six; the wreaths that hung in each one of them were not really giving off the recollected scents of fresh spruce and pine, because they were artificial. As he was inhaling these odors of Edom, as they seemed, relaxing in the warmth of the fire, which was actually too distant to be enjoyed from where he sat, a pretty waitress, wearing red doublet and green hose, ankled up and said: "Merry Christmas! May I get you a refill?" You couldn't see it yet, but business had just begun to slacken its pace; besides, Andy was a passably comely young man. And he didn't have a girl with him, so the waitress was willing to take a little extra time.

"Yes, please," Andy said. "This one was a double, and I'd like another one. But after that—singles. No matter what I ask for. Okay?"

"Whatever you don't want," she answered, and both laughed. "Are you waiting for somebody?"

"Yes, several people. But they may not come. Or they may." One lie, one prophecy. The waitress looked confused, rather than skeptical, which Andy considered a courtesy. He noted, in spite of the redundant velvet doublet, that she filled the green hose very nicely. She would make an adorable little elf, he thought. He also felt he owed her further explanation, just because she had been kind enough to believe him. "These other people—I got here late, and I may have missed them."

"Oh," she exclaimed. "They would have waited for a nice guy like you, I'll bet!" Then, over her shoulder as she moved away: "You'll see. They'll be here by the time I'm back with your drink." She was gone some while, leaving him to look over the room again. There were a lot of tables available by now; Andy considered moving closer to the fire; it was burning lower. They had stopped stoking it. The musicians had left; the barkeep had turned on a radio somewhere out of sight. The station was playing only Christmas music, this more traditional, solemn.

Now, to his surprise, a couple about his own age got down from their tall stools at the bar itself and came to him where he sat. The young man said: "Merry Christmas! Do you mind if we join you?"

The girl with him added: "I can't sit on that barstool any longer; it is taller, I think, than I am." She wasn't very tall. But she was pleasant to look at. She was dressed much like the "Plantation People" Andy knew...of, back home. She talked the way they did, too.

Now the cocktail waitress arrived, and as she set Andy's glass before him she said: "I said they'd be along, didn't I?" She turned to the others, who had taken chairs, "Would either of you like anything?"

"No, thanks," the man said, "We've both just filled up." Then he put out his hand to Andy and said, "I'm Frank."

The girl said, with a cordial smile, "And I'm Cynthia."

"Do people call you 'Cindy'?"

"All the time. But I like Cynthia better."

"It's a pretty name."

"For a pretty girl, too, I think. Don't you?"

"Frank! What do expect the poor man to say?"

"No doubt about it."

"Do you live here, Andy?"

"No, I don't."

Cynthia asked: "Visiting friends for the Holidays? Or relatives?"

"More or less. I have a friend who studies and works here. He's putting me up for a couple of nights." This did not strike Cynthia as being very festive.

"But you *do* have plans for tomorrow?"

"For God's sake, Bunn. I sat down for a chat; you're interrogating."

"I just don't want anybody to have to spend Christmas as an ordinary day."

"Well," Andy said—and he no longer found the crowd or the music or the fire quite so congenial; all these things were by now appreciably diminished—"That's exactly what I'm going to do."

"But, why?"

"Please, Bunn!"

"Because that's just how I want to spend it this year." There was silence among them. Plenty of people were still in the barroom, the fire still crackled... now and again. The waitress stopped by their table.

Finally, to head off more questions from Cynthia (*Bunn!*) and more objections from Frank—they must be engaged, if they were scrapping together so fluently—Andy decided to tell a part, but only a part, of his story. "I live out in the country, where nothing goes on. Not at Christmas, and not at any other time." He had to be fairly obtuse to think, or even say, this. But then, of course, Andy was obtuse. For he was Andy Hawkins, from the Crossroads. "My brothers and sisters are married; this year all of them are spending Christmas with their husbands' and wives' families. So it would be duller than usual." A large party got up to leave; one of them went to the bar to pay their tab, and there was some kind of little skirmish, but it was soon over. They all left in high spirits.

"What about your parents? What are they going to do, all alone?"

"It would serve you right if he told you one of them was dead and the other, in the crazy house." And, suddenly horrified at himself, Frank looked quickly back at Andy, desperate for a denial of either thing.

"They're both okay, both at home. But I don't think they'd want me."

"Of course they'd want you. Mothers and fathers want their children with them at holiday-time. Especially as the years go by."

Andy didn't know, or much care, who these people were. But, for rank strangers, they didn't do a lot of holding back. "Growing up I was a lot of trouble to them. They'll have a better time without me."

"Do they know you're not coming? They'll have a miserable time without you. Anyway, everybody is a lot of trouble growing up."

Frank intervened: "Even just-so little ladies who live in Ardsley Park?"

"Of course even those. They just get into trouble with fancier people as witnesses, so it's more embarrassing. No, you've got to go home for Christmas, Andy. You didn't do anything really horrible, so that they sent you away?"

"You don't even know whether he can get home for Christmas."

"I don't know about transportation. But I know the distance is workable." She turned to Andy: "It is, isn't it? Because you live in Jasper County, don't you?"

"Peell."

"Same thing. I recognize the accent."

"You'd better not tell anybody from Peell County it's the same thing. Or the other way round. They'll be glad to explain the difference.

"But I think the questions are beginning to pile up...."

"Please forgive me," Bunn-Cynthia said. "I must learn to curb my curiosity. Or at least my rudeness in asking people questions about themselves all the time."

"And," Frank said, "once you've got the answer, in telling them what they ought to do."

"It's not rude. Or, I don't think it is. People are usually pleased when they're asked questions about themselves, when other people are interested. It's the people whom nobody is ever curious about who...."

Idly, Andy rattled the hollow carcasses of ice cubes in his glass. The waitress hurried over. At this stage in her evening's work she had very little else to do. The public house was about to close. Earlier than usual. Andy was almost prepared to undress and show the others his birthmark, if necessary. Just to quell Cynthia's curiosity. He had not had anybody ask him so much about himself before—about himself as someone up to then unknown. To the waitress he said: "Another double, please. But remember my warning!

"I never got into 'horrible' trouble, no. But my Mama and Daddy didn't need *any* trouble. When I was worried—or scared—about something I'd done, about something someone over me thought I'd done, my father could tell. But his way was not to ask about it; he just knew something was wrong and would always talk to me in a general way about Honesty and Truth. One night, he overheard me imitating his 'Honesty-and-Truth' lecture to some friends. After that, he thought—I think—that I considered him ridiculous. So when he knew I was low, he didn't say anything in particular. He just treated me with especial kindness."

Frank said: "What about your mother?"

"You know how mothers are about their little boys."

"I guess I do know."

Cynthia placed a pacifying hand on Frank's. She said: "I have the situation absolutely clear in my mind," she said, turning to Andy, "and I can tell you with confidence what you should do."

"It will be handy to be married to an oracle."

"What?"

"You must get home by tomorrow morning."

"Since the middle of the afternoon I've been thinking some about it."

"Good! Then be on your way!"

"I can't. I have nothing to give them."

Back at Woodleigh, when he saw that his nephew was awake, Laurence

Ashfield said to him: "I've freshened up our drinks. It's Holiday time, as you said. But we do need to be fit to be allowed into the church; Bob and Alina are going to be early, so they can hold altar-side seats for the three of us."

"Am I to stay here and go with you and Aunt Lavinia?"

"Wouldn't that be simplest?"

"Yes, I think it would, if it suits you. And I don't want to go back the way I came. At least, not tonight." Laurence did not ask for an explanation.

"I stopped the car on the way over here." He no longer smiled; there was mixed into his expression a suffusion of sorrow. "The moon was high. And almost full—I don't know which side of full. It was shining on the big fields north of the road, before where the ditch crosses. The furrows left from the turning-under stretch out, I know, to the edge of the woods, but I couldn't see where they ended, because of shadow." Josh fell silent, looking at the scene again, he having retrieved it from his memory.

"And so the furrows seemed to run on forever?"

"Yes. Long furrows, travelling right up to the doorstep of infinity." He waited, looked again. "I hadn't had anything to drink, you know." Then he laughed, but only a small laugh.

"Do you ordinarily see things like the doorstep of infinity when you do have something to drink?"

"It hasn't come to that. I only see again things I've actually seen before. Sometimes they've become lovelier."

'Lovelier!' What an odd word for the boy to use. Some transformation, he hasn't been accustomed to....

Josh went on: "It could, though, couldn't it?"

"What could what?"

"It could come to that, couldn't it?"

"Yes, it could. It happened to me once. Between us."

"Your secret is safe with me. *If only my own secrets could be safe with somebody, somewhere.*

"It's a little embarrassing...why I stopped and got out of the car. The length of the furrows, with the bright moonlight on them—and it really did seem almost like daytime, although I guess the moon is well on toward setting, by now—made me think of the phrase, 'Long lay the world....'"

"Why do you say 'embarrassing...'?"

"Because it's left over from childhood misunderstanding. In the carol, 'long' refers to time, not distance."

"I thought you thought time and distance were the same."

"No, Sir. That's time and space." How should he put it? "Think of the expression 'right then and there.' There can't be one without the other."

At least he seems fluent in his conviction. Laurence had learned the two

measures as two, and not until late adulthood had he begun to see them as
one. And still he did it haltingly. Physical laws, though—assuming there
were any, for they seemed to have been varying from era to era—were less
important than his nephew's welfare. "Son, may I speak directly?"

"Yes, Sir."

"Have you started drinking too much?"

"I may have.

"But the carol: 'The world,' doesn't mean 'the land,' or 'the earth,' either.
Anyway, though, when I was a little boy, those words printed a photograph
in my mind, and became attached to it as its soundtrack.

"Tonight, I could tell the world was waiting for something, and had been
for a long time. Either that, or it already had it without recognizing it. And I
was, I felt, looking for something, too. But I feel that way a lot. Do you think
everybody does?"

"If they don't, then they're in trouble."

"Well, when I was a little boy, and Christmastime came, it seemed to
me to settle everywhere, and be at home always. And now it isn't, except off
and on.

"Somewhere, among the years...I lost that...."

"'...Nothing can bring back the hour....'"

"No, nothing can. For several years—maybe four or five—I used to be
sad when I tried so hard to reach, and couldn't. I used to go out into the night,
to look at the stars. And just to wait and see."

"Were you rewarded?"

"Not often."

"Tonight?"

"Not then. What I was really doing in the fields tonight, I think, going
down along a furrow for a while, then switching over the little mounds, to
east or to west, was looking for arrowheads. We all used to, all the time. There
were a lot of them in those fields—probably still are—and they seemed to me
to belong to another world."

"They do."

"I was searching for something from another world then. And I was
waiting for something else from some other world again tonight.

"But when I used to go out under the stars and wait, I was really hoping
to sight a sleigh...and reindeer!

He laughed again, again just a little. "Or to see a star in the East. The
trouble was that I was waiting for something that was not coming toward me
from ahead, but going away, behind me."

"And you wanted to hold onto what was receding? The Star in the East—
does it recede? Or is it—distinct from the other things, I mean—by any

chance, still approaching? Have you looked to see? Carefully?" Laurence was touched, listening to his rather massively-built nephew recounting the sweetnesses of his early childhood, the pain of the necessity of letting it go. Laurence remembered, too, from his own first years. But not from again, as Alina could, as Parker, as long as he lived, could have done. For the childless have but their own childhoods, grown so remote, with little rekindling. "I wonder whether that magic," he said, "may not be intended to evolve within us into the marvellous peculiarities of Christmas? As it is said to have begun: Angels appearing to shepherds...."

"Scaring the daylight out of them, and probably stampeding their sheep."

"...women both too young and too old bearing Children; stars guiding mages, all that. And, more than these things, what they mean, or may mean?"

"And the Virgin-birth...what do you think about that?"

"Good Gracious. The Virgin-birth? What do I think of it?" In fact, Laurence had never given to this doctrine any thought at all. "Well, not very much at all, I'm afraid."

"You weren't surprised when you first heard about it?"

"Not especially. Were you? Because when I first heard about it, I hadn't yet heard about the other kind, either."

"Do you believe in it now? Do you mind my asking?"

"Of course not."

"It is known to happen, you know. It has a difficult name...'parthenogenesis.'"

"That's not difficult; it's Greek." Lavinia came into the room. She had taken off her apron.

"Are you talking about Plotinus again? Because if you are, I've got to say I don't think Christmas Eve is the time for it." She looked at her wristwatch. "It's after nine-thirty, and I'm ready for my drink, now. Would you, Josh?"

"Oh! Certainly!" he said, getting easily and swiftly to his feet. He gathered his own and his uncle's empty glasses and disappeared into the dining room, singing: "Long lay the world, in sin and error pining."

Then he stepped back into the room and sang with exaggerated clarity the phrase, "'Long lay the world, in sin, and ere repining!' That's what I used to think it said—Fairly sophisticated, wouldn't you say, for a five-year-old?"

Lavinia asked: "What do you consider sophisticated about it?"

"That I knew the word 'repining.'"

"I consider it far more sophisticated that you knew the word 'ere,'" Laurence said.

"Did you know what 'repining' meant?"

"No, Ma'am. *And I wish I didn't know, now.* Come to say, I didn't know what 'ere' meant, either." He stood for a moment. "I suppose it wasn't so clever, after all." And he went back into the dining room, not singing anything.

"I have not been talking about Plotinus," Laurence resumed, addressing his wife. I've been talking about the Virgin-Birth. Entirely appropriate for Christmas Eve."

"What were you saying about it?"

"We hadn't got around to saying anything about it. Josh had only asked whether I believed it."

"Yes, and you said No," Josh shouted, over the clatter he was making at the drinks-tray in the adjoining room.

Laurence shouted back: "I said No, I didn't mind your asking."

"Oh," Josh bellowed.

"Let's wait until we're all in one room," Lavinia suggested, unconsciously raising her own voice.

"What did you say?" Josh shouted.

"Never mind," she answered, nearly screaming. It was because of the tarts. They were going to be a failure. She had seen and accepted that. She had stored theirs in the refrigerator and left the Arabys' on the kitchen table, with a pile of presents, for Tommy, when he should come.

The foregoing exchange had been accompanied, on what Laurence had called 'the record player,' by a splendid piece of Vaughan Williams's, cunningly inserted between two ancient lays of the Tide. This work gave new meaning to the expression "a round of brass," and was punctuated by stop/ go vocal passages, cascading all over each other, to end in a festal howl. But now the three were seated serenely about the fire, composed, speaking quietly, solemnly, soothed by the strains of "God Rest Ye Merry, Gentlemen...."

Laurence had continuously, through the small uproar, mused over the question of the Virgin-birth, and now he was ready to respond, as clearly as he could, to Josh's question. He would leave his answer at a single word, if he had to. He hated any form of obfuscation; for like a rotted timber or corroded strapping, it could not be built upon, and one was then left where one had been before: With luck, no worse off, but certainly no better, and Laurence thought life far too short for that kind of thing, becoming more firmly set in this view with each year as it passed.

"Here is a little story, told me by a dear friend who was there when it happened:

"One day, in Caracas, the square in front of the Cathedral was being paved with a fresh coat of asphalt—all the cars had to be parked somewhere else. The vendors had to remove their stalls. Passions were already running high. Actually, I think they run comparatively high there most of the time.

Just then, an earthquake struck—and the next day's papers reported 'Much Panic; Limited Damage.'

"But that limited damage included the detachment of the large Cross from the pediment between the west towers of the Cathedral. It fell, and landed in the Tarmac, which was still soft.

"Some of the young men standing by, having first taken off their shoes, either to preserve the shoes, or to incur pain—nobody knew for sure which—that stood to gain them credit in Purgatory, or somewhere like that…."

"There is nowhere like Purgatory."

"…went out into the square, as though they were walking through burning coals, and lifted the cross. When the crowd saw that it had left an exact imprint in the new surfacing-material, everyone fell to his knees, scrabbled around for Rosaries, said unnumbered Hail's Mary, and all-in-all treated the thing as a miracle.

"As for myself, I don't regard it a miracle. Perhaps it is, if you don't understand it."

Lavinia and Josh were much amused, at the story and at the way Laurence told it. But Lavinia did feel that within it there was fun being made of the Latin temperament, as well as of the Roman Catholic Church. And it was not like Laurence to belittle anything or anybody. But then he went on. "Those Caraqueños would surely have understood the physical principle underlying a heavy thing's falling with force into a soft material and leaving its imprint there. But they were not concerned with the physical phenomenon and had bypassed it; they went directly to the spiritual, or mystical one. And if we ridicule that, we degrade ourselves.

"Sometimes, when we don't completely understand a thing, or don't understand it sufficiently to set our minds at rest about it, or are not accustomed to having it happen often, then it is typically cut out from the herd, into a little corral of 'miracles,' or signal events, or whatever we are inclined to consider them. "

Lavinia had been staring at the incandescing Yule log, but she had been listening intently. "Don't you think ordinary childbirth is a miracle, in a way?"

They were quiet then. There must be respect shown for her soul, once so deeply troubled about this matter. Presently Laurence said: "It seems one when you're there, bearing the child or standing watch. Later, when you have six children, all between the ages of nine and seventeen…."

"I think," she said then, "that it is unlikely that any two people would reckon up…would recognize the same number of…."

"Number and complement," Josh said, somewhat to everybody's surprise.

"…number and complement of miracles." All agreed.

"If the Creator has wrought all that we claim to believe He has wrought, if the things we've been speaking of are acts of the Creator, it is actually entirely impossible to be surprised by anything." So they left for Church, to receive the Body and Blood of Christ, "born as at this time of a pure virgin...."

On their way, they passed close to where Mr. and Mrs. Hawkins lived, behind the hardware store of which they were the proprietors. Not in rooms attached to the building, but in a modest Turn-of-the-Century bungalow that faced the next street. All of their children, except Andy, the youngest boy, were grown and married, and all of them were spending Christmas with their respective in-laws. And without saying just why not, nor where he would be, Andy, too, had planned not to be at home for the Holiday.

The Hawkins' bungalow was by chance built to the very same plan as the Watkinses' house in New Brunswick—a popular, much disseminated arrangement of the time—but would have been worth a great deal less money; it was "on the right side of the tracks" only because all of the Crossroads and its community were on the *same* side of the tracks. The family had moved into it when it became available after Old Mrs. Paget's death. The cast-iron cookstove, which had so gravely injured that lady in her fall against it, had been got rid of. But the portable kerosene heater beside which she, when far younger, had dried and warmed her elder son after his near-drowning in Blackwater was still there, still in use; in fact, it contained the Hawkinses' Christmas Eve fire.

However, they had got a wreath for the door and placed sprigs of holly above the mirror and pictures in their sitting room. Neither of them felt as gloomy as expected, possibly just for the reason that they had prepared for gloom, to entertain it; that is, have it with them only for the occasion, as the only thing not proper to their home.

Yukoneta Browne had asked Alina if she might give the Hawkinses one of her game pies. Alina had told her to take some eggnog along with it, and a bowl of "ambrosia"—not what the word implies, but a compôte of citrus fruit, sweetened and garnished with shredded coconut-meat. And these offerings constituted their Christmas dinner.

"Well, Sarah, Christmas by ourselves isn't turning out to be so bad, after all."

"If I have to celebrate it with just one other person, then you would be the one."

"Such a sweet girl!"

"You've been calling me that for more years than anybody has ever remained a 'girl.'"

"I have noticed no change." They rose from the dining table and went back to the kerosene heater in the sitting room. "It was good when all the children were little and we had a Christmas tree—all that…."

"There is a time for everything; then the time for anything is gone. I know you're glad we had those times. Some don't."

"It was a little bit like a night of magic, the colored lights and the fireworks. Do you know there're still crescent-shaped black smudges on the walkway out in front where we used to set off those little things called 'flowers—ground bloom'? They spun like tops and went from purple to orange and yellow as they burned?"

"Well, we had that time. Maybe it will link our children's early years to our grandchildren's." She wanted to close this topic; the muscles in her throat had begun, relentlessly if slowly, to tighten. But her husband went on.

"And it was so easy to delight their hearts, with so little. That's what we had: Little. But back then, they thought the gifts they'd been given were as extravagant as any."

"Jonathan, let's don't talk about the past any more, not for a while." He didn't hear.

"We could make them so thoroughly happy then…as happy as the Ashfield children…."

"There weren't any Ashfield children at the time you're thinking of."

"When they'd got older, they saw the difference, more and more. Then they thought it meant we didn't love them as much, I think possibly. And later still, I don't think they—all—loved us much anymore. Or not as much. I guess they didn't see the signs they would have recognized, and so they couldn't draw the same conclusion. We'd just become less important in their lives. That's normal, isn't it?"

"Hush, now. Yes, it's normal. They've all been to their mates' families this year; what if next year they all come here! We won't leave anything undone!"

"Andy doesn't have a mate."

"No."

"And he won't be here." And with that a silence did fall, heavy indeed. Then: "I lost him, you know. I don't know exactly when it happened, but there came the time when I knew I'd lost him."

"Shall I give you my Christmas present now?"

" No. Let's exchange presents tomorrow morning."

The bar in Savannah had closed at eleven o'clock. Cynthia, Frank, and Andy were making their way up Bay Street, toward the Riverside Groce-a-teria. They had found out about the little skirmish at the cash register: That night, nothing any customer had ordered was charged for, and the larger party, who hadn't known this—nobody had—had eaten and drunk lavishly, and were embarrassed at first.

"When you want to give a gift, but don't have much money to spend...."

Frank interrupted her: "We realize that happens to you all the time, of course." But Cynthia had by now been scorched once too often with his tracer-fire, at least on this point. She stopped. Frank and Andy stopped, too. So did the flock of variously-patterned pigeons, who never, nightlong, gave up scavenging.

"Listen to me, Frank. If you can't deal with the few trivial differences between our upbringings, then break off our engagement. I can live with your attitude about it for a while, but not for a lifetime." And that was all she had to say on the subject. Presently, the pigeons resumed their searching, pouting, pecking, squabbling.

The three young people moved on, at first in silence, to which, though, Cynthia was not naturally given. Nor was she, to ill-feeling. "Mother always recommended choosing an expensive magazine. An expensive magazine is not really an expensive *thing*, and you can find one—at least—to correspond with nearly anybody's interests. The whole north half of the Groce-a-teria is devoted to nothing but magazines. Although some of them would *not* make suitable Christmas presents—or any kind of presents."

"Did you look at them when you were a little girl?" Frank asked her.

"As long as I could, before getting caught."

"We did, too."

"Do you think they're still open?"

"The magazines?" For Frank still remembered particular pages, heavily referenced.

"The Groce-a-teria."

"I hope so. They're usually open until midnight. And Mr. Buncombe always stays open on religious holidays, because he thinks he's an atheist."

"And because he's a Scrooge."

"Sorry thing to be on Chrstmas Eve."

Next morning, Lavinia had to face squarely the fact that "Christmas had come once more." But what to do with it? Without little children thundering down the stairs, frenetic tearing open of packages, dashes out into the grounds to look for hoofprints, what did one do? She was sitting at the kitchen table, having coffee, and asking herself these questions. Dinner had to be held at the ancestral home, even if there were only five people to sit down to it. But everything was ready. What they had, food, or company, or gifts, or song, they would concentrate and so make seem bountiful!

The day had begun brightly, but because the sun shone beneath the clouds. Now all was becoming wintry-looking. You just had to ignore the temperature, and Christmas really had come. Mary Alice Araby tapped at the door, then entered what was after all her domain.

"Merry Christmas, Mary Alice! Have you baked your rhubarb tart yet?"
"Merry Christmas, Miss Lavinia! Yes, I have. We had our Christmas dinner last night, and now we're on the way to Yemassee for the rest of the Day."

Silence.

"How was it? The tart."

"Well, I have never had one before, so I have nothing to go by."

"Are you telling me it was awful?"

"Miss Lavinia, nothing can spoil Christmas. But I stopped by to thank you, on behalf of my family, for the presents you sent us. You and Mr. Laurence are always so generous and kind; I just wanted to let you know that we don't take, and have never taken, your graciousness for granted."

"Oh, Mary Alice! If only I could show you with presents how much we... love you all!"

"Here are a few little things from the children." And she set a basket full of shiny packages on the table and went out, with surprising abruptness. But she came back inside immediately. "Miss Lavinia, Ben won't come with us."

"Why on earth not? Or does he say why not?"

"His first few months off at college—there're drink and drugs, but...."

"Mary Alice, has anything very bad happened?"

"No, Ma'am; not yet."

"What has all this to do with his not going to Yemassee with the family?"

Mary Alice broke down; she wept a bit, tried to think for a bit, before answering. "I don't know. We don't know. He never talked a lot. Now, he hardly says anything at all.

"And...I don't think it's drink or drugs—and just being away from home for the first time...."

"What, then?"

"He has seen so much hard-heartedness between White people and Colored people. That's what it is."

"But that has been growing worse for years. Didn't you talk to him about it, before he went away?"

"We tried to—both of us did. But we don't know so much about it ourselves. Living away down here in the country, seeing more kindness among people than you see where so many are crowded together...I think he just hasn't been able to take it in."

"But that can't have anything to do with how he feels about his own people—and your extended family are as close kin to him as they'd be even without your having adopted him…since you and Lilia Belle were sisters."

At this, Mary Alice instantly became completely still. The casual and minor movements of head and trunk and limbs left her all at once. Minute gestures and postural changings we don't even notice in each other. Until, unless they disappear. She looked much the same as she had to hapless Andy Hawkins the afternoon he had made the mistake of coming to the front door at Woodleigh after causing offense. She covered her face, and almost gave way to racking sorrow. But she did not give way. She took down her hands.

Lavinia saw that something had alarmed her out of measure. What, though?

"Has word come back about her? Is she gone?"

"Oh, no, Mary Alice, I meant to say: '…Since you and Lilia Belle *are* sisters.' I'm so sorry!"

"Forgive me, Miss Lavinia, for making a fuss, and on Christmas Day! Maybe some things *can* spoil Christmas." And she composed herself and added: "My grandmother will stay at home, too. She will have Ben with her."

"Is there anything we can do for them…either of them?"

"No, Ma'am, I thank you." There was no reasonable way to invoke "merriness" anymore. The two women said Goodbye.

Laurence came into the kitchen; he usually did, when he thought Lavinia was there alone. She was withdrawing the tart from the oven. "It smells wonderful," Laurence ventured. Together they studied it.

"Do you know what Josh asked me after Church last night?" he said. "While he was waiting for Bob?"

"Of course I don't know; how could I know?" She had sounded more cross than intended.

"This is what he said, right out of the blue—black, rather, I suppose. He said: 'Uncle Laurence, while we're on the subject of the Virgin-birth…'—I told him we weren't on it—'…do you believe that in Holy Communion we receive the actual, or veritable, Body and Blood of Christ?'"

"What did you tell him?" *He certainly couldn't have chosen an odder source for an opinion.*

"I told him what I thought, of course."

"Yes, I'm sure you did; but what *do* you think?"

"That a lot of learned men have considered that question, discussed it among themselves, and that in spite of it, many people believe that we do, veritably, as Josh said—others' view is that it is a symbolic union."

"Then why didn't you just tell him you don't know."

"How do you think that would have sounded. You wouldn't have been so dismissive to the Boy."

"I hope he left it at that?"

"In fact, he didn't. He went on with it. He said this: 'Well, then, whether or not...do you think Christ is God?'"

"And you answered him along the same line?" The kitchen sink was half full of Christmas greens—holly, pine, juniper; Lavinia selected a very full-leafed branch of holly and returned with it to the table.

"What kind of man do you think I am? Jesus was flesh and blood. And flesh, blood, wine and bread are all sensible creatures."

"Sensible?" She took rather listless aim at the tart.

"Apprehensible by the senses. So there is a basis of comparison of those things among each other. God is *not* apprehensible by the senses, in spite of a number of legends and claims."

"And beliefs."

"Beliefs, if you ask me, are nothing but claimed legends." They were becoming irritated with each other, the way people fond of each other often do. "Anyhow, simple transubstantiation among sensible things is at least conceivable. But to maintain that the Godhead and created man can be fused into a single, sensible being is a proposition that I don't think the mind—or, that form of mind found in humankind—can comprehend."

"Christ was not created. '...begotten, not created.' I heard you say so, or sing so, last night."

"When?" The Challenge.

"The second stanza of 'O, come, all ye faithful.'" She had picked up the gauntlet. "However, I suppose we're all heretics to some extent."

"With Church doctrine so full of self-contradictions, we are bound to be."

All of us are, who savor what is given us to eat and drink, before we swallow it. He walked over to kiss her on the cheek. It was a way they had of declaring No harm done.

Inside the beautiful fluted crust of the rhubarb tart, just bordered by a margin of slightly charred pastry filigree there swam what looked like a miniature lava-field, perhaps one in the process of cooling. Not that parts of the thing weren't appetizing to look at—glazed cranberries, with custard bubbling up among them, and so on. But some kind of butcher's offal seemed to have been dropped into the center.

"I have seen Mary Alice; they had theirs last night. Apparently its bite is going to be even worse than its bark," Lavinia said as she slammed the sprig of holly into the caldera, covering the worst, settling the whole composition.

"Ben has refused to go with the rest of them to Yemassee. So he and Miss Izora will be about."

"Why won't he go?"

"I'm not sure I know."

"What does Mary Alice think?"

"I don't know. She mentioned a lot of possible reasons. Ones that didn't seem to me particularly compelling."

"I know those people. They would want to respect Lilia Belle's trouble by treating her son with special kindness, and I think he ought to have gone and given them the opportunity." Lavinia gave the rhubarb-and-cranberry tart a look of hatred. Then she realized it had merely become the focus of all her Holiday-time anxieties, and she put it from her thoughts. "Don't you agree?"

"My first thought would have been to agree." Now the car bringing the three from Clear Creek came crunching upon the bed of crushed oyster shells up to the brick coping.

"Your second thought?"

"I didn't isolate it fully till after Mary Alice had left. Let's not let it come into being yet. Nothing must be allowed to spoil Christmas. We can talk about it at a better time." So they went out to meet their guests, their family. The shouted greetings, babble of everyone talking at once, gave the effect of a multitude, as Lavinia had planned. It was as though none of them had seen any of the others for years.

Down at the Crossroads, a thing of like kind happened. Sarah and Jonathan Hawkins had had a late and leisurely breakfast, and had exchanged Christmas gifts, when they heard a car drive up and stop in front of their house. Mrs. Hawkins hurried to the front windows, looked out and said: "It's Andy!"

"Andy!"

"Yes. Hurry! Go into the big closet. On the top shelf is a box, pushed far to the back. Get it. Bring it. Hurry!" And so Mr. Hawkins went and did as he had been asked. The container, he saw when he had found it, was a quite large one. He opened the lid; it was filled with festively wrapped presents, varyingly smaller. He hurried with it back into the sitting room; Andy had not yet come inside but could be heard stepping up to the front door.

"Were did all these come from?"

"All over the Lowcountry—I've been shopping for them for a year."

"Do you think we can still delight his heart?"

"It may be we can."

Jonathan strode over to the door, flung it open. Andy stood there, about to take hold of the doorknocker. "Merry Christmas, Son! And you take hold of the doorhandle at this house, not the knocker."

Andy held out two cylinders of white tissue paper, bound about the ends with ribbons of gold, streaming and looping in the morning light.

When all the party from Clear Creek had got inside—and it took some while—Josh, without asking or being asked, brought the drinks tray in from the dining room. Ordinarily, Laurence would have done this. He wondered whether Josh were being considerate, or whether he were merely thirsty.

Instead of the dining room, they dined in the west room, crowded around the small table where the Ashfields had many of their lunches and suppers, just the two of them; the crowding made the few seem many. To the settings, Lavinia had added all the wines Laurence had selected, in their own bottles with their gallery of imposing labels, each in its own old silver coaster. There were lighted candles and Christmas greens. No space for anything more. Only for Christmas cheer. Nobody stopped talking. Nobody stopped eating and drinking. It seemed impossible. But everybody's eyes shone, and all of them radiated happiness. Every omen was favorable: A fragment of the Yule log had survived. The piece by Vaughan Williams didn't begin until the moment when the Christmas pudding went up in flames of blue so clear and pure that the candles had to be snuffed in order for them to be seen readily.

When the afternoon had grown boozily aromatic, Bob said: "Lavinia, this may have been the grandest meal I've ever been fed."

"Thank you, Bob," Lavinia murmured, "but the credit is due Alina and May Alice as much as me."

Alina got up to help distribute table-favors, each a package identical to the others, cubes of silver foil with ribbons the green of spruce.

As Josh began to unwrap this last present of the day, Laurence said: "This is a long shot, Josh; I hope you'll like it." From the foil and ribbon and froth of tissue paper, Josh lifted a vessel, a porcelain dome you could envelope in both cupped hands, or Josh could in both his, a flat-bottom circular thing of squat elegance, a delicately lipped opening at its vertex having the graceful flaring of an unfolding flower. On its declining shoulder, an intricately incised medallion beneath the brilliant yellow glaze.

The others were delighting in their own prizes, volubly expressing pleasure and thanks. Josh held the vessel, gazing in silence upon it.

Too long a shot, Laurence said to himself.

At last, Josh said: "This is one of the several most beautiful objects I have seen…and I can't even think of any of the others—I just wanted to avoid seeming to exaggerate. Thank you very much. Uncle Laurence?"

"Yes. It was my choice."

"Thank you so much, again."

"I'm happy you like it. I used to want things of that sort when I was your age. But I hesitated to let on. I don't know why."

"Next time, let on to me! Thank you." He got up from the table. "I want to take my treasure home; I know I won't break up the party, though. Since all the rest are of a certain...no, are at a certain stage in your development, I know you have things to talk over among yourselves. While there's still time!"

Laughter and protests met these words, but, right away, Josh picked up the Testament from the secretary and according to Family tradition read the Last Gospel, that is, the first chapter of the Gospel of St. John, down to "And we beheld his glory...." Then he went around the table, kissed everybody, and made them sit down and take no part in his going. His Uncle Laurence insisted on seeing Josh at least to the door, but was dissuaded, not without difficulty. "Remember I left my car here last night, so nobody's plans will have to be changed."

Meantime, Sarah Hawkins read again the greeting card she'd found wrapped with the present from her son:

Dear Mr. and Mrs. Hawkins,

Andy was concerned because he thinks his gifts are not very lavish. I think you'll agree that they are richer than "myrrh from the forest"! No Christmas presents can have been chosen with more care—he spent, or I should say we three spent—three-quarters of an hour before he could make up his mind. (And at that, the man kept the store open late—he ordinarily closes at midnight!)

Andy thought you, Mrs. Hawkins, might like a decorating magazine; he said you enjoyed daydreaming about beautiful houses. I know I do, and I think all women do. So that was not quite as critical, Mr. Hawkins, as his choice for you. He had decided on something to do with travel. At the last minute, he found a magazine with the piece on Meteor Crater, in Arizona. He was tremendously excited. He said you had been interested in this for a long time, talked about it a lot, and that you knew *everything* to do with it. I got a quick glance at the photographs. And they *are* marvellous!

I'm writing this at my house in Savannah, where we have come to wrap the presents, and I must hurry, so I can slip it inside one or the other of them without Andy's seeing. I wanted you to know about it; I have the impression that Andy would have tried to conceal his love.

Merry Christmas from your friend,
Cynthia Rowbotham

   Sarah put the letter away. She had already shown it to her husband, who just then was kneeling in front of the fireplace, holding her silver hand mirror and a flashlight. Andy came into the room, carrying a length of galvanized iron pipe.

   Jonathan looked up. He said: "That ought to do it!" They were trying to get the damper open. They were going to build a Holiday fire. Sarah, who knew about hardware, thought the pipe was three-quarters of an inch in diameter, galvanized iron. *He may as well have dragged up a battering-ram!* But it would have been all right with her if they should end by demolishing the chimney. That could be rebuilt. She was inclined to think a lot of things could be rebuilt. For instance, she was keeping back a box of pyrotechnic "flowers—ground bloom"—You could only guess at the meaning of the original Chinese name for them—for after dark.

   Their hearth *was* cold. And it *did* have upon it the stain of congealed blood, although this had long ago been scrubbed until only a ghostly trace remained. But presently the hearthstone, like an altar-stone, would grow holy with relic fire.

IV

"You who have waited for the angry resolution
Of those desires that should be yours tomorrow,
You know the unimportant shrift of death...."

Allen Tate: *Ode to the Confederate Dead*, ll. 34-6

IN THE SUMMER, in the August before, Josh had gone down to the dock on Blackwater and waded out into the stream, thinking the thoughts of summertime, of the rich green of leaves, heavy overhead, of the cool shade they made fall all around him, of the small irregular holidays in their near-unbroken canopy, of the little figures of azure sky disclosed.

A summerwind had stirred; a cloud of hackberry leaves, already grown sere and pale—just a few, a small flight—were abscinded by the breeze, light as it was, and fell. Some of them brushed Josh's bare back, some his shoulders, only touching him—not seen—making him shudder in the changing air. And then came the echo of that shudder, fainter than the breeze itself, but real. Because when the leaves drifted ahead of him, in the lee of his breast and unwounded flank, he saw that they were already autumn leaves.

In autumn, at first, the Lowcountry basks and stretches like a cat in the rest of summer's warmth, even as the departing months are tugging it away. Then, may be the harvest moon or the setting sun, like pumpkins turned to lighted globes of orange, grown heavy, snap their violet vines of evening and plunge the world to night. And what has begun as bittersweet may end as only bitter.

Men, ever since they became men, have celebrated the harvest, then faced the cold and sad grey skies with a brave spirit, at least for a time. Later, every year, making measurements, taking sightings through slits in the walls of barrows, downward into which the sleet has scourged them, without the forged strength of iron—the metal lying all around them in the earth but still waiting, held as ore—without this iron for stylus or for gnomon; every year, from the midst of their standing stones, charting even as they must squint through snow-squalls or fog thick almost as night, they mapped the way of the light, they showed by their reckonings that the sun sank not so low in heaven today as on the days just before. They had discovered the winter station of the source of life. And they celebrated that; they thought it could be retrieved next year or knew it would return. Then, with their hearts exhausted and their plenty quite suddenly appearing only, possibly, just sufficient, it was time to wait.

As Josh Jones had stood waist-deep in the dark-gliding water and watched the fall of those pale leaves alight in their formation upon the surface, and be borne away, he took thought of all this. All this of man in winter. Time was moving on, for those to whom time applied, and he must try to see ahead. He and Mary had just spent a long weekend together at the oceanside, guests at a house party. Then they had loved each other; they had spoken, sidelong, about a future life together. But he had got nothing, so to say, in writing.

He took thought of all this now, driving back to Clear Creek on the afternoon of Christmas Day. Because he had asked Mary to promise nothing that would bind her to him safely; because she was not his—yet might have been—bittersweet autumn had ended only bitter. The solstice and the celebration of it had passed. Diversions of many kinds had been devised, but most of them were repetitive and so just markings of the settings and the risings of the sun; and another way of waiting.

How do you wait, Josh wondered, *when you feel you have nothing to wait for? Even when you know better—but just then, right then—how do you keep on keeping watch? Do you set your face, and just hold to your bearing; do you just wait? Holding tight to something, even to something material, to keep yourself upright? That* is *what you do, isn't it?*

There must be, however much society had advanced, into however many tendings it had differentiated, there must nevertheless be a degree of privation for everyone, while the cold lasted. While the sun undertook his Sisyphaean climb.

Josh reached over to the empty passenger seat. There lay the pewter field flask with its engraved and crested cipher, in its ostrich-skin case. It had held fresh water on the afternoon of the deer-shoot, although a few people, possibly from envy, still didn't believe it hadn't been fire-water.

Very well, then. It holds fire-water now, and right up to the brim of the neck. In his continuing effort to become drunken—in preparation for reading the words he was on his way homeward to read—he drew off an ample swallow. And for the first time, since he had drunk half of the libation meant to be offered for the Yule Log, the tiny, nearly atomic batons with carbon at their tips exerted the wanted effect. *Ah, better, now. I'm glad I didn't give up.* He had had encouragement in the form of example, because the four back at Woodleigh had got about as merry as gentlefolk could be rested, during the course of Christmas dinner.

The sun will have set by the time I get around to reading it. I'll think of something to fill up the time until it does. Christmas—Christmas Day, anyhow— will be over. At least the thing won't be able to spoil Christmas Day. The time for helpless waiting will have started, but it won't matter. I'm glad I put it off. Because I've had a pleasant day. And now I think I'm ready.

As he crossed an unmarked boundary between Ashfield lands and Jones lands, unwelcome thoughts bore in upon him. He was reminded of property and the inheriting of property, considerations that weighed him down and dogged his paths.

He might want never to inherit, but he would nevertheless. From his mother; through her, from his father Parker Jones—loved so deeply; lost already—from his Uncle Laurence, whom he loved and honored with the others. Whom was he going to have to lose? And now, believing that his thoughts about the day had got clearer with distance from Woodleigh, he thought he might have given his uncle offense. For, after all, he had walked straight into his house and brought out the drinks tray from the dining room, not because he had been asked to. Not because anybody else had seemed to want a drink. Just because he had himself wanted one. *And why did I have to stop him from seeing me to the door? Did I behave as though I owned the place? Owned it already? As if I wanted ever to own it! Live in it alone? I'll have to make it right with him.*

Waiting…man in winter waiting, even sometimes underground…and in that respect, waiting as the dead wait. Presently, on his right, Josh could discern, against the leaden edge of the forest, the low wall surrounding the

Paget Family cemetery, where Charles Spottiswoode waited. In just a week, though, he could renew and resume his death.

The way between the two houses was shorter than it had been on the night when he had driven with Mary beside him, for then he was taking her back to leave her; now he was on his way to claim her, part of her, her letter, desirable in spite of the bleak and lonely waiting it was going to inaugurate.

Josh laughed at his own musings, laughed a big laugh. But it lacked particular harmonics, the overtones of mirth. Nevertheless, the evil days would be burned away. Sometime.

When he had reached home, Josh fetched ice, soda, whiskey from the kitchen, then climbed up to his quarters. Yukoneta had laid fires in both rooms. He set them both alight, to see Christmas out. He poured himself a drink. The stuff was definitely working now.

He took down from his shelf of books a large volume, the text in Italian, which Josh knew little of. But technical writing seems to trip easily across language-barriers. With the book open upon his desk, he found the page he wanted, and the photograph. A Chinese brush-jar from before the time of *K'ang-hsi.* The photograph was monochrome; the description disclosed that the vessel was glazed in *giallo imperiale.* He applied a metric ruler to his uncle's gift. The dimensions matched. And on the bottom of his jar was written an accession-designation. *Good God! This must be what you give the man who has everything!*

Josh took the matchless little vessel over to his chair by the fire. He sat there, holding the jar in his hands, trying to give some shape to his gratefulness to his uncle, for he could imagine with reasonable accuracy what it had taken for Laurence to procure the thing, what favor toward himself all that effort signified.

And as he handled the object, staring into the depths of its glaze, examined the primitive "shou" incised beneath, he thought he might let all this drive from his mind thoughts that tired him.

Consciousness burned through inebriation, and resumed its tentative torture. *But that's the trouble with consciousness—it won't allow itself to be extinguished. Except over a book of contract law. No, when there is something to think about, it compels you to think about it, and takes away peace.*

He had opened a new fifth of Scotch. He had begun to suspect that if he drank it to the last drop—even if he did that—he would not sleep, but probably pass directly into a hideous hangover, with the possible diversion in between of losing consciousness, but from a deeper region in his brain than where lay the seedbeds of sleep, during all of which time "the Witch would ride him," as the local saying had it.

Josh was restless; he got up, walked across the room, looked out the east window. At first, he saw only the familiar winter landscape—the turned-under furrows of still another field, forest at the northern bound. But a small figure was moving in the distance. After a while, Josh looked again. The figure was closer, crossing the ploughland and recognizable as Ben Araby. The youth was angling over the dormant hillocks. His course lacked confident linearity. Some of the small errors and corrections were due to his having to crest the earth turned out under the harrow. Some weren't.

Josh went out onto the stoop and hailed him: "Ben! Here; over here!" Ben stood still, looking about himself. Josh raised a hand, and this caught Ben's notice. "Come over! Help me finish celebrating Christmas." And Ben started toward the Carriage House with some determination, fewer errors, those few, however, magnified by intention.

When he had got close enough, Josh said in a normal voice: "Merry Christmas, Ben. Have all of you had a good feast?"

"Merry Christmas, Mr. Josh. It was all right."

"My name's Josh, Ben. Use it, will you."

"Miss Izora would flay me if she heard me call you that."

"Well, call me whatever you want to around other people, but when we're by ourselves, call me 'Josh.' Why not? I call you 'Ben.'"

"That's different."

"Yes, it's different. But it won't always be different; and when the time comes, you and I will be ready."

Presently, they were talking together in Josh's "sitting room." This had required their bringing a stool up from the kitchen. Josh sat on it, leaving the soft leather wing-back chair for Ben. He gave Ben a glass of whiskey. "If Miss Izora is going to 'flay' you, you may as well give her good cause," Josh said, handing Ben the glass. Ben smiled narrowly. He was uncomfortable. He nearly always was. It was the behavior Mary Alice had spoken of that morning to Lavinia. And because of it, nearly everybody was uncomfortable in his company. Josh, though, was quite at ease, meaning fully to treat the boy in no special way. "Where did you get 'flay,' anyway? Everybody else says 'skin' or 'hide.'"

"I know 'skin,' but not 'hide.'"

"Yes you do. 'Hide,' as in 'You keep that up, Son, and you'll get a hiding.'"

"Oh. I didn't see what you meant, at first. Anyway, Aunt Mary Alice makes us say 'flay,' unless we're talking about a squirrel or a rabbit. She doesn't want me off at college talking like a...Colored boy."

"Well, you're *not* a Colored boy." At this, as though the film to a moving picture had snagged upon a jammed sprocket, just as Mary Alice's had done earlier when for a moment she believed in error that word had come of Lilia

Belle's death because she lived in continuing fear of such a report, Ben's posture and attitude became brittle. Suddenly, then, he leapt up from his chair and hurried across to the east window, carefully keeping his back turned toward Josh, who completed his point: "You're a Colored *man*. What's the matter with that? What's the matter with saying what is what?" But then he realized that Ben was sobbing, and he could not think what to say or do.

So, like his father, when he did not know what to do, he did nothing. Ben soon wiped his eyes with his shirtsleeve. He turned back, and shuffled across the room and sat down again. He looked straight at Josh, and said: "I'm sorry for that. When you said I wasn't a Colored boy, I see you weren't talking about my real father. You were just giving me credit for being over eighteen—a man and not a boy."

"That's right. Certainly I didn't want to make you sad or angry, not by any means. I didn't know your father. I barely remember Lilia Belle, and all I know about her is that she was very pretty; everybody loved her. She had to go away, I was told.

"But, yes, I was mainly giving you credit for being over eighteen and able to drink legally. You may have to remind Miss Izora of that, in order to keep your skin. She'll probably figure out you've had a few drinks."

"I've just had this one," Ben said, unconvincingly.

"Well, here is a second. Now, tell me about your father."

"You don't know about him already?"

"No." At this Ben was puzzled. Was the world really, after all, a place full of people he could trust? Was each bad thing about oneself not necessarily known to everybody else?

"Well, he's dead. He's been dead a long time. He died before I was born."

"I'm sorry to hear it. But now you do have adoptive parents. Ones who are close kin, too.

"And here's a word of advice: See whether you can call them 'Mother' and 'Father.' It's too late, now, for 'Mama' and 'Daddy.' But try the others."

"What difference will that make?"

"Maybe none. But I think it would make them happy for you to acknowledge what they've given you by adoption."

"I don't see exactly what they've given me." He said this without sarcasm. "They had already given me a home, and a name."

"With your father gone before your birth, maybe not married to your mother, you could have had her name, Gadsden. But Tommy and Mary Alice have given you themselves as legal, living parents, who are your next of kin. They've anchored you in the world. The world can seem a big place. A choppy harbor.

"And if it turns out you can't address them that way—and it will be hard at first, if you decide to try it; I know this because I had to deal with what to call my stepfather—then at least, when you're back at State, start referring to them as 'Father' and 'Mother,' or 'my father' and 'my mother.'"

"That's not what most people say."

"You're not going to be part of 'most people.' How are your grades holding up?"

"At first, I tried as hard as I could."

"I'd keep trying, if I were you. But it's easy for me to say that. Are you much enjoying being up in Orangeburg?"

Ben shook his head.

"Then maybe hard work can take the place of enjoyment. Or of drink and marijuana."

"I ought to do better just for Mr. Laurence. He's paying my way."

"There's nothing wrong with that. Do it for him. Do it for your mother and father. But—*do it for yourself.*"

"How did you know I'd been smoking marijuana?"

"I didn't. Are you?"

"I was."

"That's why you're not at home on Christmas afternoon...or night, by now, I guess?"

"Not exactly. Everybody went to Yemassee. I said I wasn't going. So Miss Izora stayed at home, too, since she has so much trouble getting around." He drained his glass, and stood up to leave. Josh shook his hand. Ben wasn't as greatly surprised this time as once before, with Mr. Laurence, on Blackwater. In departing, he said: "Lilia Belle didn't have to go away. She went away."

Josh, after a moment, went out onto the stoop and shouted: "Ben! Wish your folks a Merry Christmas for me."

Ben stopped and looked back. "You do the same for me, Mr. Josh!" Then he was away, stumbling across the field, but mostly turning in along the furrows, going with them where they led. The doorstep of infinity?

As Josh was going back inside, the telephone rang: "Josh, Darling," Alina said, "we've been talking it over, and Bob and I don't think we ought to drive back there tonight. Lavinia and Laurence agree."

"Too much merrymaking?"

"I think possibly so."

"Well, it's the Day for it."

"I wonder. Mama used to say she felt it a mighty queer way to celebrate the Lord's Birthday. And neither Lavinia nor Laurence...well, we're all pretty tired out. What would you think of our staying here overnight?"

"That would be perfectly all right with me."

"You wouldn't mind being alone on Christmas night?"

"It's Christmas Eve that's important."

"What do you suppose you'll do?"

"Ma'am?"

"Will you be all right there, by yourself? You could come back here, of course. We could all sit around the fire and be torpid together."

"No. I think we'd better cancel passage in both directions, for now."

"All right then, Josh, Darling. You'll find plenty to eat in the kitchen. Promise me you'll have a good supper. Goodnight, and Merry Christmas! That's from everybody."

When he had finished speaking over the telephone, realizing that it did make a difference to him that he was going to be at home by himself on Christmas night, the qualified contentment he had been enjoying started to falter. But Josh had always claimed that the glut of Holiday food took away his appetite; consequently, he had begun by dining lightly if sumptuously and was by now quite hungry. And in charge of the selections. He went down into the kitchen and there began to assemble, upon the breakfast table standing in the shallow bay they all called the "Thousand Panes," everything he had a tooth for, nothing for which he hadn't: First, cold pheasant, shot by Laurence, boned by himself and stuffed (with *pâté de gibier*) and roasted by Yukoneta.

About that time, domestically grown wines were making broad inroads, but the Barringtons were sufficiently behind the times still to keep a small cellar of only French wines. Josh uncorked a red Burgundy he was making a somewhat frantic effort to cultivate a taste for, and Champagne. He steamed another Christmas pudding, as he had been taught—this one made by different hands and from a different recipe. It was an unbalanced, curious little uncut gem of a meal—lacking the soups and sherbets and salads and courses of poached fish *en gelée* that could get to be so bothersome. But he had to hurry now, for his emotional underpinnings were buckling slightly. Was desolation closing in upon him from the shadowy corners of the room? He knew what was wrong, but he knew also that he would be able to remand it all past the liturgical end of the First Day of Christmas.

The New Kitchen was full of shadowy corners. These were formed by the strictly rectilinear and right-angular plan, realized in sandblasted granite and anodized aluminum. There were plenty of light fixtures, all let into the ceiling, wired in small clusters, though, and controlled by dimming-switches, which it took a tour of the whole room to actuate. And even then, light came back only where reflected by something fixed or by someone passing beneath the falling radiance.

Beyond the Thousand Panes, all was almost in darkness, except for the form and outline of a small deciduous magnolia, which Alina had decorated with waxen half-molds of pears, one of a terra cotta desert quail (Alina called it a "partridge") that had belonged to Parker. This was very precious, because, in spite of his wealth, Parker had owned only a few actual things, and of those most had been gifts. Like the ewer, which in New York Yukoneta had so unfairly brutalized.

Bob had applied silver leaf to the pear-shells, gold leaf to the quail. He had complained at first that he didn't know the technique, but Alina, ordering all the supplies from a place far down on lower Park Avenue, claimed that when she had told the man how clever her husband was, he had assured her that there would be nothing to it. And the whole made a very beautiful and rich gift, shining in the candle-power of the garden lights, for the First Day of Christmas. *If only my true love had given it to me.*

The tenth-myriad little squares of glass, arranged in seven lights, two to the sides, five mullioned together across the ample bay, were suddenly flecked with minute raindrops.

Josh had found the Chambertin supportive of the galantine, but he drank only half the bottle. He took the Champagne and went upstairs. There, Mary's letter stood on the mantelshelf. Josh would not look at it. He sought to orient himself to the great map that he imagined formed the walls of his apartment.

Time now, however, to leave off reading a fancied map from accidentally decorated plasterwork. Time now to read the substance of the letter. Past time, since it had arrived two weeks after Thanksgiving. The bedside lamp, a passage away, furnished no useful light; both fires had burned out to dull embers. And the letter still stood upon the mantelshelf, pale in shadow. The atmosphere was somewhat theatrical.

Josh hadn't great devotion to the theatre, where he found illusion generally poorly sustained, mainly because of unintended thuds and trampings, missed cues, botched lines (which musical setting would have remedied). However, a year before he had seen a masterly production of *The Merchant of Venice*. In a darkly fluid, totally hieratic scene, Shylock, come to weigh out his pound of flesh, standing forward, at the center of the stage, ritually withdrew and assembled his balance, erecting the post, then setting the beam to it. A Cross set up by a Jew, for the purpose of sacrifice. This was let sink in upon the audience. Then, the scales were added. The story ran its course; in this production, a good deal of redemption for the wretched character was woven into his humiliation.

And that is how Josh would weigh and judge. In one scale, the letter; in the other, his assessment of himself. For he had been undecided, off and on, about the actions, or inaction, through which he had lost, as he believed he had done, his girl, his Mary, "my life, *now that I have one again*".

Himself: *It was after that I lost her; or it was before this; or on account of something else.* The letter: *Unknown, until I find the courage to read it.* To achieve equipoise, to which pan would something have to be added? What would it have to be? The thought of flesh crossed his mind. But, whose? And how much of it?

And so Josh, who did have very great devotion to the opera, brought, in the fragile light, the letter and two iron candlesticks and placed them, the letter between, the sticks on either side; one he placed on either side of the letter, with solemnity, as beside the corpse of slaughtered Scarpia—Josh relished the notion of a treacherous fool killed by a splendid woman. Even, almost, if that fool were himself. He lighted the candles.

No Crucifix for the breast of the murdered spy! Well, but at least a Cross—at least in his inward vision, even if the Cross had to be himself, standing rapt by dreaming in the summer stream. Then the Cross became a scales. Holding suspended, on one side the Letter. On the other, the weight of his regret. And all at once, he knew when he had lost Mary, and why, and it was excruciating to know.

Back to November. Back in thought to the days before Thanksgiving. Back to the deer-shoot. Out of all the opportunities he had let slip, here, finally, was the one he had not till now remembered: The slightly unruly gaggle of youth from Clear Creek had arrived for the hunt breakfast at Woodleigh. They had bundled up the back hallway, got jammed in the passage beneath the stair-landing, and then had stopped short—"stopped short," it was well enough to say, but short of what?

Of ancient and by these days vaguely alien splendor, silent as night; alien, to a small degree, even to those brought up to it. They stopped short of Palladian Lavinia. But Mary, Mary Mountainstream, had not checked her own progress. She had known Lavinia for years, been her friend for years. So she went on. There was no need for any introduction, for any taking of hands. The two lovely women had simply smiled, murmured greetings, kissed. None of the others enjoyed this ease and intimacy with Lavinia, except her nephew Josh, so they held back, until what their Mamas had taught them had had time to take hold upon their consciences; then, they themselves poured out and forth.

Josh, who was one of them, who knew the Ashfields better than any of the others did, he being one of them, too, had hesitated for a different reason: Mary had had nothing to eat, drink, and her breath had been as sweet as sun-bleached driftwood. Her dark eyes more drowning than Blackwater. Her skin, fair, lightly gilded. All else that could be seen close-to, beautiful, radiant, in fact "lovely as the sun."

He wanted, he wanted to see it all. So, instead of accompanying her, he had let her go ahead. Ahead, to where, at no great distance, the particulars became a whole. He must see this now. He must. It was a need he could neither utter nor formulate. He didn't want to do either. He wanted to behold…and then, after a while, to hold. Then he remembered the hart, letting the hind step first into the clearing; he loses her.

The unopened letter lay before him upon the desk table; none now but candlelight. To his eye, it described a trapezoid, even though he knew it to be a parallelogram, a rectangle. Sometimes it was easy to tell appearance from reality. And sometimes it wasn't. He hefted it. It was thick, heavy, even beyond the heaviness of the stock from which Mary's stationery came. Were there enclosures? Of what? Josh slit the letter open with surgical precision and with loving care. There was no enclosure. There were two sheets of writing-paper. They conveyed a text disastrous; and that is to say the least:

H.C., Monday night

Dearest Josh,

I have thought of you every day since we parted from each other in Augusta, after *that Dance*; every day, I have known I ought to write to you. But this is such a gruesome time of the year, isn't it? When you took me back, after the hunt breakfast at Lavinia's, to Clear Creek—*your own house*, for Goodness' sake—I said Goodbye. But it wasn't a very complete goodbye. At the time, I thought there would be a change between us. And now I have found that there has been really very little change.

I ought to have said Goodnight. I felt I had hurt you; I saw you wince. But that can have been from the wound in your side, can't it have? I hope it has healed by now. I wish all wounds could heal. Well, they do, of course, but it is Time that is supposed to do the work, and I wish every hurt could be made better all at once, and then stay that way. I'm afraid I am still quite a child.

You must have seen something flicker between Edward Strikestraw and me. We had met as children, but I think he didn't remember me. He had become someone entirely different; so have I. And now, I expect him to become my life's companion.

But what I want you to know is that nothing could ever make me love you less than I have—less than I do—even if I have found someone I love even more. And I shall love you always. Not everybody would understand a feeling like that, but I know that you will. I only hope you will love me as much as ever, whatever happens to either of us.

With all my love, Mary

Suddenly, Josh fell asleep. The saintly giver of gladdening gifts and his sleigh-and-reindeer equipage, inexhaustible, completed their aërial circumnavigation. Moving westward, and away from the Star in the East.

Had the memories of childhood Christmases obscured the Star that had led, but upon its destined spot had stood?

Alina Barrington looked out on the Feast of Stephen. She looked out through the Thousand Panes. The old breakfast table and chairs glowed with polishing in their severe setting. She saw, beyond the window, nothing she cared about. She and Bob were having coffee; Alina was stirring hers, holding back.

On the breakfast table two ample, polished brass candlesticks had been left evidently to burn out, for wax and wicking were consumed down into the sockets. There was, alongside them, a half–drunk bottle of wine, and a claret glass, with dregs.

"Oh, dear!" she said, sorrowfully looking at the glass and bottle

"What?"

"Josh has been drinking, and alone."

"Josh was able to get home yesterday afternoon; it's we who had to stay where we were. A man his size ought to be able to handle a bottle or two of wine on Christmas night. And if Ben Araby was really here, maybe he helped out with it."

"There's only the one glass."

Now, Bob Barrington had been looking forward to what he secretly termed an "Ashfield-pure" day. Yet if Alina were going to be worried, then so would he have to be. "Shall I go up and look in on him?"

"Would you? Oh, Bob, please do. I want to know how he is, and I must ask him about Ben, so that I can let Lavinia know something."

But Josh was not in his rooms upstairs. "He's not here. He had company yesterday evening, though, because a stool from downstairs had been brought up."

"Thank you for seeing about him; but I do wonder where he could be."

"Darling, he is an adult male,…"

"What does that have to do with it?"

"More than you would like to think. …Intelligent, and for that matter, a member of the Bar. You've all been saying he's 'troubled.' Of course he's troubled. He may have lost his girl. It's quite painful. I've had it happen to me. But it is not a wasting illness. All—in due time—will be well."

Even to you? She looked at her husband with irony, but with satisfaction.

Needless to interpose, Bob had not mentioned the Champagne bottle and flute found upon the ledge of the washbasin, the whiskey bottle and glasses upon the table and hearthstone.

Alina's coffee had at last become cold enough to suit her taste. As she began to drink it, over the rim of the cup, through the windowpanes she saw Josh. "Look! There he is now." Bob glanced out into the garden, where Josh, looking relaxed and fit, was explaining to three young spaniels—scions of the Woodleigh pack, these named Tony, Tino, and Xanthippe—the intent of the decorations in the *Magnolia stellata*—clattering, coruscating shapes, unfamiliar to them because they didn't know the song—which had made the pups raise their hackles. The gentle Springer, after all, will lose its self-possession once in a long while. They listened attentively, but kept their hackles up. Around all of them, the tree with its ornaments, the little garden pool, seen on this day through a thin glasswork of ice, the restored sundial, all was bright and cold. "Glittering with frost in the morning...." Winter the Deceiving.

Alina, who could now feel happier about her own pup, settled back into the secure world where, ordinarily, she dwelt. She put out her hand to Bob's, and covered it. "Thank you, Darling. You help me so much with this, with everything...and you don't seem to mind."

"I haven't any children. But I had a Mother! I remember how small, usually legitimate concerns used to build to obsession, and obsession build to pain." Then Josh came inside with the hounds, who now exhibited their lineal merriment.

"Good morning, Darling! 'Christmas gear! Christmas gear!' "

"Bring it in, bring it in," her son answered.

"I'm sorry we left you to yourself," Bob said. "Christmas dinner immobilized us, I'm afraid."

"I wasn't alone all evening, though. You couldn't guess who came to see me." Alina forced herself to wait. "Ben Araby. He's a strange boy...man, I mean. But I like him."

Leading him now in spite of herself, Alina asked: "What do you mean by 'man'?"

"He's eighteen, and away at college. I gave him a couple of glasses of whiskey, and I had to remind him that it was all legal and above-board. He was afraid Miss Izora might 'flay' him."

Alina got up, and without a word went into the house to telephone to Lavinia, so that she could reassure Mary Alice.

After breakfast, climbing to his rooms, Josh found a folded note wedged between the outside door and jamb. It read: "Josh, I want to talk to you some more. I'll come back over here around four o'clock. Maybe you'll be here. Ben Araby." Josh would be there.

By now he had reread Mary's letter several times, so that he was able to recall it word by word. Or so he imagined. And this is what he recalled:

Dearest Josh,

I have thought of you every day. I said Goodbye, but it wasn't a very complete goodbye. I thought there would be a change between us. There has really been very little change.

Edward Strikestraw and I had met as children, but he has become someone entirely different.

Nothing could ever make me love you less than I do. And I shall love you always. I only hope you will love me as much as ever, whatever happens to any of us.

With all my love, Mary

The assortment of misunderstandings is not surprising. For where deeply felt and passionate love is operant, there is a loss of right thinking, which everyone is accustomed to observe: For an instance, lovers first excuse each other's faults then end by considering those faults to be virtues. All because they are to be found in the beloved. And there is a long list of further aberrations of this kind, which are often endearing initially, then speedily grow tedious.

But Josh's wrong recollection had in it one point more ominous than the certainty of subsequent disillusionment: The word "any." "Any of us." Mary had used "either." "Either of us." Josh now began a reckoning within his unconscious mind that involved not only what might happen to Mary and to himself, but also to Edward Strikestraw. That reckoning began lightly and formlessly—as a hurricane may begin far beyond the Ocean, just with the stirring of chaff in a backstreet.

At four o'clock, Ben arrived: "The first thing I want to say is Thank you for backing me up."

"About what?"

"Yesterday."

"What about yesterday?"

"That I was here, that you said I was a man, and then gave me a couple of glasses of whiskey."

"Well, you're welcome, of course. But nobody has asked me to confirm it."

"All my folks had gone to Yemassee for the day, except Miss Izora and me—I think I told you about that. Miss Izora stayed in her room."

"And you came over here."

"Not straight over."

"Not straight at all. I remember calling you in from the field; you geed and hawed a lot."

"And I told you the whiskey you gave me wasn't all I'd had."

"Yes."

"And *whiskey* wasn't all I'd had. I told you that, too. ...Well, you think you're acting in the normal way. And you can't smell your own breath. But they could. They sent Marigold and Haynesworth upstairs. They wanted to know where I'd been—where I got the liquor. My mother got into a strut... Do you know what I mean by that?"

"I do. They all get into them."

"Miss Izora went on past 'flaying' and wanted to...I don't know *what* she wanted to do, but it looked like my mother and father were going to help her do it.

"So I told them I'd been over here, you'd given me some liquor to drink, and I thought it would be impolite not to take it. That you said I was eighteen, and a man."

"What did they all make of that? Angry at me, I expect?"

"No. Aunt Mary Alice said it was all right, in that case, *if* it was the truth."

"And it was the truth. And you know—now you mention it—Mother acted rather oddly at breakfast. As soon as I mentioned that you'd been over here, she jumped up and hurried off into the house."

"What she did, I'll bet, was call Miss Lavinia, so she could tell my mother. And that explains it."

"Explains what?"

"My mother came home at lunchtime. Tommy was there and went out to meet her in the yard, and they talked together for a minute. Then they came in and got Miss Izora out of her room, and they all told me they were sorry they hadn't believed me."

"Gosh! I've never had that kind of treatment."

"You don't need it. Your folks aren't Baptists."

"You got by with a little extra, you realize?"

"I know. I don't feel too good about it."

"Well, don't feel too bad, either. But watch yourself!"

And then Ben said to Josh: "I came back to tell you about my real father—not Tommy; my real father. I thought you knew about him, because everybody else seems to know. It's why I misunderstood what you said yesterday."

"I do know about him."

"You were lying to me?"

"Do you think I'd lie to you?"

"No."

"Good. Because I didn't. Last night my mother called to say they'd be spending the night at Woodleigh. I asked her to put my Uncle Laurence onto the telephone, and I asked him about your natural father. He told me about the whole business; he said he was glad I hadn't known it already."

For after the assault upon Lilia Belle and Woody Paget's suicide, a man he barely knew had approached Laurence in the street in Ashfield and asked him some detail about the affair. Laurence had stunned the man with his reply: "If you want go around like a woman gossiping about what is common knowledge, and a thing better forgotten, I can't stop you. But you will be well advised not to refer to it in the presence of any member of my family or of the unfortunate girl's. And get the word around. Go down to the post office and tell Alma Grimsley."

"Is that a threat?" the other asked weakly.

"Yes. It's a threat. Do grasp that."

People all around, on this occasion as well as on a very few others, hated "obeying" Laurence Ashfield. But there was that straight look from the eyes they all had...Josh, Alina, and Laurence. They said Miss Allie had had it, too.

Ben had grown confident of Josh's truthfulness; he hadn't really doubted it. And now he found himself whelmed in a swell of feeling about things he couldn't clarify, either for himself or for anybody else, as a younger boy is set upon by sexual impulse without knowing what it is that drives him. There remained in Ben's mind thinly connected matter, far more general. And yet the trust he was placing in Josh made it seem to follow from what they had been talking about just before. That matter was, baldly put, Colored people and White people. He had never discussed this very much, as a youngster senses he must conceal early sexual promptings and changes within himself.

He had spoken of it never at all with a White man. But Josh—He was different; he could look at a thing from either side.

Mr. Laurence, too, was like that, Ben thought. Moreover, he would give you an answer, if he knew one. But he wouldn't make one up, just to seem fit to be the owner of Woodleigh House, fit to enjoy the reputation he had. That is why Ben had felt he could trust Laurence one day in summertime at the dock on Blackwater. And he felt he could trust Josh today.

"I want to ask you something: Do you think it's right or wrong that White people have more of everything than Colored people?" Given the era, this question, asked by a member of one race of a member of the other (for at that time there were just the two to take into account), would have been startling, and likely to produce dead silence.

And Josh was at first silent.

"Don't answer, if you don't want to."

"I want to, but I want to answer with what I think is truth." Like Mr. Laurence. Like the lighted eye within the beacon, he went all three-hundred-and-sixty degrees around a thought.

"I would say, first, that it is all right, for us, for now, to ignore any exceptions, and assume that White people *do* have more of everything than Colored people. That is wrong, not right.

"But there we're talking about very big groups of people. When you ask yourself that kind of thing, you have to consider individuals."

"What?"

"To be fair-minded, I think that you have to ask yourself at the same time whether it's wrong for one person to have more than another, for some people to have more than others. Would you agree to that?"

"I don't see how everybody could have exactly the same amount of money as everybody else, or for some to have houses each as fine as all the rest."

"I don't, either. I think that is impossible."

"Well, I'll go with you that far."

"My father thought that anything impossible was also wrong."

Josh sat back, hoping to have to wait at least a little while for an answer. Ben, who was nobody's fool, not only did not comment then and there, but asked if he could think over it.

"Can we talk about that later, after I've had some time to think it over?"

"Yes. It takes some thinking over. My father thought also that anything necessary was good."

"But you did say it's wrong…for Whites to have everything, and Blacks to have nothing."

"Yes. Now, remember, we said that, if you put it that way, we are going to an extreme that doesn't exist. Because Black people don't have *nothing*."

Ben flinched. "Black people don't have nothing" sounded like mockery. But he did not believe Josh could have meant it in that way. When he had thought about it, then he understood the reduplicated negative and said: "What do you think Black people have?"

"They have their humanity. Their strength and their gifts."

"But nobody cares about those. 'They've got rhythm,' 'They look good in bright colors,' 'Some of my best friends are Negroes (even if we do keep them in the kitchen, or out back, and make them drink their iced tea at lunchtime out of Mason jars).'"

"From enslavement, to begin with; then from unassessed repression; now from what I think we inaccurately call predjudice has come the pushing-aside of those things...."

"Of what things?"

"Colored people's humanity and strengths and gifts. What I said before. And that is wrong, too. Those trivial things you spoke of are not the Black man's gifts, but they're all a great many White people tend to see. Or, may be, care to see. Even if it is true that Whites are superior, for example intellectually, to Blacks, still you'd have to acknowledge that the intellectually inferior among Whites nevertheless have all the legal rights and social privileges—I don't mean 'social' in the sense of belonging to clubs and being invited to parties—of the superior ones. Extending these rights and privileges to Blacks amounts to the same thing, even for people who look down on them. It's inconsistent not to. All of us should have all rights and privileges—of a certain number of kinds.

"But nobody...nobody at all should misuse them. That would mean infraction, and *loss* of privilege"

The air gets unaccountably thin at soapbox-level. Josh stopped for breath, and Ben cheered sarcastically. "You ought to get that printed up, Josh. I know a lot of people who'd like to own a copy."

Josh pretended to ignore this interruption, and the nature of it, but then "Any reasoning person," he said, "would have to acknowledge that proposition, up to a point, although clever ones could get either through or around it. Of course, they might risk a Thrasymachean result."

"What's that?"

"It's something you might know if you had enjoyed the background of three centuries of wealth and privilege you seem to think I've enjoyed. If you want sarcasm."

"I didn't mean to make you mad."

"And I'm not. But what has just happened here illustrates one of the problems facing our two Races. If we say something in your favor, usually we are ridiculed for being insincere, or for arriving too late with too little."

"I really do thank you for what you said, for playing straight with me."

"But even now, with only us here, nobody else for either one of us to have to make any particular impression on, I've got to decide whether to trust your last words or the way you reacted at first. Blacks can't seem to get at what they fundamentally want. Whites can't seem to decide what they're due, or how to get it into their hands."

"It's a tough…question. Just what I know makes it a tough question, and I don't know a lot. I've spent most of my thinking-time learning to read and write and do arithmetic."

"You must believe it's a step in the right direction. Your great-grandfather probably didn't learn to do those things."

"I'll bet my great-Grandfather Paget did." Josh considered becoming exasperated with the boy, but decided against it. Josh was usually able to decide things like that.

"He did, as a matter of fact. I've seen a letter he wrote to my great-grandfather. After his own family's worst troubles began.

"Now, I'll say this, Ben; I have to say it, and you should, I think, hear it: I don't believe all Blacks know or care very much more about their inner selves than you seem to think all White people know or care. That's to say, about Blacks. I think many Blacks have almost given up on themselves. Not that there's any wonder in that.

"Do you remember a man named Edward Strikestraw, who was down here last month for the deer shoot and breakfast for that niece of my Aunt Lavinia's who was going to get married?"

"My folks remember him; he was friendly to all of us, and he didn't go too far, the way some people do, trying to show how open-minded they are. Especially the ones who really aren't. He was like you."

Can it be that what she saw in him was me? In some part? "Well, he has a very interesting theory about why Colored people are disconnected from their inward selves."

"Who says they're disconnected from themselves, in the first place?" Ben asked, tense, bristling.

"In the first place? For all I know, Edward Strikestraw. But he means just what I was talking about; that Whites don't see into the depths of Blacks, mainly because Blacks don't either. I'll tell you about it, but not now. It's something I'd never heard before. …A conclusion Edward reached—I think—not long ago."

"I've got time."

"I'm sorry, Ben, but I haven't. We've all got to go to a holiday supper over at Loblolly Place, and before long, I'll have to start getting ready."

Ben grew calmer. But he asked for a drink. Josh said: "If it weren't for yesterday's close shave, I'd be glad to offer you a whiskey."

"Give it to me anyway—I'll worry about what happens."

"If anybody checks on you this time, I'll have to say you asked."

"I don't care." Josh poured a drink for each of them. When Ben had his glass in hand, he continued: "You may be right. Mr. Edward may be right. Colored people may not be in lock-step with themselves, after so long. Maybe they don't have that famous rhythm, after all. But when they came over here, they were split up and...run. They never got together about anything. And they never ran anything for themselves.

"At college, most people seem to be acting like White people, or trying to, thinking that's the way. They talk all the time about things most of them hadn't heard of a year or two ago: 'Deans,' and 'halls,' and 'honors programs,' 'degrees,' 'course-loads.' And they break their necks to join fraternities and sororities. The men—That's what they call the boy students—wear pullovers, even when they're sweating bullets through them. The kind you wear."

"Crew neck, you mean?"

"Is crew neck the kind where the neck comes right up to the neck?"

"Yes,"

"*They're* even hotter, but they give them a lot of chest-area for wearing their fraternity pins. And you ought to see those! They look like something out of a ten-cent store. The students themselves don't have to work very hard to get by. Most of the courses are easier than my high-school ones.

"But a lot of students—even a lot of the ones that do the things I'm talking about—get drunk a lot of the time. A good many take drugs. Those are the ones who've given up, like you said. Or halfway given up. Their inside half."

"Do they tell you they feel this way?"

"They don't *tell* me...or anybody else." Josh waited. "That's just it. They don't talk."

"Not at all?"

"Not much. Some don't even seem to know where they are, or care, at least not for a lot of the time. Only when they're out pretending."

"And are you one of the exceptions?"

The answer was slow in coming: "Yes." Then: "I think so. But...I'm smarter than most of them, so it's easy for me to seem...."

"Of course you're smarter than most of them...."

And then, to Josh's stupefaction, the same tetanic-like rigidity fell upon Ben as on the day before. He shook it off, jumped up again, went again to the window, again turning his back toward Josh. "You say that because you know I'm half White!"

"Ben! For God's sake! I said it because I think it. I've known you to some extent all your life, and I think you're smarter than the average person, either Black or White. Sit down; try to get yourself together." Ben was able to collect himself. He held out his glass for a refill. "Miss Izora may flay you yet!"

"I don't care."

"Stop not caring." But he was not going to ride herd on a legal adult. That his family were Baptists was Ben's lookout.

"I'm getting used to it—all of it. You didn't even know I was stoned, when I came in, did you, yesterday or today?"

"No. But I've never smoked much of the stuff myself."

"I'll get so I can handle it, so nobody can tell. Then all I'll have to do is get hold of some odorless liquor."

"Are you trying to shock me? You have shocked me, actually. But not enough so that I'm going to start lecturing you about how this could end. I can't be your friend and your proctor at the same time. And I am going to be your friend for as long as you'll let me be."

They were silent for some ten minutes, drinking slowly, musing. Then Josh dropped back a little, and started over: "One thing you said a while back: 'Acting like White people, or trying to.' I think it means you recognize a fundamental difference. I think there is one; I just don't have a clue to what it is.

"The White man, on the one hand, can't give Blacks what they need most, most fundamentally, as I've said, and Blacks themselves don't know for sure where to begin their quest.

"And it works the other way round, too. Where Colored people have all but made a vocation of complaining about past and present mistreatment, and have let that lead them to the belief that *everything* wrong in their lives is due to White men's abuse; in that, they're wrong.

"White people are going to have to abandon their repression—every kind of it. But they can't, and shouldn't be made to abandon their tastes and preferences."

"'Tastes and preferences,' nothing. They prefer what they're taught to prefer."

"So do you. As White people come around, Colored people are going to have to take responsibility for things within themselves that need cultivating. Things that only they possess, only they can know…so, things only they can cultivate. That is where their increasing strength, and finally, maybe, their social equality, will come from."

"Then you think the two races are equally to blame?"

"I didn't say 'equally,' or at least I don't think I did. I didn't mean to. But when we're in this kind of trouble, and in as much trouble as I think I see coming—Listen! I sound like Miss Izora—it has got to be acknowledged that nobody is all to blame, nobody all to be exonerated."

"What does 'exonerated' mean?"

"It means 'freed from a burden.' Now, don't stay over here and get drunk. Come back tomorrow."

"You really want me to?"

"I really want you to. And I want you to start trusting me to mean what I say." Ben got up to go. "And, Ben. Whites don't usually see into the depths of themselves, either."

As Josh, in evening clothes, started down the stair he marveled at the discovery that Ben's father had been White, had raped his mother, who had conceived him in that circumstance. Afterward the father had killed himself, savagely; it had seemed to some, in recompense.

Ben's fits of rage, the way he felt about the races, and, in an ambiguous slip, revelation of his lack of surefootedness, were forming into something clear—clearer to Josh than to Ben. Uncle Laurence had said they were all grateful that this half-breed spawn had been Negroid, since he would be reared by Negroes. But his mother had abandoned him. His acknowledged relatives and adoptive family were Blacks. But his mother had abandoned him. And he, possibly solely, understood this.

For as Ben had turned to leave the afternoon before, he had said: "Lilia Belle didn't to have to go; she went." Josh's father had left him, but he had had no choice but to go. That had been wounding enough.

Here was Ben, Black, as far as anybody could see, living in a Black world, knowing, however, that in birth he was half White. Josh imagined it possible that those forces could war with each other for the whole of Ben's life, meaning both throughout the rest of his years, and for all those years together as the spoils of conquest.

The Ashfields were upstairs at Woodleigh, themselves getting dressed for the reception at Loblolly Place. It wasn't a plantation—instead a very comfortable house on ample acreage, occupied by friends of theirs who had moved there from Mississippi. Their names were Lillian and Brewster Holman. Lillian's family's house had been called "Loblolly Place," and they had brought the name with them to South Carolina, where it was already very much at home, along with some apocryphal family "history," but the Holmans were well liked in the County, and they entertained generously and to great effect.

"You told me on Christmas morning about Ben—that he had refused to go with the others to the gathering of the clan," Laurence reminded Lavinia.

"I remember. And he didn't go. I think you know all about that."

"I know all about it, except the reason for it. I asked you what you thought. You said your first impulse would have been to agree with me that Ben would have had an extra-warm welcome. Then you said you'd had a second thought. But you haven't yet said what it is."

"I don't know what it is, really; not with certainty. But I've begun to think that there is a wider gulf between the Races than many of us realize—a chasm. And something lies at the bottom of it, so to speak, and if it's a thing mysterious to Colored people, then to White people it's a fast-closed door."

"Are you sure you know what you're talking about?"

"No, and I said I wasn't. Shall I go on?"

"No, of course. Please do go on, because what you have to say fascinates me. It's just that it's hard to grasp."

"I don't recommend trying to grasp it. Yet. But where Colored people are concerned, there seems to me a great deal we don't see or know, and aren't meant to know. There are lacunae in it, though. And...."

"Lacunae? In a chasm?"

"In their understanding of what lies at the bottom of it. Not a good metaphor. But it's the best I can do right now....even they don't seem able to fill these. If they could, and had something complete, explicable, then I think they—or the ones we live on close terms with—might be able to speak to us freely...."

"You don't think they speak unreservedly to us?"

"No. There is a check. Think about it. We don't refer to it among ourselves so we forget it exists, but we all know it's there. Because of it, there has been no real integration—I don't mean symbolic integration, as in institutions and so on. But consider the Ferraras; they integrated themselves a hundred years ago. This chasm, then—obviously I have only the vaguest notion of what I'm trying to say—and whatever it conceals are anomalous. Because for social purposes around here, part Negro is Negro. But for *this* consideration, an essential one, part White is non-Negro. And I don't think their people in Yemassee really wanted Ben, and I think somehow they concluded they didn't, over reason, and let him either guess or know it."

"We're going to be later than I meant to be! Anyway, that's my 'second thought,' for what it's worth."

The Holmans had built for themselves an agreeable house, all on one floor, for they were preparing to grow old, and they wanted this process to affect their lives as little as possible. Outside, the building was of stucco, with vaguely but blamelessly neoclassical detail. Inside, it proved one broad hallway, every room, somewhat like an Oriental pavilion, opening off it separately. Little courtyards outside were left between every two rooms, visible through large windows, stretching down along the gallery.

Lillian Holman stood beside one of these windows with Lavinia. They were looking out onto the uniquely composed planting on the other side. It was illuminated from hidden sources: The small garden was turned into a landscape, just above *bonsai* scale.

Lillian Holman said: "I like to have the 'kept' plantings spill out into the native growth, which back here [She meant, 'back here in the East'] is some of the loveliest anywhere."

"I agree; although for good natural growth, you have to pick and choose. And here, I think it is exceptionally good. But of course that would account for your selection of the site."

"Thank you. Oh, hello, Josh."

He came up to them looking moderately magnificent, but more important, Lavinia noted, more at ease, happier. "It's a wonderful party, Mrs. Holman."

"Oh, God, Lavinia! It has begun already." She took and held for a moment each one's hand, then squeezed each lightly. She smiled, silently excusing herself. An achingly lovely woman.

Lavinia, left alone with her nephew, was not at ease. A week before Christmas, possibly a week-and-a-half, Alina had mentioned that a letter from Mary Mountainstream, marked for Josh, had appeared amid the holiday mail. Lavinia had known Mary almost from birth, because her mother had been a best friend at college. After Mary's father had been killed in Sicily, and she and her mother had moved back to Augusta, there had been frequent visits to and fro. Lavinia and Mary were alike in an assortment of respects, and became good friends, too.

Lavinia must somehow inform herself, and the need to do it made her feel ashamed. She did not want to glean "news" to put about, as some people like to do. She wished only to know what alignment was developing (or disappearing) between two young people, of each of whom she was very fond. For what she had been told and what she was observing were mutually at odds. Yet she hadn't a choice but to wait and watch. She was content to wait, humiliated by the need to watch.

Lillian was an experienced hostess, but she never took that duty quite lightly. She was always a little anxious. She cultivated this as a precaution against mishap. And so when suddenly, as she passed one of the great windows and saw the face of a man outside, she shrieked loudly. But she recovered her composure instantly. Only a few people had heard her over the conviviality; when a detail of those few came to investigate, Lillian fell in with them easily, pretending herself to be looking for the source of alarm.

Lavinia and Josh were too far away to have got involved. Lavinia struggled with what she knew: Mary had asked Lavinia to have a very early breakfast with her on the morning after the deer shoot and reception. On that occasion, she had been forthright about a sudden and complete redirection of her feelings. Now, this letter. What could it have said? Josh was too much as he had been before. Something was missing. Either Mary had changed back again. Rather unlikely. Or Josh didn't care anymore. Unlikely in the extreme. Or—what Lavinia hadn't even imagined, though it was so—Josh had not read the letter just when he had received it.

He had read it by now, though, on the evening of the day before, on Christmas Day. The last thing before going to bed. He had waited, so that Christmas might not be spoiled for himself or through contagion for any of the others.

And neither Lavinia—certainly not Bob or Alina—and, as it happened, nor Josh himself had any idea how complete a failure Mary's letter was as an instrument of communication.

"I had a letter from Mary," Josh said.

Old News. But at least Lavinia hadn't had to betray what she trusted was "laudable interest," as Miss Allie had used to put it, and not idle curiosity. Josh, with an air of having been vindicated, appeared to be waiting for a response.

"I had a 'bread-and-butter' note from her after the hunt breakfast. She's very careful, always, about matters of etiquette. Nothing newsworthy in it, though." *Was that a lie? Yes, it was. It was a black lie.* But one that had to be told, and Lavinia hoped this imperative would change it to white. "What did Mary say in her letter to you?" *That, at least, is a question that's only civil, since he's mentioned she wrote.*

"Well, it looks as though nothing has changed between us, or not much. I was afraid it might have."

Lavinia gave in to herself. "Then…I forget the name…Edward Somebody… is no longer part of the picture?"

"Edward Strikestraw. Oh, I'd have to say he's still a part of it, but just a small part now." That seemed to be the answer: Edward was diminishing, with time, as one of the "us" in "any of us,'—to begin with, a false reading.

Without warning: "Oh, my God!" Since this was the coarsest language Josh had ever heard his aunt use, looking about them for a clue, he followed her stare of shock and alarm out through the windows, beyond the little garden, and across a broad margin of lawn to the woodland. And there he saw nothing unexpected. "I'm sorry, Josh. I…I thought I saw a man standing at the edge of the woods, and it frightened me. Christmas is for some reason laying an extraordinarily great strain on us this year, I think. It must be that; I see no one now."

But as they turned from the window and started down the hallway toward one of the buffets, Josh clearly saw a man move in midnight shadow from the garden lighting. It was Ben Araby, who had come to the White man's party, too.

V

"Wide of the mark he falls, who thinks to hide his deeds from god."

Pindar: *Olympia I*, 64-5 (tr. PT)

"I REMEMBER YOUR saying earlier, when we were talking about your time at college, 'themselves' when I would have expected 'ourselves.' Can you think now why you might have put it that way?"

"I don't know—no particular reason."

"Do you not feel like a part of the student body up there?"

Tears welled up and began to slide over the boy's cheeks, like a torrent bursting over smooth rock when rain in the West causes the mountains to weep. "I don't feel like a part of anything, not anywhere."

And then the telephone rang.

Josh paid no attention. Probably the call was either for his mother or for Bob. Or Yukoneta. "Don't worry, My Friend." He reached across and placed his hand firmly on Ben's shoulder. "I'm not going to say I know how you feel…well, yes I am…I don't know what it's like to feel that way as much… down deep inside…as you do. But I have at times felt not part of anything very much." The timing of what he said next was mistaken. "This, I think, is the point at which I should tell you about Edward Strikestraw's theory. But I don't think he would…."

"Would what? Not want you to tell me?"

"I was going to say, I don't think he would want me to give his ideas the status of 'theory.' There's the making of one in them, though, I believe. Do you feel up to listening to it? Or, maybe better later."

"I want to hear it now. I'm tired of waiting for everything."

"All right, then. I'll try to do it justice, but nutshell-size justice. When the Africans were rounding each other up to sell into slavery, they were looking for pack-animals, for beasts of burden. It's hard, but it's the truth. So they took the ones who were young and strong, or pretty, and the children who looked like they'd grow up into strong men."

"Or pretty women."

"Or pretty women. That accounts for two of the three generations ordinarily alive at the same time. They left the old people. Nobody was going to pay good money for them. They had no horsepower. But to the generations who were herded away, the old people would have been invaluable."

"I don't get the point; doesn't 'invaluable' mean 'without value'?"

"No. It means the opposite—so valuable you can't attach a reasonable estimate of worth."

"Why are they supposed to have been worth so much? Old people?"

"Because they had lived their whole lives under their peoples' laws and customs. They knew in what form justice would be accepted and could be put into practice. They knew how to deal with the weather—as well as anybody does, anyhow—seedtime, harvest. And human beings will believe in God, or in gods. The elders would have been custodians of beliefs and rites. What to do about death. What to do about birth, about sickness of body or mind, sorrow, hope."

"So you mean they were witch doctors?"

"Yes, if you want to call them that. Or priests, or prophets."

"Medicine men?"

"Yes, 'medicine men' if you like. Shamans. They would have known the traditional remedies, and for more than just for sicknesses."

"And everything they 'knew' could be disproved by modern science, I guess?"

"Cut it out, Ben. People don't accept, for hundreds of years, or thousands of years, forms of treatment that don't work or behavior that doesn't make life better. Anyway, the elders would have got all this craft from the deepest ranges of their memories—those are Edward's words for it; he's very good at selecting words, I think, basing this on the few talks I've had with him.

"Our Blacks now remember it all only in bits and pieces; and they can't fit even those together."

"We're not yours anymore."

"What? Oh. 'Ours.' I'm trying to include you, not possess you. Today, anthropologists and archaeologists who have made systematic studies can't come up with much beyond what seems like childish guesswork...a few probabilities, a few possibilities. No more.

"The old people at the time hadn't any way to hand on knowledge, in their emergency, and the way of these things. And we have no key, it seems, that will open them to us. There is an historian who thinks American Blacks can't ever come to terms...with their lives, I think...until they make their peace with today's West Africans, descendants of the ones who originally betrayed them. (This historian is Black, by the way.) Those people still have in custody, at least to some extent, the authentic ways of the Black man.

"The English, when they came to the New World, brought their learning, their laws, their skills—all that—and they went back and forth, so that they could be reminded of anything they'd forgotten, or import what they'd at first neglected to bring along. The later immigrants, at first from Europe, later from Asia, brought their whole families. So they had their elders with them, and these kept the traditions. They mixed with the already-established peoples, knowing they could revisit their own ways whenever they wanted to, or felt they needed to.

"Our...the Blacks now, here, do go back to their own ways, or try to—I think it's a part of human nature to tend to—but discontinuously, incompletely. Ribbons signifying ritual intent hung on doorposts in certain circumstances, burying the dead with particular observances—particulars observed from the start, if the slaveholders didn't put a stop to them. Things done on the morning of your own birth, which my mother and my Aunt Lavinia were not permitted to witness."

"What! What things?"

"We never knew. It was a very happy time. I think I remember it, but that may just be from hearing about it. Nobody asked them to leave Lilia Belle's room, or anything like that. Two women who were your mother's kinfolk just asked my mother and aunt if they'd like to come out onto the porch and have something cool to drink. You were born in Miss Izora's house. You probably know that."

"I do know it. And I know how nice and comfortable that house is supposed to be—how old Mr. Jack...I shouldn't call him that...how Mr. Jack had it improved and added-to. And plumbing put in. And electricity after that."

"He deeded it to Miss Izora, too. He and my Uncle Laurence have kept all the houses along the Street in repair. Good structural condition. Only yours—Miss Izora's—is equipped for living in."

"For living in by Colored people; it's on the Street, where the slaves lived. There was no running water or electricity in them in the old days."

"If by 'the old days' you mean Colonial and ante-bellum times, then remember that there wasn't any at Woodleigh House, either.

"My people have consistently been known for treating all their household well. However, before you say anything in reply, I am aware that that doesn't count for much today. I can't help it if it means something to me."

Ben had got up and begun to prowl around the room. He grew flushed. With shame? With anger?

You don't get flushed with anything else, do you? Or do you? Ben was "stoned," he said, but he wasn't flushed from that. And he wasn't mellow from it.

"Edward Strikestraw," he said in hardly lidded fury, "can go to the Devil! I don't need a bunch of long lost medicine men to fill a gap in my heritage. There's no gap in my God-damn' heritage." And now he went to the desk and poured himself a drink. Without asking. Without ice. Without water, and decidedly without stint.

The telephone rang. Probably a call for Bob or Alina. Maybe for Yukoneta, but it was late for that last. Josh ignored it.

"Ben! Stop it! He wasn't trying to impugn your or anybody else's heritage. He just thinks...."

"He just thinks he's found a way to explain why the poor old Nigger is so much lower down the pecking-order than the White man!" He swallowed the full tumbler of whiskey in three gulps, one breath. "And he can go to the Devil and take your girlfriend with him!"

"What?"

"He goes out with her now. She left you for him."

"Who told you that?"

"Don't worry. I heard. I know all about it." Josh tried to put together an answer. He couldn't. Couldn't unsnarl the tangle of disjointed thoughts, couldn't work his way to either loose end of any of them, in order at least to be able to stammer out a rebuttal. He went to his desk to fetch the letter. The letter would be his rebuttal. But it wasn't where he believed he had left it. In haste he pulled out each of the three shallow drawers, rummaged through it. But the letter was gone.

Rummaging, muttering. But he ceased. Had he, he was now prepared to ask himself, in fact seen any letter in the first place? He didn't think he had imagined it, but he knew he could have dreamt it. Since he had begun to drink excessively, his sleep had been troubled by unusually vivid images, while the outlines of his waking life had been smudged in many places. He filled Ben's glass, and one for himself. They were quiet, now.

The telephone rang. They heard it ring.

"I'm sorry I said that to you, Josh."

"Forget it. I had thought that, anyway. Then she wrote to me." Josh stopped. Then, in a voice that had sunk down, he said: "But I can't find her letter anymore." The telephone had continued to ring, a metronome against rising and falling hopes and voices, against fear and trust, all of which had been running on unmeasured. *There must be nobody else at home. This is probably the same caller, and the call may be important.* He besought every power he knew within or outside himself that the caller might be Mary, that her message might repair his trampled yearning. He lifted the receiver, but could hear two parties speaking already. He listened. The conversation on the line went forward with no break in rhythm, so Josh knew he hadn't betrayed his interception. Ben was unnaturally quiet; he seemed to think no one should know he was present in the room.

"...-ssip, and I'm trying to believe not." Lavinia's voice. "I try to tell myself I simply don't want Josh hurt, or Mary hopelessly embarrassed."

"I'm sure that *is* what you want to avoid," Alina answered her, "and I'm sure it's *all* you want. It has certainly seemed to me that things weren't fitting together as they should. And today, I did something terrible. Unforgivable, really. But after what you said last night...."

"I did something unforgivable, too. I called Mary."

"I read the letter."

"What did you make of it?"

"Mary goes on a bit about how much she loves Josh."

"Josh? Or Edward Strikestraw?"

"Josh. But embedded in all that is the phrase, 'Edward will probably be my life's companion.'"

"And you say she 'went on' about how much she loves Josh?"

"Yes."

"Could he have mistaken her meaning?"

"Have you never been so much in love that you were prepared to believe that anything at all meant that your beloved loved you in return?"

"No, I don't believe I have."

"Well, I have. And more than once. And, yes, he could have misunderstood."

"He is bound to have. Because, to go straight to the point, Mary said—These are her very words: 'Edward is what I want. And he is all I want.'"

Then there came a pause, during which neither lady spoke.

Alina said: "Whatever are we to do?"

Another pause seemed about to follow. But Josh said: "It's done." And he replaced the receiver in its cradle.

Josh experienced then so fugal a blindness and deafness that all he knew of them when they were gone was that they had occurred and that each phenomenon had been complete. There followed a transient numbness affecting the arms and fingertips, the jaws and teeth. Then he was quite himself. And he had not, during the previous five weeks, been quite himself.

After all, everybody had known unrequited love; and this was no more than that—unrequited love, and not even quite that, to rely upon what Mary had written. There was nothing shameful in it. And with time the anguish would pass off. Time now to start forgetting about it, to return to consideration of the distortions within Ben's so deeply troubled soul.

Luckily, Josh's soul was no longer troubled. He could see, now that all had been made clear, that in the case of self divided, one need only look up from his preoccupation and puzzlement, and expel the less satisfactory moiety. That was all.

But the difficulty in all this was that Josh had grown thoroughly accustomed to being not quite himself—not at all himself, in fact—had got accustomed to the dark of his soul, used to ebriety, used to leading himself onto pathways that vanished as soon as his foot was set upon them. So that being "quite himself" was in fact an overwhelming *bouleversement*, and it placed him in a mentally and an emotionally more precarious state than before. Thus his believing himself to have got back to normal exposed him, and some whose lives his own affected, to peril.

"That," he told Ben, "was my mother."

"Why did you listen for so long before you said anything?"

"She's at Woodleigh, with my Aunt Lavinia. They wanted to know about something I offered to see to for my uncle." Ben said nothing. "Have you never noticed that mothers sometimes go over and over a thing they're trying to be quiet in their minds about?" This Ben did understand. He put the telephone call away from his thoughts and allowed these to batten again onto all his grievances with the world of men.

He said then: "I went to your White folks' party last night."

"Yes, my aunt saw you."

"Oh, my God! What did she say?"

"'Oh, my God!'"

The possibility of mockery again?

Josh was unconsciously turning himself into a puppeteer. Already there had arisen within him, faint as powder, faint as dust, a readiness to operate another human being, as though a machine. Powder, dust, laden with pollen from a turgid, dark, thick-stalked flower. Or bearing minute seeds from a swollen pod. The black-flowering, prodigiously ugly telephone. A twenty-year old one, like the one—long since disused—that the Ashfields still kept in the little long-legged cabinet in the Eest Room at Woodleigh.

"Josh! Tell me what Miss Lavinia said when she saw me."

"That's what she said: 'Oh, my God!'"

"I never have heard Miss Lavinia talk like that."

"Neither had I. But you scared the daylight out of her."

"Where was I when she saw me?"

"At the edge of the woods. She didn't recognize you, or say anything to anybody else. Not that I know of."

"Thank Goodness," Ben said, with a mild piety out of joint with the malevolence that was rising to swarm about them in the air like a cloud of summer gnats from stagnant ditch-water and uncut grass.

"I recognized you, though, when I looked out to try to see what had alarmed her."

"I came a lot closer than the edge of the woods."

"I assumed you had…or would."

"I knew nobody would offer me anything, so I brought my own refreshments."

"You weren't invited, Ben; what do you expect?"

"I don't expect a Goddamn' thing. Not anymore. Not from no…anybody. But they could have half-invited me, since I'm half white."

What unbelievable naiveté! *Or is rage perverting his reason?* "A lot of *all*-White people weren't invited. You have to try to be reasonable." For Josh had decided by this time that he was himself being reasonable. But the little reckoning that had softly swept through him when he had subliminally turned Mary's word, "either," into his word, "any," was already taking on the shadow of a geometric figure of negligible deformability. He must be able to bend, mould. Without consciousness of it, he had decided that the words should be interconverted again, becoming as they had begun. Mary and Josh. And no Edward. No Edward. And no real acceptance of the reality of unrequited love. No Edward, thus no need of it.

"But, Ben, I think you have got to stop regarding yourself as half one thing, half the other. Or it will tear you into two."

"Just don't tell me anymore how happy it made everybody that I turned out to look Black. What about me? Does anybody care what I would have wanted?"

"I guess it's thought that unborn children, knowing nothing, want nothing—in particular."

"The children born in Germany with deformities because of that drug their mothers took: Did they want that? Answer me that. Did they want that?"

"Before birth? At that stage, I doubt whether they wanted either normal limbs or undeveloped limbs."

"What about after they were born?"

"After they were born, after they reached an age of understanding? I imagine most of them, if not all, like the rest of us, were glad of their advantages and regretted their afflictions. But I am not sure there's ever been an instance of anybody's…going to any extreme out of dissatisfaction with himself, or purely because of what he was born with, or without. Or born as."

"I bet there has been."

"Anyway, it can't be common. I don't know of anybody's doing it, do you?" Ben shook his head. "When people commit suicide, I believe, it's because the whole shape of their lives has gone wrong. That, and because of familial ability to take one's own life."

"Are you telling me that some people are born to kill themselves and some people aren't?"

"Not 'born to,' but born *able* to. In most families there is no history of suicide—not counting, I suppose, culturally determined suicides like Roman prefects falling on their swords, or *hara-kiri*—in a few others, though, there is a history of it, sometimes a very strong one."

"Well, I'm not going to kill myself. Not my whole self."

"Good. I'm not, either."

"Why would you do it? …Oh."

"Everybody says to himself, at certain times, 'Life's not worth living.' But most people turn away from death when they're actually faced with it. Including some who ask to die, then ignore an easy and painless way out of their trouble when it's offered them."

"I don't know about all that. Anyway, would you like for me to tell you about that party last night?"

"No, I wouldn't. Thanks all the same. Remember, I was there."

"I wanted to tell you how it looked to me." Peace and quiet had returned. Ben had come off the boil, so to say, and Josh continued building the contorted notion that he was getting back to being himself again.

"No. I don't want to hear about it. The Holmans live on a grander scale than most of us, including those who are sometimes referred to as 'Plantation

People.' You'll end by working up to the conclusion that if you had been born looking the way your White man's inheritance might have made you look, then you would be an old-line Paget and live at Dodona—The Ruin—and give parties of the sort you looked in on last night."

"You mean if The Ruin had been fixed up to be as fancy as Miss Izora's house?" Taunting, goading; nearly exasperating.

"I'll tell you this, my Dark and Dark-skinned Brother: Negroes with enough White blood to make people take them for White hoe a hard and dangerous row. They get found out, and 'disaster' takes on a new force of meaning. You look Black. Be Black, and figure out how to accept it."

Josh and Ben had decided to meet at the dock; they were discussing matters not to be overheard. On the twenty-ninth of the month, Josh was first to arrive. He had been living upon uneasy terms with his family. Of the Arabys, he had seen Mary Alice, and she was behaving entirely normally. Nothing was said, as if Mary Mountainstream would not be spoken of again. The letter had reappeared upon his desk-table, and Josh had reread it, again. He harbored it in his thoughts just as inaccurately as before, but contrariwise:

Dear Josh,

I have known I ought to write to you, but this is such a gruesome time, when you look back. I said Goodbye; I knew there would be a change between us.

You must have seen something blaze up between Edward Strikestraw and me. Now, I expect him to become my life's companion.

Not everybody would understand a feeling like mine. But I know that you will, whatever happens to either of us.

Love, Mary

While it cannot be said that Josh gained much enlightenment from this—The recollected text was faulty almost to the point of making no sense, of not even construing—nevertheless one resolution had emerged: In the whole, dreadful equation—for "dreadful" was what it had become—Edward Strikestraw was to be cancelled out, along with some unknown equivalency. And that unknown equivalent was even then gathering definition at the back of Josh's mind. It had been awakened by Ben's emerging distaste.

Where was Ben? Josh didn't yet understand why, not consciously, but he needed him in alliance. He read his wristwatch and saw that he was himself early. That was all right; he could use the time.

The Fifth Day of Christmas, and most people had all but forgotten the Feast had ever come. Garlands had been taken down, or needed to be. Children couldn't play with their toys anymore, for they were already broken. Winter of the Shadows lay in wait. Winter in the borrowed robes of Photolestes, for weeks on weeks. If the days had begun to lengthen, then where was the added light? Too low in heaven to help. Everybody was being driven toward, if not into, the Close of Uncaring.

In the Carolina Lowcountry, the weather at Christmastide was often warm and bright. There could be no thought of dashing through the snow. Sweaters, tweed coats, woolen scarves didn't always look right against the radiance. They must wait until February or March to become of use, and by then nobody retained enthusiasm for them. Some retained no enthusiasm at all. People who had waited to see whether *this* Christmas would be the one to bring the Time Foretold found that it hadn't been, and leapt from bridges.

This day's weather, this day's light, though, were committed to no season. Ben arrived at the dock precisely on time. He found Josh seated upon the planks with his knees drawn up, he leaning forward onto them, looking down at the foursquare concrete boat ramp. "That's where Edward Strikestraw saved my life."

"The know-it-all ought to look to his own life. But, listen, Josh. I really do apologize for what I said day before yesterday about your girl. I had no business to do that."

"Forget it."

"I've never loved a girl; I don't know what it's like. So I don't know what it's like to lose the girl you…love."

By now, Mary's letter had got a little shopworn. Josh had it with him, in the inside pocket of one of those field-khaki coats with corduroy collars. Although the collar to Josh's was of calfskin. He handed it across to Ben. "Read this. I think everybody else has. Then tell me whether you think I've completely lost her." And Ben read the letter, comprehending it as it stood written:

Dearest Josh,

I have thought of you each day since we parted from each other in Augusta, after *that dance*; every day I have known I ought to write to you. But this is such gruesome time of year, isn't it? When you took me back, after the hunt breakfast at Lavinia's, to Clear Creek—*your own house*, for Goodness' sake—I said Goodbye. But it wasn't a very complete goodbye.

At the time, I thought there would be a change between us. And now I have found that there has been really very little change.

I ought to have said Goodnight. I felt I hurt you; I saw you wince. But that can have been from the wound in your side, can't it have? I hope it has healed by now. I wish all wounds could heal. Well, they do, of course, but it is Time that is supposed to do the work, and I wish every hurt could be made better at once, and then stay that way. I'm afraid I'm still quite a child.

You must have seen something flicker between Edward Strikestraw and me. We had met as children, but I think he didn't remember me. He had become someone entirely different; and so have I. And now, I expect him to become my life's companion.

But what I want you to know is that nothing could ever make me love you less than I have—less than I do—even if I have found someone I love even more. And I shall love you always. Not everybody would understand a feeling like that, but I know that you will. I only hope you will love me as much as ever, whatever happens to either of us.

With all my love, Mary

When he had finished reading, as he handed the paper back to Josh, Ben grew grave. "I don't see that you've lost your girl; not when she tells you she still loves you so much."

"I thought that, too. But I evidently picked and chose what I wanted to see, because that is really not quite how simple it is."

"It's just Edward Strikestraw. What kind of name is 'Strikestraw,' anyway? If it weren't for him, she'd be all yours, it looks like to me."

"It looks like it to me, too. If...."

"Well, I wouldn't miss him, the bigoted bastard!" Ben trembled at the word he had spoken, but not noticeably, from outside.

Josh's vagaries of thought kept laying on bolder strokes. And what had become of his mature, graceful capitulation to unrequited love? He said—or somebody very like himself said: "I don't think he's very fair-minded about Blacks."

"Fair-minded! I've thought about this 'theory' of his. That Negroes are no better off than they are because they couldn't have any old people brought over with them to be sure they remembered their...native *lore*; to make sure they kept up tribal practices. Does he think we'd be any better off—well, the fool probably does think so—if we painted our bodies and danced and chanted all night?

"Take young Whites—they're the ones who have barricaded themselves off from *their* elders. They don't listen to what they tell them, or do what they tell them is the right thing to do." Ben had got quite enraged. When he stopped, he realized he had reached a crescendo of more venomous pitch than he had meant to do. But it had not been of much more.

"In this day and age they have. However, their elders are just beyond that barricade. And when their own plans go wrong, they can ask for help. They may be ashamed to ask, but help is there. And when they get into difficulty, the watchful fathers will begin it, and reach across to the sons."

"You look up to your people, and so do I. I mean I look up to your people. They're not the same as the rest. Most of the rest. They've always been used to treating us like something more than mules."

Play off him; this is the third time he's cast himself categorically as a Negro. And he's looking down—or trying to—on Edward. Who was whispering this to Josh? Whoever it was, he was whispering it directly into the middle ear. Because there was no sound outside.

"In all this, have you stopped to think about Miss Izora?"

"She's a sweet old soul. She knows how to be kind…even when nobody else does. But Colored people mostly think she's half-crazy. Face it. Black people have to be funny before White people are going to take a shine to them."

"I have a deep respect for Miss Izora. And I firmly believe she sees things nobody else sees, even if she is blind and claims to see what eyesight can't. Think what just she may have to offer to those willing to take her seriously. I think she knows things nobody else knows."

"Because your folks think so."

"May be. Well, look: You told me you and your family liked Edward, the days he was down here."

"Mary Alice and Tommy liked him, and I followed along. But not anymore."

"Anyway, we didn't come out here to talk about him."

"Have you got anything to drink?"

Josh hauled out the pewter field-flask. "You're getting to be as bad as me."

"Worse, because I do both."

"Both of what?"

"Liquor and weed. I'm learning how to hide it or cover it up. Sometimes, I just stay away from home."

"They don't ask you about it? Where you've been or what you've been doing?"

"I've got around them. They think I'm 'disturbed' by the racial hatred I see at State. They think I'm 'adjusting' to the differences between how Whites and Blacks get on there, and how they get on with each other down here. So I just say I need to 'think things through,' or 'sort things out,' and they don't give me no...any trouble over it." After a little time, while both were watching Blackwater slipping past, as though swept clean, all the Old Year's leaves being fallen, Ben asked: "But, so, what did you want to talk to me about?"

"Talk *with* you, Ben; not talk *to* you. I wanted to finish about a thing we *We?* started a couple of days ago: Taking your life because you can't come to terms with what you are. I've gone over it again, to myself. We don't kill ourselves over what we're dissatisfied with in our lives, but we do try to blot out some of the things we're ashamed of, or dislike, or mistrust—I don't mean we pretend they're not there. I mean we train ourselves not to let them have any more effect or presence in our lives than we can help. Like 'dying daily unto sin'—that's something in our Prayer Book. I think.

"It's like the difference between finding out what you are, then learning to like it, on one hand, and, on the other, finding out what you want to be, and then learning to become it. Everybody has those struggles. It's not just you...and not just other people who have come into the world under the same kind of cloud."

"I'd like to kill the Black man in me."

Transfer complete! "I've begun to see that you would. It won't work, of course. I told you that, and I wasn't very diplomatic about it."

"What you said was: 'You look Black. So be Black, and figure out how to accept it.' That's like finding out what you are, and learning to like it."

"I should have done a better job of it than that. *Except that it worked.* But you see what I meant, don't you? Change what you are discontented with in yourself, if it's possible. Your being Black you can't change; but you can become a changed Black man. Only not to White. If you kill the Black man in you, you'll be left with nothing. You'll become one of those Colored people whose only aim in life is to rub shoulders with what they see as high-up White people. You know some of the ones I mean. Other Colored people won't have anything to do with them. And after they get done with tending bar at a Society party, or being companion to a broken-down old aristocrat, or picking up the hymnals and Prayer Books and leftover bulletins, and latching the box-pews in some Colonial church, they go home with nothing to keep them company but recollection and pretending.

"Anyway, when you have what you don't like about yourself bond, then you're free to build up what you do like, and go on from there to trying to become what you want *ideally* to be."

The unconscious reckoning had now got much of its form. The factors missing from the equation were now clearly apparent: A denominator on one side cancelling an equivalent numerator upon the other.

"So you think I should kill the White man in me?"

"I do. In a figurative way. You'll still have the Black man's problems. But you'll be free of the White man's. You won't keep on hoping to have what the White man has just by being part White yourself. And being White, if you could be, would guarantee you nothing. Or, nothing—or, not much of anything—that's truly worthwhile." But Josh was finding it distasteful to use forms of the word "true."

"That all depends on who your people are, doesn't it?"

"Yes, up to a point it does. You saw how many modest cars were parked at the Holmans' house? There were more people there than you would guess who haven't much money. But they all dressed and talked and generally behaved 'in the right way,' so that once you got inside, you couldn't tell who had come in the Jaguars or who had come in the 'Fifty-six Fords. Money isn't supposed to matter. Blood is.

"It's true that sometimes blood goes to the bad; money appears, steps into the breach every once in a while, and makes the old ways possible again. It's a slow crawl. Down at the bank, they can't tell new money from old money.

"Remember, Ben: A lot of White people don't have either thing."

"Either of what? Are you keeping up with what you're talking about? Because I don't think I am."

"No blood—I mean blue—and no money. Being White is not the key to a good life. There is no single key to a good life. It all depends on the wards."

"The what?"

"Never mind. But everybody has to try to find his own answer. Some never do. Some do by effort. Some do by chance. And there's every gradual in between." And then Josh stopped to listen to himself in echo. Was he really befuddling the other man?

But Ben said: "The White man in me is already dead."

"Oh, no. No he isn't. Woody Paget took his own life, but he had passed yours on beforehand. For you to become what you need to be, that has to be got rid of, too." *How, though? Even if I were certain of that, how could I tell him? And how can I sit here thinking all this? I know I can't mean much of it. I hope I can't, if I mean what it seems I do.*

"How, though?"

"If I were certain of that, I would tell you."

"But you think you do know a way, don't you?"

"I can't seem to head up into that wind…not close enough to it to be sure." Josh had once seen a way for his impulses to acquire form and life. Now, instead, he found that he himself was standing irresolute at the head of a thorny track. All this had been supposed to proceed with more fluidity and conviction. He knew it was all insane, that he must himself be. But Ben was not at all enraged this time, not insane. *Now may be the time to stop all this and go home.*

And then Ben said: "I know somebody who has killed a man."

Josh turned to look at him. "And he was arrested? He is in prison?"

"No. He's as free as you and me. Freer than I am, in a way. He feels good about it, too, because the man he killed had cut his sister."

"What do you mean, exactly, by 'cut his sister'?" For Josh found it hard to think that, even in Orangeburg, a social slight could incite to murder.

"Slashed up her face. It was over owed money…hash money. A lot of it. He got his sister to watch him do it, too. She wanted to, though, anyway. Watch."

"Stop right there. I don't want to be an accessory to murder. You are, already. It's dangerous."

But a power he had been waiting for had entered their midst. It was a dark power, but Josh would not perceive it as dark, in spite of all unconscious promptings.

Ben went on: "I could do that myself."

"Could you? Why, since you know it's wrong?"

"No. I have a reason, and a reckoning." When he heard the word spoken aloud, Josh came close to falling backward from where he sat, as he might have done if struck hard in the middle of the chest. He had thought it so often, lately used it in so many spoken and in more unspoken phrases. Yet the remarkable coïncidence buoyed him, from all around. He said nothing. "A reckoning. You know, like an accounting." Ben's eyes were blazing with fanatic fire. Otherwise, he seemed still and controlled. And this, as the vision of a terrible thing swung into their mutual crosshairs—this…intentness, coming after all the signs of Ben's instability, and possibly of hatching mania—got very close to convincing Josh that now was indeed the time to put a stop to it all and go home. However, he sensed himself no longer in charge.

"Listen," the boy continued, "a man deserves to be killed. I kill him. Do I know *that's* wrong?"

"Yes, you do." An answer half-whispered. Josh had thought he could arrange the course of things. And now he seemed to have little to do with it at all. The whole was carried by an unrecognized momentum.

"Yes, I do." A degree of mockery, in the repetition. Not a great degree. The boy was thinking, and saying with deliberateness what he thought. "I do know that it is wrong; but the only reason it's wrong—Remember, I said 'a man who deserves to die'—is that I set myself up in place of the law." And Josh rallied a little.

"You're exactly right. You would be making what would otherwise be the execution of a sentence, an act of murder."

"But how do you think I stand before the law? No! No. How do you think I *believe* I stand before the law?" And he smirked, and only with that smirk did there come to Josh the acknowledgement of mockery in Ben's parroted reply, "Yes, I do;" only then, the realization that Ben had stood, while Josh himself had remained sitting, and upon what was in effect the floor—not even in a chair. Suddenly he felt very much at a disadvantage with respect to the man he had marked out as his instrument.

Josh stood. He was at no disadvantage. He was tall and strong and quite himself. He would speak.

Ben: "Wait, though. And listen. If I kill this one man, who deserves to die, and from my one killing come two guilty deaths, then right—maybe not the law, but right—is on my side. The account balances."

"No, it doesn't. Try to think clearly, Ben," one emotionally desperate and chemically distorted man recommended to another. "You can't kill one man and take the lives of two." As he said this, Josh wondered what he could possibly have meant by making this response. Or what Ben could have meant in making his claim. He wondered, because in wondering he warded off the fact that he knew.

But, as he wondered, he imagined he saw inside a kind of algebraic gymnasium. Woody Paget, whose photograph Josh had once seen—a snapshot taken many years before the man's pitiful, atrocious death—stood to the left, beneath an elevated bar, held overhead by an athlete who, during any mathematical operations, would maintain it horizontally situated. On the right, Edward Strikestraw was standing, balanced atop the farther end of the bar. Their figures and features began to change. Each of these persons had begun to look increasingly like an amalgam of the two. Then, when they had reached visual equality, both vanished.

"Meet me here again, early tomorrow. Early. There's something I may be able to tell you. Or I may not. I have to think over it. Come early."

At this season, the earth cooled quickly with the setting of the sun. Sodden air had started covering long fetches, up from the sea, coming to mingle with the floe of winter draining from the Upcountry; Josh watched it roll into a mist, pushing upstream, overborne, falling back, holding close to the inky face of the River. He watched, without noting that Ben had gone away.

That evening, Josh sat leaning over his great desk-table, his face in his hands. His soul, if a mirror, was turned away from All-Soul, not pouring forth praise in c-swift reflection, but staring into the dusk of its own shadow. The lifeless matte of a mirror's backing was instead turned to this shining Source, covetously absorbing the radiance and converting it to heat, debased and sluggish energy—Hephaistean, subterranean subaltern to smoking forge, hammer, iron, and anvil...smitten, smitten—heat, bleeding away in blackening languor into whatever nearby mass might have room within its molecular maelstrom to receive it.

VI

"Oh, the torment bred in the race,
   the grinding scream of death
      and the stroke that hits the vein,
   the haemorrhage none can staunch, the grief,
the curse no man can bear."

    Aeschylus: *The Libation Bearers,* 453-457 (tr. Robert Fagles)

"Speak sorrow, sorrow! But let the good gain victory."

    Aeschylus: *Agamemnon,* l. 159 (end of first strophë) and l.172 (end
    of first antistrophë) (tr. PT)

"Surely as no princely hall
Furbished is my heart, this chamber;
Gloom and deep abide instead.
Yet soon as Thy grace falls, streams, and
Enters in, she counts herself

Awash in Light of day."

J. S. Bach: *Christmas Oratorio,* (Part V) no. 18 (tr. PT)

BEFORE DAWN, BEN came from the direction of Dodona and the Paget Family Cemetery, over the low hill toward the dock, moon-blind, sleepless, lunatic. Light in the sky, now; he thought he could make out that the tips of the highest branches of the bare trees were touched by a restrained red-golden light, a winter light.

Off the surface of the stream there rose, where the water broadened into its small lagoon, a close-set multitude of slowly-turning siphons of vapor. Ben thought—but could not be sure, being unsure in general, particularly of his sight and of himself—that they all turned in the same direction, left-to-right, falling upward. They were various, though, in their devotion to their source, for some, the air essayed, slipped back beneath the surface, others seemed to trip-and-glide across it in a kind of unsyncopated tap-dance, others broke free and floated, dissipated vanishing.

Then Ben saw that while he had stood watching, Josh had arrived, coming from Clear Creek, but had not interrupted the survey of the mists. He stood on the dock. He stood there as though at a helm. Ben came up and said, "Look. Look what I got." He produced a pistol. .45 calibre.

"Take out the clip, Ben. Put it away."

"Don't worry. I'm not going to shoot you."

"Good. I'm delighted to hear it. You may not be *planning* to shoot me. But the safety's off. Take the clip out. Now." So Ben made the handgun safe and put it away inside his jacket. "I hope you haven't stolen that from Tommy."

"Shump gave it to me."

"Who's Shump?"

"The man I told you killed another man. For cutting his sister over drug-money."

"Why do you have it?"

Ben, in some guiltiness, answered: "I went to his room right afterward. He was still coming to classes and living at School then. He had this gun, holding it between his knees, with a rat-tail file down the barrel. He said he'd already chiseled out the serial number. He gave it to me to get rid of."

"What did he expect you to do with it? It's hard for me to believe he told you he'd done what he had, let alone handing over the murder-weapon."

"Oh, he couldn't keep it to himself—he had to brag about it to somebody. And there aren't that many people he could brag to. Anyhow, the pistol: He showed me how to break it down. He said to put each piece somewhere different. Drop one off the bridge, throw one onto a moving train...."

"Then why have you still got it?"

"I thought I might need it."

"Listen. I'm going to choose not to believe anything you've said about all this. No! Don't say anymore. If it were true, then you'd be an accessory to murder, as I've explained to you. No, be quiet! A lot of jail time goes with that. If it were the truth."

"But it…."

"Ben! Shut up! Think, but just…just shut up."

"All right. I'll shut up. But, now. Are you going to tell me whatever it was you needed the whole night to think over, or not?"

Josh quietly slipped from within himself and stood alongside on the little dock. "Yes, I'll tell you."

"More of Edward Strikestraw's wisdom?"

"Not wisdom. But the rest of what he said."

The lurid light flared again in Ben's eyes. "What?"

"That Woody Paget did both of you a favor when he raped your mother."

"Can I borrow your car?"

Josh handed Ben the keys.

Alina and Bob Barrington always awoke very early. They liked being awake together. In their dressing gowns, one went into the morning room at the front of the house and the other—they took turns, more or less—went to fetch coffee. On this day, Alina was working in gros point, a delicate vignette, grey and gold, upon a black ground. *If only it mattered!*

Bob, being a physician, competent and straightforward, took his motto from Faustus: *Ubi desinit pilosophus, ibi incipit medicus.* But his brother-in-law had advised him to read books that taxed his comprehension. "Eventually," Laurence had warned him, "everything is going to tax our comprehension. So it will be best if we're prepared." Therefore, Bob had got a book on classical physics, which he had learned once but since forgotten, and was at that time trying to grasp exactly why a body moving in a circle at a fixed velocity must be undergoing constant acceleration. *If only it mattered! And by now it has probably turned out to be not even true.*

As they sat, close to each other and close to the fire, which Bob had poked up, they heard the sound of a car motor. Then they saw the roadster emerge from around the southwest corner of the house and move away down the Magnolia Lane.

"Where on earth could he be going at this hour?"

"Oh, I imagine over to Woodleigh."

"Do you think I ought to telephone Lavinia?"

"No. Laurence will be up and about by now. He frets over the Pankeytown Hounds, because he thinks it's wintertime."

"It *is* wintertime."

"Not wintertime a mongrel hound would notice."

Alina, in her worry, half-stood, then sat down again. The work slid from her lovely lap. The needle, which was of larger calibre than most we see ladies sewing with, trailing its coma of yarn, lodged momentarily in her leg, just below and outside the knee, then fell away with the other paraphernalia. It was followed by a surprisingly full trickle of blood.

Bob laid down his book gratefully, and went off to his "workroom" for disinfectant and bandages. On inspection, the wound was as one made by a sewing-needle. *You might expect more from a negative scratch-test.* But Bob knelt and with great expenditure of time cleansed and dressed the little division within the superficial layer of skin, as though with enough care he could heal harsher wounds, from which he knew Alina suffered. For so did he himself.

And then he took her into his arms, and said: "I could never have taken the place for Josh of his father; even if I could, I would not want to. Having no child of my own, I don't know for certain. But I think I love him as much as I would if he were of my flesh and blood. If he should be lost, I would not want to go on myself, except to stay and take care of you the best I could." Alina's emotions were completely destabilized by this speech. They had needed to be. Then, as she was drying her eyes, the telephone rang.

"Probably that is Lavinia," she said. Bob went to answer.

"Bob, this is Lavinia."

"Alina thought it would be you."

"She often knows things she has no apparent way of knowing."

"I've noticed it. How are the two of you."

"We're well enough. Now, Alina always knows a lot of things; see whether she knows anything about this: Rennie and I just saw Ben Araby drive around the house. In Josh's roadster."

"I can tell you she doesn't. We thought, when the car passed by us, that it was Josh, driving away from here, and probably on his way over to you."

"No. It was Ben. And he parked among those hybrid hollies that screen the swimming pool. Rennie went out to the kitchen house, and he saw Ben hurrying on foot down The Street toward Miss Izora's house. But you don't know anything about it?"

"Nothing. Let me see what I can discover, and I'll let you hear."

"May I speak to Alina?"

"Will later be all right?"

"It was Ben in the roadster. It seems he parked off, then went toward home on foot.

"Not Josh, then."

"No. Ben, in Josh's car. So I'm going up to see about Josh, if he's here."

Before very much longer, Bob returned to the little sitting-room. "Josh is at home. In bed. Coccooned in comforters, and sleeping peacefully."

"Oh, Dear Bob! You've taken on all this trouble so willingly."

"It's nothing. Were you listening to what I told you just now? What if I were still alone?"

"You've never been alone."

"There may be a sense in which I haven't. There's always been somebody to love me. There hasn't always been anybody for me to love. Now there is. Compare the two states, and you'll find that trouble in the second circumstance is better than freedom from it in the first."

"Well, Josh is all right. With that settled, I can worry about his car later."

"Or not worry about it at all. It's just a car."

"Yes. But it may have Ben inside it."

Driving away from the settlement that had been his beginning and his world, Ben fled along under an overarching canopy of oaks, trapped in darkness, like a moth held onto the pavement by the cupped hands of a Gargantuan child, curious, but intending no harm. He bawled out crazed songs; he shouted passages from the most vindictive of the Psalms his great-grandmother had made him learn: "'Up, Lord, and help me, O my God; for thou smitest all mine enemies upon the cheek-bone; thou hast broken the teeth of the ungodly.'

"Oh, de shoulder-bone connected to de neck-bone...de neck-bone connected to de jawbone...de jawbone connected to de cheek-bone....'" His feral cries resounded in the forest, to which they anyway belonged; they were mazed among the trees and hanging moss. But the dark swampland set free upon its wing no echo.

Josh had gone back to bed upon returning from his meeting. But he was not sleeping peacefully, and, when Bob had looked in, not sleeping at all, but pretending. He had awakened from a dream, and upon awakening had recognized it as the forgotten fourth dream that had visited him during five nights sometime before Christmas. In this originally mislaid dream, Josh had stepped from a humid passageway into a series of chambers, each entered from the one before through a series of doors. These and the chambers were coated with pitch, darker than night. When he left the last of them, he awoke. He knew then that the chambers were those of his own heart.

So he thought over the series of five dreams, to see whether they made sense together. The deadly anger, the sexual fury, the sorrow of which he could not gauge the depth, now this journey like the *descente aux enfers* from an epic not destined to be written, and finally the unwilled but enforced departure. But if they constituted some progression, any continuity it possessed had escaped him. He was in any case imprisoned in the aftermath of the fourth. His heart. His dark, still, hardened heart. How had it got that way? Or when? He may have had some inkling why.

For then, in waking, there came to him some words, chanted, he thought, as though in Church. Not Anglican plainchant—he'd have recognized that. It seemed less complex than Gregorian. Or, he thought so. But the words were certainly chanted, not said:

> *And I will remove from your body the heart of stone*
> *And give you a heart of flesh.*

He did not know where he had heard it, or what it was, but as the words circuited his thoughts, after a while the notes came to him correct and complete, so that he could chant it himself. And he began to do this, over and over

When the Gargantuan child opened his hands a little so as to inspect his captive—that is, when Ben drove out of deep forest and onto a section of highway with ploughed fields on both sides—the sun had risen quite. He stopped, opened the roof. Then, as he went, he still shouted and sang: "'…they do but flatter with their lips, and dissemble in their double heart.'"

Off to his right, far off, was a steading, still in shadow of the woods. He noticed it, because just then an ammonia vapor lamp, raised on a pole high above a barnyard, flickered out. Soft, warm incandescent light shone in a window; smoke rose direct from an inapparent flue. And for the first time Ben felt lonely. Because wilderness is not of itself a lonely place. But if vestiges, or if knowledge of man's presence be found in it—seen either to be at unapproachable distance, or known to have been but be no more—then solitude turns to loneliness. Ben shouted: "'He hath graven and digged up a pit, and is fallen himself into the destruction he made for other.'"

Josh sat wondering for a long time. When he had dressed, he pulled on his *bottes sauvages*, for the shortest way, by foot, to Woodleigh lay at one reach through swampy marsh. Then he set out.

Alina and Bob caught sight of him crossing the great field through which Ben had come and gone so often in the last weeks. "He must be going to Woodleigh to see about his car." His car, of course, was no longer at Woodleigh, and no one had seen—or at least, no one had reported—Ben's departure in it. But Josh was in fact going there to look at his Grandfather's Bible. *'The sorrows of death encompassed me, and the overflowings of ungodliness made me afraid.'*

This Bible had an index of words and phrases at the back, so that sometimes you could find a passage just from here, when you remembered it only in part.

All out of season, a serpent, a moccasin, struck from the slough as Josh was treading through it and sank its venom-teeth into the heel of the left boot. Josh saw it when it moved to strike. He placed his weight upon his left leg and foot and deftly crushed the creature's head with his right. He did not believe the fangs had penetrated inside the boot.

When he reached the Kitchen House at Woodleigh he removed his footgear, and having plucked two straws from one of the brooms that always rested against the outside door-casing, he sounded each of the punctures, and was reassured. In stocking-feet, he followed the brick-paved walks to the house and went inside. Nobody was there except Mary Alice. She was sitting at the dining table, polishing flatsilver.

"Merry Christmas, Mary Alice! I hope you and your family are in one piece, after the Commotion."

"I hope you and yours are, too, Mr. Josh. We're not, though. No, we definitely have a piece missing, and it's Ben. But I'm not going into all that anymore."

"I came to look at Mr. Jack's Bible. Do you know where they keep it?"

"No, Sir, I don't." She didn't know *whether* they had kept it, after the Old Man had died.

"I don't want it for dates, or anything like that, that he might have written on those blank pages they put in at the front. I'm trying to find a passage. Grandfather's Bible had that index in the back."

"Could you tell me what you're looking for? It may be I could help." For, reared as she had been at Miss Izora's knee, Mary Alice was in herself perhaps the most nearly complete concordance to the Bible in all of Peell County.

"Yes. This is what I can remember: 'I will take from your body the heart of stone, and give you a heart of flesh.' That's all."

"But I think I know it—or something close."

"You know it? Where is it written?"

"See whether you think this is the same thing: 'And I will take away the stony heart out of your flesh, and I will give you a heart of flesh.'"

"That's got to be it, in a different translation."

"I remember it because it comes just before the story of the Valley of the Dry Bones."

"All I know about that is a song...a rather foolish one. What actually happened to the Dry Bones?"

"Oh, nothing so much...not for the Maker. Ezekiel found a slain army—nothing but bones. The Lord told him to prophesy, and bone came to its bone, sinews connected them, then they were covered with flesh. That's why I remembered the part you told me. When I first learned it, I thought the Maker must have been in a humor to give out a good deal of flesh, around then."

Pounds and pounds of flesh!

"Then skin, then the four winds brought the breath of life."

"Thanks, Mary Alice. I don't see how you remember all those things, much less how you keep them straight." So after they had parted, when Josh got to the back doors, he shouted over his shoulder: "We'll save Ben. The Lord will keep him."

He went down from the verandah wondering whether, of his own accord, he had ever predicated anything of "The Lord" before. He pulled on his boots at the kitchen-house, and stumped off with what seemed to be a fantastic spur at his left heel.

By the time Ben had reached Orangeburg, it had got colder, and the sky was blanketed with cloud. Soon it began to snow, lightly as usual in those parts, when it snowed at all. Ben pulled off the street and put up the roof of Josh's car, taking every care. When it was in place, he got inside again and tightened the two chromium-plated knobs that held the top fast. Then he drove on, muttering. "'Up, Lord, disappoint him and cast him down.'"

Orangeburg, with its population of twenty thousand, was home to two colleges: Claflin College, and South Carolina State College, both dedicated to the higher education of the sons and daughters of Africa. But Orangeburg had no flavor of a college town. There were the two campuses, adjacent; across a railroad embankment, a street of which a block-and-a-half had shops and restaurants catering to the students, all Black. Nobody outside the institutions knew or saw anything else.

Ben, himself transformed in the days since he had been there before, found congenial the metamorphosis of the town that the flurries of snow had wrought out. Lines of white powder made backbones along the pair of canon, removed from their carriages and now at rest upon dressed blocks of granite, aimed westward, where the ground fell away to the River, along which the public gardens lay; guarding, they were, the figure of a Confederate soldier atop his *Sigesseule*. Yes, atop his victory column, for Southerners of many sorts believed, and do believe, that true Victory in the Civil War alit upon the prow of the ship of the Confederacy.

Soon Ben was bumping and dodging through the complicated intersection that led him across the railroad and to his alma mater. The legislatorial vision had been splendid; the appropriations had been wanting. Through the pale curtain of snowfall you couldn't see that the color of the brick was wrong, verging towad purple, and from a distance you didn't know that the columns and corbels and cupolas were made of impressed metal, not sawn and planed and carved and routed wood. The lampposts shone, in spite of the morning hour: The photoelectric cells that controlled them were seeing what we see, looking directly up into a snowing sky: Grey, soiled by what looks like falling ash.

One of these lighted globes had been broken. The shard had fallen to the inside.

The silhouettes of the buildings were authentic. Illusion made it seem to be Hanover, if not quite Williamsburg. A little imagination, and Ben might have stood in The Yard itself. The flakes had spent themselves by now, and, as he walked toward his dormitory Ben crossed the shallow roots of pinoaks, snaking along, enclosing pools of hard-packed sand, and from close-to he noted certain other physical shortcomings of the place.

Lights were burning in roughly a third of the windows on Ben's side of the building. That meant plenty of students had already returned from vacation. He knew that a few wanted to have an early start preparing for examinations, which at that time were administered after the holiday break, before late January. He knew, though, that others had come back because college was for one or another reason better for them than home. To others still, it didn't matter where they were.

Two students were coming along the hallway toward him as Ben stepped out of the stairwell. He knew them by sight. "Have you all seen Shump around?"

One answered: "I never heard of anybody named Shump."

"Then how did you know it was somebody's name?"

The other boy spoke up: "I know him. To see him. I've been here since right after Christmas; he's not around." And the two went their way. They had all three been standing beside a partly-opened door, and now the occupant of the room beyond opened it wide and beckoned to Ben to come inside.

"Shump's gone. They kicked him out."

"Why? Do you know?"

"Every reason. He cheated, and still his grades were no good. He was a pain in class...when he went. Drank, did drugs, got caught."

"How did you hear he'd been kicked out?"

"Nobody said so. But I know. He always stays—stayed—in the dormitory over the vacations. That shack of his across the River, behind the old Chemical Plant...Do you know it?

Ben remembered the things Josh had warned him about earlier that same day. "No. I don't know Shump myself, either, except by sight."

"Then why are you looking for him?"

"To...um...give him a telephone number. Somebody asked me to do that if I saw him, but I don't know what it's about. No, I don't know the shack. I don't know Shump."

"Well, it's not fit for a swarm of cockroaches to live in. But that must be where he's staying. He hasn't got anywhere else."

"No folks?"

"Not many. Nobody ever knew who his father was. His mother left him and his brother with their grandmother, so she could go to some big city up North and make money whoring. The brother had a bad drug habit. Cocaine. He killed their grandmother to get her money. A hundred and thirty-five dollars! So he's in the Pen'.

"And I haven't told you everything I've *heard* about Shump, but I told you what I know, except that he's supposed to have a sister, too, somewhere, and it's enough. You ought to go out there and stick that telephone number on the door, and then get the Hell out. It does have a door. The shack." Ben thanked the boy and said he'd follow his advice. Then he went out to the car. The other student looked down from his window, once he had heard the stairwell door slam and catch, and watched Ben emerge from the building, walk across the dead or dormant turf, and get into the conspicuously expensive car and drive away. *So, that's what he wants. Well, Shump's got plenty, I guess.*

Josh was starting back to Clear Creek, a long trek over land that would be his own. *'The lot has fallen unto me in a fair ground; yea, I have a goodly heritage. I will thank the Lord for giving me warning.'*

Ben drove back across the River and turned south on Bacon's Bridge Road. This way he followed to the Chemical Plant, and with misgiving drove around behind the disused buildings and tanks on towers, looking for a tin shack. He had vowed in his soul what he would do. In his mind he had twisted wrong a turn further, into righteousness. Still, he knew his resolve was going to be assaulted, and he knew he must arm himself against this kind of onslaught. *'Thou shalt destroy them that speak lies...their throat is an open sepulchre.'*

Well, there it was. The shack. That must be it, a small ready-made accessory building. People bought them for their backyards, to house tools and gardening implements, sometimes to serve as workshops. Aluminum. Seamless. Pitched roof, but rounded where ridge and eaves would have been. This one rested upon eight cinderbocks. Unless it had been late afternoon, Ben could not have seen the light inside, for its dimness.

"So," Shump said, "you've got a job to do."

"Yes. And I'm going to do it."

"And you're afraid you won't be able to go through with it. Is that the problem?"

"Things get harder to do, the closer you get to doing them. You know the danger before, but when it comes to it, the danger can reach out and touch you. Or, you feel like that."

"And you don't want to feel like that."

"I can't afford to. If I turn back, I'll be turning back to a life I don't think I can live."

Shump stood up, moving from some kind of bunk—It looked like nothing more than a pile of fleeces—and went over to a small table, on which the only light, a kerosene lantern, burned. He fumbled about with a small tumbler, a bottle, spoon, some packets. He started talking softly, as though to himself: "There's something they've found out about, something you can do to this stuff. It makes it a lot more powerful." And these words themselves made Ben feel that danger might be reaching out to touch him already. "Come over here and sit down at the table. This is on the house, just a little bit to try, so you'll know. Now, mix this much of the powder in this bottle of liquid. Don't worry. It's mostly just rum."

When Ben had drunk it, soon afterward he felt confident of being able to slaughter anything that might slither out of the swampland around the North Fork of the Edisto River. As he left the shack he noticed for the first time a Christmas wreath on the door. Not like Shump to do that. Maybe the offended sister.

At home, Josh took down his own Bible. It was of course the Authorized Version, or, as it was known by most people in Peell County, the "Saint James" version. He'd forgotten to ask Mary Alice where to look.

She had mentioned Ezekiel—a figure known to Josh only by name. And from that zany song he remembered: "Ezekiel connected dem dry bones...." And there was another he thought he remembered: "Ezekiel saw the wheel, 'way up in the middle of the air.…" *You grow up accustomed to all these figures, without bothering to think how bizarre they are.* But, sure enough, looking at the table of contents, he found: "The Book of the Prophet Ezekiel, p. 763." He found and read the consecutive passages about the hearts of stone and of flesh, and the Valley of Dry Bones.

In over a month of nearly unremitting regret for his loss of Mary Mountainstream, of nearly unremitting drunkenness, he had plowed a furrow longer than any he had followed before, either on that same afternoon or by clear moonlight on Christmas eve. A deeper furrow, too. His share had become entrenched.

He poured himself a copious drink and was about to sit down with it to think again of his girl. Now, though, he found himself strongly inclined to do this while looking outside, outside his rooms and outside himself. Because for the first time in weeks, he thought of trying to see beyond. There was no balcony, though, and the stair landing at the back would not accommodate a chair—at least not one with Josh sitting in it. Besides, it was on the wrong side of the Carriage House—he wanted to look westward. Like John Donne.

So Josh took from behind his desk the light but sturdy chair and placed it in the passageway connecting his sitting room and bedroom, his back to the bath, facing the tall window. Here still hung the immense globe of mistletoe, still fresh, still trailing its comet's tail of colored ribbons. It had until January fifth.

Josh sat down and looked out. The view was overlaid by a faint reflection of himself and the chair. With a long draught, he began to ponder things.

How is it I felt this morning that I was walking through my own, pitch-lined heart?

A distinct voice, to his surprise, came from somewhere outside himself: "That is really two questions. First, you have diminished your being, are so much less than yourself; that is why you seemed to be moving inside yourself. And the pitch? It was not so much lining the passageways of your heart as sealing them, letting very little either in or out."

Has my heart then become a heart of stone?

The clear voice answered, "It is well along the way to becoming like stone. You know that pitch, unless you set it alight and make a torch of it, gradually sets up, hardens, and becomes brittle. And at that point, it may as well be stone."

How have I diminished myself so far? Now the sun was low, shining from under the clouds. With greater light outside, the reflection of a man sitting in the chair grew faint…faint to disappearing.

"By dulling your senses, and your ability to integrate them, with drink, and with grief and doubt; by fixing what attention you've left yourself upon a single misfortune; by edging out of your thoughts any but some scraps of your good fortune. That is how."

What has taken me over?

"You're not a half-wit. Or, you didn't start out as one. You think you've lost Mary. And you think you love her. But you haven't, and you don't—at least, not to the extents or in the ways you suppose." And now the sun was beginning to set; the windowpanes were ablaze, whether seen from inside or out.

It is true. I haven't lost her. She won't become my "life's companion," but she loves me just as she did. She said so. The light—not heat—seemed to liquefy the windowpanes. Blazing, consuming, revivifying, silent. *Let this burn the pitch away, out of me.*

If I loved Mary truly, then I would want her to have what is best for her. I would pay in money for anything that could make her life good, and I'm going to have to pay in another way for this. Edward is best for her. It hurts me to have to think it, but the man better for her has won her.

When the sun had gone down and darkness was falling outside, the lighted passageway transformed the windowpanes practically into mirrored planes, allowing Josh to recognize his interlocutor. With a heavy hand he replenished the glass, but with a heart—Was it possible?—grown lighter. A little more supple? A spark held to the fuel? He returned to the chair. He didn't want to sit in his arched window on display. Particularly not beneath an enormous ball of mistletoe. So he put out the light in the passageway and sat down again. The lighting in the garden below had come on automatically. It was dim, and it balanced closely the light spilling into the passageway from the bedroom to Josh's right and from the sitting room to his left. The reflection was thus nearly transparent, but it was there again. Or still?

"Here," it seemed to say, "is a heart of stone," exhibiting a pale, smooth river rock, about the size and shape of a human heart. "And here is a heart of flesh." Beside the stone, Josh, or his reflection, laid a human heart. It was a recently resected one, red mostly, covered with tissue-fluid. Josh-of-the-Chair recoiled a little, and took a walloping slug of whiskey. He had never seen a human heart cut out of the body. He had not seen any heart, for that matter. Not from the outside.

"You can *see* a difference, of course. But do you *know* the difference?"

The stone one has pitch inside?

"No. There's no inside to it—stone, stone all the way through."

Then what is the difference...at least, the difference you're looking for?

Reflection-Josh took up a short staff, no longer than eight inches. It was copper-colored, and it had a curious sheen. Josh-of-the-Chair saw, bending forward for a closer look just at the moment when Reflection-Josh in his turn bent forward to proffer, that the staff was wrapped in a close coil of fine copper wire. It was sparkling, burning densely within a minute spheric space at the end of the rod. Reflection-Josh then bent down over the hearts, just as Josh-of-the-Chair bent over them to look more closely. When the intense fire-fountain was held to the stone, a glittering webwork of sparks flickered over the surface, weaving and twisting in bright threads among each other, and this continued until the stick was withdrawn.

"Electrons, applied to what won't conduct them, repel each other, out onto the surface. There, they keep repelling each other, but the repulsions cause collisions, and that's what we've seen scuttering all over the rock, like sand-fiddlers when the tide is dead low"

I've seen things like that before.

"We all have. Now the same charge applied to a living heart…."

That's a living heart?

"Yes. It's on loan."

A normal living heart?

"Yes."

With nothing inside it?

"Not anything that doesn't belong there." And he applied the charge to the heart of flesh. After a short time, it began to beat. Josh-of-the-Chair thought blood might spurt out, but none did. "When the charge enters what will conduct it, then it flows along in a little bustling, regularly bumping sort of current. Current electricity, when there's a dependable flow of it, can make things that are sensitive to it do their work. But you're still wondering about something."

Yes, I am. What if the living heart had got something viscous—or even brittle—inside it? Would it still work?

"The current travels through the muscle-tissue, which is particularly formed to conduct it efficiently along specialized pathways. It would work, but it would work less well."

One-Josh had nodded off to sleep, and awoke, startled, only just as he was about to spill the contents of his glass onto the floor. He drank it, instead. There was no more reflection. Had the lights in the garden got brighter? He ambled off to bed, and, again and finally falling asleep, thought: '…*Then will I sprinkle clean water upon you…then will I cleanse you.*' …*Less well, but it will work.*

Next morning, along Orangeburg's main street, before the stores had opened—the few that were going to—there seemed to be only three people about. One was Ben, who hurriedly entered the First National Bank. Its giltwork clock on the sidewalk was chiming half past eight o'clock. It was

New Year's Eve; everybody at work there so early would go away at eleven; nobody would be in the next day.

The other two people were Johanna-Maria, daughter of the proprietor of the small grocery store on the corner, under a defunct hotel. She was a dark beauty of Mediterranean descent, and her smile was like the Mediterranean sun. She was talking to Shump as she unlocked the front door to the store. He was dressed remarkably in a long knitted cap, red, green, and white, with a pom-pom, and a tailored topcoat, inset sleeves, of dark grey stuff in a herringbone pattern.

Ben came out with all that had been in his account, the greatest part being two hundred-dollar bills, in a gift-envelope provided by the Bank, decorated with poinsettias and snowmen. There was beneath the unsealed flap an oval cutout, for displaying the presidential portrait to the fortunate recipient of a gift of money. This, of course, was not a gift.

Shump said goodbye, as Johanna-Maria went into her father's store, and he sauntered up to Ben, taking from his coat pocket a package wrapped in embossed silvery foil and royal blue ribbon; he held this out to Ben and said cheerfully, "A late 'Merry Christmas,' and a Happy New Year!" Ben handed over the envelope, and Shump sauntered off in the direction of the River, singing—or singing at—a popular Holiday tune:

> Oh, the weather outside is frightful,
> But the fire is so delightful,
> Da da da da da da da…Blow;
> Let it Snow, let it Snow, let it Snow.

When Josh awoke on the morning of New Year's Eve, he realized that he had not become "quite himself" at all, and that in order to think straight, as he put it to himself, he would need a "little tot." *'Then will I sprinkle clean water upon you, and ye shall be clean.'…Then I shall have a heart of flesh…it will work, and work well again…the Water of baptism…drowning me dead to sin.* He held up his glass, looking through the liquid inside. *And getting me free of this poison.* He added an Augustinian "But not yet."

The best water to drown in, the deathwater that wouldn't mix with any other stream, with any living stream, was Blackwater. Josh pulled on whatever clothes lay nearest to hand.

On the dock he undressed again and dived into the River. He swam underwater. He swam to the bottom. He dug his fingers into the sandy streambed in order to be sure he was completely immersed, completely dead. In order that his choked heart might become completely dead, so that when it lived, it could live in movement free.

He came up out of the water, stood on the dock, waiting to be dry. But as he stood there, his thoughts turned to Ben, where he might be, what he might be doing or be about to do. *Why have I waited?* Josh got dressed and ran all the way back to Clear Creek, hammered at the back door, even as his heart hammered inside him—from exertion, urgency, and from fear. Alina, just now awake, came to let him in. "Darling! What is the matter?"

"Bob." It was all he could say, for breathlessness.

"What about Bob?" No answer. Josh was still panting for air, leaning against the doorpost with his right hand and arm. "Bob. *Bob!*" Alina turned back into the hallway, leaving her son where he stood.

Bob appeared instantly. "Josh! What are you doing? Training for a Marathon?"

"Can I have the truck?"

"Sure. The keys are in it. Tank's full."

When Josh had driven away, and Bob and Alina were alone in the morning room, Bob took in a deep breath, and tried to think where he had left the various pieces of the Armor of Light. Alina took a sip of coffee, and, as she found it still warm, set the cup down, took up her needlework. She said: "Bob, I do not want you to worry or exert yourself over whatever is taking place. I'm not sure of much, but I'm sure of this: The matter is out of our hands entirely."

Bob tried to distract himself with further exploration of the simple phenomenon of angular momentum, but failed. He looked at his wife. She was wonderful to look at, he thought. He said: "Why don't you go ahead and drink your coffee? You really do not need anything that *macht schön.*"*

Presently, Josh reached Ashfield and drove around to the north side of the Courthouse, where, in the basement storey, were the County Jail and Sheriff's office. Merrimon Baker was still at his post, unchanged by the nearly twenty elapsed years, except that the margins of his cleanly trimmed sideburns were now perfectly white.

"Good morning, Mr. Jones," he said as Josh to an extent erupted into his office. "Can I help you?"

"Good morning, Sheriff. Yes, please. I think my car's been stolen." The Sheriff drew a ruled pad to within easy reach, and asked Josh to sit down.

"Could you give me the particulars, so I can decide on the best way of finding it? Is it your roadster?"

"Yes...Sir. I leant it to a friend; he hasn't brought it back."

---

*Allusion to a German *Sprichwort: "Kaltes Kaffee macht sch*ön," or "Cold coffee makes one beautiful."

"When did you lend it?"

"Yesterday morning." Since his plunge into the River, he hadn't had anything more to drink. He was glad of it, because he hadn't wanted his parents to know, and he didn't want Sheriff Baker to know he had been drinking at sunup, if it could be helped. He had awakened with the remarkable realization and conviction that drinking had already got to be dangerous for him, that he must stop. But he desperately wanted something to drink—not much; only a little—and as soon as he could get away. He felt humiliated by the urgency.

"So, then, about twenty-four hours ago?"

"Yes."

"Who is the friend?"

"A boy named Ben Araby."

"I know who that is. When were you expecting him to return the car?"

"I didn't tell him to bring it back at any particular time."

"Did he tell you how long he meant to keep it."

"No, Sir."

"Then I'm afraid we can't regard that as a stolen car, but…."

"There's more I need to tell you. Can this be just between us?"

"I'll certainly keep it that way while I can. And if I have to divulge anything you tell me, then I will let you know in advance. Is that good enough?"

Josh nodded. "He has a pistol. Loaded. He has started drinking and using drugs. I think he has gone up to Orangeburg—He goes to college there—to restock, and then I think he will head toward Wilmington. North Carolina, not Delaware. That's all I can say. But I may know what he'll do if he gets so far, and I have to try to stop it. I mean, whatever I have to do."

"Did you know all this when you leant him the car?"

"No." Josh didn't feel quite right about saying No, but when Yes and No are both true…then, surely, it's all right to give the more expedient answer. "I put it all together during the day, and last night…and this morning."

Merrimon Baker listened closely to this statement. But he did not write it down. He had not asked for any elaboration. No clarification. No signature of acknowledgement. He stood up, and Josh got to his feet. "Have you ever been sick, Mr. Jones, and gone to a doctor who didn't know what was wrong?"

Josh must think over this, but then said: "Yes, at school."

"You'd be surprised at how often people of whom I ask that answer: 'He didn't know,' or 'He wasn't sure,' and from what you have felt able to tell me about your car, I cannot make a diagnosis."

"I'd tell you more…."

The Sheriff held up a silencing hand. "No. That's not what I want. You've heard the expression, 'Going by the book,' of course. Yes. Well I don't always do that. The letter of the law does not always provide the best solution to a problem. Not the surest Justice, nor the greatest Good.

"I will deal with what I know. That a car—which I will describe and specify—may have been stolen. If it is seen by the Highway Patrol, or other peacekeeping agency [*Is he making fun of me? Of the Law? Of himself? Because he is sending something or somebody up*], then it ought to be stopped and the driver held for questioning. I'll transmit it as what we call an 'All-points Bulletin.'

"Where can I reach you?"

"May I telephone you at intervals? I'm going after him, myself."

"Do you have any reason to think he'll harm you?"

"I'm supposed to be in his good graces. I'm not part of what he's after. So, no, I haven't any reason. I mean, any reason to be afraid of Ben."

"Good. Don't exceed the speed limit." They grinned at each other, following this somewhat formal exchange, and shook hands. Just as Josh was going out of the office the sergeant—not Sergeant Wilson who was working in Ashfield when Woody Paget had been held overnight in jail there, but a new one, named Lunsford—came in. Baker felt, as they said Good Morning, that Lunsford had worked himself up to something or other, and felt it could have to do with information he had about Josh's car. Or it mightn't be anything. The sergeant sat down at his own desk, in a corner, but close to the other window. It faced Sheriff Baker's.

Presently he stood up, and walked to the pencil-sharpener mounted to the door casing next to the way to the prisoners' cells. He began to grind away at a pencil. Without turning around, he said: "Are you a married man, Sir?"

"No. I assumed everybody knew that. What makes you ask?"

"Aren't you wearing a wedding ring?" Still he didn't turn to face his superior, not even to verify the observation he believed he had made. He had certainly seen a ring there before.

"Yes. Yes I am." Baker took off the ring, which had been his uncle's, and put it into the breast pocket of his uniform. "Sometimes I do."

"Widowed?" The pencil sharpener had stopped turning. The Sergeant just stood, not moving, his back turned to the man he was supposedly addressing.

"No. I've never been married. So I guess the ring does require an explanation."

At last Lunsford turned. His face was slightly flushed. He didn't seem able to raise his eyes. "Sir, you don't have to explain anything to me. It's none of my business. I don't know why I asked you."

"Well, I think I do know why, Tucker, and I'll be glad to make it your business: Occasionally, when I go away, I wear this," he said, tapping the pocket, "to discourage anybody from…approaching me."

"Oh, I see what you mean. Streetwalkers…or queers." He was by now leering conspiratorially, but still discomfited.

"No. It's not that simple. I'd be as useless to 'queers' as to 'streetwalkers.'" Lunsford became baffled, and looked to be. He turned away to see whether there were any of the pencil left for him to pulverize. "I was injured, a long time ago."

Lunsford remembered then something his predecessor had told him about. Baker had got the Congressional Medal. And the Purple Heart. He never talked about it.

But now the sergeant had probably *forced* him to talk about it, just from a salacious wish to know whether the Sheriff were homosexual, as once in a great while somebody, usually somebody with a grudge—even if the grudge were only envy of physical, mental, or moral superiority—claimed him to be. He had known quite well that his intendant had never been married. But he'd prodded him. He'd reopened a wound. Likely one that had in any case never quite closed.

Daylong, he hoped to be called away, sent away, got away from the office and jail for no matter what reason. When the workday came to an end, he stood up, walked across to the Sheriff's desk, and began an apology. But his words got entangled as he proceeded. Then the Sheriff held up the silencing hand again, saying: "It was completely reasonable for you to ask me. When things don't square with each other, a good policeman looks for the reason."

"And you gave me your reason; and I had no right to it."

"I gave it to you willingly, but now let's leave it." The two men were about to step out into the evening, just as a radio transmission came in. The Sheriff turned back. "I may know what that's about," he said. "I'll take care of it. Good night, Tucker. Happy New Year."

"Good night, Sir. Happy New Year."

Once back inside Bob's truck, Josh had drunk from his flask just so much (he told himself) as would bring him "up to snuff." *All these little phrases, euphemisms for doing wrong and enjoying it, and all the more, probably, because of his* 'certitude de faire le mal'! Then he set out for Wilmington—for New Brunswick, rather—and not for Orangeburg.

About then, Ben was setting out, also for Wilmington. The farther he traveled in Josh's car, the more conspicuous, the more exposed he felt. The man and the machine were indeed not matched. But he concentrated upon his goal. When the fuel gauge had fallen as far as Ben thought he ought to let it, he pulled into a filling-station. After he had pumped what gasoline he thought his budget would bear, he went inside to pay. A large White girl, with densely cascading, artificially blond hair, let him have a roadmap of North Carolina. She had beautiful green eyes. Feline ones. Ben asked for the key to the men's room. She looked right into his soul with the green eyes, and she handed over the key.

Ben, once closeted, was relieved to find the door lockable. So often, the very public ones weren't, due to vandalism. And there, having prepared it with care, he took a fourth part of Shump's elixir. He waited. Nothing changed. Then suddenly, there it was! He could carry his design through to the end. He was astonished. He found it hard to believe something you took that way could change the whole world, and change your place within it.

He also found it hard to believe that the ample young woman, when he was returning the key to her, didn't know what he had been doing. The green irises probed, constricting.

Ben drove on. He kept within the speed limits; he could not risk being stopped. Or was the green-eyed girl calling the Highway Patrol even then? But why should she? Because of what Ben was by now convinced she knew about him? At first, he had thought her accommodating. She had been. And now Ben concluded that she had been too accommodating not to have had some ulterior prompting. He began to look for a satisfactory place to pull off the road, to conceal the splendid automobile that any fool could at a glance see was not his own.

He was caught in the grip of uncertainty and drove far before he could make up his mind to leave the highway. There was a small church of white-painted clapboard, set well back, affording a spacious parking area, at that time empty. Ben cruised slowly around and behind the building and found himself in a much smaller clearing full of rough tables, all set askew with respect to each other. The ground beneath them was covered by layered oyster shells, these, however, not crushed.

He stopped the car and got out. He had the unsettling feeling that someone was about to arrive in order to align the tables. Why? And of course there was no definable reason for this concern. An overgrown lane led out of the picnic area, through a narrow stand of sedge into the wooded land. Ben followed it. It curved well out of anyone's sighting, and so he returned to the roadster and drove it into cover.

He could tell that he was sensing more things, now, and each in more ways. Was he fearless? Yes. Was he fearful? Equally so. He felt sure of his ability to carry out his principal purpose; crouching behind a dense growth of yaupon holly, where the lane met the clearing, however, he had a heightened sense that a trivial mishap would wholly sabotage his scheme, yet confident all the while that no such thing would actually occur.

And through all these branchings of provision, he realized that the drug was producing them, so he threw over any plan against the kind of contingency he imagined. He elected those propositions that fit his purpose. For he was a clever young man. And it was not the drug that had made him that way.

Walking out to the highway he noted that the windows of the church were of the ordinary sash type. But the panes were painted in different color-washes, to suggest stained glass. Above their squared tops were triangles of casing, meant to evoke the two-point arch. Upon the roof was a small bellcote, with louvres on all four sides, topped off with a two-by-two shaved into a pinnacle, whitewashed, sun-splintered. *Nigger Gothic.*

Holding the roadmap folded within his jacket pocket, Ben Araby fared out on foot, on the way to making himself a free man.

Josh thought it time to try to make sure that he was, literally, on the right track; and so he telephoned to Ben's dormitory after another unproductive call to Sheriff Baker. At the time when these things took place, very few college students had telephones of their own. There was normally a coin-operated telephone at one or the other end of each dormitory hall, or it might be halfway along. When it rang, no one wanted to answer (unless he were expecting a call—usually no one was). And so, when any call came in, ordinarily the telephone rang and rang and rang, until some one of the residents could stand it no longer, broke down and answered. And usually regretted having done it.

"Is Ben Araby there? May I speak to him?"

"What?"

"Ben Araby. Do you know him? Is he there?"

"Wait a minute." But in short of a minute the voice returned.

The young man who answered hadn't left the telephone at all, but had just stared through a grimy window at the scene across the grey railroad-bed and -tracks, at the grey things and Black people on the other side. Trinity Church. Imposing, but with something faintly wrong. For, after all, this was earth and not heaven. The steeple surmounting the west end of the nave, which in fact faced east, had succumbed to the imperfection of life below, for the timbers carrying the copper sheathing had bowed or expanded unequally—not much so—twisting the Cross on the pinnacle a bit to the south from east. Steel rails, granite fill, coals—different shades of it, but all grey. Some persisting snow? Sullied sand? It didn't matter. It was hard for the boy to make things matter. It might start to drizzle rain. But that would be grey, too.

"Hey! Mister!"

"Yes?"

"I don't think he's here. But he was yesterday. In a smooth car, too."

"Well, I wonder if you could have a look at his room. To see whether he's there. Or whether his gear…."

"What?'

"His stuff."

"What about it?"

"Could you see whether he's there, whether he's unpacked?"

"Yeah. I'll go do that."

"Or somebody named Shump? Is he there?"

"Wait a minute." The handset had evidently been dropped hanging upon its cord, to clatter back and forth against the wall.

Josh was beginning to think he was wasting his time. The respondent was a simpleton, or had done something to himself to make himself seem so. But now a different voice came onto the line: "Mister, I don't know who you are."

"It doesn't matter."

"Shump."

"Yes?"

"How is it you know him?"

"I don't."

"You don't sound like somebody who would. But I'll tell you this, Mister: If you don't know him, then don't get to know him. And Ben Araby, I don't kn…." Some kind of scuffling could be heard over the line.

The telephone receiver had become an object of contention. The original voice, phlegmatic or desensitized, depending from guesswork, returned:

"His stuff is here. But it's all still packed up. Just piled on his bunk. But he's gone."

"How do you know?"

"His car's gone. If it's his car."

"How long has he been gone? Do you know?"

"Last night, late, the car was here. This morning, early, gone."

"Thank you."

"You're welcome, Mister."

Then came the more attentive voice again. "He's right, uh, Sir. Ben's not here. Shump's been gone a long time. And like I said, I don't think you know Shump, and I don't think you'd want to know him. But if Ben turns up, if you'll give me your name or 'phone number…."

"No. No, and I thank both of you very much." So Josh kept on as he had been, not wanting to be stopped, either. For the journey was demanding replenishment of fuel. Three compounds of it, too, between the two travelers.

After the broad meadows of Awendaw, before he entered Georgetown, Josh crossed the South Santee River, the sacred delta, the North Santee, which Hopsewee commands, cradle of expectation, beholder of the depths and of woe.

One way or other, he must either overtake Ben, or warn Edward. The telephone in Thomas Strikestraw's study rang repeatedly, each time Josh had stopped and tried to place his calls. And he was partly thankful there was no answer. For, if he had reached Edward, what could he have said? "Be on guard?" "Leave this place?" Then what explanation might he have given? At any rate, when he got to either Edward or Ben, he must explain what he hardly knew how to explain; perhaps confess, though he could not envisage any precise confession; perhaps, if he could at all, atone?

Josh might have rested these musings; a buckler was set about the innocent; atonement writhed and thrashed, awaiting the guilty. Since the morning, though bright with early sun, with the Sheriff's clarity of purpose, with his stepfather's graciousness steady at his back as a favoring wind, still, good hope had been gradually corroding. Winter light was withdrawing. Josh could not raise Edward on the telephone; Ben had eluded him. Where was the roadster—not that it mattered a great deal—but where was Ben? Ben, who had certainly been a dangerous man when last seen, and might be yet. If not warned, how else was Edward to be shielded?

Clouds of rice birds, high above, where it was brighter though day was beginning to close, swept back and forth ahead, darkening the sky when seen all together and full-on, nearly disappearing when enfiladed to the eye, like Venetian blinds opening and closing. Like the blades of an Aldis lamp.

For reliable auspices, you had to know the number of birds—and these were numberless—and the direction from which they appeared. And that kept changing. Josh was desperate for augury, since none of his telephone calls to Sheriff Baker had so far been answered with any news.

There is no cause for worry. He will have come to his senses by now. By now he will have abandoned any plan for an act of crazed vengeance or execution of justice, since he seems to consider it that. He has the two ideas conflated in his mind. The fury in his head, yesterday like a flood-tide, will have ebbed by now. I'll run him to ground before anything can happen, anyway. I'm wearing thin; I need a little something more to drink; as long as it's not too much; I can maintain a steady state, can go on until I catch up with him.

But the swallow of tonic proved to be *le vin triste*—wine of sorrow. His conviction abated. A ring of pallid daemons tightened their formation about him. He knew a way out of this. He had no true thought of following it. Still, he kept thinking of the early morning, before he had set out.

For in Ashfield he had noted the appearing of some of those who by day populated that city without citizens. Death must hold it by night, and now night was laying hold upon Josh.

Ben ambled along the verge of the highway, unaware that ambling was a conspicuous thing for him to be doing, then and there. He took out the map to try to discover where he was, where he must be headed. A pickup truck, one that resembled Sonny McCallum's, but black, passed. In its bed were a crew of day-laborers lying upon and sitting among some crates, being taken early to a rendezvous-point, for home and celebration. They all looked at Ben after they had passed by. Ben expected them to start whispering to each other. About himself. But they seemed to ignore him, all laughing, cuffing each other, miles away from Ben, miles away from where they were going, miles outside themselves—because tomorrow they would no longer be themselves, but would be the children of an Other Year. And Ben could see this.

The turbulence from the passing truck blew the map closed, the lie of the land vanished, then open again to a broad stripe of wrong counties. Ben found his place, he believed. Then, looking ahead, he saw a sign: "Shallotte 3." It was the name of a town, which on the map seemed bigger than the others indicated as near to it—nothing to do with those things Mary Alice—no, "My Mother"—was always making him chop to bits in the kitchen house at Woodleigh.

From there, provided his money held out, he must be able to take a bus to Wilmington. For you could see at a glance that Wilmington was a city that dominated the region. He wasn't deliberately hitchhiking, but he couldn't help looking back when he heard a car coming up. A pretty young woman stopped and offered him a ride.

"I'm just going to Shallotte," she said, pronouncing the name in an unexpected way, "but I can at least take you that far. If you like."

Ben got in. "Thank you, Ma,am. That's where I'm going. To the bus station."

"I go right past it on the way to my folks' house." They were there in no time. "I'm going home for New Year's. I had to work at Christmas, so I get off for New Year's." She told him she worked in a restaurant in Savannah, Georgia. "It's a bar, really."

She let Ben out, and after him shouted: "Happy New Year!"

"Happy New Year to you, Ma'am, and thank you."

"Oh, you don't have to say 'Ma'am' to me; it makes me feel old."

"You're not old," Ben answered. "Not old at all. But you're a White lady." She shrugged her shoulders, but still smiling. She winked an eye, and vanished.

Josh pressed on with a measured but steady speed. He had a roadmap, too, limited to two dimensions, a third left out by the terms of its printing. That made three. There was supposed to be, classically, at that time, only one other. But in this case there were redoubled "When's." One, his, measurable from his wristwatch. The other, Ben's, only to be guessed at.

Josh made about a dozen guesses. They spanned a period of many hours, thus were useless. During that interval he drove past the ramshackle church behind which his car stood concealed. This lone circumstance was going to doom his search, for it was the roadster, with Ben inside, headed north on the Ocean Highway, that he hoped to sight and then overtake.

Several times he thought he had spotted it. Each time, he accelerated, got nearer, saw his mistake. Once, when he was getting very near to Wilmington, and trying to think what he should do if he actually reached the bridge that lofted the highway into the City—stop and wait, in case for some reason Ben had lagged behind, or go as quickly as he could on to New Brunswick and find the Strikestraw house—he overtook a Queen City Trailways bus. The road was not good, and the bus had looked like being difficult to pass. He drove on, thinking. He knew the practice must not and could not continue, but he drew from the field flask, which he had placed beneath the driver's seat, meaning to relegate it to the truck-bed next time he stopped.

North Carolina Road 211, making its way from Southport to Lumberton, is carried upon a viaduct over United States Highway 17, south of Wilmington. On either side of this bridge, a Highway Patrol car had been parked. The two patrolmen had got out and met to watch the traffic and have a little space of relaxation, before New Year's eve got to be New Year's Eve, so to say. For a few minutes they stood together, leaning over the railing on the south side. Traffic was light, and the early afternoon was clear.

"That's a good sign," one of them said.

"Yes, a good sign, unless it's a bad sign."

Sagely: "I know what you mean."

The only traffic in the northbound lane—the one that could even now be bringing nighttime calamity into town—consisted of a tractor-trailer—and, at a safe distance behind it, a pickup truck. Behind that came a bus, driven with care, as usual. None of the drivers was speeding. All were directing their vehicles properly within the lane.

The two officers turned to saunter across the lesser road and assess the flow of southbound traffic. Then there came titanic concussion, instability, and slippage. The first officer: *There's been an earthquake; the bridge is giving way.* The second: *The bridge is giving way,* and, glancing over his shoulder as they ran toward the nearer embankment to the east, he caught sight of the tractor-trailer emerging, and the bus following, but swerving from the oncoming back into its own lane. Each, while they ran, remembered hearing a clashing sound that was wrong and close to bringing sickness.

VII

"'Arise my son, follow
Here in the wake of my voice to the place frequented of all.'"

Pindar: Olympia VI, 62,3 (tr. Richmond Lattimore)

"We watched, silent, numb, as the giant crystal ball made its slow descent. It all seemed so frightening: the screaming crowds, the frigid air, not knowing if our father would live through the new year."

Anderson Cooper:: *Dispatches From the Edge: A Memoir of War Disasters, and Survival*

"The New Year waits, breathes, waits, whispers in darkness."

T. S. Eliot: *Murder in the Cathedral,* Part I, l. 11

E VEN FROM THE back of the bus—Ben had chosen a seat here for the sake of isolation; there were few people aboard, and no one else had taken a place at the back—the harsh sigh of compressed air bleeding into a cylinder could be heard. The door swung open somewhat wildly, recoiling from its hinges and stops. Ben stood up and began to shuffle out behind the others. He put on his new gloves. These, and the second fourth of the tincture that he had found privacy enough to prepare and consume, made him feel close to invincibility.

The average man, when he wears gloves, experiences a feeling of mass added to his hands, and perceives it as additional strength—possibly a vestige of a more primitive belief in the acquisition of power of the wild beast whose hide the hunter has put on. Flexing of the fingers and carpal bones is restrained by gloves; this may be interpreted by the wearer as muscle-binding. Moreover, when your hands are armored, you dare touch things you otherwise wouldn't risk: Contact with greater heat, more mordant cold, contagion.

The tissue of these gloves, however, had come from a cow.

The boy, when it was his turn, stepped lightly down the lozenge-bossed steps and onto the concourse, beneath a metal canopy supported on steel posts. Outside the station, the air was cold. And while everything looked almost familiar, still nothing looked entirely so. This place would not welcome him.

How, from now on, was he to disguise himself? By his behavior and manner. He must smile a few times, little smiles. He must not laugh, but mustn't look unhappy, and certainly not afraid. Appear to have a place to go, yet not look in any particular hurry to get there. Sure about finding what he sought, and about what he would do when he found it. The worm-like menacings he could, when he recognized them, keep at bay, so that they might not undermine what he had in hand.

He went inside the terminal. The first thing he noticed there, hanging upon a wall, was a map, this one in large scale, so that all the places upon it seemed more broadly scattered. Transparent red lines indicated the bus routes. There was none connecting Wilmington to New Brunswick. The map-key didn't even make the smaller town seem at all an important one—and not one out of which so much wrenching agony, one would think, was likely to have sprung. Just as the average traveler rarely pauses to reflect that each little square or dot, perhaps with a quaint or odd name—Round O, Green Sea, Lone Star, Walhalla—pays out to time so much birth, death, sorrow and joy.

Ben went up to the ticket-vendor's stall, asked whether, and had it confirmed that there was not, any bus service to New Brunswick.

"Is there any other way to get there?"

"You might get a cab. Or you might hitchhike, but I wouldn't try that, not at night, and especially not on New Year's Eve."

"What's the matter with New Year's Eve?"

"Oh! On New Year's Eve, everybody goes out to parties. They drink until midnight. Then they shout, and hug and kiss each other. They throw streamers into the air, and blow whistles and horns. As though a war had ended. Some stay on. Finally, they try to go home. But they either run their cars into the ditch. Or they plough into telephone-poles or trees and get killed."

"Those, anyway, don't have to stay around to fight another war."

"Huh? But, well, see if you can get a taxi."

Ben returned to the concourse. His bus was still there, its motor running, its driver absent. Power without direction. A thing to be shunned.

There was a taxicab at the curb. Ben walked over to it; the driver rolled down the window. "How much would you charge to take me to New Brunswick?"

"Ten dollars."

Ben reached for the dwindling contents of his trouser pocket and counted. There were four one-dollar bills, and some coins. "I don't have that much."

"I'm sorry, Son. But I have to get my full fare—Christmas nearly cleaned me out. Either my full fare, or knock off. See, I live in Burgaw...in the opposite direction from New Brunswick." Both felt awkward. Ben, for being short of money; the cab-driver, because he wanted to accommodate the boy. Then, from the sidewalk along the street where the bus station stood, a tall man came toward them. He was elderly, had a slight limp, but was making good time with it. He wore a camel-hair topcoat and a muffler of silk the color of chestnut-wood, with little medallions of gold, coral, and ivory printed in a neat pattern. Ben thought: *They have Plantation People up here, too.*

The old man said to Ben: "Are you taking this cab?"

"No, Sir; I don't have enough money."

"Where would you be headed? Maybe I can give you a lift. I certainly don't want to benefit from somebody else's misfortune."

The driver rolled down the window farther. "He wants to go to New Brunswick, Mr. Hammond."

"Get in, Son. I'm going there myself. My wife deserted me, so I need a ride, too."

"I could put in my four dollars."

"No, no, Son. It's on me." Then Mr. Hammond said to Ben, under his breath: "Maybe you could give him a dollar or two when we get there, as a tip." And soon they were settled into the taxicab, driving through the darkness, all together. They crossed the high bridge in the other direction, then turned away from the highway along which the bus had traveled.

"What's your name, Driver? Since you know mine."

"It's Joe. Joseph McIntyre."

"McIntyre!"

"Yes, Sir. Maybell McIntyre was my Mama."

"Good Gracious! I knew she'd passed on, and I was saddened to hear it. If she had retired before I did, my office would have just quit running...so then I guess I would have had to retire, too." He turned to Ben. "This man's mother worked with me for forty years! It's a small world, particularly around here. What name do you go by, Son. Do you live in these parts, too?"

"Ben. No, Sir. I live in South Carolina. In the Coastal Plain," he added. Because, although nothing was ever said about it directly, people from South Carolina who live in its coastal plain feel themselves chosen, all but anointed. Just as all other people do, for other but like reasons.

"You're visiting for the Holiday?"

"Yes, Sir. My aunt...my great-aunt."

The driver spoke up: "Who's your aunt, Ben?"

This potential dilemma was forestalled. Ben had been careful, if not to formulate a full cover-story, at least to gather together an assortment of "cover-details," ready when they might be needed. And he was canny enough to produce smooth linkages. For Ben was a clever young man. "My Aunt Rhodë. She works for the Strikestraws."

"Canon Strikestraw is my closest friend in the world!" John Hammond said. "But his wife is dead—there aren't what you'd call Strikestraws." He emphasized the plural.

"I was counting in Mr. Edward." Ben's position was authenticated.

"Of course."

They went along, with the wind, the stars, and the Year brushing past them in the night. When they had got almost to the limit of town, there appeared on their left a stand where fireworks were being sold, outside of town, and so legally. It was brightly lighted by strings of clear bulbs, hung from poles. Young children with their fathers and mothers were lined up to buy sparklers and Roman candles; boys old enough (important enough, too, they felt) to be out on their own were there for firecrackers and rockets; ruffians, for "cherry-bombs," stiff green fuses joined to bright red balls of considerable explosive power, since outlawed. All the customers were going to take their selections back to within the town limit and there light them off, illegally. There were already flashes and sharp and muffled reports, near and far.

"It will be hard for most in town to fall asleep before one or two. But we live in the country, thank Goodness."

"Mrs. Hammond...she'll be out there when you get home?"

"Oh, yes. She only deserted me for the afternoon. We went to a luncheon party in Wilmington. She just got a little tired of my company and left earlier."

Luncheon party! I don't think even Miss Alina and Dr. Barrington stay at luncheon parties until six in the evening.

"Now, Ben. I don't believe I know where your great-aunt lives. Can you show us?"

"The best thing to do, Sir, if it suits you and Mr. McIntyre, would be to let me off in front of the Strikestraws'...Canon Strikestraw's house. I have directions from there. It's not far."

"Good. I know Rhodë has always walked to and from work."

By now they had entered the part of town founded in Colonial times. Like Nevers, "It was built like a capital, yet a child could walk around it in a day." During the Civil War, parts of the earth had been pleated into incomprehensible redoubts. Joe McIntyre turned the taxicab onto Front Street, the esplanade on their left, the several tributary streets opening, by blocks, on the right. The broadest of these was marked Church Street. As they passed it, Ben could see the lighted façade of Christ Church at the far end. They pulled up before the gates of the Strikestraw house, and Ben reached over and handed Joe McIntyre his four dollars. "I know it won't go far to making up for getting cleaned out; I hope it helps some."

"Well, thank you Ben! Thank you verykindly, but it's too much." And he tried to give back some of the money. But Ben refused.

"I want you to have it. And I thank you, Mr. Hammond. When you take, you ought to give, too, I think. Happy New Year." They all reached around and shook hands; all said Happy New Year. Ben got out and stood before the prophetic iron gates until he saw the taillights of the taxicab disappear around the bend at the south end of Front Street, back to the west. Then he ventured just within, and brought the gates together behind himself.

Ben Araby now stood upon a threshold of uncertainty. In night-games of his boyhood, he had always felt more uneasy when seeking than when being sought. Then, you had to move out on your own, instead of just holing up. He felt that way now, as there came suddenly the sound of a great explosion— surely not very far away?

The reports of firecrackers had worked themselves into the fabric of the night. A rumbling. Brilliance of a silent stream of fire whitened the sky. Ben looked up at the thunderburst of stars; trails of splendor, falling like a song. As he watched, a few drops of rain touched his face upturned. Streams of light, radiating outward from a now-dark center, seemed to die, too, at their perimeter. But just as they faded, at the end of each radian another star expanded, softly coming down like the rain, darkening gradually and sinking in quiet. And now it was raining through the stars. The spectacle would recur in the coming hours, green of fire, sometimes, blue, red, gold, or again and again, moonsilver.

Ben turned so that he could watch on. The cursive iron of the gate, with the blaze lapsing slowly, soundlessly behind it, registered trippling stripes of light and shadow. These wrote dashes and dots, too, to Ben enciphered; but he could transpose and read them simultaneously, as an accomplished clavecinist can shift key, playing with no loss of fluency, in order to avoid twitching a note he remembers is jammed, in order not to have the music be interrupted: *We will give you light for the deed; we will supply darkness then to shield you.*

Crackles of sound went on, waxing and waning in frequency, as youthful pyrotechnists now and again decided to save back their stores, then gave in to the unequaled excitement little boys derive from blowing things up.

First actually to arrest Ben's progress was the appearance through the back door of a grand-looking Black woman. She must, he thought, be his "great-aunt" Rhodë Harmon. She had been there late because the Strikestraws—for inside were two men by that name, and two women who were soon going to take it—had given a luncheon party of their own. And this one, too, had gone on until six o'clock.

Ben escaped notice by his spurious relative, and once she had passed by him along the brick-paved driveway, on her way home, he continued around the house. He found that the southern side of the building was one with the brick wall that separated it from the next property. And so he turned to retrace his steps. This time, when he reached it, he turned aside into the front garden.

There had been four automobiles parked behind the house, and light came from windows in all the front rooms. Ben must know, if he could, who were there. In shadow, he took off his shoes and placed them carefully on the third step up to the verandah. Then he went on, up and across, keeping to the wall of the house, edging near and nearer to one of the two windows on the northern extent of the front. Both windows were half-open. The night was milder here, closer to river and sea. Raindrops had now begun to fall in sporadic showers, like curtains, matching the tiers and fountain-sprays of light in the sky. Matching and redoubling them, and carrying their brightness all the way down into the shaded earth.

Eventually, Ben leaned forward and around and caught a glimpse through knotted edging of the window curtain. Inside, they had let the fire begin to die down. Overnight, it was expected to die out altogether. There was Miss Mary. The fact was, she was the most beautiful White girl Ben had ever seen. There were an older woman and man. The man must be Edward's grandfather; he had a stiff white band about his neck. The lady—who could she be? In a way, the same type as Miss Lavinia. She was entirely composed, but nevertheless struck Ben as ready in the next moment to break free of any degree of composure. *Not* like Miss Lavinia.

Edward wasn't there. Had he gone back to college? But then Miss Mary wouldn't have stayed, not without him. Besides, who drove all those four cars parked behind the house?

And as Ben pondered all this, Edward came into the room. He carried a waiter with glasses and champagne in a wine-cooler. He poured flutefuls for them all and handed them around. For a while, except for Thank you, none of them said anything. Finally, the older woman declared: "I've seldom been so bored in my entire life." No one was moved to comment. After a pause, she went on: "We've spent half the day eating and drinking; visiting with friends." Another pause; the others seemed rather torpid. "What's left? Do we just sit here, waiting to wish each other a happy New Year, drink our champagne, and at last go to bed?" Still, nobody seemed inclined to say anything. "What's midnight, after all? Nothing actually happens. There's not even any liturgical significance to it; or, Thomas, is there?"

"None, my Dear," the older man said, the Feast of Holy Name having begun at sundown. "I think we do this in order to say a grateful farewell to the Old Year, and to bring in the New Year graciously."

"I know, Darling. I'm merely tired. But, you know, midnight tomorrow night—every midnight—will end a year itself, and begin another—just not ones on the calendar."

"All have agreed, Alenda, upon the one on the calendar."

Now Edward spoke up. "A year, Alenda, is just a chunk of time. And it shows you what time really is. Does it seem to pass too quickly? Too slowly? You can slow it down my making it part of a bigger chunk—say, of a decade— or speed it up by chopping it up into seasons, or into months, weeks, days."

"Talking of chopping up time," Mary said, "Does any of you know why the telephone kept ringing, off and on, all afternoon? "

"I don't know why," Alenda said, "but several times I thought it might drive me round the bend. However, this is not my house, so I didn't answer."

"It is as good as yours, my Dear. But, I agree that it is not your responsibility to answer the telephone."

Edward said: "Since Mary is here, I knew it couldn't have been anybody I especially wanted to talk to."

"Maybe Rhodë answered it. Did she say anything about it to any of you?" No one replied, except to shake his head. "Of course the calls could have been for Rhodë herself."

"That is unlikely. I have several times overheard her accept personal calls...."

"How does she handle that?"

"In such a way that the particular caller would not be likely to try it a second time."

"There were a lot of people here. Maybe the calls were for one of them. Or for some of them."

"Maybe they were for one of us. And we didn't answer."

"If so, we shall probably find out about it soon enough," Thomas said, getting up and going to stand with his back to the dying fire, reflecting that in the process of dying it was only yielding to time. "The truth is, time is never far from the foundation of anxiety. And so we try to speed it up to get it over with, or to slow it down enough to become unaware of its passage. In the end, though, all of us must simply wait it out. And that is for the best, I think, because we are unprepared for eternity. Though it will come to us. In due time, of course.

"Don't you think I could spend the night here," Alenda asked, "I mean, since Mary is here?"

"Of course. No one pays attention anyway."

"Then I think I'll go up." They all said Goodnight.

"Are you too cold, Grandfather?"

"No...no. Although I can't say the fire has much comfort left to offer."

"I'll close the windows." And he began to walk toward the one nearer the corner. "Are the ringers going to ring a peal for the New Year?"

"Not that I've heard about."

"Well, then, I'll go up to the church and toll the Old Year out. That only takes one person."

Mary asked: "Shall I come along?"

"No need. You've seen the tower already. And now it will just be cold and gloomy." Down came the corner-window sash, slammed hard. Ben could still hear what they were saying. "Snuggle up in a warm bed. Start the New Year that way."

I bet you think you're coming back to snuggle up with her. To start the New Year. But you won't come back. No, you won't.

Ben shrank into himself. Edward was coming, presumably to slam shut the window outside which he stood. Yes. Here he came. Knowing all the while that Colored people couldn't get on with White people because they wanted their share of what the White man had. *But, oh, no. The real trouble between Colored people and White people, according to what Edward Strikestraw went around preaching, came of Blacks' thinking they wanted what Whites had, wanting to do what they did and be who they were. What Blacks had to do, according to* Edward Stirkestraw, *was find out, from some lost racial past, what they* really *ought to act like and think like, and go their way and leave White people alone. Here he comes.*

Out of Ben's ken a candle was burning. Edward bent to put it out, after closing the window, and then Ben saw clearly written in his face a proclamation of kinship with Satan. His face, who had claimed that Woody Paget had done both of them a favor by raping his mother and begetting himself.

'I'll go up to the church and toll the Old Year out.' This would be Ben's opportunity to separate Edward from Miss Mary, in fact to isolate him completely. He was hesitant, he found, to consider that God was on his side, but Fortune clearly was.

And I'll do this between the Years. I'll do it outside of time, and it won't count against me, even if it had been going to in the first place. Nobody will be able to pinpoint when it happened—not in 1963, not in 1964. It won't have happened at all.

Ben felt now that the powers of the universe were abetting him in his aim. They were confirming it as right. He had known all along that it was right. It was a wonder he continued to be so uncertain. Well, he felt ready.

Then he started convulsively when he heard the key turn in the front door latch—he expected the door would open, and himself be discovered.

But it was being locked for the night, for Edward's everlasting night. For Ben glanced through the window and saw him pull on a down vest, then kiss Miss Mary, Mary Mountainstream The Beautiful, goodnight, then his grandfather. He would be leaving now, and from the back of the house. Even if he drove—He would drive; Ben heard the car door close—Ben could be in the churchyard before he had got there, rung the bell, and come out again. Still, he hurried down the steps, unnerved in spite of a bracing draught by the frequent passage across the sky of drenching light. He crouched in a planting of helpless boxwood and vigorous Cape Jessamine. Edward drove slowly down the driveway and turned into the street. Ben set out to follow on foot.

Two things he had left behind forgotten: The empty bottle and packet he had bought from Shump, behind the house, and his shoes, on the verandah steps. There was no one to make sense of these items, if it should come to that event. Ben was himself unaware of it; in all his imaginings and calculations, in all his planning, he had not one time thought of the aftermath of his design, not even whether he would survive and come away from it.

Ben was a little out of breath when he slipped into the churchyard. Edward's car had been parked at the curb. A dim light shone through a round window in the tower, and the little sacristy at the back of the building was brightly lighted. Edward must have gone in that way and have reached the ringing room, so Ben looked for a position commanding the door through which the little cortège had passed so many years before, on its way to obsequies for the drowned sailor.

At the same time, Edward was in the tower examining, alternately, the bell-rope and his wristwatch. He found that all the bells had been rung up onto their stays. One of them he had expected to be set, for he had asked that it be left so. This was the bell that would be his, if he ever learned to ring well enough to join the others. She weighed seven hundred and fifty pounds and was tuned to A-flat.

He took the rope into his hands, took out the slack, said to himself *She's going,* pulled with some force, felt the rope slacken again as the bell came off, free, and said again, in the brief silence before clapper and sound-bow clashed, *She's gone.* And, for the Years, *Farewell, all Ye.* A muffled note sounded in the bellchamber above.

Not that the bell herself had been muffled. Ben heard her shed, through white-painted louvres, her clear, bright music over all the township, falling to the rooftops, darting among the streets. He continued his quest for a vantage point. He had been in ancient churchyards before; he had seen ancient tombstones before. Some had cherubs' faces, with flanking wings, others had death's heads. But now he discovered a dark stone marker surmounted by a wingèd skull. Seeing in this combination, for whatever reason, a further favorable omen he chose this tablet for his general cover and one of its shoulders as a rest upon which to steady the barrel of his pistol. He waited, huddled.

In the ringing room, Edward, after the bell had spoken three times, used all his strength to effect a pause. It worked. He was learning better bell-control. Then he let her sound again. He would have to go through this once more. Then, after the third group of three rings, he would have to set the bell, and this operation would require a delicately administered decrescendo of force.

Below, Ben, among the Bloodless, was startled by the first break in rhythm, since he thought that was to be all. He was already in an unorthodox firing-posture, on both knees, with his left hand on top of the gun-barrel, clamping it down hard upon the stone, thinking this would steady the pistol, when only ease was needed.

He decided, in order to be ready to fire as soon as Edward came out, to place his right index-finger within the trigger guard. But this had not been designed to accommodate the thickness of hide and stitch. The trigger was depressed. The pistol discharged. At the same time, the bell sounded again. Ben was close to fainting. Some of his emotional tension was released, however.

In the tower, Edward had barely congratulated himself for having achieved the break, when it was time to think about the next. This time there was the option of setting the bell briefly. But that could make the pauses uneven.

Ben did not hear his first, accidental bullet strike anything. In fact, it had ploughed into the earth above the drowned sailor, who, with all the others who slept, was to waken for the closed cleft between the exchanging years. This annual renewal of death went some little way toward approving Edward's earlier statement about time and the Year. It invalidated Alenda's pronouncement about the coming midnights, as well. But the phenomenon was unknown at that time in the world of men. Generally.

Edward, in the tower, strove mightily. No supernumerary sound was made. He turned out the lights and left.

The remainder of the tolling had given Ben time to reconsider. He removed the glove. Again he took aim. And he let up on the pressure of his left hand; the strain had induced a tremor. The report from the pistol had not distracted him, a loud crack and whine, among so much other midnight clamor. Besides, it had coïncided with the note of the bell, and by now the sound of other bells poured from their throats all over town. Other churches, the Town Hall, the Firehouse. Were they ringing out the Old Year, or the New Year in? Ben was satisfied not to know, for not knowing strengthened in his mind the exculpatory belief that the ever rolling stream of time would stand still for his act of murder.

The light in the sacristy went out. Just when Ben had expected that Edward would step through the sacristy door, light appeared in the church itself. For Thomas had instructed his grandson, after he had closed both windows in the library at the house on Front Street, to leave the church lighted and the doors open for the remainder of the night, in case anyone might want to come in.

Ben went in fear to the sacristy door; he found it locked. Edward must be about to come out through the front doors of the church. Ben hurried, crouching as he ran most of the way, toward the street. Here he improvised a post, which proved more natural, comfortable, and, he thought, more apt for the kill. He took up his position.

From the unceasing ringing of bells and explosion of fireworks, the sound of laughter emerged, and a group of people, all of them talking at once, came down the sidewalk, apparently bound for the church.

Edward heard them, too, and went to meet them on the steps. They were the ringers, come unexpectedly to ring a peal. Edward knew all of them at least by name. He wished them all a Happy New Year, then explained that he had been tolling the Old Year out using the A-flat. Miss Bena Lucas stepped forward: "I'll ring her up, unless you left her as you found her. She's my bell."

"I did. How do you manage that thing, Miss Bena?" For by now she had become a frail-looking old lady.

"After managing you and Bobby McCallum, that bell is little or nothing." She kissed him. "Happy New Year, Edward!"

The ringers started making their way into the church and up into the tower. Edward went down the steps and along the walkway, looking over his shoulder, saying Goodnight.

When he had got halfway to the gates, Ben took aim, squeezed the trigger. He was unprepared for the recoil, but kept his balance. He aimed again, fired again.

As when the layers of the retina detach and a dark shadow or curtain seems to unfurl into the field of vision, although the detachment occurred far back in Ben's brain and not in his eyes, so now he began, not only in sight but also in hearing and awareness generally, to recede into detachment from the world around him. But as he fell backward, he saw Edward turn, stumble, and fall forward onto the side of his face. Earth to earth.

The two patrolman from the viaduct had joined another Trooper, who had been dispatched to write out an official report of the accident. The three men stood upon the margin of the Highway.

"Not fast at all, as well as I could make out." The Trooper looked toward the other for confirmation.

"We were just comparing notes on our districts…looking down at the traffic, enjoying the sunshine. They weren't speeding…."

"Definitely not speeding. Other traffic was passing them, in fact."

"What do you mean by 'Them'?"

"There were three vehicles that seemed to be moving together…."

"Looked like they were deliberately matching speed…."

"The boy's truck, and a bus behind it, and…I forget what was in front of it. Of the truck."

"A tractor-trailer."

"That's it."

"Could either of you see whether there was anything in the road to make him swerve suddenly. Like a blown-out tire?"

"No."

"I couldn't, either. When we got down the embankment—when I did, rather; Bud was on the radio calling for an ambulance—I didn't see anything like that…not besides parts that had been knocked off the truck. There were a few things thrown out of it, it looked like. Papers, an old Army-issue canteen, manuals, a pair of sunglasses. I gathered up those things in a plastic bag."

Bud confirmed all this, and said: "I looked particularly, too, because there didn't seem to be any reason for the crash. And yet the boy could have been killed."

"He may *have* been killed. We'll have to see whether he makes it to the hospital. Could you identify the victim?"

"Yeah. We sent his stuff, including his wallet, with him in the ambulance, but Bud copied down his name and address from his driver's license. The dispatcher has already tried to get a telephone number, but there's no listing for a John Jones in Ashfields, South Carolina. She says there's an Ashfield, South Carolina, too, without the 's,' but he's not listed there, either."

"Don't worry about it. I'll put my girl on it, and she'll be able to find his folks. But, now, listen, you two: Was he weaving from side to side, at all?"

"You mean, like he was drunk?"

"Yeah. Like that.

"All three vehicles were moving along straight as a die," Bud said.

"Straight as a plumb-line," Vernon added, surmounting, for once, his peer.

"Did you search the vehicle for drugs, alcohol?"

"Thoroughly."

"We didn't find anything."

"Then I can't figure out why it happened. Look. He cracked this concrete pillar over here." The Trooper had walked over to the steel-reïnforced structure, reached out, as to a deadly thing, and touched it. "He must have been going too fast."

"He wasn't, though."

At the edge of the Emergency Department accession-bay a young physician and a nurse stood waiting for the ambulance doors to open. The nurse was the vision that all lascivious convalescents entertain, top to bottom, as people occasionally express it. The least forwardness with this young lady, though, and the enchantment was cancelled on the spot. And the wanton convalescents didn't even see her with her long blond hair down—it was brought up somehow and fixed beneath a little coif whose design signified the school where she had got her training. The doctor was tall, unreliably handsome, intelligent enough to have learned his craft well, skilful enough to apply it to good effect. For the most part. Thompson was his name.

These two were members of the hospital staff. Farther back and well to one side stood two older men—one older still than the other. Dr. Smoot, the elder, was a neurologist; Dr. Knowles, a neurosurgeon. They were both in private practice, both dressed in tweeds for a luncheon party, from which they had been called away just before sunset. They were waiting for historical and physical data about the patient before Smoot gave an opinion and Knowles went up to scrub for anticipated surgery.

Two orderlies inside the hospital were rushing toward the doors with a stretcher.

A short while before, Nurse Whitman and Dr. Thompson had bent over the radio equipment, crowded into a corner of the emergency room, trying to communicate clearly with the approaching ambulance. Dr. Thompson had said first: "Is he conscious?"

"No, Sir."

"What kind of unconscious is he?"

"I don't know what you mean, Doc."

"Can you get him to open his eyes?"

"Yes."

"How?"

"By telling him to open his eyes."

"Do you have to shout at him?"

"Loud. LOOK AT ME. OPEN YOUR EYES."

"And he opens them?"

"For a second or two."

"Can you get him to say anything?"

"Not words. Let me try some more." And raised voices were heard through various kinds of interference. "He'll make some kind of…."

"Phonation?"

"Yeah, Doc, but no regular words."

"And his blood-pressure and pulse are as before?"

"Yes, Sir. We're watching a rhythm strip, but we got a full twelve-lead cardiogram."

"And that looks normal?"

"Yes, Sir. It does to both of us. The driver, too. He says we're about five minutes out, now."

"Good. One more thing: If you grind the sternum with your knuckles, how does he respond? Or *does* he respond?"

"He just bends a little at the elbows and knees."

All through the day, Alina had practiced what she had, at its beginning, recommended to her husband. But the concealing of her grief and desperation was draining her strength away. Lavinia had asked them to Woodleigh for drinks and an early supper, as a distraction, but the Barringtons both thought they should be within hearing of their own telephone. After considering it, Lavinia and Laurence thought so, too; so they took a picnic to Clear Creek before sunset.

To the west of the Tennessee and Ohio Valleys, high pressure in the atmosphere had dug in its heels against warm air along the Eastern Seaboard, with no force driving moisture from the Ocean or Gulf. Sasanquas had bloomed, and profusely, right through the Holiday Season, as they sometimes will, and similarly, all of the ornamental trees were in early bud. It was like spring, but a spring without promise.

In Ashfield, Sheriff Baker had turned back into his office to receive a radio message, feeling sure that Josh's car had been found. God alone knew what they would have done with poor Ben Araby. "We haven't found the car you reported missing, but we've found its owner."

"Josh Jones? Where?"

"There's been an accident, south of Wilmington. If Josh Jones is the same as John A. Jones."

"He is. Has he been hurt?"

"He's unconscious. They've taken him to the hospital."

"To which hospital? Can you give me the number?"

"New Hanover Memorial." And he gave the Sheriff the telephone number. "We couldn't get hold of any of his people. Believe it or not, there's no Jones listed either in Ashfields or in Ashfield."

"It's under 'Barrington.' His stepfather. How did the accident happen? Any other vehicles involved?"

"No. No others. And we don't know. He seemed to be driving along completely normally—two patrol officers saw it happen. Well, not exactly; it was underneath an overpass where they were standing. He suddenly ran off the highway and hit one of the supports. Of the roadbed where the patrol officers were."

The sheriff telephoned the hospital to see what he could learn, how he might protect.

Back in Wilmington, Dr. Thompson began his questioning and examination, even while the paramedical auxiliaries were lifting Josh onto the stretcher. He attempted to confirm the data given him over the radio, noting first a developing ecchymosis, or bruise, over the left side of the forehead and temple. "He struck his head against the windshield?"

"We thought so, from the way he was positioned in the wreck. The glass was smashed."

"You've drawn blood specimens? Good. Give them to the nurse. And give me the cardiogram and all the rhythm strips you've run." He started toward the two older physicians, saying, over his shoulder: "Miss Whitman, would you fill out the usual requests and take or send them to the laboratory along with the specimens. Get skull films and an ultrasonogram of the brain, before he goes up to the General Operating Rooms." To the orderlies manning the stretcher: "I don't know which operating room they have ready, but you'll find out when you get him up to the floor. Get the ultrasound done in the elevator—the apparatus is portable." And here he actually stopped and turned to nurse Whitman, seeming to give her his full attention: "Look at the pupils, will you? I think I saw a sluggish reaction. Tell me what you think." And he went on to report to the private practitioners, who then went in to the patient.

Dr. Thompson wanted all the nursing staff—all female, at that time—to be smitten with him. Miss Whitman was not, and he knew it. Therefore he regarded her as a medical technician, and nothing more. Very irritating, he thought. (He also wanted to be taken on as a social equal by each of the private practitioners with whom he at various times worked; they, however, could hardly wait for him to be replaced and move away.)

Julie Whitman—her name was Juliana, but abbreviated and recast during her early childhood; she got called "Judy" a lot—went after the stretcher and halted the orderlies. From the pocket of her apron she took out a small flashlight. They could not get Josh to open his eyes, so she held the lids apart, first on the left, then on the right, directing the ray through the pupils onto the retinae. Each time, she was sure she saw the iris contract, slowly, yes, and only a little, to be sure. But the finding was definitely present. Then, Josh opened his eyes spontaneously, and he looked at her. He sank back immediately into coma.

Julie stood where she was and indicated to the orderlies to carry on. She started back out onto the accession platform to report to Dr. Thompson, who, though, at that moment shouted: "For God's sake!" He strode over to the ambulance, where the paramedical auxiliaries were beginning to put things in order and pack their gear. "You—one of you—said the cardiogram was normal! You call this *normal!*" And he held the tracing up before their faces, up to each one in turn, including the driver, also a trained medical technician. For he had concurred with the others.

"Yes, Sir. We thought so. I guess it's not?"

Another said: "We're not doctors, Sir. We're trained to recognize the major arrhythmias...."

"Do you think you could recognize asystolë—cardiac standstill?"

"His heart has been beating ever since we got him aboard."

"Yes. A little over *thirty times a minute!*" He stumped away, greatly irritated. *Somebody could see these tracings and think I failed to deal with the bradycardia.*

Nurse Whitman came toward him, walking as buoyantly as he was ferociously. The doctor was so agitated that had no clear idea of where he was going. A possible blot on his record! But when saw her, his next anxiety had to do with whether his physical findings had been corroborated. "Miss Whitman! What about the eyes?"

"Sir?"

"What about the patient's eyes?"

"Oh...blue," she said absently. Then, quickly: "I found both pupils round, and sluggishly and minimally reactive to light."

"And did you think you smelled ketones on his breath?"

"I wasn't sure of that." She was sure instead of something else. "Do we know of any reason for him to be in ketosis?"

"No. Well, thank you."

The doctor's self-confidence was restored. A balm had been poured onto his injured pride. Nurse Whitman did not say that the patient had seemed to open his eyes and to look at her. She had not been in a rage, but some kind of balm had been poured out, anyway. She must get off to herself and think about it.

Dr. Thompson was proud of himself for having asked her to check behind him. It showed what a good sport he was. It showed he didn't think he knew everything. Since he did know nearly everything, he could afford to give this impression, occasionally.

Barringtons and Ashfields heard a car coming along the Magnolia Lane, toward Clear Creek. They were sitting in the back garden. The car stopped in front of the house. Bob got up and walked around to see who it was, and found the Sheriff, who in few words told him as much as he knew. "But it's my duty to tell all this to Mrs. Barrington, since...."

"I know. Come with me." They joined the others. "Mrs. Barrington, I'm sorry to say I have unhappy news." Alina got to her feet, not easily. "About Josh."

Alina walked directly up to him, and she said: "I'm ready to hear it." But she didn't look ready.

"He has been injured in an automobile accident. He is alive. They need your consent for surgery, verbal consent. Over the telephone. Here is the number, Dr. Barrington."

Bob said: "I'll put the call through, get rid of the preliminaries and so on; but I think Alina will have to give the actual consent. So could all of you, some…I don't know…help her into my work room as soon as you can?"

And when this business was finished, Bob telephoned to Brewster Holman, who had an airplane. He kept it at the primitive-looking airstrip outside Ashfield, its runway entirely adequate, however, for light aircraft. "Brewster, this is Bob Barrington. Are you free tonight?"

"Let me put it this way: I'd like to *get* free. Have you got an excuse?"

"Josh is in surgery in Wilmington. North Carolina, not Delaware. He was in an automobile accident. He's been injured seriously, and possibly, I'm afraid, mortally. I wondered whether you could possibly…."

"Fly you and Alina up there? Of course. You all come to our house now. I'll get to work on a flight plan. By the time you get here, we should be ready to drive right on over to the airfield; they'll be shut down tonight, but Wilmington won't, of course. I'll file with them"

"Do you have enough fuel?"

"I top her up every time I land back here. Come ahead. I'm very sorry about Josh, but until we know worse, we'll hope for the best. Tell Alina. I'm sure I won't be taking you up there for nothing. Goodbye." And he hung up the telephone.

Within a half-hour, Alina, Bob, and Brewster Holman were in the air. They could see a lot more light in the sky; the darkness below them had got denser. They were able to identify clustered lights at first, but soon lost track.

Lavinia and Laurence began the long drive; they both hated driving at night but gave it no thought now.

On the accession platform there remained only Dr. Thompson and the personnel from the ambulance, taking up their task where it had been interrupted. The doctor, whose work was done, unless victims from other disasters should come in, watched the team. Before, they had all been talking animatedly as they worked. Now they moved about the bay saying nothing to each other. As he watched, absently at first, he began to feel heavy-hearted.

He was still holding, tightly holding, crumpling the cardiograms. Suddenly, as though set in motion from outside himself, he walked up to the others, and said: "You men did good work. I congratulate you all. That boy, if he lives, will owe you his life. If he doesn't live, well, then I'm here to say Thank You on his behalf, for the effort you've made."

One of the men, the one who had given data over the radio, the one who had reported a normal electrocardiogram when the patient was in fact exhibiting an abnormally slow heart rate, startled, looked up and said, "Sir?"

"I just said the three of you have done a fine job."

"I thought we'd botched it." Now the others came up. "Over the heart rate."

"It would have been better if you'd told me about it. But no harm was done, really. His pulses were full all along, weren't they?"

"Yes, Sir; they were."

"His systems got an adequate supply of blood, then. He just needs the pressure in his head relieved, and that's—I presume—being taken care of now. It seems I need the pressure in my head relieved, too. I overreacted."

"Bad day?"

"No, not really. But on this date you spend the whole time expecting the worst."

"Well," the technician who had originally declared the tracings normal put in, "the mistake I made…."

"We all made."

"…Goes to show we aren't given enough training for what we have to do… or might have to do. I wish I did know the right way to read a cardiogram."

The doctor asked whether they had received any other call. "Then give me a minute, and I'll start you off. You see," he continued, as he unrolled the strips of paper, "this really is a normal tracing, except for the bradycardia. But you can read duration of time from it—that's why the tracings are run at a standard speed. That's why the manufacturer prints the big and little grids onto the tape. The little boxes are four one-hundredths of a second long. The big ones are fifths of a second." The men were rapt. Here they were being treated as educable by the most scornful medical practitioner in New Hanover County. "The complexes themselves are normal. Shall I quickly tell you why I say so?" The four bent attentively to the markings.

Floors above in the operating room, Dr. Knowles and his assistants, guided by the results of such imaging techniques as were then available, had made a burr-hole in Josh's skull, in the suspect area. They encountered clotted blood. Now they knew with certainty the nature of the injury that had imposed the state of coma. So, after paring almost loose a portion of the calvarium, leaving a broad section of the scalp undivided, through the outermost membrane covering the cerebrum they made an opening through which, with suction, mechanical manoeuvres, and irrigation they were able to remove all of the lightly coagulated mass. Two sites of blood-seepage were noted and staunched. Gradually the heartbeat had returned to the lowest rate regarded as normal. Bob had got there; he was able to assure Dr. Knowles and the anesthesiologist that this was normative for their patient, who kept himself fit.

Alina was told that her pup would survive, but to expect improvement no sooner than she could see it. For now, this was enough. It was for a parent a great deal more than enough.

In scanning the results of the laboratory tests, of which all were negative or normal, Dr. Knowles wondered in passing why the blood-alcohol level had not been measured, but imagined that the nurse had assumed this would be included in the toxicology panel. Anyway, it had all seemed to turn out well.

Downstairs, the platform was at last empty of people; everyone had done his duty and retired from the field. "Look at the beginning of the complex that represents the heartbeat. There is a small upright wave—rounded, as it's supposed to be. At least, it is in this part. This is the impulse generated in the atrium; it initiates a heartbeat. It goes up, then down, smoothly. It takes the right length of time. Then, we lose sight of the impulse, because it is traveling to a relay at the top of the ventricle—the heart's pump. But you know that. This also occupies a normal interval. Then, here is the very tall spike, showing the contraction of the ventricle. See how thin and needle-like it is? All the way up and all the way down again, using up only a little of the time line. That's because specialized tissue spreads out and delivers the impulse, in this patient's case, to all of the cardiac muscle tissue at once. Then this pause. Then the long, rising-and-falling marking, concordant with the spike. What? Oh. That just means they point in the same direction—in this case, both go up from the baseline. That's the muscle fibers resetting themselves to be ready to contract for the next heartbeat. Too bad it took it so long to get here!"

"Did you have to say that?"

"I had to say that." Dr. Thompson laughed at himself. "Anyway, happy New Year, all of you."

"Thank you for the lesson, Doc. And happy New Year to you."

"Thanks. You'll run into deformed versions of this pattern, then you'll see how beautiful the normal one is. Remember, the slow rate is due to pressure on the brain; this patient has a normal heart. Goodnight."

In the little collection of leaves and discarded paper things, cloudlight things, released by the wind, thwarted as it encountered a wall of brick, built there to conceal bins of often-remarkable refuse, lay the tracing of Josh Jones's heartbeat, like the yellow seeds of sea oats at a certain time in summer, dropped from the inconstant ocean breeze to rest in dry sand, cupped by the passing, retracing feet of bathers and surf-fishers.

This patient has a normal heart.

To anybody who has begun to cherish listening to them, changes rung on a peal of fine bells by competent ringers have begun the integration of complex and progressively complex sequences, with voices which seem to grow in the splendor of their authority every time they issue from the bronze-throated, occasionally homicidal, giants suspended in their tower.

To the rest, who try merely to hold on until the end, they're just terrible racket, becoming more and more disordered with the minutes as they pass.

Ben Araby, rising toward then breaking the surface of unconsciousness, felt that he was drawing his first breath of post-mortem air—What else could explain what had happened to him than that he had died? Died, and resumed consciousness only at the tocsins of the coming of the Judge?

But with a little time, his surroundings took on recognizability, if not familiarity. He recovered recent memory. And now uncertainties were crowding in upon him. His unconscious mind had copied, from the patterns of light and dark rippling along the front gates of the Strikestraw house, rosters of Dreads and of Expectations, and before he made the slightest move, he needed, he knew, to entertain them one by one. Then decide. His thoughts raced. His first measure was to note that Edward's body had been taken away. He was surprised that the bell-music had been allowed to continue, after such a tragedy.

He sat there, behind the basalt slab engraved with the particulars of an earthly life long since completed, only for a few moments longer, then he stuffed the pistol back inside his jacket and started to run, out of the churchyard, onto the sidewalk. But it occurred to him that his hurry would attract attention; if no one cared what he was running from, inevitably somebody would wonder what he was running toward. He slowed to a walk. He tried to look impassive, but this effort resulted only in strabism.

He came to a deep ditch. The channel was conducted under the roadway by a culvert of concrete.

He slid down the nearer embankment. The ditch was almost dry, and, in any case, the bed of it was several inches below the lowest level of the mouth of the tunnel. Ben crawled into it. He found that sitting sidewise was comfortable, and, if he put his feet across and flexed his knees, then the curve at his back was agreeably restful.

The bell-music, coming to him now seemingly from very far off, suddenly ceased. Ben thought that, possibly, whoever had earlier come to the church, found and undertaken the removal of Edward Strikestraw's body had returned to make the ringers stop. Out of respect for the dead.

In fact, they had reached the end of the peal. And Ben had reached the end of his endurance. He fell deeply asleep.

He awakened to find the morning of New Year's Day as brilliant and clear as the sound of the bells that had rung it in. He looked about. To his right the culvert stretched away into shadow, then darkness, with light at the end: a big, round aperture, admitting a dim glow of uncommitted color, shapes beyond still only vague, indistinguishable. An unspecified planet, it seemed, seen through a telescope. To his left, the near mouth of the tunnel let in a splendor of gold. Directly before him was a ledge, receding shelf-like from the inner wall, lighted, now, through a shaft going up to a grate covering the storm-drain in a gutter alongside the street.

Looking again to the right, he could make out a pale nimbus coming from the corresponding drain on the other side of the road. He looked again at the small niche before him. For there was something resting on it: A brick, and on top of the brick a cylindrical object, elongate, at once greasy and rusty, with a spherical apparatus—maybe a valve?—at one end. It looked like a discarded part from an old automobile. It also looked a little like the instrument the County Nurse looked into your eye with, when once a year she visited the schoolhouse back at the Crossroads.

Ben was a good deal less wary than Shump would have cared for in breaking down the pistol. He threw a piece out through either end of the culvert and put two more on the ledges under the drains. And he left it at that.

Afterward, he wasn't sure what to do. He had laid no plans for afterward. Why? Did he believe that killing a White man, and with him the White man in himself, would leave only half of himself—half a man, that would dwindle away in dust, before he could be mirrored by another Black half? Did he? He couldn't remember. And he couldn't, because at no point had he given thought to any of these matters. Well, here he was, and there occurred to him two things he must do immediately: He must get out of the tunnel and stretch himself. He had been away from home for two nights without leaving word. He must concoct an explanation for that. The hundred questions that were milling in his brain he would have to deal with later.

Above ground, all seemed undisturbed. He walked in stocking-feet until he found a filling station. It was closed for the Holiday, but the public telephone was outside. He had enough pocket-change to initiate the call but had to reverse the charges. When Mary Alice answered, recognized his voice, she burst into a flood of tears. Cannily, Ben kept shouting, as jovially as he could: "Happy New year, Mama. Happy New year to Miss Izora, and to Tommy, and to the little children."

"Where are you?"

"At school."

"Where have you been?"

"Right here." *Amazing, the fluency of lying!* "I've tried to get through several times; the circuits were all busy."

"But I don't know how many times we've called your dormitory."

"Nobody ever answers the hall telephone."

"Somebody did a couple of times; they said you weren't there."

"They meant I wasn't in the dormitory; I was probably in the Library. That's where I've been most of the time, studying for exams." *Lying, lying.* The sound of Mary Alice's weeping waned when she brought out words; waxed otherwise, and deteriorated now into slow, deep sobbing. So Ben forged on: "I mainly wanted to wish everybody Happy New Year. I also wanted to ask you to let J...Mr. Josh know that his car's in safekeeping, and to explain why I left without saying Goodbye...." This claim set his mind racing, for there was no explanation he could give, himself understanding none. But he was preserved from the necessity. For when he uttered Josh's name, Mary Alice began to wail truly very loudly. At this, Marigold and Haynesworth started wailing too, Miss Izora began screaming something, far in the background, and then Ben heard the telephone receiver slam against the wall or floor. Tommy came onto the line.

"Ben?"

"Is something the matter, Father?"

"Something surely is the matter,"—*This time they really* will *flay me*—"and I don't know how to tell you...or even what to tell you. But I think Josh may be dead."

In its turn, Ben's stunned silence fit plausibly into the exchange. Because it was an exchange of misapprehensions, lies, and incomplete information. Finally, he asked, "Did you say Mr. Edward? Mr. Edward might be dead?"

"Mr. Edward?" Silence. Then, "Oh, Mr. Edward that took Miss Mary. No, Son. *Josh.* Mr. Josh. He was in a car-wreck, in North Carolina. They had to operate on his brain last night. We don't know whether he lived through it, or not."

"Oh, Mighty Jesus!"

"Watch your mouth, Boy. Particularly now, because the Lord is our bulwark...only bulwark."

The evening before, when Julia Whitman, who was Sarah Elkin Whitman's daughter—she who had so kindly nursed Mr. Bennie Ormond at Thanksgiving time—reached her apartment, she found that her two roommates had gone out, as she had expected they would have done. She had not looked forward to being alone as the New Year came on.

As it was, though, she was glad to be to herself. The roommates, Sissy and Beth, had left a note on the door saying there was a bottle of champagne for her in the refrigerator, and wishing her Love and a happy New Year.

She had thought of telephoning to her Grandmother's house, where her family would be gathered. But she would drive over and see them all the next day, when they would return. The ones who hadn't thought it best simply to remain. These changes of mind had come about because Juliana believed she had fallen in love with John A. Jones. And at that, knowing practically nothing about him, including whether he were dead or alive!

Something connected to this had caused her to fret since late afternoon. She had got off work at eleven o'clock, report hadn't taken long. And so here she was at home, at twenty minutes to twelve o'clock, with lights either dimmed or put out, drinking a bottle (bottle?) of champagne, and grappling with this new emotional dilemma.

It wasn't that she was surprised—or very much surprised—at falling in love with a comatose stranger at first sight. When she had reached an age of being able to figure it out, she began to suspect that her mother and father had fallen in love, and madly so, immediately upon seeing each other, and independently. She had once asked her mother how long it had taken her to fall in love with her father, and Sarah had replied: "Oh, you would have to find that out from the Naval Observatory in Washington. Or from the Bureau of Standards."

No, Julie's problem was that she had long thought that all really dependably handsome men had brown eyes. Eyes that could see through you. With her second glass of champagne, she let her golden hair fall about her —what could have honored the New Year more!—and wondered whether she hadn't been mistaken.

She had not been. For with her next glass, she realized, just at the stroke of midnight, that Dr. Knowles's patient, John A. Jones, who had beautiful (she thought) blue eyes—eyes that *she* could see through and into *him*—was not a really dependably handsome man. Which was of no consequence to her. So simply was Julie's dilemma resolved!

Gosh, she thought, *I certainly hope he has survived the surgery.*

With this charitable sentiment, she came to the end of the Year of Our Lord 1963.

VIII

"O Friends, I have come
At the bidding of Love
To the lordly threshold
Whereon convene
The benisons of whoso lives, and of who dies."

Giacomo Puccini: *Madama Butterfly*, Act I (Libretto: L. Illica, G. Gicosa) (tr. PT)

"Some enchanted evening,
When you feel her call you
When you find your true love,
Across a crowded room.
Then fly to her side,
And make her your own—
Or all through your life
You may dream all alone.

Who can explain it? Who can tell you why?
Fools give you reasons; wise men never try."

> R. Rogers and O. Hammerstein, II: *South Pacific,* "Some
> Enchanted Evening,"

"You will rise again; yea, rise again,
Dust of My Body, after quickly-passing rest.
He Who summoned you will give you
Life…never to die."

> Friedrich Gottlieb Klopstock: *"Aufersteh'n,"* ll. 1-5 [Known
> principally for their inclusion in Gustav Mahler: *Symphony Number
> Two, in C minor ("Ressurection"),* fifth movement] (tr. PT)

"And the Word was made flesh, and dwelt among us, (and we beheld his
glory, the glory as of the only begotten of the Father,) full of grace and
truth."

> *The Gospel according to St John (AV),* 1.14

"And a self-contradiction does not cease to be meaningless by seeming
sublime."

> A.O. Lovejoy: *Great Chain of Being: The History of an Idea*

"Let us, then, state for what reason becoming and this universe were framed
by him who framed them."

> Plato: *Timaeus, 29* (tr. W. Hamilton)

"Batter my heart, three-personed God; for you
As yet but knock, breathe, shine, and seek to mend;
That I may rise and stand, o'erthrow me, and bend
Your force to blow, break, burn, and make me new.
I, like an usurped town, to another due,

Labor to admit you, but oh, to no end;
Reason, your viceroy in me, should me defend,
But is captived, and proves weak or untrue.
Yet dearly I love you and would be loved fain,
But am betrothed unto your enemy;
Divorce me, untie or break that knot again,
Take me to you, imprison me, for I
Except you enthrall me, never shall be free,
Nor ever chaste, except you ravish me."

John Donne: *Holy Sonnet XIV*

"OF COURSE I'M looking forward to dinner with the family, Grandmother. It's just that I can't be there by eleven o'clock."

"Did you go out with a rough crowd last night? Have you a…hangover?"

"No, Ma'am. But you know that all my uncles, who *are* coming there at eleven, have them. They'll start in drinking Bloody Marys…."

"My dear, you are too young and lovely to talk like that. Can't you call them 'tomato-juice cocktails'?"

"Granny, I don't even have to talk about them. I'll be there by noon. I worked evenings yesterday, and I've left a few things I must do."

If I show up at the Hospital dressed for a family dinner, then all the staff will wonder what I'm doing there. If I go in uniform, I won't be noticed. But then I must come back here and change.

Juliana Whitman set her hair and cap in place, and then she drove to the Hospital. The parking lots were less than half full. *Amazing how many desperately sick people find it possible to stay at home during holiday seasons! Amazing how many physicians, in spite of their crushing case-loads, can discharge so many patients just in time, and admit no or so few more until afterward!* She parked, and walked up to the building, entering through the main door. She crossed the lobby to a house telephone, asked for patient information.

She was informed that a John A. Jones had been admitted the day before, attending physician Dr. Knowles, in room 346. *Well, that's an encouraging beginning. He has undergone emergency surgery, and survived. He has stabilized, and lived through the night; he's still in the close-observation unit, but that's expected.* So Julie thought a little more seriously about the possibility of having fallen in love; she knew of people being in love with other people who were dead, but she felt that would not be rewarding.

Then, in the elevator on the way to the third floor, this occurred to her:

Post-surgical patients somehow spend amazingly little time in close-observation around Holiday time, before transfer to a regular nursing unit! Dr. Knowles had better not take any shortcuts. It did not strike her that this reflection had diagnostic value. The elevator doors opened. Room 346 was ahead, through a pair of automatically operated doors, then to her left; Julie knew this because the layout of all the patient floors was the same. She noticed a young Colored boy standing at the doors, but making no move to go in. As she drew closer, he hurried away, or she thought he did.

So she knocked softly. From within came a woman's voice: "Come in, please." So she opened the door and stepped inside the room. A middle-aged woman and man, carefully dressed, stood up when she entered. Seeing that she was a nurse, the woman said: "Good morning; I expect you want us to leave you with your patient."

"Oh, no. No. Not at all. It's just that I was on duty last evening when they brought him in. I wanted to know whether…know that everything had gone well. Please sit down. I'm Juliana Whitman." She offered her hand.

"I'm Bob Barrington, Josh's stepfather, and this is my wife. His mother." Alina mentioning her given name, they all shook hands, ignoring the patient, who was lying still, with his eyes closed. Julie wondered how much obtundation had persisted. *Some patients with subdurals don't even lose consciousness.* "It is very gracious of you to be enquiring."

"Yes," Alina added, "it certainly is. I can't imagine how much else you must have to do. But, thanks to you all and thanks to God, he has survived his injury; Dr. Knowles has told us not to look ahead for recovery, but he admits at the same time that, theoretically at least, it could be both speedy and complete."

"How wonderful! I'm very glad for you. May I go over and speak to him?"

"Of course, but he is very, very drowsy still."

Julie approached the bed, saying softly: "Mr. Jones. Mr. Jones, can you hear me? Are you feeling better, now?"

Josh opened his eyes. He looked directly at Julie, and said distinctly: "Yes, I am. And I remember you from earlier."

Alina and Bob moved swiftly to the bedside, for Josh had up to now not been nearly so responsive. Julie introduced herself, and Josh slowly but deliberately put out his hand, his left one. Clinical interest began to operate: "Is he left-handed?" Julie asked, turning to Alina.

"Right-handed. Why?"

Josh had taken her hand by now, and was saying: "I'm Josh Jones."

Bob and Alina exchanged glances of wonderment; these were the first clear words their boy had spoken.

"I wonder, Mr. Jones...."

"'Josh,' if that's all right."

"...whether you can give me your other hand?"

"Too?"

"Or instead; whichever is more comfortable."

"Oh, yes, I think so," he answered, easily bringing up his right forearm, in which, however, there was fixed an intravenous line. "But there's this thing hooked up to it." He took her hand firmly.

Bob said quietly to Alina: "You can't tell for all the bandaging, but the injury is to the left side. I'll tell you about this later."

Josh had not relinquished hold with his left hand. So there they were, holding each other by both hands. Julie's clinical interest was suddenly gone. Josh had never had any. She wished fleetingly that she had let them "leave her alone with her patient." Josh spoke again, just as clearly:

"I remember you. Yes. I remember. Are you going to stay with me, now? Before, you went away."

"Actually, it was you who went away—or were taken away. But I will come back again very soon. I'm so glad you're better." To Bob and Alina she said: "He has not been this lucid?" They shook their heads. "Then I'm sure Dr. Knowles will want to know right away." But she was unwilling to go herself to the nurses' station. She thought for a moment. Then she left it.

"Don't you think we should contact Canon Strikestraw?" Lavinia said. The four of them were staying in a hotel in downtown Wilmington. They had a suite. The hotel, like so many just about that time, had been built as a grand showplace, but had seen far better days. Would it be one of the ones to be knocked down, or among those destined to survive into the coming era of interest in preservation?

That day, it was Josh's destiny, and that only, that the four gave any thought to. He had been so clear-headed that morning, or had seemed to be. Bob and Alina had considered the possibility that they'd imagined it. But the nurse had noticed it, too, and seemed surprised. When they had told Dr. Knowles, he, also, had sounded surprised. (He had, right away though with difficulty, reached Julie Whitman by telephone in order to confirm the finding.)

"Or do you think it wouldn't be a good thing? I mean, having a priest visit."

"Well," Alina answered, "I think it would be a good thing to have a priest come in; but the connection to this particular priest...."

"Not only that...any priest. Any priest at all, on second thought, could alarm him. Does any of you remember that harrowing passage in *The Magic Mountain?*" But Lavinia was the only one of them who read fiction. "A little girl in a tuberculosis sanitarium is thought to be dying, so they fetch a priest, a Roman Catholic one, naturally, to administer the Last Rites to the child. She knows exactly what is going on. She goes mad with terror of death…of her own death."

Bob said: "But we don't have the Last Rites."

"Oh, yes we do have. It's not called that, but at the end of the order of Visitation of the Sick, there's that ghastly prayer that begins, 'Depart, O Christian soul, out of this world….'"

Laurence stood up. "This is ridiculous. I'll call Canon Strikestraw now. Will he have to drive a long way? Doesn't he live just across the River?"

"Darling, you can't ask him to swim here. Be tentative yourself, and ask him to be very candid about it. Maybe there is a Hospital chaplain." So Laurence telephoned to Thomas.

"Canon Strikestraw?"

"Yes?"

"This is Laurence Ashfield. We have never met, and I don't believe you know who I am, but…."

"Oh, indeed, I think I know exactly who you are! Weren't you my grandson Edward's host at the deer-shoot in November?"

"Yes, I was. It's remarkable you have me catalogued correctly!"

"No. I think that visit was very critical for Edward—critical, in the Greek sense."

"Of course. I know my wife has invited you to come and visit us, and we both hope very much that you will. And before it gets too hot.—But today I have telephoned about something else."

"I hope it's to say I can be useful in some way."

"It is, if the inconvenience will not be too great. My nephew Josh Jones has been in an automobile accident. It was a catastrophic one; he nearly died in it."

"Good Go…racious! But he has survived?"

"He has, in spite of your grandson's not being on hand to preserve his life a second time. We did wonder whether you could come to see him, maybe in a day or two, hopefully in connection with something else that will have already brought you into Wilmington?"

"I'll come at any time—that's military time—if necessary. If, though, he continues stable, then would tomorrow be all right; say, early in the afternoon?"

"Of course, and we can't thank you enough."

"Shall I see you then?"

"Not if all is moving in the right direction; we'll be going back home as soon as possible. We left without making any kind of preparation; but please bear in mind how much we are looking forward to meeting soon. Thank you again."

"It is nothing."

On their drive back to the hospital Bob explained: "All that business about 'You can't be rid of the Caucasoid half of yourself by murdering a White man; you can't survive the slaughter of the Negroid half,' or whatever he was babbling about, when we thought he was delirious early this morning, was part of something he'd read in a novel, he just told me over the telephone. He was only napping, apparently, and dreaming about it."

Lavinia asked: "What was the novel?"

"I didn't think to ask."

"He certainly does remember a lot of things in patches, it seems to me, and forgets a lot of others."

"After head injury, that's expected," Bob said. "Usual after simple concussion, and virtually inevitable after any degree of coma. What is new to me is this rapid alternation between sleep and coma—or, rather, commutation among those two and the total lucidity of waking. If we get there before Knowles, I'm going to make a screening neurological examination."

"No, Bob," Alina said, as she patted him gently on the knee, "you're not."

At midnight, Ben Araby, stowed away in a utility room since late afternoon, having noted a lot of coming and going of nurses about an hour earlier, realized now that things were settled, quiet. So he inched the door open, to see what he could see. Each of the uniformed women seemed to have something she must do; all were generally silent, concentrating upon their tasks. Two of them had come out into the hallways, pushing trolleys with little drawers in them. They seemed to be visiting each room in turn. They would take up small plastic cups, or syringes filled with liquids, tap on the doors and enter without hesitation. The nurse on his side of the floor went into Josh's room as third in her rounds. After she had come out, Ben slipped inside.

The lights had been dimmed in the hallways. Inside the room, a nightlight burned. Ben's eyes adapted quickly. His attention was first held by the curtaining partially drawn about the bed; he had not seen this before, and he wondered what it meant. He went up to the bed. Josh lay still, and his eyes were closed. His head was bandaged economically, a military, a cut-cap effect. Ben went to the far side of the bed, so that he could duck down out of sight, if anyone should come in; he had to hold back the white canvas hanging, in order to reach where Josh's head was pillowed. "Mr. Josh, Mr. Josh," he called in a low voice. And Josh opened his eyes, for he had not been sleeping, although neither had he been entirely awake.

"Who's that?"

"Ben Araby."

"Oh, Ben. Do you know where we are?"

"In the hospital. In Wilmington."

"Oh, yes. I can't keep it straight for very long at a time; I have to be reminded. But the Doctor told my folks I was recovering well." He reached for a glass of water; the drinking straw seemed to have a little accordion at the neck—it could be bent, Ben saw, without being pinched. "What are you doing up here?"

"What are *you* doing up here, Mr. Josh?"

"I came looking for you...to tell you to...not to.... I thought we had dropped the 'Mr.' part."

"We had. But we never should have. I won't ever be able to understand your background, and I can't get the right sense out of what you're saying about mine."

"Everything in my head has got bashed about. And they are giving me medicines...."

"I'm not talking about now. I never have understood you rightly, before the wreck, anytime. And I ought not to have tried to."

"The wreck. Wait just a minute."

"You know you were in a wreck?"

"Yes. I know it. I can remember some of that now. I have been wide awake a couple of times—at least a couple—since they brought me here. Mostly, though, I just...'drift' is the best word.

"You haven't seen the girl, I don't suppose?"

"What girl?"

"Never mind. What did you say you were doing here?"

"Never mind that, either, for right now. When you hit the overpass, were you trying to kill yourself?"

Josh closed his eyes; Ben could tell he hadn't fallen asleep. "No. I was not trying to kill myself. I was *not* trying to. No. It was the rice birds—an enormous flock of them flew right at me, from the left. From ahead, and the left. They were going to smack into the window on my side of the truck."

The door opened; Ben had time to crouch beside the bed, out of sight.

The nurse called softly: "Mr. Jones?" But Josh lay still—motionless and silent. The nurse went out and made a note in his chart: "Resting without distress; talking in sleep occasionally; will not awaken until due for vital signs."

"Jesus! That was close," Ben said.

"Yes. Somebody or other pops in here constantly. You can't be sure of being left alone. Birds. I veered to the right, and, just then, the birds turned... they turned away from me—you've seen them do that? All hundred or so, at once. When they do it, they seem to disappear in the bright sky, and...like a shutter opening: There's nothing but light. There was nothing but light; just before, a black cloud of birds were coming toward me."

"Mr. Josh! You're going to sleep. But I have to tell you something... and you have to be wide awake. Nobody can be here. When should I come back."

"Come back anytime. Tomorrow. Tomorrow afternoon. In the morning, they're all going home...."

Ben slunk away. He had got his shoes, anyway, but he was not having a comfortable stay in Wilmington. No, not a warm welcome at all. And the early signs had been so promising!

Except that there hadn't been any early signs. He could see that now, along with the realization that there hadn't been any all along. He couldn't have expected to kill the White man in himself...or be justified in killing another White man by claiming therewithal to kill the life of Woody Paget that was living, and would always live, inside himself.

No. None of the things he had talked himself into believing was true. And now he wasn't at home or at college—the only two places he had any business to be. Mr. Josh's car was stranded God knew where...if it was still even there. He had shot Mr. Edward to death, watched him fall, touched, even, his blood as it congealed upon the walkway to the church. And now he didn't know fuck-all about what would, or even about what could happen next.

But that was a good thing. He had left his life behind, with the result that he could see nothing ahead, either. He began to think, dispassionately at last, as one may in that intermission between being awake and falling asleep, about the livingness of his father, Woody Paget. For he had found that he mourned him, to a point, and to a point was prepared to defend his memory. After all, he was his father.

Mr. Laurence and Mr. Josh had each told him about the handing-on (or not) of his father's life to himself. They might have been telling him the same thing in different words, or they might have told him two different things. Mr. Laurence—and Ben knew that he had said what he had in order to make Ben able to feel free of the attainder of his parentage—had told him that he and his father hadn't even been alive together at any time, because fertilization lags by many hours behind coupling. Where, then, was he during this period? Was he far away? Far, and journeying from eve and morning?

Later, when Ben had said: "The White man in me is already dead," Mr. Josh had answered: "Woody Paget took his own life, but he passed yours on beforehand." Did that mean he had already come from the Winds' Twelve Quarters to the Crossroads?

Sight of a very old colored janitress in the hospital stairwell brought to his mind the time when all his own people had forgotten it was his birthday… except Miss Izora, his great-grandmother. She gave everybody else a chance to remember first. But nobody had availed himself. So she, who could hardly walk, had yet come upstairs at midnight, had sat beside his bed, stroked his head, sung him a little song: "The old grey goose is dead."

Iambs. Ben didn't know the term, but he knew the foot. And that memory and meter made to coalesce the phrases that had just been flaring among his musings like flambeaux—ones that were either very small or very distant. They were bits of a poem Mr. Josh had taught him. No. Of a poem *Josh* had taught him:

> From far, from eve and morning
> And yon twelve-winded sky,
> The stuff of life to knit me
> Blew hither: here am I.
>
> Now—for a breath I tarry
> Nor yet disperse apart—
> Take my hand quick and tell me,
> What have you in your heart.
>
> Speak now, and I will answer;
> How shall I help you, say;
> Ere to the wind's twelve quarters
> I take my endless way.*

Ben didn't understand all of the ways the words were used; he knew, for an example, that "stuff" didn't mean what he himself meant by it. But he knew the writer was saying that he had come from, and was going to, a place nowhere. *Just like me.*

Nothing to fix his thoughts on. He felt free and clear of all of it. He

---

*A. E. Housman: A Shropshire Lad, XXXII

slouched down onto a sofa in the Hospital lobby, and he went easily to sleep.

Every morning, form half past seven until nine o'clock, the hospital cafeteria was made available, in addition to hospital staff, to relatives of patients—and relatives only; you had to write down your relationship to the specified patient opposite your name—for breakfast. The Ashfields and Barringtons were seated a small table. They were dressed for travel. There, at that time, for them, this meant dressed as for church or for a small daytime wedding. That is how it was. They were going to see Josh, then leave for the Crossroads. It had all been discussed the afternoon before with Dr. Knowles, who, aware of the level of discomfort they were subject to because of their sudden departure from home, told them that Josh was simply going to get progressively better ("No. Now I can't say just when he can be moved"). They might as well go home, returning prepared for a convenient stay. Alina, naturally, was the problem. She had been assuaged. Or they thought she had been. But at breakfast, she had begun to paw the earth again. To every objection she raised to The Plan this morning, the others all just said: Nonsense, this, or Nonsense, that.

In the staff dining area, another little "discussion" was taking place among three young nurses, of whom one was Julie Whitman, who, though, had not begun but been drawn into it. Remarkably, the subject was Josh. Nurse Augustitus, who worked on the unit where Josh lay, said, as she finished her Cream of Wheat—this preference had already put Julie off; she ranked that comestible alongside tapioca pudding—"Well, Julie, we have certainly enjoyed seeing you on our wing lately."

"It is gracious of you to say so, Palomba," Julie responded, not quite icily. Not quite.

"Why have you been on Three West so much?" the third nurse, named Hortense, who circulated in the Operating Rooms, asked.

"I have been there twice."

"Are you sure that's all?"

"I am entirely sure."

"...Because Miss Palmieri—she's the Charge Nurse on my shift—said this morning she wished you'd come oftener...that Mr. John Jones rallies miraculously *every time* you appear."

"'Every time' is an exaggeration. I believe I said I'd been there twice." Julie had been holding a cup of black coffee...so long that it had got cold. Now, she prepared to replace it in its saucer with perfect accuracy, set them down, and, entirely composed, to rise and excuse herself. But, no. Cup and saucer clattered as they struck the table surface aglance, the spoon rattled from the saucer, and some of the coffee splashed across onto Hortense, who could actually use a little *kaltes Kaffee*. Not much; but a little.

Palomba Augustitus didn't know when to desist: "Well, all I can say is, I'd marry him just for those eyes!"

"If," Juliana retorted, with lack of complete clarity of meaning but to great effect, "that is all you can say, then why not just spend the rest of the morning saying it? Sit here, and keep saying it. Over and over. It will spare your patients your incompetent ministrations." This would have had still more effect if Nurse Whitman had turned abruptly and walked away, which in fact she set out to do. But she wavered, looked back, and said in a menacing voice: "I don't know what you think you know about his eyes!" *Then* she embarked upon her *Bucintoro*-style withdrawal, once more.

But she found herself face-to-faces with Josh's family, who were just getting up from table. And of course they all greeted her warmly, to Julie's chagrin and to the ratification of every scrap of Nurse Augustitus' innuendo.

Ben had roused himself early and gone outside the building. He found The Ashfields' great black Buick easily, and then a point of vantage from which he could keep an eye upon it. When the imposing-looking party had boarded the single large make of car to escape Miss Allie's anathematous "Showy," and the car had glided from the Hospital grounds—under power, as it were, rather than full sail—he went back inside. Visiting-hours were liberal, but excluded mealtimes. Ben sat in the lobby until three minutes past one o'clock, then he went to the reception desk to request a visitor's pass. Although the clerk had addressed him (pointedly?) as "Sir," for the Civil Rights Movement, which in the summertime would result in law, had caught on sooner in North Carolina, Ben advisedly wrote, under "Relationship to Patient," "Employee." Just in case.

He rapped on the door of Josh's room.

"Come in, please." Ben opened the door. No one but Josh was there. "Hello, Ben. Come ahead in. They've left."

"I saw them go."

"Sit down. Have you had lunch?" Ben had eaten nothing for two days. "Because I have no appetite at all—I think, because of the medicines—and I haven't touched my lunch. Why don't you have it? The food here seems good, believe it or not." The moment of the message he had to deliver, great as that was, was displaced just then by Ben's hunger. So he had lunch as Josh's guest.

When he had finished lunch, he put aside the tray, dusted a few crumbs from his jacket, then asked Josh to lend him some money. "So I can take the bus back to near where I left your car, so I can get back to State...to Orangeburg."

"Sure. I'll have to give you a check, though. They take away your money... watch, wallet...things like that. Cash the check in the admissions office here, so they can call me and verify I wrote it. Where is the car, anyway?"

"It's hard to explain, but I can get to it."

"Never mind about it, then. Now, tell me what you're doing up here."

Ben sat up in his chair, as more alert, with the dignity of a herald. "Do you remember that I was here last night?"

"I do."

"Three times you've asked me why I came up here to this part of the country, and so far I haven't given you an answer.

"I could give you a complicated answer. A week ago, I would've. I was messed up with drugs and being a halfbreed. You were crazy with drinking and losing Miss Mary. Then, neither one of us said anything that wasn't complicated. Except that I'm not much good at complicated talk.

"I wish we'd been thinking and talking straight. But that's done with. I came up here to kill Mr. Edward. And I did it." Josh started, turned his head farther to the right, to look directly at Ben. "I shot him to death. At midnight, between New Year's Eve and New Year's Day. I watched him fall. I saw the blood."

Josh, for a moment, neither moved nor changed. He mumbled, low, so that Ben had to lean over to hear him. "It's the deepest wrong...it's the wrong of ...wrong of the... burnt-out fire, or snuffed flame... the dark of the barrow." More, he said not.

Poor Benjamin Araby! He was to suffer more things that afternoon than that largely unsung prophetess, Lady Pilate. And, like that Dame, considered himself to have suffered them in a dream. He hoped it were, anyway. For if the memories of that day that he carried away with himself should turn out to be wide-eyed, waking realty, then the world and the people in it were in for a worse time than he had thought, worse than he thought *they* had thought.

Still at his post at Josh's bedside, Ben was caught off guard. The door was opened after a pro forma tap, and on the threshold there stood for a moment a beautiful young woman. As beautiful as Mary Mountainstream, if in an entirely different way. Come to think of it, nobody could rival Miss Mary with any success ...not at her own onyx-and-amber game. But this one could beat her at gold-and-copper.

And if this young woman were coming to see Mr. Josh, too—he looked down at his friend: What was there about him that kept on drawing beautiful women? *Mr. Josh is right nice-looking, in the kind of way, say, that Mr. Laurence is. But nothing special. Maybe they all know about his money.* (Although Ben himself hadn't but an inkling about that.)

She nodded to Ben, then bent over the patient and said: "Mr. Jones. Can you wake up!" So Josh opened his eyes, looked directly at her, said, "I *am* awake. I'm happy you're here."

She does *know him, she's come to see him. The lucky bastard! It's got to be the money—and the Family.*

But Julie looked up at Ben (*her* eyes were like topaz). "My name's Julie." "Mine's Ben."

There came a knock at the door. When Juliana turned, Ben crouched down again beside the bed. This time, while the nurse was giving her attention to admitting some visitor, he managed to get himself all the way under the bed, where he lay gratefully upon his back, to await the next development, whatever it should be.

"Canon Strikestraw! You won't know me of course; I'm Juliana Whitman, and Sarah Elkin is my mother."

"My good child!" Thomas exclaimed. He took both her hands. "I saw your mother not very long ago; she told me about you. I knew you were practicing here, but I had forgot, and I certainly didn't expect to see you today. You are every bit as lovely as your mother, and that is not a little. But how did you recognize me?"

"Well, there's the collar. And your name is on your visitor's badge." This was pinned to the violet shirt.

"Oh, dear. We get so foolish when we get old. At least I can console myself with the dubious consideration that there is by now little wit left to lose. But how is your patient, whom I've been invited to call upon?"

"He's not actually my patient. I work in the Emergency Room, and I was on duty when they first brought him in. I've just stopped in to say Hello. He's a little drowsy right now, but he needs to be awakened—not to sleep too much by day, for fear of a wakeful night."

When she had lied to this goodly cleric, she looked back to make sure to cut Ben off, if he should be about to say the wrong thing. She hadn't seen him slip out, but obviously he had done so. So she conducted Thomas to the bedside, and said: "Mr. Jones! Wake up. You have a visitor."

"Josh. I thought I'd asked you to...."

"The Hospital requires all staff to address the patients with courtesy. Here," and she turned toward Thomas, "is Canon Thomas Strikestraw; he's the vicar of Christ Church in New Brunswick, just across the river."

"Not for long!" Thomas said with unexpected relish.

"Our families have known each other for a long time." She started to go out, in order to leave them alone. "But I must get back to my post."

To Thomas Josh said: "How do you do, Canon. It is very good of you to come." He held out his hand. To somebody. His mentation and speech were still a little slowed. To Julie: "And I would like for you, Miss Whitman, to come back soon. When you can stay for a while...just for a little while." So Julie left and Thomas stood by the bedside alone. As he thought.

By now, Ben, lying under the bed, had pieced things together: *This is Mr. Edward's grandfather! And I just killed his grandson. I reckon the preachers have to put on cheerful ways for the sake of the sick people.*

"How do you do, Josh? A great deal better, I should think. You look very well."

"Thank you, Sir. But what do you think of my hat?"

"Well, I believe I can say truthfully that it is remarkable."

"That, at the very least. I admit, though that I'm a little leery of seeing what's beneath it."

"Well, at least they've been able to put it all back together, and in working order."

"Thank God! Oh, sorry, Canon,...."

"No. That is what I was about to say."

"Ah, good. But it's not all quite in working order. I can tell I make little mistakes."

"Isn't that supposed to be a good sign? That you can tell?"

"Yes, Sir. They say so."

"What brought you up our way in the first place, if I may ask?"

"One of the strangest parts of this whole thing is that I don't know."

Under the bed: *That's a relief. And probably a lie.*

"Do you, by any chance, remember my grandson, Edward Strikestraw? I think he visited your aunt and uncle, the Ashfields, late last year?"

Under the bed: *Oh, Jesus!* And then a great many suppositions began swarming in Ben's brain, and his was unimpaired. Or, more or less so. *Oh, Lord God! Is the preacher getting ready to tell him Edward's dead? Does Josh remember about what I said to him? Is he going to tell the preacher about me... and that it was me that killed Mr. Edward?*

The two White men had gone on talking with each other, but Ben wasn't listening, and anyhow couldn't have heard them for the ringing in his ears, growing louder, growing louder, coming in rushes, one right after another. *Maybe Josh doesn't remember.*

The ringing stopped, and Ben stopped thinking about the killing. Because, at his feet, a motor had begun to whir, and the bed above seemed to be folding up, kinking upward and away, about even with Ben's knees; downward, just over his chest. Just when a crossbar was about to make contact, the whirring and the deformation of the bedding both stopped. Ben was not hurt, but he was fixed in position. First, cupped under the hands of a child-giant; now pinned down like a butterfly, fresh from the kill-jar. Either way, a bug. A *bug!*

The priest had finished the social part of his visitation, and was embarked upon the sacramental portion: "...and of the Holy Ghost...; beseeching the mercy of our Lord Jesus Christ, that all thy pain and sickness of body being put to flight, the blessing of health may be restored unto thee." Josh and he together said: "Amen."

"Thank you again, Canon."

"It has been my pleasure and my honor. I will tell Edward you are here. He will want to stop in, before returning to the North."

"I'd like very much to see him again. To talk to him again."

Wedged under Josh's hospital bed, Ben was "knocked winding," as some say, by Thomas's casual, entirely cheerful reference to his grandson, and to a possible visit from him, who therefore must be alive and well. Then, as Ben was beginning to question what he thought he himself had done and seen in the churchyard, and to pour out from his battered yet apparently pardonable soul praise for deliverance, he heard another voice. Not one from within himself, which wouldn't have surprised him—for by then, what might have?

Ben heard, apparently as Canon Strikestraw was going out, a clear voice, coming from the hallway.

"Grandfather! I found your note. How long have you been here? Does anybody know for sure what has happened to Josh Jones?"

"Oh, yes, absolutely. He received a severe head-injury, in an automobile accident on New Year's Eve."

"I hope it wasn't because he was drinking."

"Oh, by no means. It happened in the afternoon. That had nothing to do with it.

"Anyway, Son, garrulous as I've got, the fact is I'm in a bit of a hurry. John and I are going to try to get over to see Benny Ormond. "

Thomas had evidently been ambling back toward the open door with Edward, who was making his own way there, because their voices had been dropping in pitch, yet were easier for Ben to make out. "I thought Mr. Benny was dead!"

"We did, too. But he's not. Although we may be too late for a visit today, we're not, as it turns out, simply...well, too late."

"Before you go, Grandfather...do you know why Josh had come to Wilmington?"

"No," Thomas said, with uncharacteristic succinctness, provisionally sensing danger. He started off down the hallway apparently, and Edward came into the room. "Josh?" he said tentatively. Ben should have been prepared for the flesh-and-blood, having heard the voice, but he wasn't: He fainted now, indeed, but soon came around.

Now Mr. Edward was walking up to Josh. "I'm sorry to hear about your smash-up, but, at least, here you are!"

"Edward," Josh said, a little wearily, "Thank you for coming here; I'm glad to see you. We're going to have to skip 'How were the Holidays?' and 'When do you go back to school?' Do you mind?"

"Not at all. It's what made the little we said to each other before Thanksgiving count so much."

"I don't recall saying anything that counted much. But I'm not very imaginative."

"And your skull has been bashed-in. But I know. We've got to talk about Mary. I want to be sure you understand something: I didn't—wouldn't have let myself fall in love with her, if I'd known she was your girl. By the way, I think she may still be your girl."

"No, she's not. And here's why not: After the breakfast, I took her back to Clear Creek. She kissed me on the cheek and said, 'Goodbye.'"

"Do you remember what you said when I asked you whether 'your girl' was someone you knew, or just a 'Please-call-for-Miss...'?"

"No."

"You said, 'She's my life...now that I have one again'—something like that.

"She's pretty splendid, you know—She knocked me cold. But I've been there before. A lot. And if I'd known, I could easily have...I could have let it go at that. I'm very sorry, and very unhappy, that I didn't. But I didn't know."

"Did I really say she was my life? Because after I knew I'd lost her, I did lose my life...in a way. I lost hold on it. I drank a lot, got drunk a lot. My folks, I think, were desperate; I should have been man enough to buck up, if only for them.

"There were two complicating factors...."

"Two, at least, then. Maybe a third."

Josh seemed not to have heard.

"The first has to do with a friend of mine. Although I doubt if he'll call himself my friend anymore."

Under the bed: *All I said was, I thought I ought to go back to calling him 'Mr. Josh;' he ought to quit trying to get me to understand his world...or my world, by way of his. He's got to be my friend still.*

"It's Ben Araby. I don't know whether you remember him—he remembers you."

"Of course I remember him."

"He came to see me in my rooms on Christmas afternoon. I live in the carriage house behind the big house."

"Woodleigh?"

"No. Clear Creek. I'd come home early from the family gathering. Ben's a child of rape, and he knows it. A State congressman, White, of course. And Mary Alice's sister. She delivered him, and went away. And so we drank together over our confusions and conflicts, and he doped a little. We fed off each other.

"Then—and I swear to you it started in an effort to help him see his life more accurately and hopefully—I told him your ideas about the severance of American Blacks from their ancient cultural founts."

Edward waited.

"By that time both our minds were sickened with drink, and, respectively, with either hatred or sorrow."

"And he took it the wrong way."

"He did."

"Everybody does. I still think it's correct, but it's either unpalatable or somehow off the mark. Do you think it could be taken as...in some way... demeaning?"

But Josh was not ready to digress. "The second of the complicating factors was a letter from Mary. It had come two weeks earlier, but I waited to read it until the Yule Log and Midnight Mass and presents and Christmas pudding were done with, because I expected to be plunged into bitterness by it, and I didn't want that rubbing off on my family, spoiling the Day. Actually, we had a wonderful Day. I had been trying since the night before to get drunk, but soul and body held out against it...until Ben came and we talked. After that, I read the letter."

"Can I know what she said?"

"Of course. To the extent *I* knew. The thing is, I edited it for myself as I read it. I hung onto what I wanted to know. Let the rest go."

"As everybody else does."

"She addressed me as 'Dearest Josh,' said things weren't greatly changed; she said she loved me as much as she ever had, that she always would.

"Like a fool, I saw hope of things' being the same again. Looking back, I saw it when it couldn't be, and besides, when I don't think I really even wanted it to be anymore.

"And here, Edward, is where I'm afraid my friendship with you has got to end, and I'll regret it for the rest of my life."

"What have I done?"

"It's what I've done, and I am so ashamed of it that it is going be hard for me to…even to speak about it. But it's my duty, and it's my loss. I began to build on Ben's having taken your thoughts other than as they were meant.

"I tried to discredit you. I don't know why I thought discrediting you with Ben would discredit you with Mary. I was clearly insane. But I don't plead Not Guilty by Reason of Insanity. I don't trust that defense."

"Why don't you?"

"Because we can't accord the insane—even the temporarily insane—the privilege of being greater nuisances to society than the sane, yet letting them get by with it. What they do—we do—is nevertheless done. I tell you that I neither expect, nor even want to get away with what I've let myself do.

"Ben had got up with some bad sorts at State. That's South Carolina State College. He's a freshman.

"Finally, he got to the point of seeming to want to work you woe. And I abetted it. Now, before I finish—and I'll be finishing myself—I want us to shake hands a last time. Because I'm sorry.

"I told him you'd said his natural father had done both him and his mother a favor when he raped her."

Under the bed: *I knew to Hell that was a lie. Why aren't they saying anything?* They weren't, because Josh hadn't control of his emotions. And tears were slipping down Edward's lacerated cheek. (No two of the bricks forming the walkway to the church were at a level, it seemed).

After a little while, Edward said: "Josh. Josh, turn back; look back at me. Listen to me. You have done nothing to hurt me."

Presently, Josh said: "I did nothing *in order* to hurt you; not for that reason of itself. If you could try to remember that…will you try to, as the years go by? But you could've been hurt, you could've been killed."

"In fact, though, I haven't been. And I won't be. Because I have the feeling the danger is past."

"It is. No. Thank God it's turned out that way. I've hurt only myself. By making myself a dastard, a liar, and a fool.

"And when I told that lie to Ben, I was trifling with questions he had concerning himself that were about to—really just on the brink—about to tear him apart. No madness to justify that is known to psychiatry. Legitimate psychiatry. You will learn, by the way, that not all is."

"Josh, leave it. And I'll take your hand any time you're willing to offer it. And we're friends until *you* say we aren't."

"You mentioned a third—anyway a third—complicating factor."

"Yes. Mary and I thought we had fallen in love."

"I think so, too."

"So, after the Thanksgiving vacation, I went down to Roanoke. It wasn't exactly picnic weather, but not exactly not. We trekked out into the mountains. It was the first time we'd been together by ourselves.

"When it was time to go back, she said, 'You know I still love Josh.'

"I thought it was an odd time to bring it up, but I answered that I assumed she must…still love you. If there'd been reason for it before, then I couldn't see that anything had happened to undo it. I don't think it was the right thing to say, as it turns out. Yet I still love the small handful of girlfriends I've had. It seems, though, not a sure thing, trying to say the right thing to Mary."

"I never—now I look back—said much to her. So I guess I didn't run afoul often. One thing I probably should have said is: 'Will you marry me?' But I didn't."

Ben, once the shouting and tumult had died, once the whirring had recurred, bringing the hospital bed to a level, had finally ventured out. Josh, left alone, had given in to exhaustion and gone immediately to sleep.

When he thought it nearly time to return to his earth for the night, Ben had awakened Josh and had said: "I ate your supper."

"Good. Then they won't come in and badger me about it."

"Do you remember that I was here before?"

"In a way."

"Do you remember what I told you? You ought to."

"I don't remember."

"I told you I had shot Mr. Edward and killed him."

"But you couldn't have, because he's alive."

"I know. I was here when he was here. Under the bed."

"You were under the bed, then, during the coming and going?"

"Yes, Sir."

"You don't say 'Sir' to someone who has lied to you. If you weren't willing to talk to me at all, now you know what I said was a lie, I wouldn't blame you."

"I heard you telling Mr. Edward about it. I heard you say it meant we couldn't be friends anymore. You and me."

"I said you wouldn't have me as a friend anymore. I do ask you to forgive me…sometime…when you can. But what I said about Edward Strikestraw and Woody Paget was a vicious thing.…"

"Mr. Josh, you might have told me a lie. You probably think it could have…that it did make me do something that might have been terrible.

"But what I tried, I was going to try anyway. I believe I was. And I told you lies, too. And maybe you told me some other lies you've forgotten. Or didn't even think were lies. Both of us have been …messed-up lately.

"But if it'll make you still be my friend, I forgive you right now. I love you, Mr. Josh. I know you don't want me going on about being half White, but…inside me…I am. And you are the only White person to have given me much more than the time of day. And you have given me away more than that. You've looked at me, talked with me, until you'd figured me out. And that way you—nobody…nobody else—got me to look at myself. See what I am. Where I am."

Josh lay still. But his breathing was awake. His eyes were open.

Ben finished: "So, can we still be friends?"

"Friends to the end." They shook hands. The next morning, Ben cashed his check without difficulty, traveled by bus to Shallotte, by foot to Calvary Baptist Church, and by Mercedes-Benz 190-SL all the way to the Crossroads, where he had begun.

Of particular importance, once the Ashfields and Barringtons had got home, was the state of things that resulted from this letter, largely self-explanatory:

Dear Mrs. Barrington,

First, I think I must reïntroduce myself, although I hope that you will be able to remember me. My name is Julie Whitman. I work as a nurse at New Hanover Hospital in Wilmington, in the Emergency Department. I was on duty when your son was brought in following his automobile accident, and I stopped in to see him the morning after his surgery.

That is when I met you and Dr. Barrington.

I've made a new paragraph, but I don't know exactly why, or how to express what I feel I must. A friendship sprang up between your son and me during his hospital stay. I visited him several times, even though I had no professional duties toward him. The other nurses have been beasts about it; one would think they were still in high school.

In any case, the rumor reached me one morning that Josh had called in a local jeweler—*the* local jeweler. When I visited him later, that same afternoon, he asked me to marry him and offered me a splendid ring, which I thoughtlessly accepted. It was in a way the natural thing to do, since I had already fallen in love with him when he was still unconscious. I hope you will find it possible to believe that. I shouldn't, in your position

Soon he will be on his way home. I have begged him not to speak of our engagement, until he knows whether you shall have read this letter (I'm afraid that may be a tense that doesn't exist, or, if it does, that I've not used the right form of it—You can see I'm a little low on self-confidence at the moment).

All of us, I suppose, know of "whirlwind engagements," but two terrible concerns have arisen to make me think this one may be so ill-advised as not to be allowed to continue. First, I did not know Josh was heir to wealth. Thinking of the ring, I asked him about it. Second, if anyone chose to think of me as that particular kind of woman who marries a man for his money—I won't even use the expression, but I'm sure you know the one I mean—a good case could be made for my abuse of abnormal mental status (which Dr. Knowles, who is an old friend of my family's, assures me is no longer present).

I love your son with all my heart, and my fondest hope is to spend his life with him, and make him as happy and safe as the world allows. But I can only imagine how all this might be interpreted.

Now to a matter that is practical (I'm much better with these): All you need say is something like, "Wouldn't it be better to wait?" I will understand your message and I will not feel rebuffed, because I really can put myself in your place, and I should think it hurried, too, and suspect.

Yours very truly,
Juliana Whitman

Alina read the letter, much moved by the delicacy of feeling—and evident care taken in the rearing—of so young a person. So young a woman, that was. The next thing that occurred to her—and she was very much ashamed of it—was that Julie, who now knew that Josh was rich and possibly groggy, did not yet know that he was "on the rebound" from Mary.

Alina herself, however, did not yet know that he was not. He had cut Mary loose, and himself free, before laying even sightless eyes upon Juliana. Alina had said to herself, the moment Julie had entered the hospital room—neat and pretty and golden-haired—*If only Josh could fall in love with* her. *And she with him!* She had even tried to get a look at the girl's left fourth finger. Talking of things done at high school level! There had been no ring. So Alina straightway fell to fretting over the possibility that married nurses didn't wear their rings to work—particularly not to work in an emergency room.

She had gradually realized that what Josh wanted, early on in his convalescence, that all he seemed to want was for Julie to be near him.

Something must be happening on a very occult plane. When Bob had told her, after she had finally torn herself from her cub's bedside and come home, that Josh had telephoned to ask him to find out the most reputable jeweler in Wilmington, her heart had "turned over," and her hope had risen. Now she went looking for Bob, to show him Julie's letter. Then the two of them got hold of Josh to see what he would have to say for himself. And this is what he said:

"I want you to know, first, how well *I* know how carefully you have looked after me and how much you have cared for me and...I think...loved me. I mean both of you. So I'm not going to say to either of you, 'This or that, no matter what.' But unless there's a good reason for it that I don't know, and can't imagine, Julie is going to be *my* life's companion."

At the uproar, Yukoneta hastened from the kitchen, through the dining room, to the East Room, where the two had been talking. Alina was so overjoyed she couldn't speak. Bob said to Yukoneta, who looked to be good for swounding again, to bring champagne and to telephone to Woodleigh. "But telephone first. Mr. Josh is going to marry!"

"Bless Cush! Miss Mary?"

"No. Miss Juliana."

"Lord *God*, bless Cush! Cush the Benjamite!"

A month afterward, Alenda sat upon upon her verandah, drinking tea and remembering. Remembering the recent days when Thomas had been in the throes—throes necessarily shared by his flock—of composing and delivering three homilies, a series beginning just after Christmas Day and meant to infuse into that low period some buoyancy.

He had written something and asked Alenda to read it. When she had done so she had come to him and said: "Well, Tommy, Darling, I have thought of an epitaph for you."

"I'm sorry to hear it."

"Why do you say that? I'm merely trying to be helpful."

"For one thing, I'm sorry you anticipate our needing one so soon."

"Oh, no. That's not it, not at all. It's only that I think these things ought to be mentioned whenever they come to mind. Can you imagine our having—or somebody's having—to think one up on the spur of the moment? It would be bound to be unsatisfactory. But, anyway, would you like to hear my suggestion?"

"No."

"Very well, then. Here it is: 'Thomas Grantly Strikestraw,' and then the dates, 'Priest and Heresiarch.'"

Thomas thought over this, but not at any length. "The other reason I'm sorry to hear it is that I'd already composed one for myself."

"Then in that case, we shall certainly use yours. May I hear it?"

"Of course: 'Thomas Grantly Strikestraw,' and then, as you suggest, the dates, then, 'All that Work for Nothing.'"

"Oh, Dear. Well I do have at least a small bit of information that will make the whole thing easier. Lucille and Joe Watkins have gone to Michigan for the Holidays, and they won't be back until early in the New Year."

This homily was delivered by the Reverend Canon Thomas Strikestraw, in Christ Church, on December 29, 1963:

"In the Name + of the Father, and of the Son, and of the Holy Ghost."

"*Amen.*"

"Dear People of God,

"On the Sunday in Christmastide, I have usually spoken to you about the Church's Doctrine of the Incarnation, that is, the Word of God becoming flesh, taking on the nature of man, and dwelling among us. In the early Church, there was a great deal of discussion about this matter, because many people believed that Jesus was truly man, possessing in some measure the nature of God, but yet not truly God. When the dust from this had settled—for the discussion had been an extraordinarily spirited one, and a great deal of dust was in fact raised—the Church had concluded that the truth of the matter was that Jesus was "very God of very God," as well as very man.

"This belief depends from a concept of God as having created, out of His own impulse, both the world and, in it, man—man in His own image, and good, therefore without knowledge, or any need of knowledge, of good and evil. How vividly all of us recall the outcome! Man disobeyed, and drew down upon himself a curse for his disobedience. But God relented, and took upon Himself—that is, upon Himself in the Person of His Son—man's nature, then offered, as it were, Himself to Himself as a sacrifice sufficient for the redemption and salvation of mankind, otherwise doomed.

[Here there occurred a minor stir among the congregation, as some strove to be sure the unfamiliar expression of the idea actually squared with their beliefs. Thomas sipped a little cool water.]

"Nearly all religions—and, I believe, some cultures, apart from any institution that we would describe as a 'religion'—have their own creation-stories. I have just alluded to our own, one which was nearly spoiled by that sly pair, Adam and Eve, through their misuse of apples and snakes.

[There occurred another, fainter stir, as there sank in upon everyone present the realization that this was going to be another of their Rector's highly "characteristic" homilies. From this point onward, everyone kept quiet. Or, nearly everyone did.]

"But there is a story of God and His creation of the world that has never come to characterize either any religion or any culture, even though the story itself has been told and retold over many centuries. It is a remarkable story, and not, I think, an easy one to understand. Reference to the original sources of it is printed in your bulletins today, and will be on each of the next two Sundays.

"In it, God is Good. That must come as no surprise, since we are accustomed from childhood—for instance, when we say, at grace before meat, 'God is great, God is good…,' and so forth—to think Him so. But we acknowledge other of His attributes: Lovingkindness, compassion, mercy, indeed, but vindictiveness, wrath, and jealously as well. The philosopher's God—as I shall refer to God in this other story—is Good, and here the word is a noun, not an adjective. It does not *describe* God. It attempts to *represent* God, and to come as close to stating what God is as our speech, thoughts, and intellects can do.

"There is no intent to belittle those or any of man's other faculties and gifts. The intention is to express how much greater God is even than we do imagine or are able to imagine. He is *the* Good. Good, wholly good, and only good, for nothing else is needed at the degree of perfectness. Beauty, truth, courage, and all the other virtues—even Justice herself—are subsumed into it.

"In this other story, neither is man made in God's image. For the Most High God has no visible image, and is beyond the reach of our other senses. Which is not to say that He is beyond reach.

"And being all complete and in need of nothing, the philosopher's God desires nothing for Himself. I have said before that I myself cannot think that man, product of the dust of the ground, could supply to the Godhead either any pleasure—I'm afraid I went so far as to liken us all to mere toys, in such a case!—or any other benefit. But, again, uselessness is not the same as worthlessness.

"In this other story, God is One. For, can there be two—or any other plurality—of 'Highests'?"

[Here there did occur an interruption: Little Alice Barnes, remaining convinced of the importance of dialogue on all occasions, shouted. "No, Canon. There can be only one Highest!" And poor Mrs. Barnes was soon halfway down the aisle with her obstreperous brood taken in tow.]

"Exactly right," Thomas said, preserving the tempo of ordinary conversation. "And if this One, Highest Good be so far beyond us men, and if we cannot perceive Him by the senses, then we refrain from thinking of him as a Person. In fact, thinking is the only link we have to him—we perceive him by our intellects. When we think, we produce ideas, just as we produce music when we sing. And so we speak sometimes of the Idea of the Good. We do all we can to show God's transcendence beyond man. In the world, then, of being, we have the Idea of the Good (except for a little surprise, which I shall save for later) and the Ideas and patterns of all the other things we can think about. These, too, are timeless, heavenly, changeless. They originate from the Idea of the Good, not by means of will and surely not by means of work. Good is fertile, and a property of good is to produce good. And in the not-easy story I am telling, evil, if thought of at all, is the marked absence of good. It is barren, produces nothing, and its fate is to not be. (I see an esteemed schoolmistress in the congregation, and she will be displeased with me for splitting an infinitive off from its introductory particle. But I did not want to say of evil that 'its fate is not to be.' That might suggest something different, perhaps that 'evil' at some stage enjoyed the possibility of being or not being. No, in the philosopher's story, the lot of evil is to *not be*.)

"It is an idea rather like that of cold. Our high school students who are studying the natural sciences, which some of their parents—and grandparents—may not remember so well, know that there is no cold; only heat. And cold is the relative absence of heat. So in wintertime, when we say: 'Keep out the cold,' a very strict physicist would prefer, 'Keep in the heat,' because to his expert mind, one thing is possible, the other, not.

"Now, in this comparison, I do not mean to minimize the dreadful distresses that have come upon many of us, at one time or another, and will doubtless come upon some of us again and upon many others in time to come. All of us encounter tribulations, and we are inclined to label them as 'evil.' But thinking of these woeful things, it may be worth at least a trial of saying—to ourselves, of course—'This state of things is markedly lacking in good.'

"Next Sunday, if you will come back and hear me, I will say how it is that a perfect and heavenly Idea, dwelling without change in a realm of pure *being*, may benefit by translation into an earthly world of existence, where there is change and *becoming*. That is, I shall say how, to the best of my understanding.

[A distant wail sounded from little Alice. Thomas winced. He took another sip of water, only to find it, to his surprise, lukewarm. Or had it got actually hot?]

"But, in advance, let me say that the Ideas (that is with a capital 'I'), heavenly, eternal, and good—and each a perfect pattern of the kind of thing it is—are nevertheless yet patterns.

"I assure you, Good People, that, as well as I am able, I am hastening to the end. Nor have I forgotten that this is Christmastide, and that my message must have to do with it. I have not presented the first part of this other story to you in order to ask you to believe it, or to believe in it. A building dedicated to Christian worship and hallowed by more than two hundred and seventy years of Sacrament and prayer would be no place for that, in any case. But I think—unless we can look upon such a story, in which God is not so much 'our Maker, Redeemer, Defender, and Friend,' at least as someone else's hypothesis—if we cannot briefly entertain this idea of the Godhead as 'Wholly Other' than ourselves or than anything else we may know or know of—if we cannot accord these challenging ideas at least a moment's contemplation—I think that then we may be taking the transcendence of the Almighty, and the near-unbelievableness of God's becoming Man, too lightly.

"Some of you may recall that I once suggested you include in your meditations the phrase from the *Gloria in excelsis*: 'We give thanks to thee for thy great glory….' And even if for nothing else. Thus, we should consider whether it would not be reasonable that the Highest Good be worshipped, even if unaware of His worshippers. Which I believe, as you all do, that He is not.

"Now unto God + the Father, God the Son, and God the Holy Ghost be ascribed, as is most justly due, all might, majesty, dominion, power, and glory, both now and forever."

"*Amen.*"

John and Helen Hammond, all the way home from Church, had exchanged few words. They had mentioned the weather, of course. They had commented upon the haste with which many people, following such protracted anticipation, abandoned Christmas and its trappings.

But after they had sat down to midday dinner, Helen asked, apparently very much by the way: "Do you think, Dear, that Tommy is all right?"

"Yes, I think he is perfectly all right. I imagine you are wondering about the sermon today; he likes to call them 'homilies.'"

"I wonder why? Although they are unlike any other sermons I have ever heard. For the most part."

"He told me once. He said something like this: 'A "sermon" suggests the traditional preaching of the Gospel, and I do not consider myself qualified to undertake a thing of that kind.'"

"That seems to me a remarkable thing for a clergyman to say."

"Tommy is a remarkable man."

"Do be assured, John, that I esteem him as highly as you do. It's only that I understand him less well."

"Oh, I don't say I understand him. But I trust him. Personally, of course, but also as a priest. The reason for it is that in or out of the pulpit, he is trying, when he speaks, to tell you something. I have heard eloquent sermons that, when later I thought about them, meant nothing…or nothing beyond what we've all heard a hundred times. If not 'Ten thousand times ten thousand,'" he added, being in a churchmanlike humor.

After a brief interval, he added: "Chewing their cud—That's about all you get from most of them."

After an interval only slightly longer, Helen Hammond said: "That is definitely not what we got this morning from Tommy."

Toward the end of dinner, the telephone rang. It was in the hallway, just outside the door to the dining room, where it had always been, if a newer instrument—as far out of usual earshot as possible. "Shall I answer?" Helen offered.

"Please do, my Dear, if you will." He prayed silently that the caller not be his sister. He looked, then, with loathing remembered at the wound-down clock on the mantelshelf. His sister always wound it for them.

Helen's voice came to him from the hallway: "Hello? …Oh, hello Minnie. How are you? …Good; and Michael?…Grand!" And then John stopped paying attention, since his sister's name was Iryse.

"That was Minnie Collier. Funnily enough, she wanted to know whether Thomas were all right, and she was sure you would know."

"Well, I do know. But I hope you didn't quote me as having said he was."

"I just said he was quite all right, as far as I knew."

"What had made her think he might not be? Or do I want to know?"

"I doubt whether you do, but I'll tell you anyway. She began by saying she thought it puzzling that he was marrying so abruptly; she couldn't understand it, since Tommy has known Alenda for thirty years without marrying her then suddenly is doing it at his age…by which she meant 'advanced age,' of course."

"She has no need to understand it. It will not have any effect on her, to be sure. Furthermore, for the first twelve of those thirty years, Alenda was married to somebody else, and for seven more after that, Thomas was married to somebody else."

"And the middle sixties, or late ones, are not an especially advanced age. Plenty of people marry then. And have completely satisfying marriages, in every respect."

"She expressed another concern. She and Michael have begun to feel that his…commitment…to Christianity as we know it is possibly less fervid than it might be. She couldn't tell what this morning's sermon was about."

"All due respect to people I count among my friends, and so forth, but

Minnie and Michael should probably both be going to Sunday school, rather than to Church."

"John!"

"I'm simply saying what I think, and to my own wife. And in my own house."

"Well, there's something else. Do you remember that parable Tommy read one Sunday? I was a good while ago. Two stewards with lamps, going out into the desert at night? Or something of that kind?"

"I remember it rather well. And I do, because I was unfamiliar with it and found it interesting. I spent a lot of time trying to interpret it."

"Well, Minnie says it's not in the Bible."

"Tommy gave the Book, Chapter, and beginning verse, as I recall."

"Still, it's not in the Bible."

"What has brought her to this conclusion?"

"She wrote to a cousin of Michael's who teaches at Sewannee. He researched it. And it's not in the Bible."

"And so she telephoned just to tell you that? Although, I must admit I'm surprised that Tommy said that it was in the Bible; that is, if it really isn't. We ought to get the opinion of someone at Davidson—sounder scholars there."

"That is not exactly all she called about. After this morning, they wonder whether something ought to be done."

"Did you ask her what measures they have concluded would be appropriate?"

"They think they ought to mention it to someone."

"In that case, let them mention it to Tommy; they're all friends."

"John, you know they can't do that."

"That's what they ought to do. If they can't, then they should keep quiet about it. Or they could go and tattle to the Bishop."

"What they're doing is tattling to the Senior Warden."

"Well, then. You've done their tattling for them."

"Will you speak to Tommy about it?"

"Certainly not! Besides, what could it lead to, beyond Tommy's removal as Rector. The only decent way for a parish to do that is for the vestry not to renew the incumbent's contract. And Tommy will have retired before it would be time for that to happen anyway.

"Forget about it now, Lunn, and spend the afternoon figuring out what this morning's homily meant. For apparently there will be a sequel."

On January fifth, 1964, Thomas Strikestraw delivered this homily in Christ Church:

"In the name + of the Father, and of the Son, and of the Holy Ghost."

"*Amen.*"

"Dear People of God,

"Hear the opening words of the first verse of the One Hundred and Twenty-seventh Psalm: 'Except the Lord build the house, they labor in vain that build it....'

"This morning, I intend to show you, if I can, how it might be that a heavenly, therefore perfect, thing—that is, an Idea, since only through intellect can we perceive anything in or about Heaven—stands to gain by being placed here, in an imperfect world, one that is subject to time and change. For in the end, whether we are speaking of the God of Abraham and Sarah, or, to use the expression I used last Sunday, the 'philosopher's God,' the God of All does not bring about anything, unless it is, essentially, a good thing.

"I have quoted those words of the psalmist because they speak of a house, and I intend to do the same. They suggest that laborers on earth may build a house, but, unless their work is somehow confirmed in heaven, the house will not be established.

"In order to illustrate the relationship between Idea, on the one hand, and, on the other, a 'real' thing, as we might wish to call it here, in the world of sense and becoming, there seems no better example than the plan for a house. For this represents the architect's idea—though, of course, in this case it is not a heavenly one. It is perfect, in a limited way, because the lines are straight, the corners are square, and so on.

"Such a pattern may give rise to many actual houses, when carpenters build according to it. So the architect's idea has acquired multiplicity. And because builders, like the rest of us, have their idiosyncrasies, the realized plan will gain in realized variety.

"The floors of these houses are seldom quite level, though; the 'right angles' contain more or fewer than ninety degrees, for the carpenters are building on earth and not in Heaven. And how earnestly I wish I could cast these thoughts in the clarity and fixity of the heavens!

"At any rate, by exalting this notion in our minds, beyond the words in which I have expressed it, this actualization, or construction from lines drawn on paper, we may liken to the Creation, where God's intentions are brought about. They serve, though, but for a time, then are gone. Others take their places.

"When young, I found a good deal of satisfaction in things I did, particularly if they amounted to improvement upon things I had done earlier. In my later years, I have found either that accomplishments are often less gratifying, or that tasks I have undertaken have ended in results falling farther short of expectation. This process is that of becoming: Initially seductive, eventually wearying. One seeks a resting-place.

"With this in mind, I want now to comment on the realm of Ideas, as it were from below, from our world of ceaseless change. Imagine an engineer, as an example—and it is a fine one, for engineers have often seemed to me most efficacious among professional people. And let us take in particular a builder of bridges. Because bridges are eminently useful, especially in the shortening of arduous journeys; they are sometimes beautiful, as well. In fact, for me, certain bridges stand among the most beautiful edifices in the world. They have, too, the near-mystical property of joining together what were separated before, and of doing so without making use of that which lies between. Except, of course, for space itself. And we must beware of thinking of space as 'nothing.'

"The builder creates a bridge widely acknowledged to be both sound and in appearance pleasing. He is thus employed for the construction of other bridges. And into each he will incorporate structural and aesthetic features from the ones before. But not all—only those that have proved best. Yet, no matter how far he refines his craft and art, would we expect him ever to stop and say: 'This one is perfect; I shall build no more, at least none differing from this.' He will not say so [Thomas must answer his own question since on that day little Alice Barnes was not present], unless through some intellectual perversion he has failed to grasp that each of his works has been a stepping-stone to the next, and each next, better than the one preceding it. Ideally.

"But the process in which the bridge builder has got caught up must end. All our journeys do. Here, the end is a bridge with every good thing about it that a bridge can exhibit, so long as that feature appears nowhere else. For we remember that perfectness of type is not shared, but belongs to one [*Take that, for little Alice!*].

"This we see only with our feeble intellects (I absolve in advance everyone who will repeat this phrase, wittily changing it at my expense). But our intellects are the only eyes we have for examining pure Being.

"Well, we have looked downward from Heaven, in a much-flawed manner, and upward from earth; we may have seen but little. But we are destined to see more, I think.

"I shall close, now, reminding you all that I am telling you this story only because I hope it will help you to be sure in your own minds how far above earth is Heaven, and above us men, God.

"For we have completed our observation of Christmas, the Birthday of Christ, and we embark presently upon another feast and another season, Epiphany, the Manifestation of Christ to the Gentiles. In each case, we see, in the words of the beloved Carol, 'veiled in flesh, the Godhead.'

"And it is my earnest hope that we sense the ineffable in this occurrence, which we do not hesitate to celebrate each year, sometimes, I am afraid, perfunctorily. But I accuse mainly myself."

"Now unto God + the Father, God the Son...."

"I wonder, Darling, whether you are familiar with a practice called 'tarring and feathering'?"

"I don't know what you may mean by 'familiar with.' I have never either suffered it, nor taken part in inflicting it, but I do know what the term means. And it is—or was, because the thing has fallen into disuse—typically followed by the riding of the victim out of town on a rail."

"Good God! Tied, wrists and ankles, across a pole, the way they sometimes sling deer? Is the subject unconscious? Not dead, surely?"

"Oh, no. The victim was made to sit astride the rail. Very unsettling. I understand some of the Central American 'governments' still use a similar form of torture for punishment of political opponents. They're blindfolded, I think, and their hands tied behind their backs. So there is really no safe way to dismount. They call it, I believe, 'riding the *caballete*.'"

"How gruesome! Anyway, not to stray, if you had not been born here, had not belonged to a respected family, and were not personally so widely loved...In other words, if you were some vicar just shipped in, and took to delivering homilies like your last two, then in that case I believe you would be tarred and feathered."

"And ridden on a rail."

"Yes, and ridden on a rail."

"Well, let me tell you that I cannot help the circumstances of my birth, nor the position of my family. But I do think I have earned the loyalty of most of my parishioners; and, whether I have or not, it never hurts to give a bit of a shake to those whose meditations may have grown stale."

"A bit?"

"So much as is necessary."

"Necessary to what?"

"To their examining their notions of what it is for us to be men and for God to be God."

Alenda arose, and, before leaving the room turned back to her future husband. "Shake them, then; batter their hearts. I shall be on hand, of course, in case I may have an opportunity to be helpful—splinting, that kind of thing!" She looked rather wonderful, as she nearly always did. She wore a black dress that was really dark purple, and, around her slender waist, a shimmering sash the yellow of lemon quartz. Thomas felt she had probably tethered a *caballete* outside their door.

Thomas Strikestraw, January 12, Christ Church:

"...I did introduce this as a creation story. And so it is. But because the creation story we know best is a Bible story, we have tended to wince a little, I think, finding this to be anything but Biblical.

"In this connection, as some say, it only gets worse; for in the complete form of the philosopher's account, God did not make from the primal Chaos the world, as our religion teaches, but Heaven, in order for it to serve as a pattern for the universe of all existing. And, again to tell this story in it most fully developed version, the Godhead dwells not merely in the realm of being, but is conceived of as dwelling beyond even pure being. In short, we are meant to be all but exhausted by thought of His transcendent glory.

"Yet the Idea of the Good, being perfectly good, is in human terms without envy. His will is, therefore, that every conceivable thing be, and be as much like Himself as possible. And to this end, all Ideas—for they are really categories of things—though not necessarily at once, are granted existence, that is, becoming and not only being. Multiplicity and variety can thus emerge. As each kind of existence gains in goodness, it approaches to the perfection of the corresponding Idea and reaches forth toward perfect being. This is all.

"Repeatedly I have declared that my purpose in preaching this non-Gospel has been to lead our thoughts toward the transcendence of the Godhead—even as in these Seasons He seems to have become so much our own—and away from an over-zealous tendency to claim for ourselves any other relationship to our Maker than is consistent with His nature, and with ours. And whenever we predicate anything about the Almighty, we must remember that in all but a few cases we are more likely to be wrong. For of Himself He is considered by many to have said, merely, I AM. No subject complement. [Miss Bena Lucas nodded, smiling to herself.]

"What may all this have to do with the Incarnation? That, in order to accept this other view of God and the universe, and at the same time to embrace a doctrine of incarnation, it would be necessary to suppose that the Highest Good—for inscrutable, not explicable reasons, but ones necessarily ultimately good—accepted existence, in addition to essence, and ultra-essence, for Himself, and became sensible and changing Man. But as One *becoming*, and in time; simultaneously, as One *being*, and in eternity, if not beyond even that.

"And what may there be for the Highest Good to become? [*Alice?*]

"To my mind, which is not a fertile one, the only possibility is simply All Things. ...By Whom all things were made; who all things then became. That God is everywhere and in everything is not a new concept. I was taught it as a child in Sunday School. And it is a primary tenet of some religions and systems of mystical thought.

"To the philosopher Plotinus, especially, among the proponents of the story I have been telling, the distinguishing characteristic of the possession of soul is the ability to move without the aid of other force. If God, the All Soul, is in all things, and in Human Person has become all things, then all things must move of their accord, even the seemingly still stone within the frozen forest.

"And all things do so, though we may have to look to subatomic particles for evidence of that motion. And if that does not satisfy us, then we may look—for those familiar with it—to 'zero-point energy,' or to Background Microwave Radiation, relic of the Primal Light. And many of you will live to see the necessity of looking deeper inward, or farther outward. The Necessity, most likely, of doing both.

"I do not consider, for my own part, that even such insensible motion and energy would be present apart from a degree of indwelling Soul, and the presence of God, having entered and *become* the Creation by joining with Man, subject to time and becoming."

"And do not be discomfited by thought of two moments of Creation. For there is but one Moment at all."

An awful hush fell within the old Church, where an old man was speaking of things he only barely grasped, willing to do so because he knew that beyond the "last" wall that Duzey Blanding had told him of—knew that in every successive wall there is an opening; that when one passes through, then the wall is gone…even if another looms ahead.

It was a kindly hush, and it held Thomas in its hands. And it allowed him to go on:

"And now, beloved and patient friends [The Watkinses had returned from Michigan; so far, Joe had held his peace; even though he suspected that he ought to be getting really infuriated over something, he could not quite see through to what that might be], let us return to the way we all actually go about our days thinking and feeling. We do sense that our God is with us, that He watches over us, that He hears our prayers of praise and supplication. And we picture Him in our imaginations. To me, for example, He becomes almost palpable when, in another Season, one that will be upon us sooner than we may expect, on Palm Sunday we sing, in the hymn indispensable to that Day:

> Ride on! Ride on in majesty!
> Thy last and fiercest strife is nigh;
> The Father on his sapphire throne
> Expects his own anointed Son."

"Then I see the Father, surrounded by the Host of Heaven, coming forth to take His ceremonial place of governance, awaiting, as any earthly father might, His once-imperiled son [There was a tiny phonemic deficit at the end of "son," unnoticed, as Thomas clutched the edges of the pulpit, momentarily staring straight ahead, through the clear glass, along the street, down to the Great River, shining], whose safe return is nevertheless assured.

"If I have asked you to stray, it has been in order that from a perhaps illicit place of vantage you may see the Sun a great deal farther away than previously thought, yet infinitely brighter. And now I leave with you a line of verse by John Donne, Priest. Lifted from an intricate context, I think it nevertheless safe:

'I turn my back to thee but to receive....'"

After all this, Alina's teacup was full of sand, her memory exhausted. She must welcome home now the unique man to whom, against odds, she was married. There had been Bill. And the one other dream, like a mist; not a mist as at great altitude and at that seen from above, appearing discrete and self-consistent. A sea-level, a Trade Wind mist, frayed of border, various in substance, thinned in places, worn by time.

IX

> "…Where's
> The gain? how can we guard our unbelief,
> Make it bear fruit to us?——the problem here.
> Just when we are safest, there's a sunset-touch,
> A fancy from a flower-bell, some one's death,
> A chorus-ending from Euripides,——
> And that's enough for fifty hopes and fears
> As old and new at once as nature's self,
> To rap and knock and enter in our soul,
> Take hands and dance there, a fantastic ring,
> Round the ancient idol, on his base again,——
> The grand Perhaps!"

Robert Browning: *Men and Women*; "Bishop Blougram's Apology,"
ll, 179-190

"And till Moses had done speaking with them, he put a vail on his face."

Exodus 34; 33 (AV)

IN ITS COURSE the day came for the journey to Bewley Island, the visit to Mr. Benny Ormond, and the inspection of the improvement he claimed to have made to the Old Light. Thomas, John Hammond, who knew their host's life's story, and Dr. Harper, the Unitarian clergyman, whose friendship Thomas had begun to cultivate, who did not know it, formed the party. They set out in midafternoon, in John's little motor boat. The sky was clear; there was a steady breeze, and the water was chopped into very small, very uniformly disposed seas. But the boat was too minor to achieve smooth sailing over this only coarsely homogeneous surface.

Dr. Harper warmed John, who steered: "Do be careful; it would be mortifying for three elderly gentlemen...."

"All pillars of the Community," Thomas added.

"...To be drowned in plain sight of everybody for miles around."

"And we shouldn't get to see the lighthouse, or its new fitting...whatever that is."

"*And* I would never hear Mr. Ormond's tale. And it is one I want to hear."

But they accomplished the crossing, and Mr. Benny, who had seen them approaching, went out to meet them and to help them beach their vessel and disembark out of it. Thomas thought he noted that the skin of Benny's face—all that was visible, for he wore gloves as part of a prescribed "occlusive dressing"—was exceptionally clear. After introductions, the four walked to Mr. Benny's cottage, and were invited in for coffee "or something a bit stronger, if it's not an offense to offer it."

And yet again, Mr. Benny recounted his story. But now with a clear brevity that made it seem fluid, seeking its conclusion steadily as the river seeks the sea. "When I was stricken at last, I thought my folly had brought me up short, and as an old fool. We're supposed to be the worst kind in that class. But then I was spared again. I hadn't expected to be. The doctors hadn't expected me to be, and they told me so."

Dr. Harper said: "Mr. Ormond, the events of your whole life long would compel anybody. Compel him I don't know quite to what."

"We Unitarians go to Church and worship God. But we are not Christians, as many think we are. Therefore, I understand less than you others," taking in John and Thomas with his glance, "what you appear to be held apart for. In other words, not, within the organization of my understanding and belief, for the Last Judgement. However, that does not produce in me at all much doubt that you are being preserved for something. And not having a ready-made answer, I have to ponder more carefully."

"And further," Thomas said, "and that is just why I haven't come to see the real meaning of it. I did have a ready-made answer. But now my acceptance of it is gone. Largely gone."

Dr. Harper said: "It is hard, if you profess Christianity, to escape the notion that some will not yet have died by the time of the Last Judgement (Now I do realize that that idea was to the first Christians an all but present reality). For in either of the creeds you commonly recite there is the explicit implication: 'From thence He shall come to judge the quick and the dead'; and 'He shall come again, with glory, to judge both the quick and the dead.'"

"Yes, but note 'recite.'"

"In that case, we're left with your possibly living this life forever to some other end than the Last Judgement. I can't think what that might be, although...."

"Not 'forever,' Doctor, Sir, but just for maybe a long time, ending in some way besides in dying. But excuse me, because I interrupted."

"Often necessary," Dr. Harper said, smiling. "I was only going to say that the Bible, just as a single example, contains several instances I can remember, of life in this world ending other than in death. There's Enoch, 'taken by God,' giving rise to the doggerel 'The oldest man that ever lived,' meaning Methusaleh, 'Died before his father did,' meaning that Enoch did not die; Elijah ascended into Heaven in a chariot of fire, I think. There are the ascension of Jesus and assumption of his Mother, following her dormition—which I don't think is in the Bible but in Roman Catholic fancy."

"Not that it's not all very interesting," Thomas concluded, "but what is important, I feel, is that this life need not invariably end in death."

They walked over to base of the Old Light, opened the door, and started to climb. They could see their way. Nobody carried a lamp of any kind; Thomas felt that either the door below or the hatchway above had been left open. Neither had been. Mr. Benny, leading, turned to say something to them, and Thomas had a strong impression that his face, clearly visible, was giving off the light by which they were proceeding.

All this was forgotten once they had entered the lantern chamber; there stood in its midst an object of such simple grandeur than none of them thought to say anything until several minutes had passed. "Good Gracious," Thomas eventually said; "It's beautiful!"

And although only a lamp, it and its glazed site together, mirrored shimmering. The object could be described as a large spool with sturdy axle, set vertically, fashioned of gleaming brushed stainless steel. Between the peripheries of the discs at each end stood twelve equally spaced tubes of heavy glass, faintly violet-hued, as though iodine had been made to sublime within each, the vapor not fully extracted.

And within each graceful cylinder was from above attached an elongate bulb, an exquisitely coiled filament, seeming of gold, though not, falling through its length. There were a great many other features—separating sleeves, connecting rods, lock-washers, nuts, cotter-pins and clevises, skeins of electrical wiring and their bindings and connections.

The apparatus , thirty inches tall itself, was suspended the same distance from the floor of the chamber, with the result that it was seen against the windows of this little eyrie, beyond which the dusk of that day was settling in rose- and persimmon-colors.

Among the men there was only murmuring, and that of things said only through need of saying something. Dr. Harper and John went to the windows, to try to identify places on the ground and among the waters below. But Thomas stood gazing at the Central Glass, Steel, Gold. Mr. Benny had begun to consult his wristwatch, when, all at once, he shouted "Canon!" and, averting his eyes, for they had been changed, tried with his left shoulder to shove the priest out of the way. Light!

A few minutes later, Thomas found himself standing at a south-facing window, positioned as though looking out, the others moving about solicitously and softly enquiring and encouraging. But Thomas was blind— totally blinded.

Outside the sun was setting, about to plunge the earthbound world to night; possibly time, possibly the closer correspondence between intensity of light streaming over the priest's retinae and the ability of those organs to convert and transmit—at any rate, something produced dimmed, flaring arcs of blunted tints to appear in Thomas's visual fields. Blood flowed. Chemical standings in the rods, cones were gradually reversed. "I can see, but I cannot see any thing."

And then Thomas did see a thing: The paired towers of a distant city gate. He wondered whether he were going toward it, to enter in. Then this sight was obtruded upon by still, shining water below, ranges of trees, now darkening, and above them dun clouds, recognized only by the chaplets of defining sparkle with which the sun still edged them. "Now I can see normally." With expressions of relief for Thomas's recovery of sight, of admiration for the potent lamp, the men began to file down the stairs.

"Where did you get the lamp, Benny?"

"Well, in a way I designed it and had it built."

"Why, 'In a way'?"

"My grand-nephew helped me with the particulars, when I'd shown him what I wanted. And...but never mind."

"No. What?"

"He's in the Coast Guard. And he's a lawyer. So he not only cleared the way for me, but, too, he helped me get a Government grant. He says if you know what you're about, you can get a Government grant for anything...as long as it's of no real importance."

Thomas did not expect to see normally quite yet, of course, but he did wonder whether the blinding flash were now making it seem that Benny's face was emitting low light, though enough to see clearly by. No. He had noted the same effect on the way up. Perhaps he must use some kind of ointment that luminesced.

When they reached grade, it had got a lot darker, and a lot darker than just minutes before in the lantern chamber. They walked to Benny's cottage and were invited in again. John and Dr. Harper wanted to know all they could learn about the lamp. And it was a thing indeed worthy of study and richly able to repay curiosity. But Thomas, who it should be remembered had last seen Benny when he thought he was seeing him for the last time at all and been wrong, was interested in the way his disease had been brought under control, if not indeed cured. So, when opportunity offered, he asked: "Would you mind, Benny, since you were desperately unwell when we last met, telling me how it is you've got so much better?"

"Not at all, Canon. If I did half what they told me to do when I was discharged out of the hospital, then I'd spend all day *schmieren und salben*, as some poor Kraut prisoner used to say...he had a lot of sores, and that put pluck in us all. It was just before the Plague struck."

My God, the things people will remember!

"But that's about all skin-doctors can do, as it turns out. You see I wear gloves. Not to bed, though. They're supposed to keep one of the salves in close touch to my skin."

"Must you do anything about your face?"

"Two things: Smear some ointment all over it—not the same one. And then I'm also supposed to wear a beekeeper's hat."

"Beekeeper's hat!"

"Veil, I think it is. But I feel like a jackass when I wear it. I'm supposed to wear it when I'm outdoors. But however bad my face may look...."

"It doesn't look bad at all, but...."

"...I'm sure I'd look more startling in this thing."

"...But...."

"I suppose you always wear it in the tower. It's bright enough up there. If the Light should come on unexpectedly as it did this evening, I imagine the exposure wouldn't be at all salubrious."

Mr. Benny didn't have to worry about what "salubrious" meant. He said: "That was not unexpected. A switch brings it on at set times.

"I don't wear the veil when I'm in the lantern chamber. I am supposed to wear it outside. But, no. Never in the lantern chamber."

"But, Benny, this ointment for the face...Does it glow in the dark?"

"Once I thought so. But not in the dark. It was by daylight. I came down from the tower, then went in to shave. In the mirror, it...my face...did seem to shine. But I had been working with the new lamp, my eyes were right bedazzled, so I put it down to that."

Twice more the Banns of Marriage had been published, in Christ Church but by the Bishop, and nobody had found cause, or just impediment, why Thomas Grantly Strikestraw and Eleanor Alenda Thornwall Lucas should not be joined together in Holy Matrimony. Accordingly, they were now joined together in it. Edward had stood up as Best Man for his Grandfather; Alenda had had as her attendants her new daughter-in-law Martha Trimble (Lucas), Matron of Honor, and Mary Mountainstream, Maid of Honor. William Lucas and Rhododactylë Harmon were the only ones not in the wedding-party asked to be present. After the ceremony at high noon, Alenda, and Martha and William, received special guests at Alenda's house. They did it *very* grandly: Those passing nearby assumed three times the guests there as were.

When the last had gone, Alenda handed the housekeys, one to Martha and one to her son, and said, "It's all yours!" Then she kissed Wisty, who had kept house for her for eight years and would stay on to take care of "the children," saying "Lord! I'm going to miss you, Girl," took Thomas's arm, and they walked together through the gentle middle March afternoon to the Strikestraw house, preceded by a quartet of pipers.

They sat on the verandah, and Thomas said: "It's odd, but I assumed that once we were married we would go inside."

"There will be plenty of days and hours for inside."

"It is to be hoped. Already, though, I have had more than my share of contentment."

"Do you think you will continue to be content, now you're without a church to call your own."

"Without a doubt. Now I have you to call my own."

"You won't miss your priestly doings?"

"I imagine I'll be called upon to christen, marry, or bury every now and then. I'm not going to, though. Not for a year. The new rector must put his hand in, and not just once in a while."

"What about Church?"

"—About what aspect of it?"

"Attending it."

"Not until after a year has gone by, just as for the other things. We might go to Communion when we're out of town." How contentedly Alenda began to look forward to the coming year!

As Edward climbed the stone stair that twisted from bottom to top of Henry Tower, he wondered, in case Sandy had already returned from Christmas vacation, how much guff he would have to take for the bandaged laceration over his right cheekbone, the abrasions and bruises that clustered round it.

Sandy had returned. He had dropped his luggage in the middle of the floor; he had not turned on the lights. He looked around, when Edward opened the door, from the leaded casements through which he seemed to have been staring into the mist from the lake; entirely ignoring the evidence of facial trauma, he said quietly and with unsettling solemnity: "Edward, I have something to tell you; I don't know how you will take it, but I want an honest response.

"I'm not going to medical school."

A stick of dynamite might has well have gone off. Edward was stunned. For three-and-a-half years, both of them had been trying, with steadily increasing effort, to equip Sandy—or so Edward had believed—to answer that summons of the heart which once was called "vocation." By that time, however, your "vocation" meant simply your job.

Before the holiday, Edward had even, at merciless invitation, vetted essays on application forms—ten of them! So he said in reply, "Why not?" And he thought he had done well to come out with even that.

"An issue of *Newsweek*. Right after I got home, I read an article in it that said there was 'sharply decreasing' demand for doctors, that already there were too many. It said their average annual income had dropped 'significantly', and that it was expected by some to begin soon to 'fall steeply.'"

"It does seem a lot of people have been crowding into medical schools."

"That's why I applied to some of the third-rate places I did."

"Everybody does that—as a 'safety-net.'"

"Oh. But, I'm not worried about being admitted. Well, yes I am...."

"Everybody is, naturally, until it happens."

"And, by the way, which law-schools are you applying to?"

"In alphabetical order?"

"Just answer me." Sandy had wanted to know from the beginning; all during the fall semester he had tried to be first to pick up their mail (expediently delivered by being thrown onto the middle of the floor of their sitting room) and sort it, presumably taking note of the return addresses.

"In alphabetical order, then: Duke, Harvard, and Vanderbilt."

"You didn't want to throw in Yale? As a 'safety-net'?"

"Don't be an ass." Edward was too overborne to continue. Only now did he take off his topcoat and the other, alien things you wear in winter in the North: Gloves, muffler. Then he set a fire and lighted it. Each of them pulled a chair up to the fireplace, which was finished like the top of a two-point arch. They sat looking at each other. The most Gothic thing about the Tower at that moment was probably Sandy.

Edward, for his part, doubted that what his roommate was telling him really amounted to a decision. "Will you fill me in? Starting from the article in *Newsweek*?"

"Yes. I read it, and I decided."

"Then and there?"

"Yes, then and there. And I felt a great freedom and a great optimism after I'd done it. So I knew I'd made the right decision."

"The freedom. Do you think you haven't, deep down, wanted to study medicine in the first place? Or, possibly, that you have come not to want to?"

"It used to seem to me the perfect profession—a lot of income, without having to work and wait a long time for it; respect in your community, without having to work and wait a long time for that, either; the opportunity to settle down wherever you chose."

"I don't think any of those things goes automatically with the territory anymore, if it ever did. But I do understand what you mean; I can see how you could have expected all that from it, some years back."

"Six…yes, six years ago—or five-and-a-half—when I first started to think about it, all that seemed entirely plausible. I knew people whose experiences had been exactly that.

"Not now. The money is certainly not there. People are readier these days to criticize and blame and sue doctors than they've ever been before."

"And I'm afraid you'll find you have to go where you can get the best deal."

"The article mentioned that, too, as a matter of fact. Desirable communities are glutted. I didn't see it coming. Any of it."

"And, Sandy. Look: You have to wait seven years, before you start practicing."

"Five."

"One year of post-graduate training won't make you very much sought-after, I don't believe. Although I don't really have any way of knowing."

"Well, I slept on it. Then I went to my parents and told them."

"How did that go?"

"They've always been skeptical of my becoming a physician. My mother thinks I don't have the right temperament for it. My father wants me to come into his company—no expense, he says, no preparation, no waiting."

"You're not interested in that? I sometimes wish I had a job to step into."

"I'm not at all interested."

"What do you think you want to do now?"

"Study law."

Again, Edward was stunned, and momentarily speechless.

So Sandy went on: "I can apply now. I can change at least two of my spring semester courses, I think—I have an appointment on Monday with Luddy...my faculty advisor! God!...and I can make up the rest over the summer in Athens [by which he meant the City where the University of Georgia is situated]."

Well, I've never heard him say "I can" three times in a row before now. Maybe this is his real beginning.

Sandy continued: "I can see the handwriting on the wall. And I'm not going through all that, if I can't finish and then get out and have the life I want."

"Sometimes we have to take what we get, remember. 'Lawyer' comes right after 'doctor.' And before 'Indian Chief.' All those positions are changing, probably in parallel."

"Why are you going into law, then?"

"Only because I know there are progressively fewer openings for Indian Chief."

"Seriously, you would make a...remarkable physician."

"I'm going to study law in order to see what opportunities I can find to have the law approach more closely to Justice. And to earn an honest living"

"More Plato?"

"There can never be enough! But the optimism you felt. What about that?"

At this, Sandy put his head in his hands; when he took them away, his face was flushed. Edward thought his eyes might be glistening. "I had to modify the optimism. Claire put up a fuss over my decision."

He's holding to the proposition as a decision. "How much of a fuss?"

"You be the judge. When I told her about it, she made me stop the car. She got out and walked home. I didn't understand it, and I still don't. She will have plenty of money of her own, whatever happens. But in the next Sunday's paper there was an announcement breaking off our engagement, 'At the request of the bride-elect.'"

"Her parents went along with that?"

"They must have."

"Have you talked to her since then?"

"Yes. Once. And face-to-face. She said she thought she was marrying a man who would be a doctor; she said that was still what she was going to do." Edward, experiencing an upsurge of disgust, opened his mouth, about to speak, but Sandy cut him off.

"Please don't say I'm better off without her. I heard that twenty times before I left home." He smiled, staring out through the leaded casements. If the mist had cleared, by then it was too dark to tell.

"She will be less well off without you."

"Thank you." He lifted a suitcase onto his bunk. "I never liked her much."

The Barringtons and Ashfields of Peel County were looking eagerly toward the Easter visit of the Strikestraws. It had turned out that none of them had yet met, face-to-face, either Thomas Strikestraw or his Bride. But with all that had taken place among them, all that had cloven Edward and Josh—that is, "hewn apart" and "made cling fast," the two old verbs having conveniently come together (again?) in the modern forms—everyone felt, along with "laudable interest" in the prospect of meeting strangers, also the comfort of reunion with the almost-lost well-known.

Thomas's and Alenda's arrival in the southern coastal plain was as Edward's had been—only across the earth's career around the sun. In the marshes, where the sandspits rose high enough to break the surface of that same violet water, the year's growth of marshgrass had appeared, tender, bunched shoots the green of the sky, when the sky is green. Overall the land seemed upborne on the Waters Under the Firmament, but again, the old creeks and oxbows seemed moveless—welling only. Now they reflected the clear daylight of spring, as they wound serpentine far and away and out of sight.

Katabatic. That odd word with no good stand-in. Downward and seaward. All bitterness of winter, the sere leaves and pods—some from the High Mountains—all sunlessness, joylessness seemed to the not-quite-yet-jarging newlyweds to have been lanced and drained to the Ocean for cleansing at the Equator. Neither had all through life been oblivious of the Poles. But they were unmindful of them now, as though the two hubs of the world, too, might someday soften and grow lovely and whisper the leafy prophecies of springtime. Such a resting-place, though, is born of searching fire, long since deep in green.

They followed the same improbable-looking directions Edward had followed, likewise finding them not to fail. They drew up onto the turf before the narrow stretch of ploughland, now sending up a little crop of millet.

Laurence came down from the verandah to welcome them, and Lavinia followed him. They all walked toward the house through a precinct of age-burnished rebirth. Even the liveoaks were dusted with new green, although never having lost an appreciable number of their older, darker leaves at a go. The banks of azaleas were in heavy bud. *Thank Goodness the things are no closer to actual bloom,* Lavinia said to herself. In the woods as well as in the garden, white-flowering dogwoods were first to catch the eye, seeming the most beautiful. And mysterious: No two had "come along" in the same degree. "It's just a matter of whose spirit dwells within the particular tree," Lavinia explained, and all of them were content to leave it at that.

Each of them felt from the first entirely comfortable together with the others, and—oddly—somewhat accustomed to each other.

Josh met them on the verandah steps. Out of courtesy to Thomas, he had waited to thank him again for his ministration, before leaving for Wilmington, merely, insofar as he knew, to spend Easter with Julie and her mother. The engagement had not yet been announced, but was about to be. And as in confidence, the happy tiding was divulged to Alenda and Thomas.

The hosts and their guests watched the cloud of dust sink slowly behind the roadster, as Josh followed his destiny toward and through the night.

When the visitors had got settled, all met on the front verandah for refreshments. It was a congenial party, everyone in a communicative frame of mind, and plenty of subjects for discussion.

Thomas, for example, wondered: "Did Mary know, when she first took up with Josh—if you'll forgive my asking—that he stood to inherit, as he does?"

Lavinia answered: "For one thing, your asking doesn't need forgiving... this is exactly as I hoped we could all be together. And, for another, when they 'took up with each other,' neither had any idea even what inheritance was." And she explained the connection that had brought them close as young children.

Meantime, Alenda was uncharacteristically quiet, but of course only Thomas noted it.

"Well, I must say," he resumed, "I have never known another young man who attracts such wholly agreeable and strikingly beautiful girls."

"What, besides the usual," Alenda managed to ask, "have you put into his drink, Laurence? I have known him to be crass, but not often, and never so blatantly."

"If he is drugged, Alenda, it is off those two girls. And I am equally intoxicated. By the way, Josh is going to Wilmington to meet Julie's mother… for the first time, believe it or not."

"He has met none of them? Her family?

"Do you know them?"

"I don't imagine anybody knows all of them. There are so many. But I know her mother very well—Julie's father was killed early in the War. Second World. Early in our part, I ought to've said. And I know a considerable number of her relatives." If only Thomas had thought to add: "Our families have been friends for a long time."

Now there hung, suspended in air, a question inevitable in the Southland of that day—inevitable, because it was (through error) considered to be of supreme importance. But for a little while, nobody seemed inclined to put it. All of them were tired, all at peace in the legendary quietude of Woodleigh, the cool fragrance from the woodland mixing seductively with the smells of the flooding marsh.

Alenda again broke her relative silence. "Lavinia?"

"Yes, Alenda?"

"Could I see over the house? Would you mind terribly?"

"Certainly, you may," she replied. "Anyway, we want you both to consider it your house, while you are here." She stood. "Let's go. Tell me where you'd like to start."

"It is grander, but it reminds me of my childhood home." Then, with Lavinia holding open the screened door, Alenda turned and said to Laurence: "Julie's and Josh's marriage will unite two of the proudest, loveliest families we know."

When inside the house, Alenda gave herself up to what had beckoned to her; on her earlier entrance, climb of stairs, freshening-up after the day's travel, then going immediately downstairs again; she had heard, but not replied. Something within must settle—either within the house, or within herself. She could not distinguish. Close identity with a house is more reckless than many would think.

She sat down in a straight chair that had been pulled up to the round table beneath the austere sixty-three branch candle-holder, as it hovered from the ceiling. She looked slowly around, at first as though lost, then as oriented. Lavinia said to her, "Would you tell me about where you grew up, and about the house there?"

"In Barbadoes. We grew sugar cane. Of course, everybody grew sugar cane, then. The name of our house was 'Windward,' as it faced the eastern coast. The Trade Winds blew upon us constantly, like a beast with no need to draw breath. But they brought in a varying climate. Just as everybody supposes, the Island, being tropical, lies mostly under bright, pleasant weather. Occasionally, it is cold, but not often.

"When we are struck by hurricanes—there is supposed to be some kind of cycle, I think, but, I think, too, that I didn't live there long enough to endure a complete one—there is Hell to pay. When one is a small child, it can seem exciting. Like an ambulance passing by. So long as you're not the one in the back whose heart has stopped beating. For example." Both laughed a little at this. Alenda appeared crestfallen, a thing few had ever seen.

"How long did you live there?"

"I was born there, in 1898. You can be sure I'm not fibbing about my age—1898 is too long ago! The idea was for me to go to University in England when I was sixteen or seventeen. But the War made that impossible. Instead, I eloped with an American I met in Bridgetown. My parents had already foreseen that I hadn't much future in Barbadoes, the man proved to be of good family, and there was some money.

"We returned immediately by aeroplane to America—the flight would have made the passage to Shangri-la in *The Far Horizon* seem soothing.

"But you asked me about the house, not about the story of my life. It was shaped like this one, smaller, but with the same way of attaching the siding-boards: Edge-on, not overlapping. My great grandfather, who had to import nearly all of the materials, insisted these boards fit together like modern-day floorboards."

"By means of tongues and grooves?"

"Yes. And over and over, through the years, the hurricanes left it standing, we thought because of this interlocking. It was a sparely furnished house, like yours, but most of the furnishings were light and lovely—refreshing touches of opulence in what was becoming a sleazy world. If you'll forgive the expression."

"I hope you and Thomas have some of them in New Brunswick—it can be sad to remember, sad not to."

"No. I have nothing from there. My parents died simultaneously and otherwise, too, somewhat mysteriously, in 1935. I think of the house as still standing on its sugar cane-filled plateau above the sea. But that is unlikely."

"Well, then. If you would like to see over this house, why not do it alone? It's entirely at your disposal. Mary Alice has gone home, and I will go back outside and try to forestall Laurence's dragging your husband through the rice fields."

"I accept your offer with gratitude; it is most thoughtful. And, Lavinia...."

"Yes?"

"It *is* sad to remember, and sad not to. Thank you."

Thomas was talking to Laurence about his nephew, his bride-to-be, and about her family. "Julie's mother used to live with her own mother and father, and younger sister Gillian. I would speak with Sarah regularly...but not face-to-face; she operated the telephone exchange in New Brunswick. We tried to be very cosmopolitan, each behaving as though the other were only a disembodied voice."

"And now, that's exactly what we are to each other—disembodied voices. Before long, there'll be no telephone operators at all."

"Well, Sarah certainly was one, and not a disembodied one, either. She was charmingly pretty when young, growing into real beauty. She met her husband, Halbert Whitman, at the pavilion on Wrightsville Beach—that's near us. They fell instantly, and I think very fundamentally, in love. They awakened Sarah's parents at six o'clock in the morning, after singing and dancing together all the night through, to say they were going to marry. A license was obtained somehow, because it was wartime, and by ten o'clock the deed was done."

"One of the truly romantic stories from that era."

"And one of the most tragic. They had less than a month together, before Hal shipped out. The transport was torpedoed while in convoy. Hal was killed.

"But, do you know, Sarah has told me many years afterward that so far as she is concerned she had—even at that—had the best of everything! She has not married again. She went to nursing school, then, to help with the war-effort. Graduated too late, though."

"Did she ever practice nursing?"

"She does, still." The men looked again over the marsh to the pine forest, now a tawny ribbon in the blue dusk. "I believe," Thomas added, "that it is necessary for her to work."

Lavinia came outside. "Alenda is touring the house by herself. That way, she can poke about wherever she feels inclined to...open doors, drawers, pick things up to look at...all that. But we did have a talk about the two houses, especially hers, in Barbados. Laurence, it was called 'Windward,' because it was on the Island's eastern coast, facing the Trade Winds. Isn't that charming...evocative?"

"It is. And Barbados is, I think—Thomas, isn't it?—the easternmost of the Lesser Antilles."

"I think so. I do know for sure that hurricanes were…presumably still are…slamming into it all the time."

"But our conversation kept returning to her life—facts of it, not her impressions or emotions. So I sent her off alone, because I felt there were memories she had let fall, and now wished to gather up."

"I'm very glad you did that. I've known her for thirty years. Now I've married her. She was a close friend, a confidante, of my first wife's. Grace. And still, her past is largely a mystery to me." An owl could be heard, speaking in the wood. His call seemed to intensify the stillness around them rather than break it. "I think that is because a lot of it is a mystery to herself."

"She told me about the death of her mother and father. Is that what you mean?"

"That, and other things."

"By now," Lavinia said, "she may want company. She may have questions. She may have thought of things that want telling." She got up, and went back into the house.

Both Laurence and Thomas heartily enjoyed their whisky, in company. More, if the company did not include their wives. They spoke a little further about Julie's families. Then about Josh's. Thomas intended to let Laurence pass on about the parents…*But they aren't the parents…* whatever he might choose. In this connection, Thomas said: "I'll meet your sister, won't I?"

"Oh, yes!"

"And her husband."

"Tomorrow at dinner."

"What sort of man, though, was your sister's first husband? If I may know."

"Parker Jones. Alina and Josh loved him very much. So did I. His family were obviously cultivated gentlefolk, from New England. They were all gone by the time we knew him. He was quiet, but very emotional on a deep level, like the water-table when it rushes underneath us. Like carp in a garden pond in autumn, when they reach for the lowest depth; amber themselves, dark as the water has become. But his feelings were stronger, more closely controlled, than the arabesque a pond-carp's tail makes at the end of an exuberant dash. Complete sureness about things, as he understood them, or had formulated them; complete satisfaction with his understanding." This speech had brought about near-total stillness. "Otherwise, he'd alter the way of his understanding, never with any fuss.

"He'd come to me and say: 'Rennie, I do not think 'X' can be so. It's not consistent with 'Y.' The 'Y' would be something he considered essentially valid. But he might change that, too. In the meantime, though, he could be both confident and ready to be dissuaded."

Laurence replenished their drinks. "Parker's dead, you know. Not divorced from Alina, whom he widowed. None of us could have let him leave us under any other circumstance."

"He had a sense of humor, to go with that gravity?"

"The keenest."

"What kind of thing would he take so much thought over?"

"Anything. Whether ash were better for an axe-handle; whether Evil existed or not."

"Better than what?"

"What? Oh; than beech."

"And to go with it, a concern about metaphysical matters?"

"An overwhelming concern. He said to me once that some things were for use during the day, and other things were for use at the end of the day. He believed our life here made a difference—at the end of the day, or when we looked into mirrors to take stock of ourselves."

"Interesting about Evil."

"Yes, it is. And odd."

"How do you mean, 'Odd'"?

"He and I carried on an unusual dialogue on that subject. Our wives were intermediaries, without knowing it. He and I never spoke much about these things face-to-face, and we really didn't mean, I think, to discuss metaphysical things together at all. Other than in little clipped observations.

"An example will make it clearer. Lavinia told me that Alina had told her this—or something like it—that she had got from Parker: He didn't accept any doctrine of original sin, but nevertheless he felt that mankind stood in need of redemption. A very specific kind of redemption; not that which the Church teaches."

"Jesus!"

"What is the matter?"

"Here you are my guest, only weeks retired from pastoral duty, and I'm trying to make you 'talk shop.'"

"My dear Laurence! If you suppose that the things you're saying constitute 'talking shop,' then you are very much mistaken. At least with regard to my Shop. The phrase 'not that which the Church teaches' is music to my ears. At one time I became so fed-up with orthodoxy, burdened as it is with all its limitations, that I invented a Biblical—or Biblical-like—parable. I actually passed it off as Holy Scripture, and I did it from the pulpit!"

"I wish I could have been there. Except that I wouldn't have recognized it as bogus."

"I finally got caught, too, but it wasn't until ten or fifteen years afterward. I was already about to retire when the cat got out of the bag. So to say. It was too late for anybody to do anything about it; besides, my parishioners were uncommonly faithful to me."

"That comes as no surprise."

"Thank you. In fact, two rather close friends were the ones to figure it out."

"How did they take it? Once they had figured it out."

"Well, not being very adventurous folk, they thought I had *dépassé les bornes*, as you French say."

"I am only of French ancestry."

"Well, with a middle name like *des Champs-Locuplétisis*, I'd play it up for all it's worth."

"You admire the French?"

"The *French* are a little hard to admire, but I do admire *France*. So these people, looking upon my 'work' as they did, first began to ask everybody we all knew whether I were 'all right.'"

"As, of course, you were."

"As much so as I've ever been; at any rate, the thing had been put over on all of them years and years before. But I've said that."

"How did it end? Or has it ended?"

"They finally let their discovery be known to the Senior Warden. The Senior Warden happened to be my closest friend, and he had got quite interested in the fake passage anyway. The Bishop had known about it almost from the beginning."

"How did he find out about it? But perhaps I oughtn't to be asking all these questions."

"I told him, that's how; he is an old seminary buddy. But, do, please, ask away. You'd be welcome to, anyway...no holds barred in metaphysical discourse. But this isn't very metaphysical, is it....?"

"What? Oh, yes, please, if it's not too much trouble, and if you're going to join me. Thank you so much. As it is, though, the parable—It's called 'The Parable of the Two Lamps.' Very Holy-Writsky, don't you think?"

"Eminently."

"Where was I? You see, I am in fact *not* all right. I'm losing my mind. However, no more precipitately, so far as I can tell, than anybody else, and it has been coming on gradually for years. My old friend the bishop can no longer say the Lord's Prayer by heart! Think of that! Well, but the business about the Parable was the most fun I had in all my career. So I very much enjoy talking about it.

" But please do go on about your brother-in-law." And then the secrets

Thomas knew almost overcame him. Still, the fresh drink was helping to smooth things over.

"He didn't simply reject the notion of original sin.

"He told my sister—and Alina doesn't argue with much, but never with *anything* Parker laid down—that sin would require the existence of evil, which he thought not possible."

"He really did think the existence of Evil to be impossible?"

"He did."

"He was well-advised to say so only to his wife."

"Why is that?"

"I once, within a homily, told an entire congregation of the faithful that evil doesn't exist. Are you familiar with the American term 'clobbered'?"

"Well, yes; and you do know that I'm an American myself? So many people in this Country seem to be."

"Yes, of course. So am I, for that matter, but my mother was English. Oh, dear. I do hope most of this is due to the whiskey."

"I'm thure it is, Thomas. Whisky does strange things to people."

"I was clobbered, almost. And by my own flock! I simply wasn't the *bonus pastor* that day."

"Parker started from the 'man's first disobedience, and the fruit/ Of that forbidden tree' business." Thomas was suddenly sobered; this condition had been threatening him, already. "I forget just how it went, but Parker told my sister that such a thing would imply either that God had created the world using imperfect components or had built it according to a faulty design. He said either was impossible.

"So I told Lavinia there was a broader idea of evil than just the snake and the arple, and I wondered how Parker felt that bore upon his conception of things. Because I had thought, really since boyhood, that God, being omnipotent, would destroy evil, if it existed at all. And now I have refined that opinion—but not recanted from it.

"Later on, I found out—through the usual channel—that Parker thought that, too. Almost that. But he really felt that there never could have been any evil in the first place."

"I have myself come to think there can't have, because, in Plato we realize that here we are only becoming—not being. Just working ourselves up to it."

"In the realm of eternity and pure idea."

"You find Plato cogent on the point?"

"Totally. But you can wring a little extra conviction from Plotinus."

"I've heard that. I must hurry, if I'm to digest Plotinus. Already, there can be no more question of reading him in the Greek—for me."

"Nor for me. I studied a little Greek in school, and I've since tried to teach myself more. But it won't work—not for me, either, and decidedly not if it's a question of Plotinus."

"For a long time I thought the Godhead lived in that realm we've mentioned. Purely in Being. But no sooner had I got used to that than I found out (through your Plotinus) that Plato considered the Godhead, Idea of Good, *ens perfectissimum*—all that, however it should be thought of—to dwell *beyond* Being. I checked back, and it's so. He did."

"I'm frankly amazed!"

"By what?"

"By what we've both gone through to get where we are. And most people would think we haven't got anywhere at all, I'd bet."

"Parker knew all about this, too; I think he came to equate Good with Being. And so he went on to conclude, I'm pretty sure, that hypothetical Evil would match up with not-being. Thus he thought there could be no evil."

"I wish the three of us could have—Oh, thank you very much; we'd better take care, though—got together to talk it over. These are the most important of all considerations…by the way, don't you think those arrangements of stars ought to be called 'considerations' instead of 'constellations?' '*Sidus*' is so splendid, whereas '*stella*' has unsatisfactory undertones, like 'parlor.' Perhaps not [Laurence, in unusual inversion, knew 'little Greek and lesse Latin,']…, and yet they are nearly universally passed over."

"At the end of the day, I should certainly be nowhere without them."

"I mentioned that I once tried to convince my parishioners that evil does not exist; further, I proposed that the dreadful things that happen to us are merely degrees of want of Good."

"And they took it—how?"

"Badly."

"I don't wonder."

"Alenda had read over the draft. That led her to compose an epitaph for me. She asked me after my next effort, which she had only heard about, whether I were familiar with the practice of 'tarring and feathering,' just as I asked whether you were familiar with the term 'clobbered.'"

"Well, here come the huntresses." Loud, uninterrupted, entirely mirthful laughter could be heard coming from the hallway, drifting out through the screened door, and presently Alenda and Lavinia came out onto the verandah, scarcely finding opportunity for speech or breath. For this is what had happened: Lavinia had found Alenda looking out from the window at the end of the upstairs hallway. She seemed sorrowful. So Lavinia had decided to guide her through the house. And she told some of the little stories that connected it to American Colonial history.

During their passage from room to room, beneath the gallery that carried the stair landing across the hallway, wonderment at views from the upper windows, Alenda had continued rather quiet. When they reached the Kitchen House, she sat down at the central table, put her face into her hands, and wept. But just briefly.

Remarkably, Lavinia had said, "You need a good, stiff drink." (Momentarily rousing in Alenda the horrible possibility that she was about to say, "You need a nice cup of tea." For as a girl, Alenda had always waited until the maid had gone out, and emptied her early tea through a window.)

Lavinia returned with two good, stiff drinks, and Alenda said: "Thank you. I have always tried to tell myself that the place, as I knew it, ceased to exist when I left it. But it has arisen in my thoughts in mordantly beautiful detail. I'll tell you tomorrow."

"Is the land where it stands—or stood—still in your family?"

"No. And God knows what has become of it."

But while they were on the subject of houses, Alenda decided to reveal her suspicions about "Woodleigh House," noted at the head of Lavinia's letter to Thomas. "We always said Such-and-Such 'Place,' or So-and-So 'Hall.'"

"Much more dignified."

"Much more pretentious." By the time she had got to the part about tuberculosis sanitarium and insane asylum, both women were shrieking with laughter. If they hadn't been away off in the Kitchen House, their husbands would have come running. Instead the ladies poured two more good, stiff drinks and went to join the gentlemen on the verandah. And when all had been made clear (not counting the existence, or not, of Evil, and for certain excepting the subject of natural parentage), the four began to speak of arrangements for the next day, which was Easter Sunday.

"We go to church at a small, very old foundation. It is one of three served by a single priest; he normally conducts a service at each, nearly every Sunday, and when he cannot, all three parishes have platoons of layreaders who can read Morning Prayer, if all else fails."

"This year, though," Laurence put in, "all else has failed. One of Mr. Sallopp's churches is Old Sheldon Parish. It is possible you have heard of it; for its ruin is large, it is reputed to have been very magnificent when intact, and it has some claims to fame, which I forget. Only a ruin. But with devoted parishioners.

"The vestry there have had a firm of architects and a pack of 'archaeologists' who are really primarily decorators, research and draw up a plan for rebuilding. So they have invited all three parishes to join in an unveiling of the designs, and a festival service. To raise money, of course."

"Of course," Thomas agreed.

"*Laurence!*" Turning to the others, Lavinia announced: "But we shall be going to our own church; a friend of some parishioners, a retired Presbyterian clergyman, has graciously offered to conduct a simple service for us. Of course, he will not be able to celebrate the Holy Eucharist."

"That would be available here at Woodleigh."

"How generous of you, Thomas. We accept."

"Really," the reprobate Laurence continued, "I hate to miss the Service at Sheldon, in a way. They're going to have a harpsichord and a *portativ*. The noise from the generator will certainly drown the notes of the harpsichord, if not of the organ."

Alenda asked: "Are you a musician yourself, Laurence?"

Brightly, uncharacteristically maliciously, Lavinia overrode his immediate demurrals with: "More than that! He is a composer of opera!"

On Easter morning, Lavinia and Laurence went to church, far out in the countryside. When they arrived, Alina and Bob had already got there and were waiting for them in the Family pew.

This was the same place where Lavinia had once come in distress, if not terror, to ask God to take away her "reproach among men," to render her fertile, to let her bear a child. Even if—She had said this in her heart, in despair of soul and possibly in some derangement of mind—it meant she must survive to look upon the death of that child. The greatest joy, sought at once with the deepest sorrow.

But all that was well over. Even the tiny blight of envy she had noted upon the green leaf of her friendship with Alina, who could bear a child, had been put by, years before she had learned—for she had learned it only very recently—that Alina was herself barren. That is to say, physiologically barren, for outwardly she appeared as foetant as the Earth itself.

Sunlight filled the little building on this Day; the Altar Guild had outdone themselves, employing ingenuity wherever there had occurred a dearth of flowers and greening sprays and trails. The sacred furniture was covered in white, worked all through with symbols and vignettes in gold thread. Some of this was Lavinia's own work. Some of it was Alina's, some Miss Allie's.

The Strikestraws had remained at Woodleigh. Thomas had bits of consecrating to perform; Alenda sat in the sunshine and began to piece her life together, starting at the beginning, not at the end of the day of the span of man's years.

Away, away in Wilmington, Josh Jones and Sarah Whitman were full of happiness, because each had found great liking for the other. Josh had been told that after Church—both sides of Julie's family were Presbyterians, and all of them considered being Presbyterian of the utmost importance, although few ever grasped the point of attending Church services—they would be going to Julie's Grandmother Elkin for Easter Dinner. Josh had not, however, been told that the entire clan—churchgoers and non-churchgoers—would be on hand as well.

But mother and daughter were uncommonly sagacious and had not told any of the family that Josh would himself be there, either, and neither of them had the slightest intention of introducing him as Julie's fiancé. However, Julie, from first being given it, had not yet worn the ring Josh had presented to her. It was of restrained—or partially restrained—magnificence. Today, she put it on. An emerald with diamonds all around it. As they walked the three blocks to the church, the precious stones seemed to Julie to become a little heavier and a lot bigger with every step they took.

Meantime, the service was beginning for the Ashfields and most of their fellows, although a few had defected to take in the spectacle at Old Sheldon. The gracious stand-in minister appeared of a sudden upon the chancel step. He wore an academic gown, black, as most of them are, with the three velvet doctoral bars on each fluid sleeve.

"Probably just an honorary degree," Laurence whispered to his wife, who pretended not to hear.

The cleric held up both arms, and seemed to shout: "Please stand, and let us sing, 'Christ the Lord is ris'n today'!"

Laurence bent again and whispered: "What happened to 'Jesus Christ is risen today'?"

"Laurence, you are behaving like a petulant child. I think the two hymns are very much the same." But Lavinia was beginning to lose patience herself. If there's one thing Episcopalians know—or knew at that time—it was when to stand, when to kneel, and when to sit. Bob attempted to appear impassive. Alina stared at the little vaults in the ceiling, thinking about where the curves might end if produced.

Under ordinary circumstances, the Presbyterian service consisted of an ample and often wide-ranging "Pastoral Prayer," and the sermon, with filler at the beginning, in between, and at the end, this consisting of hymnody, the giving of alms, announcements of various kinds, and a benediction straight out of the Old Testament, there being nothing wrong with that…in itself. Only, it had no Christian flavor about it. And this was the most Christian Holy Day of all.

At least there was no possibility of including that Sect's one other regular feature, it being a Production Number by the choir, known as the 'offertory anthem,' a precocious form of sacred entertainment in return for which the auditors were expected to part with a bit of lucre.

The Pastoral Prayer had left many in the congregation believing themselves unlikely to withstand the sermon, but they were destined for a pleasant surprise, or for a surprise. Now, once again the minister raised his arms, saying as he did so, "Please stand, and let us sing...."

Suddenly, Lavinia turned to her husband: "*A bat*! That's what it is. He looks like an immense bat!"

Upon entering the church, the worshippers had been handed special service-bulletins, and it was a good thing. They were double-folded; on the obverse of the first leaf, one saw this lurid device: Upon a purple ground-cloth lay a Bible, open, over which had been set a fistful of Easter lilies (*Lilium regale*). Underneath, in blackletter, but not black blackletter, was written, "He is Risen!" and athwart the whole fell the shadow of a Cross. Inside this pamphlet, in the order of service, the sermon was given a title: "The Stone is Gone!" The delivery, by contrast to the insipid and interminable prayer, was spry; the title-phrase was used repeatedly, "gone" rhyming with "stone." Could it have been intended as a kind of mnemonic? No one knew.

The disquisition was full of arcane material. It had to have been arcane, because nobody could make head nor tail of it. The peroration concluded with the loud command, given with forefinger and bat-wing pointing to the church door: "Now, go forth to behold an EMPTY TOMB!" An incredulous hush ensued. Then the small remainder of the service got underway, and finally it was all over.

They walked out of the church, Lavinia—never before exposed to anything of this kind—staring vitreously ahead, going right past the clergyman in the narthex without batting an eye. She walked straight to their car and got inside.

Laurence exchanged some Risen-indeed's, spoke briefly with the Barringtons, then went to the car and began the drive back toward Woodleigh. Halfway home, Lavinia said abruptly. "Stop the car. I heard a trumpet."

"I didn't hear one."

"Well, I did. Stop the car."

He stopped, and she got out. There were fields all around them, no one to see. Lavinia listened. "There! There it went again!" So Laurence got out, too, and they both listened. Finally, Laurence said, "I don't hear anything."

"I don't hear it either, not anymore." They drove home in silence. In silence, for a few minutes, they hesitated inside the parked car.

Then Laurence said: "We all have our little aberrances, Lavinia. That will teach you to ridicule *Il Struggietore*."

Laurence had pulled up to the front steps; Alenda and Thomas were waiting for them upon the verandah, but waiting without impatience. As they came up the steps, Thomas asked the Ashfields how they had found the service, but neither could think what to say. "Well, at any rate, The Lord is risen."

And they all answered, "He is risen indeed; *Alleluia!*" And this made them feel better, at one with the Holy Catholic Church the world over.

Laurence went into the house. The others sat rocking lazily in heavy chairs with unnumbered coats of cracked and crazed dark-green paint, enjoying the peculiar silvery luminence of late morning in early spring. Lavinia was preoccupied; not upset, she told herself; she merely wondered what had happened, and why.

Laurence came out again carrying a tray with four glasses. "I've prepared gin-and-tonics for the ladies. For you and me, Thomas, I have gone all-out and made a drink from a formula passed down through generations of my family. In honor of the Day, I have called it the 'Anastasia Special.'" Thomas's heart sank as he took the tumbler, tightly wrapped in its linen napkin, the way bartenders at country clubs used to do it.

For her part, Lavinia, who could not recall even so much as hearing of the ancient family recipe, began to think that possibly, even though she couldn't put her finger on the precipitating factor, something had pushed her over the edge.

Thomas set his drink down gingerly, and talked about the *anástasis,* the Resurrection. "In spite of things you hear, during modern times it has not been known to occur. In Christian circles, Christ as the Lord of Life cannot be bound by death. If Jesus's Resurrection were the only instance of it, I think we could work better from that idea. However, to leave the Old Testament aside, it happened also in the case of Lazarus."

To everyone's surprise, Alenda said: "Yes, but Jesus brought that about. I grant you, the Scripture makes it noisomely clear that Lazarus was definitely dead. And subsequently, he was definitely alive. But at the agency and command of Jesus."

"Still the Lord of Life. But at the moment of Jesus's death on the Cross, 'Many bodies of the saints which slept arose.'"

"...Connecting resurrection with Jesus's death, it would appear. I wonder who ran that part in?" Alenda had recovered her usual manner. And appearance: Oddly lovely, evidently ready for anything diverting. She was for once not wearing black—not on Easter Day—but white, which drew attention for the first time, or for the first time in a long time, to the wonderful olive tone of her skin. She did, however, have on a black sash, embroidered in vivid purple. "From what Thomas leads me to understand, though," she added, brandishing her gin-and-tonic, "almost nothing was past believing in the First Century. No doubt the author—or the author of this tradition—thought that having the dead get up and walk about town would contribute to a sort of *Dies Irae* mood. Quite suitable, I should think, for Good Friday."

But they all felt inwardly that they were speaking of Scriptural avowal, and not about events. Though it hardly mattered to them—they felt, each in some unspecified way, that life would be replayed; that death would fold after one night, due to unfavorable reviews.

By this time, Thomas had calculated he could defer drinking the Anastasia Special no longer. He tasted it, and found it quite palatable. So of Laurence he asked: "This is very agreeable. What is in it?"

"Well, soda water."

"And?"

"Scotch whisky."

"Nothing else?"

"No."

"That would account for it, then."

Now Alina and Bob arrived. Thomas had been making himself important by worrying over the dramatic irony his meeting them would entail.

However, by the time introductions and greetings had been completed, by the time they had by universal consent agreed that the Morning's service would not be spoken of, Thomas was so much under Alina's spell that all else vanished for a while from his thoughts.

He plucked her drink from the waiter Laurence bore, forgetting his own replenished Anastasia Special, and offered it to her with ceremony. It was how you treated a goddess. He had learned a lot about goddesses from *Les pêcheures de perles*. And a little more while at seminary, but not from operas.

They fell easily into conversation. "How is your son? Fully recovered, I hope. He seemed quite fit when I saw him last evening."

"He's doing very well, thank you Canon; and he is going to be married! We are all rather wild with excitement, but we have to contain ourselves—or try to—since Josh is just now meeting Julie's family...He had to get well first...but of course, you know them I expect? Juliana Whitman?"

"I do; and I don't think you could find a lovelier girl or better people anywhere. I've known Julie's mother longest; she is a gallant woman. Since her husband's very untimely death, she has put herself through nursing school, and then—without accepting a penny to help—did the same for Julie. But only after having sent her first through all four years of college."

"How remarkable! I should never have been able to do anything like that for Josh, except that...things must be different for her and me."

"I'm sure, if it had been necessary, that you would have done the same—the equivalent, rather. I must say, Josh seems a fine young man, as it is…."

"You'd have said nothing of the sort if you'd met him three or four months ago. He was like a whipped dog. You can imagine why: His girl fell in love with your grandson, Edward. And now…."

"Yes, now they've got engaged, too, and will be married in May. And Josh is going to be Best Man, which I find improbable, but wonderful."

And then, essaying an offhand attitude—difficult for a man who for all the years of his life had yet to be offhand about anything—he said, following a little silence, which he thought would strengthen the illusion but proved instead dismally artificial: "How old a man is your son, now, to be taking a wife?"

"Old enough to have taken one sooner. Except that if he had, it wouldn't have been Julie."

"You all approve?"

"I do. And I'm the Mother of the Groom."

Are you, indeed?

"The others?"

"I'm merely being facetious. We all expect to love her. But we've just been introduced—no more."

"Josh began his journey to this world while you and Mr. Jones were living in New York, I understand. Was he born in New York?"

"I don't know where he was born; Parker and I adopted him."

Mary Alice came out and summoned Laurence to the telephone. He went in, and Lavinia introduced Mary Alice to the Strikestraws. Then she returned to her duties. Which included keeping an eye upon Yukoneta, who, since she had no plans for the weekend, had come to Woodleigh to lend a hand. She leant it, for the most part, to a little refreshment she had brought along, "To honor the Master's overcoming sin and death."

It was Josh who had telephoned. "Uncle Laurence, there must be a hundred people here! I really don't know what I'm supposed to do."

"Where are you?"

"At Julie's Grandmother's house."

"Do you know why you were invited there?"

"For Easter dinner, I thought."

"Has anything specific made you think you were invited there for anything else?"

"No, Sir."

"Then, what you're supposed to do is have dinner."

"And that's all?"

"I should think so."

"Thanks so much, Uncle Laurence! I've got to dash. I'll call back later, to wish everyone a happy Easter!" And he hung up the telephone.

This reassurance from his Uncle changed everything. Josh had begun to get "nervous" about being a bridegroom-elect, and had come to think that he must be one actively and at all times. Relieved of that burden, he went to find Julie and her mother, and they began to serve themselves from the buffet.

There were considerably fewer than a hundred people at old Mrs. Elkin's, but it was true there were a lot. Tables had been set up everywhere. There was at least one candle burning on even the smallest folding card-table (disguised under napery), because it was Easter.

In the middle of the feast, one of Julie's great aunts, and at that by marriage, registered from across the rooms, as Julie was laying down a fork, a ray of brilliant green, a flash of green light.

When dinner ended, this lady mentioned Julie's ring to several dozen of her nearest table-companions. Someone went for the newspaper and found the modest announcement. After that, all was changed. To the extent that Josh was prepared to be driven away even if in a rat-drawn pumpkin. The women bore in on Sarah, the girls all had to see the ring, and at once. Julie's male cousins and younger uncles procured after-dinner drinks and wandered outside. A couple of them got Josh in tow. In small groups of one other or two, as they wandered about the garden, smoking, drinking, talking, listening, watching, they "shook Josh down," he barely realizing it. All concurred: He was a man, and a good man.

There came toasting and joyousness. The girls all said they knew exactly what Julie meant about Josh's eyes, and everybody asked hundreds of questions to which there were not yet answers. The young men stayed until dusk, became quite jolly, and decided to hold an Easter egg hunt. This marked the official end of the festivities.

The next morning at breakfast, a day off duty for the two Angels of Mercy, Josh told his ladies that he loved Julie's families and was eager to become a member of each one.

At Woodleigh, before Easter dinner at three o'clock, Thomas gave them what he called "battlefield Communion," as they knelt on sofa-cushions. The feast was served in the dining-room, the traditional roast leg of lamb, accompanied by all the things the Earth bears first, once she begins to bear. Afterward, they went directly into the East Room to have coffee. They had all rather anticipated Josh's second telephone call, but it never came. None of them was surprised. Possibly inauspiciously, Bob quoted: "Your son's your son till he takes a wife...."

At first, the rest were a little sorry for Alina; for, if she had not borne Josh, yet nevertheless she had reared him from the day next after his birth. Recollection of those early days was bound to make her think of Parker, her companion in the boy's upbringing. The dining room suddenly felt the shadow as of a stone and seal across the archway into the entrance hall, where afternoon light had been pouring in.

Alina herself felt nothing but delight, and gratitude that her son would not have to journey on through life alone. "Lavinia, we must light the candles. It's Easter! My boy is engaged to be married with one of the loveliest girls I've ever met. We must toast the couple!"

Easter fire sprang up everywhere. Easter joy abounded. Josh had returned not only from the "sickness unto death," but from a dark, cold, close place. From asystolë, cardiac standstill. By what Power he had been brought forth, none of them knew...not specifically; but all of them really did know, each in his way.

The ladies all wanted to begin to plan the wedding, but knew they must refrain. The men walked about outside in The Circle, Thomas and Laurence with rapt interest in learning from Bob all the particulars of Josh's injury. "I think," Bob finished, "he should have formal cognitive-function testing, but I can't find it in myself to bring it up to Alina."

"Why not bring it up to Juliana, after they're married. Then she will be his next of kin. Or talk to them both about it."

"Yes. I will. It's their business, and there's little to be done about it, anyway." Alina came down the verandah steps, saying: "Bobby, time to go home. We must begin living just the two of us together."

"That ought to be agreeable."

"Yes, it ought. And it will. What about Connie? How is she to get back?"

"'The God of peace, who brought again from the dead our Lord Jesus Christ' will, I'm sure, help us find a way."

"My God!" Alenda said. "Will it have come to that? I mean, she won't have.... Oh, never mind!"

After the Barringtons had driven away—they were all to be together again later in the sojourn—Laurence asked his bride (He thought of Lavinia that way, and sometimes he called her that): "Have you and Alenda any plans for the rest of the afternoon?"

"We do have, in fact, now you ask. Alenda is going to tell me about Barbados, her home there, her life there."

"Good. Thomas, why don't we have a walk, a long one. Along the paths Josh and his father used to follow."

"Wonderful idea! And you can finish telling me about redemption."

When the men had got well out of hearing, Lavinia said: "*Laurence* is going to tell *Thomas* about redemption!"

"I can't see why he shouldn't."

"At least he won't be dragging him through the rice fields."

The sun was beginning to sink; the appeased light seemed prematurely to fulfill the promises of later spring. For a while, Thomas and Laurence spoke only a little—the afternoon was ravishing. Moreover, each man was preoccupied with something he had determined to talk about to the other.

Thomas began: "Are these, then, the places Josh and his father haunted?"

"Yes. These and a lot of other ones. Primarily, they liked to be together. Secondarily, they liked walking through the woodlands together, naming the plants and trees. Often—all the time—they came back to some specimen, bringing me along to identify it. I'm not sure why they thought I could. But most times I knew either the, or a, common name, or the taxonomic one. They were particularly glad of those. Afterward, Josh would use them in casual conversation for weeks." Again they fell silent, Thomas was inclined to ask some of the names himself. But he didn't.

"I do hope you'll be willing to tell me about Mr. Jones's unorthodox view of redemption."

"I mean to. Last night I found myself trying to remember all I could about it, just in order to be able to give his thoughts the way he thought them." They walked on. "But, may I tell you something else about him first? About Parker?"

"Of course."

"It's inconsequential. But I've wanted to recount it to someone, sometime. There are not many seemly candidates."

"I'm honored to be chosen."

"I told you, I think, that I was very fond of Parker myself."

"You said you loved him."

"I did, and there came a time when I wondered whether I loved him in an unsuitable way."

"There is not an unsuitable way to love."

"Even so, I began to think my happiness when he came in, or my pang when he went out were other than as they should have been. It worried me."

"I've just said there is no unsuitable way to love.The circumstances, of course, can be awkward. And lust is nearly always a mistake, but you are not talking about that. Besides, I don't recognize any sexual perversion, except deliberate celibacy."

"I need never have been concerned about it, though...."

"No."

"...And resolving the thing proved as 'easy as falling off a log;' it was brought about by exactly that—falling off a log."

"Who fell off?"

"We both did. And you and I are coming to the log we fell from, just beyond that *Ilex vomitoria* up ahead. I have never seen one grow to that size this far inland; Little John was ecstatic over that name. Is this beginning to bore you?" For those desperate to disclose are often anxious of the attentiveness of their listeners.

"Even if it were, I should have you go on. It is apparent that what you have to say matters."

"Only to me."

"Then it matters to me, too."

"We three had been on a rather long expedition, so we sat down on the log to catch our breath. Josh decided right off to go on the rest of the way home. As Parker and I were sitting there, talking of nothing important, a rather dismal-looking and large insect came buzzing up and alit on the back of the shoulder of his coat. I told him to keep still; I would brush it off. But I leant back too far and started to fall. Parker put out his arm to steady me. But he lost his balance, and we both fell backward and onto one of each other's arms. Our knees were still crooked up on the log. It must have been ridiculous to see."

By now Thomas and Laurence had got to the place and themselves sat down.

"Our arms were pinned beneath each other. When we could stop laughing, Parker said: "We have to put our free arms over each other, and push ourselves up a bit, to get our other arms loose." And that is what we did. But it brought us breast-to-breast.

"He held me tightly for a second and said, 'Ah, Rennie.' We got disentangled, and back up onto the log. And all my misgivings had disappeared."

"Could you tell why?"

"He had hugged me, and called me 'Rennie,' which he rarely did. And I realized that all I really wanted to know was that Parker liked me better than any of his other friends. And now I knew he probably did. All along, that's all I'd wanted. But it does sound like a kind of jealousy."

"May be. Anyway, I'm glad you told me. I think you weren't quite finished with fretting over it. You should be now, though, because that kind of thing is natural, normal, and ubiquitous, if not universal. I know from speaking with hundreds of parishioners. Over what seem like hundreds of years, I may say."

"Good...good. Now, before it gets too late—for us to get over there and back—I want to show you the spot where your grandson saved my nephew from drowning."

'My grandson, your nephew.'

They walked farther, saying nothing, until they could feel a coolness that Laurence knew came on gentle breezes off the River. Thomas said, then: "I am glad we aren't having to talk only about trivial matters."

"Why might we have to?"

"Just that I've found that it's as much as most people wish to get involved in, with strangers."

"First, I don't consider you a stranger. Besides, a lot of people really aren't able to talk about very much more."

"No. I'm sorry to say, they are not. As to our not being strangers to each other, what should you think if you discovered that we were kinsmen?"

"I'd be surprised, of course. But, of course, pleased."

"It is good of you to say so." They walked along some way, until they saw glinting water, barred among the treetrunks, the surface of that New World River without Kindred. "I know we must not be too late getting back.

"But I have learned a story. At first, I thought I wouldn't tell it; I left the barest of particulars sealed in an envelope. I thought Edward could open it someday. But now that won't work. Alina has 'scooped' me regarding a part of it, but there is more. And I find I must relate it all.

"And, yes, I am rambling. And I don't doubt a spot of dottiness has crept in. But, unless I take a once-upon-a-time approach, I shall not be able to make it much clearer."

"Do you mind sitting down on the dock?"

"Not at all. Is this the river Josh nearly drowned in?"

"Yes."

"It would have been an even greater loss than we thought."

But this time Laurence answered nothing; he only looked with requiring eyes. Thomas began: "My son's father-in-law was a snob. And the '*sine*' was orders beyond the '*nobilitate*.' Not a charitable thing for me to say, but the simple truth, nonetheless. His daughter found herself pregnant. Bunny—well, someone you once knew slightly, didn't Edward tell me? Bunny Singleton— took the whole problem upon himself. Nobody, nobody at all knew about it otherwise, not even the girl's mother. Bunny, being what he was, insisted that the adoptive parents be socially impeccable. He also insisted—and only Bunny could be this great a fool—insisted also that the natural father be someone socially impeccable. You'd think he'd realize the futility of that, but

Bunny was unique." Thomas noted that Laurence was not looking at him as he listened, but into the dregs-dark water.

"All went well, discounting how hard the girl was on herself about it. But she recovered with time, met Robert, and they married, just as we were getting into the War.

"My son, who was a Naval Lieutenant, once when at home on leave, after they had got married, told me all this. He defended her to me—needlessly—and said she knew without question who the father was; that the conception had occurred through isolated impulsiveness."

Laurence had laid his face in his hands. He said: "Your son was quite right. Anne was the most virtuous of women." Staring into the tar-dark water. But a feeble or wavering light, a sheen, a shimmer, as perhaps of crystalline kin to unwrought Rheingold, was just now to be seen in the depths, although the tremulous play of earlier strokes of sunlight had flown.

"One day, after both Anne and Robert were gone, after even Grace—my first wife—was gone, I became beset by determination to find out who my grandson's half-brother or -sister was. It is still, and will always be, a tarnish on the mirror on my soul the cruel means I employed to wring those names from the pitiful wreck Bunny had got by then to be. And in the end, when nothing had intimidated him, including the barrel of a revolver…for what had he to fear in his extremity?…a last-ditch appeal to his snobbery had effect.

"He told me the names of the father and of the adoptive parents. I recognized none. I wrote them down, and put them away for Edward, in case he might come to wish to pursue the matter.

"Then Bunny asked me to shoot him.

"Then he asked me to bless him."

They set out upon the trek back to Woodleigh. Laurence asked—for in his darkened heart glowed yet an "ember furled in flame"; had taken this away with him from the depths when they had left Blackwater behind—"What has happened to revive those names?"

"Your wife wrote to me soon after Edward's visit here for the deer-shoot. In her letter she mentioned your nephew, Josh Jones, his mother, Alina Barrington, who, I assumed, was at one time Alina Jones. She also mentioned you by your Christian name, and of course I knew the surname. The three names caused something to stir in my memory, so I went back to the letter I had left for Edward."

Having got to this point, neither man seemed to feel that he could any longer grapple with the matter, not judiciously. Laurence had at several times made conjectures. But he could not get them all to fit together. Thomas had found that there was no one to whom he could tell his story whom he would not hurt by doing so. He had delayed. But now the dice were cast.

Thomas: "I had supposed it would come as a surprise to you to learn that Josh had been adopted."

Laurence: "Three months ago, it would have. But in some kind of transport of sorrow, on our way here from Josh's bedside in Wilmington, Alina told us. That he had been adopted. As they had been away for a year, and had never spoken other than strictly truthfully, none of us had suspected."

"I gather that this is now generally known."

"Josh doesn't know. Only Lavinia, Bob, and I. What had you written to leave for Edward?"

"I had written:

My Dear Son,

I don't know whether it will ever be of use or particular interest to you to know that you have, or have had, a half-sister (as I think) or a half-brother—I don't know which—your Dear Mother's child. The adoptive parents' names are Alina and Parker Jones, of New York City, and the father's name is Laurence des C.-L. Ashfield, of Peell County, in South Carolina.

S. M.T. L.
Grandfather"

"It has only now occurred to me that Bunny must have been content to have things his way, after all."

"I am one of three children; the other two were my elder brothers." With this homely statement, Alenda began upon the promised story of her girlhood in Barbadoes. "We were all instructed together in the early years—our ages spanned a little more than four years—by governesses. Then my brothers were sent to boarding-school in Bridgetown. But I continued to be tutored at home, even though…"

"You were the cleverest," Lavinia supplied.

"And from early on bound, according to my parents' wishes, for university. But, as I told you yesterday, the Great War made that not possible."

"Were you very much disappointed at not being able to go?"

"Only because it meant I could not travel. I was convinced I could acquire as much—or little—education as I wished. But, in spite of what I look upon as a happy youth—in general—and a great fondness for my parents, I wanted to see a bit beyond the shores of Barbadoes."

"Were you fond, also, of your brothers?"

"For me to say Yes would be true, but not a complete answer. There were not many White young people...well, in fact there were not a great many White people at all, and some families were beginning to leave the Island; the Blacks stayed and proliferated.

"Still, there was surprisingly little 'carnal commerce,' if you will, between the races. I suppose it was because all of us were of English extraction. There was the expected amount among white youths, when the time grew ripe... although I should be hard pressed to refine what I mean by 'the expected amount.'"

To this Lavinia answered: "I have the distinct impression that if anyone could judge it rightly, it would be you. But I say that only because I suspect you have very acute powers of judgment."

"Who can say? But I am sure—or nearly so—that there was an excessive incidence of that kind of thing between brothers and sisters...and between sisters and between brothers, probably. But in those cases, conception was not a threat...and 'incest' seems not applicable."

Alarm at what Alenda might be about to disclose dampened Lavinia's eagerness for the rest of the tale; Alenda's sense of a burden lifted caused her to wish to savor the moment. And it was a lovely moment; the breeze had wrung loose a petal from an early-booming dogwood, and it drifted down to prod the earth further awake. The women watched. It seemed deliberately to prolong its flight, and when it touched the ground, it was as though a great fugue had found all its ways and met at once, resounding music struck from the land.

"I assume such a practice had no effect on you? Otherwise, I believe you would not be telling me." She had spoken too soon, for the chord had not yet completely died away.

After it had, Alenda resumed: "It did. It had a very tragic effect, but I think not the one you fear. And, to be truthful, even in that case I think I *should* be telling you. I don't know why. My younger brother James—the younger, but still older than I—and I were playmates in childhood, and later grew into *copains*. My elder brother, however—his name was, possibly is—Iain, stood somewhat apart, and seemed to watch over us. And his vigil elevated him, decidedly, and apparently gave him an onlooker's perspective."

"I wonder whether he feared racial disturbance. Two centuries ago, there was an immigration, especially into South Carolina, of Barbadians of British origin. Like us, they had acquired African slaves, who were discontented. Here, we always sensed a...threat, even if it was only imagined, shapeless... and shadowy, actually. There were only a few, abortive 'rebellions,' but in Barbados I think there were more."

"There were. And the proportion of Black folk in the population, growing steadily, led to greater anxiety among those of us of British descent who had remained."

Now Lavinia waited, since she knew that Alenda had something she must speak out about.

"To get back to naughty boys and girls: I was considered the prettiest girl in our province. That is because there were only two others. Otherwise, I shouldn't expect you to believe it." Lavinia was about to protest—for if any of her present enchantingness had sprung forth, Alenda would surely have been the most tempting young girl in the Lesser Antilles—but chose again to wait. "Iain had decided to spend all of his last year of schooling in Bridgetown—he returned to us for none of the holidays.

"At the end of the year, he came home. He had become a man, and by no means a poor specimen of one. James was all I had to compare him with, of course, under the circumstances.

"The year was 1915; I was sixteen, almost seventeen—of all the banal ages for a young girl to be! Mother Nature and my own mother, the redoubtable Augusta Thornwall, were in their influences impelling me in opposing directions. Upon a single dimension, of course. There was no question of a flanking maneuver. Mother Nature, it goes without saying, cannot be outflanked.

"I had been desperately looking for someone to fall in love with, but with no luck. Until I saw Iain, and he was my own brother, so that was impossible. Or, at least it was supposed to be—although I knew of instances of it, as I've said.

"Nevertheless, I ate little, cried all night—that sort of thing."

"Yes. I used to do all that from time to time."

"Over Laurence?"

"I knew I'd marry him, so no. Not over Laurence. He didn't excite me then."

"He didn't?"

"Not until after we were married. Then he did."

"Altogether a better arrangement.

"I did hit upon one positive thing with regard to…my brother, positive anyway to an adolescent girl: I could dramatize myself. But to whom? I thought of writing a novel; pure of page, but with every bit of the salaciousness implied."

While she was speaking, Thomas and Laurence came out of the western woodland, crunching upon last season's dried leaves, riffling through what brittle ghosts of annual underbrush were left over. They were both looking not-quite-grim. When they had come up onto the verandah, Laurence growled: "We're going to have drinks and shut ourselves in the East Room until suppertime. Is that all right?"

"Of course. Are *you* all right?" And…suppertime? Ah, supper*time*.

"Yes. We are all right." Unexpextedly, Laurence leaned over and kissed Lavinia.

"Since you're being so sweet, would you bring us drinks first?"

"Certainly. Alenda, what will you have?"

"Two double whiskies, each with a lump of ice, if I may." And then, by way of clarification: "It will save at least one of us an extra trip."

Once they had taken possession of their refreshment, the ladies moved noiselessly to the west end of the verandah, so as not to be directly outside the windows where the men were apparently going to confer about something deep and dark. When they were settled, they heard the sashes in the East Room, first grinding within their stops then thudding onto the sills.

"You must tell me how it ended; I'm sure you mean to."

"Of course I'm going to tell you—what I know. The standoff went on for a few days. I imagined I saw signs of requital. Iain spoke to me with a kind of restraint; looked at me in a way I hadn't known. All night, each night, I expected him to come into my room. I think I wanted him to—so long as he didn't.

"But, no. It happened in broad daylight. I was sitting at the end of the Promontory, an extension of the lowest terrace in front of our house, and not planted. The sea was roaring around me, but I heard him. I turned. He looked down at me and told me he had fallen in love with me.

"I told him I had fallen in love with him. We discussed no details. He took my hand, pulled me up, and kissed me. He knew what he was about. I did not. Just when I was expecting to lose consciousness, he let me go, and said: 'It is impossible, you know. *I* know it is.' And he walked without hurry or misstep back to the house. I watched every footfall. That's how I know. I can replay it all, as though it were film from a motion picture. I didn't follow him. He didn't want me to.

"I looked back out over the Ocean and imagined something very odd. The sky was clear blue. I saw venom, coming from The Scorpion (I knew that the stars were still in the heavens, even if outshone by the sun), falling and falling. It fell toward the earth and toward me. Dark as blood. Then, I imagined, just as it came into the way of the bright disc of the sun, it encountered an invisible layer, high and cold, where it spread and congealed, blotting out nearly all of the day.

"As far back as I can remember, everything Iain did or said was 'from honest motive purely.' So I didn't follow him. Both my highballs seem to have evaporated!"

"I'll get you another."

"Two others, if you please; these have had only physiologic effects." *Easter! Resurrection—but for all of us? Or only for me?*

Lavinia returned with the ubiquitous small waiter. This one held two glasses and linen napkins, ice and tongs, and a faceted crystal pitcher of whiskey. She had laid across it a flowering branch of dogwood, and an Easter lily.

"How beautiful! How festive!"

"Do you mean that? Are you sorrowing?" But before Alenda answered, Lavinia had gone back into the house for candles, for it was now growing quite dark.

"Night was reaching for the promontory and for me. I went back. Iain had 'had to leave,' as he had told them, but had left me a sealed letter. Through it all, no living person had seemed so...*null* to me as poor James. In the letter, Iain said he had loved me for a year. He thought the impossibility would make it evaporate.

"He had told them he had taken a summer job with a grading company. He had.

"I knew I couldn't be with him; I could not, though, stay at Windward without him. So I gave our driver my gold fountain pen in return for taking me overnight, secretly, to Bridgetown—not to follow. To escape. The ass wanted to know how he was to make up the petrol-difference. I know. I call it 'gasoline,' now. Sometimes just 'gas.' Then, for a while, the two women sat in silence, each staring ahead into the darkness, toward the Ocean, which was twelve miles away, to windward.

"I can't imagine what you felt. Or what you thought lay before you."

"Neither can I. I had no legitimate way to spend the next day. Or night. I was sitting on a bench in the park. A rather dashing-looking man in uniform—United States Air Service, as it proved—invited me to lunch. And I said I was running away from home and accepted the invitation.

"And now, Lavinia, you must pay close attention. Because Chapter One, although it is dramatic in an unseemly way, can hardly touch Chapter Two, which is twice as dramatic, outwardly, even though I can remember clearly only a single important detail from it, and fourfold as unseemly."

Lavinia, still sipping her original gin-and-tonic, glancing across at the tray she had brought out, was surprised to see that the pitcher of whiskey was still at least half full. The paraphysiologic effects must have begun to take their hold.

"As this man, whose name was Bill, who seemed to me old enough to be my grandfather in spite of his being half my father's age, and I walked in the park after our lunch, he asked me to marry him, and I accepted that invitation, too. We found a sufficiently empowered official. By late afternoon we were—without authorization, I've always believed—in an aircraft, preparing to take off for Miami. Of all places! Miami! But, looking back, I thank God it was as close as it is. I had never flown before. I came to suspect that Bill hadn't either. And he was piloting the thing! We were without doubt flying through some kind of tempest. But I can't think that alone accounted for all the terrifying jolts and jogs in our progress. I knew there must be noise; but I could not discern the expected roar from the unexpected changes of pitch, scrapings of metal (I didn't really think there ought to be any of those at all). We landed somewhere not at all near the tall buildings and bracelets of lights. I considered the possibility that I was smuggled goods.

"I didn't have a passport, but I was Bill's wife by that time."

"Is that the one significant detail you still remember?"

"No, it's not. The detail I remember…is…." Here Alenda, whose self-possession had seemed complete, even when she had claimed to feel the effects of strong drink, rose abruptly and walked quickly across the board floor, down the steps, and out into the darkness.

For the last thing she had seen with clarity, through the small eisenglass-filled port in the aircraft, before the machine made a last, slewing effort and got from ground to air, had been her brother, bent to shoveling rubble into the bucket of an earth-moving tractor at the edge of the runway. He had slipped out of his shirt, but without removing it, merely keeping it out of his way by knotting the sleeves around his waist. His face and shoulders were drenched in sweat, and Alenda, craning her head around as the craft gained altitude, could make out for a long time—it seemed—him gleaming, otherwise indistinguishable, up first through dust then light cloud, long after he was recognizable as a man. And she had never seen him or heard either from or of him again.

"I am already regretting my decision, Laurence. Now I feel I ought to have spared you…your having to deal with it."

"You must not regret it."

"I could have destroyed the letter I had meant to leave behind, and kept my own counsel."

"Could you have?"

"It would have made me acutely uncomfortable being your guest."

"That is enough to make me grateful to you for telling me, and there is more than that. No one else knows of it?"

"Alenda knows that Josh and Edward are half-brothers. But that is all."

"Considering all things, I can't see what other course you could have taken."

"I couldn't see, either. Because I thought it would make you happy to know you have a son. It is news that you have a claim to, that you own. I couldn't see that I should be right in keeping it to myself."

"The shameful thing is that I have already started to feel deeply gratified, knowing that Josh is my begotten son, as you have put it."

"I should think so."

"It hasn't taken long for gratification to displace shock, has it? My heart... you know...it is very full."

They sat intently staring into a fire that was in point of fact not burning in the grate, just as Miss Izora sometimes did, while the blessings of their lives sprang up and washed over them as though they were statuary, bathed in an unstinting fountain. But they knew that their good fortunes came at cost, were qualified, and would lead each of them whither they would lead.

Eventually, Laurence said: "I must stop thinking about my new gladness, before I start handing out cigars; I must think about each of the others. How they would be affected, each, by knowing what you have told me."

Thomas answered: "That is what I tried to do. But I was afraid—for you—of the difficulties. My part ultimately seemed to be to bring the news to you. Perhaps together we could...."

"Yes. I will need you to help me. And first must come Lavinia. Do you agree?"

"Unless, Alina."

"No. If I have a son, and Lavinia is not his mother...."

"Do you think that, now, so long afterward, with, I assume, a good record since, she would be very greatly disturbed by reflecting upon the infidelity?"

"A perfect record. Since. That is not the most important consideration, although I was troubled by it for a long time afterward. But you will see how that waned, when I tell you how the whole thing happened."

"It's as you wish, of course, but it doesn't take much speculation to gather 'how the whole thing happened.'"

"No. Yet there are some peculiarities. Right after my sister and Parker were married and settled in New York, I traveled to Philadelphia—or nearby—to see about having the old ironwork from the trunks in the ricefields replaced. I had an appointment to show some drawings to a forger in bronze.

"At the last minute, or so I've tried to tell myself, I put the smith off a day and cancelled my plan to visit the Joneses. I was 'motoring up,' as Bunny would say, and could change my itinerary at will. I turned aside from the straight way, to pay a visit to the Singletons. The minute I did all this, I realized I had given in...to something already alive in my brain.

"Bunny and Libby were cordial, as always. Anne was at home."

"Had you and she...been, ah...romantically allied? Though I suppose it is out of order for me to ask; you've already seen me breach good form that way."

"No. Oh, no. When we were young and that house was the center of a lot of, well, merrymaking, Anne had always been a member of the party, but much in the way of one who stands guard, to fend off danger from the rest.

"After dinner that evening, she and I walked out to see the nags that by then made up Bunny's stable. The smell of saddle soap and harness and dander took me straight back to those tack-room days. Anne rode very little… although Peggy was always on horseback…that is, when not on her own back. I beg your pardon. I so often and so…greedily wanted to spend Anne's off-time with her. But I never did.

"That evening, it seemed neither of us could think of anything to say to the other. So we said Goodnight.

"Around midnight, I went to her room, assuming she would throw me out. Otherwise I shouldn't have gone."

And now neither man could think of anything to say to the other. Laurence tried unsuccessfully to come up with some way of filling the void other than, for once, by pouring more drinks.

"But, Lavinia. We have shared so much, nearly all. She at one time desperately wanted a child. She even made a compact with God. She accepted in advance what actually overtook you: She believed she was willing to survive a child, 'To look upon its death,' she said. If only one might be given her. A child of her own. And since Josh cannot be that, then she must not know he is mine. At any cost, she mustn't. If she can't share my happiness, then she is not to know of it."

"What about Alina?"

"I can't explain this rationally, but, although she of course knows she did not conceive and bear him, she regards Josh as fully her own. And I don't think it will in any way do for her to find that her own brother has a more legitimate and after all prior claim. It would be cruel enough, but unthinkably cruel to shut Parker out."

"I understand all your reckonings; I can sympathize with your feelings completely; I simply had no way of knowing what they would be. And I assume you mean to have Bob know no more than Alina?"

"Don't you think that the most sensible thing?'

"Yes, I do."

"I don't believe it would have much effect on him, one way or the other, except through my sister's anguish." But in this supposition, Laurence's sensitivity had not come fully to his aid.

"So, with Anne gone, Bunny gone, and Robert gone…."

"And Mr. Jones."

"And Parker, of course. I think only the brothers themselves are left to learn or not."

" It is probably my responsibility to decide about Edward. Yet, whether to inform him or not must depend upon what you decide about Josh. Neither need know he is the other's brother, or both must know."

Laurence stood up. "I can't handle any more of this right now. I imagine you can't, either. After all, matters stand as they have stood for a quarter of a century. This last decision will have to wait."

Meanwhile, with spring and Hurricane Season drawing on, the Lesser Antilles linked elbows, tried their footing. The great house at Windward, long vacant, looked past her prospect of ruin, out across the sea; waiting, trusting, she gazed steadfastly through the ceaseless wash of the Trade Winds, sheltering her own secrets while she stood. It was what she had been set there to do.

"I want you to be sure to know, Grandfather, that if you were not a priest and an officiant at my marriage with Mary, I should of course have asked you to be Best Man," Edward said solemnly.

"Thank you, Son. The same thing happened in connection with your father's wedding." They were sitting on the verandah in New Brunswick, watching Mayday shed her manna of petals down into the garden.

"I wonder how many people think it's odd that I'm asking my bride's former boyfriend?"

"I wonder why you ask. Do you yourself feel any awkwardness about it?"

"No."

"Does Mary?"

"No."

"Does Josh?"

"No.

"Good. Well. In regard to your choice of Josh as your Best Man, I do have something I feel I must tell you." Thomas allowed Springtime herself to provide an intermezzo, then he said: "It is something I tell you for yourself; after a long while, others may know it, but for the time being, you will be—and you must remain—one of five informed. And this is what it is: You and Josh Jones are brothers."

To his announcement there could be only one response. And it came: "*What!*"

"It is so. Half-brother, he is." Flowerets fell from trees, blossoms stood open at the extremes of their petioles. The air rested upon itself in cool layers. "You are about to ask me how I know, and I will tell you, even though some parts may be painful, others will be astounding. But there has been no conspiracy. To cover it up—not by me nor by any of the South Carolina Folk.

"Are you telling me this now, so that I'll know that my Best Man is my brother?"

"In very small part. However, most of it has come to light only in the past several months and weeks.

"It was your own father who told me, before you were born, that Anne, who became your mother, as you of course know, had borne a child already. The child was privately adopted, and only your other grandfather knew by whom. Your Mother demanded not to know this, or even the sex of the child. During her confinement she sought to lose track of time; she did not want to know the birthday. She was a conspicuously virtuous girl, and she punished herself severely."

Then Thomas related the entirety of the story. Including the revolver. Edward was stupefied. But more curious than stupefied: "Do you think, Grandfather, that there is a close linkage in such situations?"

" Do you mean one such as yours to Josh? There is of course the genetic... rewriting."

"Anything more than that?"

"In the absence of knowledge, I may say I think, particularly where the mother is the parent in common, there is somehow much more than that."

At Woodleigh, Laurence was entertaining Josh in the East Room, who had come to make him a short speech, which he delivered with gravity: "Uncle Laurence, I have to assure myself that you know these things, and not leave the matter to chance: No one has been kinder, more generous to me, or more watchful over me than you have been; I include Aunt Lavinia in all this, of course. And I am closer to you by blood than to anyone else but to Mother."

"You are very good to say all that, Son. We have done nothing more for you than simple duty requires. But it does go, I hope without saying, that we would reach as far beyond the call of that duty as our strength and resources would afford."

"Not everybody...not anybody else is dutiful, in that case. What I want to tell you, though, is that if I felt I had an entirely free hand, I would ask you to be my Best Man."

"That choice is entirely up to you, Josh. No other person has any business questioning it, and you ought not to question it, either, within yourself."

"Thank you, Sir. Good. Well, I'm going to ask Bob. Because he is unavoidably so much on the outskirts of the thing. I want to bring him into it as much as I can. I believe it would please Mother, too."

"It would please her, I think, tremendously, and it pleases me. It shows a fine sensibility."

But the question was not to be so easily settled.

"Laurence?"

"Yes?"

"This is Thomas Strikestraw."

"Hello, Thomas. How are you?"

"Embarrassed. You remember we decided that we would tell the boys?"

"Yes."

"But that you should decide when."

"Yes. I remember we said so."

"I didn't keep to the bargain. I just this minute blurted it all out to Edward. He was, I think, rationalizing his choice of Josh as his Best Man. So, before I remembered our agreement, I explained that there was an excellent rationale, ready and waiting."

"Don't be concerned about it; I'll just get hold of Josh, and explain the matter to him right away. Funny that you were talking about that...the Best Man. Josh came over here this morning and made me a very touching speech on the same subject. He's going to ask Bob, my sister's husband."

Thomas, in his perturbation, said nothing. The New Brunswick birds twittered over the wire to the Peell County birds, who twittered back. Eventually, "Remember, I know perfectly well who Bob is." Then silence, except for some further rustles of spring. "But how will it affect Josh, to know you're his father?"

"I'll let you know."

"At once?"

"At once. But remember I have no control over the time his reaction will take up. You mustn't hold your breath."

"No. I have made a point of warning Edward that he himself must not make any disclosure to *anybody*, although I expect him to tell Mary, once they're man and wife. I recommend you tell Josh the comparable thing. But, then, who am I to set rules? All I've done so far is break one of the ones we made."

"Don't be harsh with yourself. None of it is all that consequential. Although I begin to wonder what Mary will feel like, when she knows."

"God Almighty! Oh!" Pause for thought and words. Then: "Well, anyway, not '*triple*-turned.'" Neither the pause for thought, evidently, nor yet the one for words, had been long enough.

The marriage of Mary Mountainstream to Edward Strikestraw took place on Saturday, the Eleventh of May, 1964, in Augusta. Many pages could be allowed a tally of the preparations for and details of the wedding. In the newspaper, many columns in fact were. But it is enough to cite the adage: "If vows are exchanged, then the wedding is a success." All that tended to mar the ceremony was a pack of little boys, deceptively angelic-looking in their bowties, blazers, and white ducks, who sat together in the organ-loft and kept maliciously breaking wind. They were later pardoned at the request of the bride, who traditionally gives law upon her wedding-day.

The couple (*At home after the fourth of June, Six Wendell Street*) postponed their wedding-trip, because it was going to be unique and required planning. It required a good many other things, besides.

After they had kissed the bride, danced with her mother, and eaten (in Laurence's case) a mint shaped like a calla lily and (Thomas's) a spoonful of caviar, Thomas said: "I am only an officiant, for purposes of this reception. I believe I can get away now, don't you think?"

"I do. And, so far as anybody—or anybody much—knows, I am really nothing at all. Why don't we ask Alenda to take Lavinia back to the hotel when they're ready, then go off ourselves and relax for a while. We have things to discuss." And soon, they were sitting together upon a park bench, watching the stuccoed faces of the old Medical College meet the color of the afternoon sun halfway.

"You said that 'as far as anybody knows' you are nothing in particular. Will you tell me about your informing Josh? Because I have come to realize that the shock, for him, and the awkwardness, for you, will have been far greater."

"That is how it was."

"When I told Edward about the reshaping of the Family Tree, I took nothing from him…but merely applied a graft. The mother and father he had grown up believing were his, were his still. He just had to accept a small error taken by his mother, before she was his father's wife. That the error compelled him to have now to regard Josh, to whom I think he is devoted anyway, as his brother, can't have been what you'd call 'devastating.'"

"And that is all?"

"Not exactly. But Edward is not troubled—I say so, because after his visit to your home and family, he told me you were a man he would have been happy to have had as his father, if he couldn't have his own. By that I mean to convey that the whole connection makes him happy."

Laurence's voice was checked; how full could the heart become before it burst and bled away? And his talks with Josh had ultimately left it weakened in places—'areas of dyskinesia,' Bob would likely have termed them. In his own fleeting muddle, he said: "But there was no confusion? For example, he doesn't think *I'm* his father, does he?"

"No, no. All of it is perplexing to an extent, but I got him to understand exactly who was who, and to whom, and who was not who."

"What did you say?"

"I don't remember, exactly. We'd better move along from here. It's cooling off."

Abandoning the park-bench, the grounds, waning warmth, and deepening shade of the stately Structure, Thomas and Laurence ambled without purpose along a street, and when they saw a sign reading "Bar and Grille," they turned in. The tone of the place they found a little surprising. When they had sat down at a vacant table—But there were not many, for it was Saturday afternoon, and getting on toward "bullbat time"—a gifted waitress came up and asked for their orders. Unsure of liquor laws in a different State, Laurence asked: "Can we get a glass of whisky here?"

"Honey, in here you can get just about anything you want. I like you boys' get-ups!"

So they sat in the agreeable twilight and quiet hum of conversation from other tables, where the patrons must have got "everything they wanted," until the waitress returned with their drinks. Laurence was wearing a box-back coat, and so was Thomas, but with the addition of the canonical violet and a "dog-collar."

"After I had spoken with you over the telephone, I decided to walk across to Clear Creek. It was a beautiful day. I had never visited Josh in his rooms in the Carriage House, except by invitation, but I went up to the stoop and knocked. Josh answered right away. I think he had seen me coming over the field in back of the building. He obviously felt an unease, which he was trying to hide. On the walk over there, I had had time to realize what a cruel thing I had set myself to do.

"I even thought of skipping it. But, knowing that Josh and Edward were already friends, I knew with equal certainty that both had to be told they were brothers as well. We'd been over that.

"I said to him: 'Son, I think I should have told you this earlier today. And as it is, I don't know where to start. So I think I'll get over the worst of it first. Has your Mother told you they adopted you at your birth?' Because I felt there might be a slim chance that, once she'd told the three of us—Lavinia, Bob, and me— she would soon afterward have explained to him as well how things stood.

"But she hadn't.

"Josh was quiet, but that is not unusual. He was quiet for a long time. He stood up and paced about, stopping to look out through each window. He was obviously shaken, because he said: 'Do you...do you mean to say Bob adopted me, when he and Mother were married? No, then I'd be Barrington. No. You said "at birth." ' It was painful to watch him; I knew I was wrenching out of his grasp a lot of what he loved most. Or needed most...or was constituted of. Does that make any sense?"

Thomas said: "It makes far too much sense. I should have kept everything to myself. And I *knew* I should have. From childhood, my Mother admonished me to try to become 'not quite so communicative.'"

"No. We've talked about it and agreed. You acted in the one honorable way, as anybody would affirm."

Laurence, ready for dissociated surprise, incredulousness of the matter, skepticism about the provenance, had had no guard up against the bewilderment his declaration inflicted upon Josh. The boy had abruptly seemed—sooner than one might think he could have taken in what he had heard—familiar with nothing in his surroundings. As though he had been living beneath an enormous churchbell, one even bigger than the biggest of the real ones, with all he had ever acknowledged somehow represented inside the vast throat and bow. As though a full company of ringers had tugged a mighty rope across a block and drawn throat, bow, and mouth right up above him, leaving him to a scape of eye and mind in which all was unknown. Where everything should have been known, but nothing was.

Josh began again to walk around the room, this time tracing, with an index, a filled crack until it disappeared or branched; or covering, with his broad palm, a patch of raw plaster, skimmed smooth, or of old work, its coloring burnished, nearly effaced. Engaged in this, he disappeared briefly into the bedroom, all throughout his searching behavior making no sound. Along no fissure did his tracing finger come entirely to rest, but moved on; over no tract did his palm flatten and cease, but continued a slow *effleurage*, cupped, light, circling.

He came back into the sitting room. When, in order to sit down, he must withdraw his hand from the wall, still he moved it gently until it was free altogether of the obsolete mapwork, with its undependable ways and boundaries, its discrepant keying.

He looked hard at Laurence, then said: "Nothing tends to make me believe it."

"Thank God! That, at least, I can understand." For he had not understood the examination of the walls, with little wonder enough. "Your Mother... Anne...Anne Singleton, your Mother...was one of the most beautiful young women I have ever seen. She may have been the most beautiful. With her, you soon stopped being aware of her beauty. Because it all went past that. But none of the young men in her circle—no man at all—would have thought sidewise of taking any liberty with her. Even though you felt more manly when alone with her than at other times.

"Then one day…one day and one night…she made an exception to her virtuousness, and she was got with child. Only her father knew about it. He made all the arrangements, and she went away for a long while, until the baby was born. …Anne Singleton's baby…."

"And the baby was me?"

"The little child was you. And Alina and Parker, who were living in New York, and wanted to have a child, found they could not.

"And it was they who adopted the child of Anne Singleton, subsequently, as I believe you realize, the mother of Edward Strikestraw."

Laurence had been entranced, clearly, but now he turned back to Thomas: "And there we sat, with darkness falling. Josh didn't say anything; he didn't seem able to say anything. I kept waiting, but he only sat quietly. I was afraid he was going to begin to cry, or to do something else equally unnerving. I had no idea what to do.

"So I said: 'Are you going to offer me a drink?' and he answered: 'No, Sir.'

"I blundered on: 'Do you want to hear anymore about this?' and he said again: 'No, Sir.' So I got up and went out. I turned on the lamp on the table by the doorway as I left.

"When I was halfway down the stair outside, Josh came out onto the stoop and said: 'No more, just for now, Uncle Laurence, if you please.' Going back to Lavinia that evening seemed one of the hardest things I've ever had to do."

How could he have done it?—my own father; but he wasn't my own father. Still, how could he have misled me for all those years? Misled me, and let me believe all I did believe, and say all I said, and hear…?

Then Josh fell to brooding, as we have seen him do before. As we have seen him brood so deeply, in great pain and confusion. *I remember I felt betrayed when he died. It was foolish; nobody can help dying…for the most part. But all I thought he had given me; all I had wanted to send him away from me with—and he wasn't my father and I thought…he let me think…he told me he was. Or did he? Ever?*

Josh went down the outside stair, into the great House, and up the inside stair to the room that had been his when a child. *Maybe it wasn't his decision, or not his entirely, not to tell me.*

"Open this, if you really need your father," came to him in echo from across the years. He went to the windowsill, to which the stoppered bottle had been restored, idly, thoughtlessly, one day by Yukoneta, after she had spotted it lying upon the tabbywork of the Magnolia Lane. He broke the seal. He meant to read the note inside. If it were a note. Suppose it contained a consecrated wafer? Because it had become sacred for him over the years. No. He remembered, he thought, seeing writing througe one fold, when the Gift was new. What, then if it said something like this: "There can fall no... Orphanage upon those Children to whom God is Father."* Could this, or any such thing, be enough?

But he sat cradling the vessel in his hands. After a great while, having grown calm he stood up and put the little flacon back in its place, knowing that he could trust without knowing, and that he could wait.

Alina had been surprised by Josh's request to paint his quarters, after the passage of so many years. "Of course you may, Darling. The paint, even, is still somewhere about the place. You do mean 'have it painted,' don't you?"

"No, I want to do it myself. In a certain...order. But I would like you to get the painters back and have them brush down the walls—no more abrading, no more chemicals—and tape the window casings and cover the furniture and floor. I'd do it myself, but I'm leaving for Wilmington tomorrow morning."

"Oh, I'd love to ask them to come and make it good! And I shall have them stir the paint, if Connie can find it, and be sure it's still useable. And if it isn't, I still remember...I think I do...the name of the color. They find the most fantastic names for paint-colors. But then of course they have to differentiate among fifteen tones of grey, and so on. How nice it will be!"

"What was the name of the color?"

"Something like *Weasel Walk*, but it couldn't have been exactly that. That ought to be enough for them to go on, though."

"Or you could make another choice. A new one."

"You're right, Darling." She put her arms around him; she kissed him. "It seems a time of new choices."

"But I hope Yukoneta can find the original cans."

"I've always said Connie can do anything."

"Anything, yes; but she can't do everything."

"You may be surprised!"

" 'Bye, Mother." He kissed Alina. For he loved her.

---

*John Donne, *Lett.* (1651) 108

"I was unpardonably rude to you the day-before-yesterday, Uncle Laurence, and I wanted to say I'm sorry, before I go. I was a bit startled, to say the least, to lose genetic kinship with those I have thought my parents. But one really needn't be limited to just two parents; so their figures only tottered from the collision, then held their positions. And I am un...unspeakably content to know it was my own brother, whom you *found* for me at that same time, who saved me from drowning."

"You were by no means rude; you have nothing to be sorry about. I was hardly able to make myself tell you what I had to tell you. Your behavior was gracious, compared to what mine would likely have been."

"Thank you, Sir. But it hardly squared with the speech I made, last time we were in this room together. Anyway, have you got time to tell me the rest, before I go?"

"Oh, *time*. I've got *time* enough."

"What else will it take?"

"Courage. Because I have to take an uncommon risk. But you must be on your way, so here it is:

"The information I have given you came to me, of course, through Canon Strikestraw."

"Yes. I had decided it must have."

"His own son, Edward's father, had told Thomas what I have told you about Anne. Years later, he decided to go to Virginia and extort the names of the father—there having been but one possibility—and of the adoptive parents from...from your natural grandfather. The names held no significance for him. But he wrote them down, and sealed them up in an envelope marked for Edward, thinking either that he might need them somehow or that he had, or would have eventually, a right to know them.

"Then Lavinia wrote to him—that's to Canon Strikestraw—after Edward's visit here for our deer-shoot. In her letter she referred to 'Alina,' not very usual, 'Josh Jones'...some others, I think. They stirred his memory. He retrieved the names and made the connections."

"What about my natural father? Was his a name anyone recognized?"

"Yes. It was."

Of the foregoing, Laurence went on to tell Thomas those parts he knew. They left the Bar and Grille, assuring the waitress that while there they had indeed got all they had wanted.

"Those parkas are too cute," she said.

"The best-man question had not by then been laid fully to rest," Laurence told Thomas as they looked for their way back to their hotel. "Josh came home from Wilmington, having decided that he wanted two best men; I told him that was against tradition. But he was unmoved.

"Then I pointed out that it would diminish the courtesy to Bob, and that convinced him."

"So he will have one Best Man, as is usual."

"Yes. And that will be Bob. But Josh has had his name changed from John Ashfield Jones to John Ashfield-Jones. He did it now so that he would be married with that name. I thanked him for this act of family loyalty. I recommended that he might eventually want to drop the hyphen, but by all means to consider 'Ashfield Jones' his and his issue's surname."

"Excellent form, all around. I wonder whether his Bride had to be given a full account of his reason for wishing to make the change?"

"He says not—just that otherwise I'd appear to be *fin de ligne*—but I expect he's lying." A pause. "In strict privacy, he calls me 'Poppy,' something your son, I gather, used to call you sometimes." There was a moment left aside for removal of various discreetly overwelling tears. "Not very manly sounding, though."

"Who gives a God-damn?"

X

Text scribbled in pencil on paper, found lying near
the wastepaper basket in a classroom high up in
Sever Hall. Kept by the finder not for its obscure
meaning, but for the music of its consecutive dactyls.

A T THE END of summer there came another wedding: Julie's to Josh. But
because of extreme reticence and a high degree of exclusivity, it went
almost unnoticed by the press. There was, by design, a very discrete
three-line notice printed, and, through chance, a large photograph on the
front page. The elder strikestraws had a good deal of merriment out of it.

On Sunday morning, September 14, 1964—as part of his stretching-cat's
kind of languorous delight in having decided not to attend Church, Thomas
reminded himself that this was also Holy Cross Day, and still he wasn't going
to Church. He sat upon the balustrade of his verandah, sidesaddle, leaning

---

*"There exists, so to say, something that undermines joyfulness."

against the pillar behind. Alenda half reclined upon a *chaise longue* drawn to within inches of the way to inside the house.

From etched stems they were sipping *eau pétillante*, glad to have a little time together, yet somehow ready to acknowledge passersby warmly...and slyly. Thomas wore a white linen suit, which wrinkled but wrinkled right, and a splendid silk bowtie. This ornament seemed from any distance at all to be vaguely silver or gold; looked at closely, it exhibited narrow diagonal stripes of nearly any imaginable misted but lustrous color. Thomas had inspected it closely and had found that none of the hues could be identified with *any* liturgical color, Sarum Rite included.

Alenda had chosen a dress less severely cut than usual for herself and she wore, withdrawn from a battered, velvet-covered box, stamped in gold with the discrete blazon "Asprey, London," a set of two combs and a necklace, an astonishing collection of pigeon's-blood rubies and exotic horn, gleaned from some wild corner of the Empire, very dark. The stones of the necklace were set in a rare agate that matched the horn. Alenda's grandmother, bred to it, had hated Edwardian flash. She had balked even at the narrowest, plumbline-straight bezels in gold which the jeweler had found it necessary to employ. This lady didn't like Edwardian richness, either. But, here, she was stuck with it. Thus, it was as looking like nothing seen before in Brunswick, New Hanover, and Onslow Counties put together—or Beaufort, or Jasper, or Peell—that she, roused from a light rêverie, heard Thomas greeting someone. "Oh! Good morning, Minnie, Michael...On your way to Church?" Alenda agreed with John Hammond that the Colliers ought really to attend Sunday School, not Church.

"Thomas has just told us you have house guests, who are away at brunch."

"Yes. Two at one place, three more at another. For the wedding, you know."

Minnie, before she could check herself, asked: "Which wedding is that?"

The Strikestraws exchanged a brief glance. Then, they began to laugh lightly, musically. Making it clear they were enjoying Minnie's little quip: Which wedding? Ha, ha. Which, indeed! So amusing, they seemed to imply. They resumed their places, waving Goodbye. Minnie and Michael Collier drifted away.

"I can't say I hope there won't be any further interruptions, for there is so much to convey by appearing to know nothing," Thomas said; "however, I do want to find an opportunity to ask the Ashfields about something we never seem to make time for."

"It's that business about redemption, isn't it? So I suppose you and Laurence will drag Plato into it."

"If, my Dear, we are able to *adorn* our thoughts with some teaching of Plato, then we shall be closer to Truth, and better off. But, from what little I've heard, I think this subject will be eccentric to all that."

"Wait, Thomas. I think some of them are returning now." And, as she spoke, an automobile, but as it proved an unfamiliar one, pulled up to the curb, and a lady and gentleman, whom they recognized vaguely from pastoral days, got out and came up the walk. The lady seemed—possibly not quite, but close—to be in what Ben Araby would label a "strut." Thomas leant forward, reaching for a straw hat, which had a band of dusty periwinkle blue, held it above his brow for a moment, then replaced it upon the railing. He had tipped his hat to the lady, he reckoned.

It occurred first to Alenda who they were. She got up and crossed the verandah in a slow glide, at the same time saying: "Good Morning, Mrs. Maxwell, Mr. Maxwell. Been to Early Communion?" The intensity of the strut lessened as the Maxwells gazed onto this other world, as it seemed to them, and, truthfully, might have seemed to many.

"No," she replied, "we haven't."

"But I should have thought that close as Sarah Elkin and I were in school, we'd have been invited to her daughter's wedding."

"And you were not?"

"No, we weren't." Mrs. Maxwell was evidently indignant, and nursing a grievance.

"My Goodness," Alenda answered, lying luxuriously. "Almost everyone was. It would have to have been an oversight."

Mr. Maxwell was a little embarrassed. Additionally, he wouldn't have cared if he should never in his life be invited to another wedding. But he had this to get through for his wife's sake: "I said to Jean I imagined you had conducted the service, Canon."

"No," Thomas said. "The family—actually, the families—are great friends of ours, but the Whitmans are Presbyterians. I was asked to add to the rather bare service a couple of liturgical flourishes, which their...Order of Worship is without."

"Will you come up and join us for a few minutes?" Alenda asked, then, when it appeared they might actually take her up, she quickly added: "We do have house guests, who will be returning from brunch at any minute."

Thomas put in: "In fact, when we heard the car we thought you must be they."

Jean Maxwell, therefore, stood where she was, but plunged recklessly on: "Of course, my only concern is that Sarah might think we had received an invitation but not responded to it. As though my upbringing would allow for such a thing!"

"Oh, I'm sure she knows better than to think *that*."

"Actually, we've come mostly out of concern for them in case there is anything...the matter."

"Matter?"

"Yes, matter. I can't put together all the secrecy and haste. Is Juliana going to...I mean, is there anything irregular...."

"Well," Thomas mentioned, "I must say, as they have been engaged since January, I hadn't thought to ask about it. But I can tell you this much: If young people engage in sexual intercourse, then naturally that sort of thing will happen every once in a while."

A kind of hush fell.

Thomas then said: "It's the Creator's way. But why not settle for reading about it in the Paper?"

"It isn't in the paper. That's another thing."

"I shouldn't know, in any case. We don't take the Paper."

The two turned to go, Jean far from being satisfied. She looked back: "Why not? That is, if you don't mind my asking."

"We have practically no need of it."

Alenda called after them: "Do glance at the front page, and then inside the last page!"

Wondering, they went away.

Finally, the Barringtons and Ashfields returned, having brought along Carlysle McClure, coming one by one up onto the verandah and commenting variously upon the *chic* with which Alenda and Thomas were greeting the day.

"We were inspired by your own *panache* when we saw you leaving," Alenda said, "and sought to imitate it. We've been drinking fizzy water and misleading everyone about the wedding." Alina and Lavinia glanced knowingly at each other.

"I thought as much. It was clear, where we were, that somebody was doling out bits and pieces of information."

"What was Laurence talking about?" Alenda asked of Lavinia—He was just now coming up the steps, followed, Alenda saw to her dismay, by the dear and honorable Howells, Anne and Ashton.

"Oh, nothing so much, I believe; we were being entertained—beautifully, too—by Julie's father's people. A young man, whom I momentarily supposed was Josh, burst in shouting: 'Why has this Town got it in for our Family? The entire account of the wedding was deliberately left out of today's Paper!'

"His mother, Julie's great-aunt, took him in her arms, signaled for Champagne, and said: 'Neither Julie nor Sarah nor Josh nor Mrs. Barrington wanted anything in the paper. No one has it in for us. There is only the Notice, which almost no one uses anymore, except for deaths. It used to include births and marriages, too. "Hatches, Matches, and Dispatches," everybody used to call it. Like the *Carnet du jour* in *le Figaro*. I will show it to you. But, now, drink your Champagne while it's chill, and join the happiness all around." Lavinia completed her characteristically kind, unerring account:

> "**Notices**. *Marriage.* Juliana Castlereagh Elkin Whitman to John Ashfield-Jones, September 13."

"What under Heaven are the Howells doing here?" Alenda seen once again in a rare state of perturbation. "For I could never slight them, no matter what. Good afternoon, Anne. Is Ashton with you—Oh! Here he is." Alenda had a little inner preparation that she carried out before doing something she must, otherwise would avoid like an adder. "Do come up and have a glass of sparkling water with us."

By this juncture, the five out-of-town guests had gone inside to refresh themselves. Laurence, for example, was wearing a raw silk vest the color of a roe's coat. He looked very opulent and *soigné*. But the cloth, heavy, fitted, was making him hotter than Hell itself, so he wanted to get out of it. The others had similar aims. Lavinia had noted Alenda's quiet rubies and so decided to wear her golden pearls—pearls were suitable for daytime, she reasoned...even ones this color...even ones this large. What on earth was overtaking them all? The sense of near-pure festivity was what.

Upon the verandah, as they took chairs, Anne spoke first: "We don't want to interrupt, but we did want to bid your guests welcome to New Brunswick and to hear that all went well with the wedding. We know the Whitmans very pleasantly but very slightly and of course would not have expected to be invited."

"Well, I lent an ecclesiastical hand to what was a mercifully brief service. The clergyman, in hope of getting him to cut short the extemporizing, had been led to believe that the wedding was to be little more than an elopement. And it worked. Up to a point, of course."

"The church looked lovely, simply decorated in keeping with the small scale of the ceremony; somewhat misleadingly simple, I think, given the evident deftness of the decorator's touch ." *Now I've actually begun lying for fun.* For Alenda herself had been the "decorator." *I can't help it. People's reactions are really ridiculously malleable; I'm sure mine are too .—So diverting!*

Ashton then asked this matter-of-fact question: "All of us must have seen the front-page photograph of the wedding party coming out of the church?"

"We didn't; we don't subscribe to the paper."

"It was quite imposing: Bride and Bridegroom, Bridesmaids, elegantly turned-out guests, all spilling grandly down the church-steps. But the caption was puzzling. It said: 'Juliana Whitman was married to John Ashfield-Jones'—I think the hyphen was a misprint; 'Ashfield' ended one line, and 'Jones' began the next—'on Saturdayafternoon, September thirteenth, First Presbyterian Church, Wilmington. The bride wore her family's historic diamond pendant, a bridal tradition. Other details were not made available.' What do you make of that? Because I went through the whole paper and, sure enough, there were no other details."

At this moment, Alina reappeared. There seemed to have been made no change in her costume, but she looked fresh as morning. "Please don't anybody get up. I believe Carlysle McLure, who'll be down shortly, can explain a little about the photograph and caption."

"Ah," said Ashton, "Good."

"By the way, Alenda, I wonder what the Bridegroom's family must have thought of such a...an atypical wedding."

"So far as I know, they are quite content with it."

"What sort of people are they, do you suppose?"

Alina, writing for the Court: "As in all families, I believe, Anne, there are some members who are quite cultivated, others who are country clots."

Laurence found he could not undo the bone buttons to the waistcoat, so, following a mighty effort, which only made him hotter, he gave up and went downstairs to join the others.

Alenda asked whether Carlysle could elucidate the photograph and caption.

"To an extent, I think. Seated next to me in church was a very old, charmingly diminutive lady. Presbyterians allow themselves to converse in church, before the service, so that I was able to learn that she was Cousin Sue McQueen, or Miss Sue McQueen, depending. I had to help her up when the Bride came in, because her feet didn't reach the floor. When I had done this, she looked back, then turned to me and whispered loudly: 'Oh, look! She's wearing it!' I looked; you could see the object through the veil, that it was rather magnificent, so I asked why Julie might choose *not* to wear it.

"'Juliana,' Miss Sue McQueen declared, 'is a dog of her own trot.'"

Carlysle had looked over his shoulder again, for the confection of earthly beauty he saw did not seem well-characterized in this way. But Miss Sue was herself a dog of *her* own trot, and she knew whereof she spoke.

"When the service was over, I helped her off the pew again and escorted her outside. She was slow, and we were among the last out of the kirk.

"I had rushed ahead," Alina explained , "to see just how the folds at the back of the gown had been pleated successively to suggest a small train. It was, I thought, extremely elegant."

Lavinia concurred: "It was stunning; I'd never seen anything quite like it. But very classic; not at all *outré*."

"I'm damned," Alenda said, "if I could see anything from where I was stuck away."

Carlysle went on: "There were three bewildered-looking press photographers standing about. Miss Sue went straight up to them and said: 'I trust you got a good photograph of the diamond pendant; it has been in the Family for *centuries* and is worn *only* by brides at their weddings.' So they all wrote that down in their notebooks, and I got Miss Sue down to the sidewalk and into the nearest Limousine.

"Anyway, I think that's what's behind it all."

"Why do you suppose the photographers were there in the first place?"

"One had come from Savannah and another from *The Ashfield Astonisher.*[*] They didn't know not to. I think, when the people at the local paper got wind of press photographers hanging about on the church steps, they thought they'd better send somebody out, too."

The Howells said Goodbye and went home. Thomas said: "For a small wedding with no to-do, this one has turned practically into a full-time job, and I have other things on my mind...Laurence?"

"I'm prepared—at least, I've continued to go over it, point by point, as well as I can remember them. But since Alina is here, we'd better let her tell us what she remembers, for she is closest to being a primary source."

Alina said: "Don't suppose I don't know what you're all talking about; it's that thing about redemption. I think you're about to make a quagmire out of a hogwallow."

"It's all they ever do," Lavinia said, lofty in her purple dress (the one from the hunt-breakfast, shortened) with the chain of sun-golden pearls about her neck.

"Well, it mustn't be so worthless an undertaking, my Girl. If Plato can be trusted, it's what Socrates did for a living. Of course, on the other hand, I don't think he ever quite earned a living. But Thomas and I have earned ours, and certainly Parker had earned his."

"All right. Here we go." For the mention of Parker's name always rearranged things in Alina's heart. "We were talking about our wedding.

---

[*]Popular reference to the Town's newspaper, unhappily called the *Ashfield Informant*, rather than *Ashfield Informer*

Before it took place, but, of course, after it was destined to. I suggested a very straightforward service, since I didn't think Parker was very religious.

"His whole temper changed...that is, he became very grave. He said he thought it would be 'very wrong' of himself or of anybody else to be irreligious...that he understood that part of being human, with exceptions, was believing in God and worshipping Him. Therefore, he said he felt, that impulse, because seemingly intrinsic in man and persistent, must amount to an adaptive advantage. Otherwise it would long ago have been bred out. That's when I realized orthodoxy was not going to be part of the picture.

"He waited so long, looking at me so eagerly, that I asked what the advantage he proposed might be. And he said 'redemption.' I knew he had long since rejected any notion of what we can gather up under the canopy of 'Original Sin.' So I taxed him about any need for redemption. Then we didn't talk about it again until we were married and settled in New York."

Here Lavinia declared: "Nobody, except some Sectarian Christians, thinks redemption is one particular thing."

"I wonder," Thomas said, "because so many of us call it by this one name and use the word in the same way."

"Even so," Palladian, lovely Lavinia went on, "we use it—when we use it—within a narrowly circumscribed reach of thought, so that it may seem we mean by it the same thing, yet not. Like the familiar example: We agree an object is blue, but we have no way of knowing each other's actual visual sensations when we make our examination and pronouncement."

"That is a familiar example?"

"It's been around as long as I have. I've heard of it all my life."

Laurence: "A fleeting moment in time." Lavinia smiled broadly, characteristically sabotaging her magisterial look and demeanor. "But we've got off to an unpromising start, if, about to discuss a notion of redemption, we can't agree that we can agree what redemption or anything else, I assume, is. Among ourselves."

Bob: "Of 'blue,' remaining objective, we can only give examples, or specify a range of electromagnetic wavelengths. Affectively, we can describe it. But surely more can be said about 'redemption,' and we can go on to specify what we mean by it. Because, as I suspect Thomas is going to tell us in a minute or two, 'redemption' is not 'sensible' but is perceptible only through the intellect. Blue's out."

"We can. And there is a big difference between the meaning of 'meaning' in these two cases, but I am eager—and I've waited patiently, I believe—to hear about Mr. Jones's 'horizontal' kind of redemption."

"The word means buying back or buying again.

"But I don't think Parker was quite satisfied with that; he retold a story from a sermon he'd heard as a little boy. He appears to have been made to go to 'Divine Worship' a lot. It's true, though, I must tell you, that in that connection, for Parker a little could be a lot. Anyway, a child had lost a sailboat that later appeared in a store window. The child's father insisted they 'buy it back.' Parker said he thought that might have made a church-school lesson, but was too flawed to be delivered from the pulpit. Who'd have thought he cared! I doubt that, at the time, he did.

"But he went on to ask me whether, if the toy had been found by another boy, one better able to care for and use it, the boat would have *required* redemption. I said I thought not."

Thomas dismounted. "I might have put money on it! I think he thought redemption meant movement from a place not very well suited to oneself—or oneself to the place, of course—to another, where congruence was more nearly approached."

Alina said: "I believe I remember he said as much."

Thomas: "But he specified a movement sidewise?"

"Yes. He said, 'Not vertical, as from the pit of Hell to the height of heaven, but laterally.' Yukoneta was dusting; I could see she had been getting increasingly agitated, but at that point I thought she had got apoplectic. That's what happened to the Ewer—the Georgian one with the Kyrillic inscription. It's at our house in the ballroom. You've all seen it, haven't you? With the dint?"

Thomas answered: "It seems to me he may have considered redemption to be justification—in the sense of becoming or being made more nearly just. Or just. Did he ever say?"

"Not in those words, not that I can remember."

"Think of not leaving this world, yet entering a part of it where you could usefully give something you possess, but not proper to you: Of intrinsic worth—coral, ivory, gold; or of crafted worth because useful or beautiful; of knowledge, understanding; of enlightenment on a point, or the gift of the ability to enlighten. Or entering another part in which you could recoup those things in each realm, proper to you, but lacking before!"

Alenda, following a draught, for the fizzy water had been put by: "My Dear, if you suppose I don't know that's out of Plato, then you must think me a greater fool than I appear."

"My Love, you appear quite a goddess. Further, you have always known I think so." Alenda couldn't come up with a reply that wouldn't spoil the compliment. She'd be damned before she'd do that.

"Well, then, I wonder. Should you say Mr. Jones's view was like Gnosticism turned on its side?"

"I have always viewed myself," Alina said, "as a country girl—not a 'clot,' exactly—with limited education. But Gnosticism, I do know, depends on the notion of an imperfect creator. That's why they think they have to scrabble their way up to redemption, and be ready for salvation. Or something of the kind."

"The Demiurge," Bob said, in order to remind them that, although a tradesman, he was there, and all there.

"Do you think your first husband would have accepted the notion of an imperfect creator, Alina?"

"In fact I know that he would not have. From this: He didn't believe in Original Sin or any similar doctrine because, as he said, that would imply that the Creator built the world from a defective plan, which he said was impossible. When I mentioned I thought sin had appeared right *after* the Creation, he rejected that, too, as impossible, since it would imply the Creator had used defective elements."

Thomas turned to his bride: "Then, No, Dear. It's not horizontal Gnosticism. Mr. Jones was not thinking of a means of salvation, which the Gnostics thought, I think, was the ultimate reason for redemption through their *gnosis*…knowledge achieved."

Bob said: "We may lose precious time, if we continue to limit this in four-dimensional terms."

Thomas answered: "I think so, too, and I think we may stand to lose more than that."

They were all rather glad to see Duzey Blanding coming up the walkway to join them.

"I'm afraid I couldn't keep up with any more than four," Alina said.

"I'm sure you can, Allie," Lavinia answered. "I think…I don't know much about either physical or metaphysical things…you just give up that framework, but then don't try to replace it. Later, meditate. Though I think you're probably too…alluring easily to be thought of as meditating. But it's not a solely monastic activity. Is it, Thomas?"

"For years, I assumed all people meditated regularly. And for all we know, they may."

"But I don't much think so."

"Neither do I. Anyway, the difficulty in it to me, at the moment, is this: Whether, if you are removed to the better, you vanish from where you began and appear somewhere else? None of us has known of either thing happening. Or, I haven't. And I don't think Mr. Jones, who was obviously not wanting in subtlety, meant anything like that.

"A few have begun to tender the notion of, first, other worlds exactly like our own, the universe being handily great enough and time sufficient in its own extent to make this more probable than improbable. Second, that there are a number of dimensions besides the ones we know, so that the like worlds could even be coincident. That I can tell what they're talking about, alas, doesn't mean I grasp it."

Laurence, whether thoughtlessly or only lost in thought, rattled his unbuoyed ice cubes. Bob, as the youngest and most agile, responded. Laurence nodded his thanks, began clawing absently at his waistcoat buttons, and then said deliberately: "Parker, if he lacked anything, did not lack sinuosity of thought, even though he kept it isolated as we would a winding snake. I have said many times—and drawn often unbelievable, or maybe just unbelieving, responses—that what we can see and touch are not the totality of the world. And I mean Of this world."

"I think you must have become impatient of the sensible world earlier on than most of us. You guessed there must be other…parallels?…other lanes. Yes, I believe 'lanes' will serve. Yes. Starting out together, moving together, leading in the same direction. But not confining.

"I'm afraid that's about as non-dimensional as I can get." Thomas had finished his speech; he turned to his refreshment.

"But we must keep our ideas as far away as we can from what we're accustomed to. Parker once said to me this: 'Rennie, if we let linkages among our beliefs remain mystical, then I think we'll end not making such great asses of ourselves.' And he meant 'to ourselves,' since he sought no followers."

Bob returned, attracting everyone's notice by allowing the screen door to slam shut behind him. He had removed his blazer, and strode along with it slung over his left shoulder. "I heard that. It would have been a vast relief for me to have known my predecessor; in my line of work, linkages were considered essential. They had to be proofed before a—say, a differential diagnosis—could proceed. Two years later, the 'proofs' were 'wrong.' Medicine—a struggle in the dark, and bound to the senses. That's why physicians take up only where philosophers leave off."*

"Then suppose I found myself more nearly true-hearted, or even true-hearted. I would have got to a clearer lane in my life and could see better how to go on. What about the other people and things formerly surrounding me? Because surely I wouldn't have left them behind. For, if I should've done that, then I wouldn't be still in this world."

"I think that for their better or for their worse, they'd have been replicated. Fully. Versions for the new dimension…or dimensions. And the things around you would be mostly the same. Other than the ones accompanying or having preceded you toward redemption."

---

*Christopher Marlowe: *Doctor Faustus*, sc. I: *Ubi desinit Philosphus ibi incipit Medicus*

"Leaving empty simulacra of themselves behind?"

"No—other selves of themselves behind."

"Which self is Me, then?"

"They would be—to borrow language not my own—so closely nuanced as not to seem a plurality."

"Wouldn't that necessitate a near-infinite number of replications? One for each 'lane-change,' by me or by anyone...."

"Or by any thing." For Duzey Blanding had sat through a lot of it, unnoticed at the eastern end of the verandah.

"Yes, I expect so."

Alina, country girl and all, said: "Wouldn't that be wasteful?"

"No. My grandson...well, Edward, whom you all know...studied the classics in college, and therefore naturally came up against the Greek philosophers. He suggested, later while in law school but talking among a group of graduate students in philosophy, Mr. Jones's conception, and was ridiculed for it. Primarily, I suspect, because he was a 'mere' law student. Philosophers will both say and listen to anything, among themselves. He let the jibes die down, then said: 'But it seems to me a terrific means of reaching the Plenitude.'

"So everyone wandered away."

"People are always wandering off, or drifting away. Where do they go?"

"Thus, Alina, it would seem, to me, not wasteful."

"But Creation would have to be going on continuously."

"I've always thought it did, anyway."

Laurence then asked: "Numberless worlds would have to come into being anytime anyone...."

"Or any thing." Duzey.

"Or any thing inched nearer to its redemption? Staggering, but certainly only for us and not for the Creator."

"—Who is underwriting the whole process, anyway. Nor staggering for the worlds."

"We may do our best to find a way to true-up our hearts—maybe our souls, too—when we see them off level or out of plumb. But the actual jog would be implemented by the Godhead."

Bob finished thus: "Belief in Whom and worship of Whom discovers for us this adaptive advantage.

"But we've done it again—slipped back into thoughts depending from dimension. I don't think we'd have to 'leave' from anywhere or 'arrive' anywhere else to edge closer—Note 'edge', not 'rise' or 'descend'—to redemption. 'Look for the God within you.' Or imagine an archway, through which you thought you had to pass in order to be inside. Then realized you *were* inside, and what you saw through it was outside, basking in its own, outer sunlight."

The discussion continued among the men and Alina. Lavinia retired to rest. So did Alenda, to whom Lavinia said, once they were inside: "Thank you so much, on Sarah's behalf. I know what a faithful mainstay you have been to her through all this. And I'm the one who referred her to you for advice."

"It has been nothing but a happiness. It has been a little tiring, though, but less so because your delightful friend Dr. McClure seems quite naturally to have become Sarah's right-hand man, from the moment of his arrival. I don't even know how they met, so early on."

"I bet I do. Carlysle was wounded horribly during the war."

"It doesn't show."

"It never did. He was wounded over here, not over there. If you see what I mean. He couldn't get overseas soon enough. He was supposed to be non-combatant, as a physician. But they could do nothing with him; he disobeyed orders all the time—as though trying to get himself killed.

"And he has never been...out...with a woman, at least not a reputable one, since returning. That is a long time."

"Do you know about Sarah's husband?"

"Only a little."

"Sometime I shall tell you."

Lavinia went upstairs. Alenda followed, after taking fruit and cheese biscuit out to the verandah.

Alenda lay where Grace had lain, imagining the scent of hyacinths. As she sought to empty her mind, yet thoughts of the wedding, oddments of thoughts, came and went. When, for instance, Thomas had got the ring—the one with which Parker had married Alina—it had clacked loudly when he placed it upon the undraped Communion Table..."Bless, O Lord, this Ring, that he who gives it and she who wears it...." Josh, by prior arrangement with Thomas, recited, not taught by the Priest: "With this Ring I thee wed; with my Body I thee worship; and with all my Worldly Goods I thee endow." The formula borrowed from the Prayer Book of the "C. of E.," as Thomas would have it.

Thus, the bride, whose mother had hardly afforded her wedding reception, arrived at it potentially the richest woman present—in a not uncompetitive field.

The thought how, at this reception, modest and stately, modeled after Anne's and Robert's engagement party a quarter-century before, Julie had gone up to her mother, asked Carlysle McClure to hold her glass for her so that she might have both hands free, and lightly thrown her bouquet across to her Mother, to applause.

Thought of the nostalgic dance afterward at the restored Lumina (open next day to all without charge for admission, attractions, refreshments, in honor of the new Patron's Bride).

And five blocks down the street, Josh's wedding present to Juliana: Her family's old cottage, put back as it had been when her mother had been a girl. A pledge that at vacations she would always be able to come home.

Sarah and Carlysle McClure! He would soon become her left-hand man. From the prospect of the officiant.

Downstairs, the Barringtons and Carlysle had gone to their lodging, the pack had lost the scent and were harking back.

"However much redeemed, we're still Man."

"Yes, but made better."

"Yes. But marked."

"A macular dimness at noon with the sky pure of cloud."

"A brack in the cloth of the cut of our days."

"*Est quasi laetitiae vitium.*"

"There is a thing I have to consider: I have been asked to preach at the Unitarian Church. What do you think about that?"

It had taken Alenda only a moment to gather the prospect of a Church-pure year, when before their marriage Thomas had promised it, and though the period had lapsed, she had fully reckoned that state of things in among her happinesses. Now, this! "Thomas! Retirement is retirement. Besides, you are neither cut out nor qualified to take that on!"

The early roses had begun to bloom. Thomas looked steadily at them. Alenda continued: "And there, too, you are bound to encounter some degree of orthodoxy."

"But they don't have—or so I've been told—very specific doctrines."

"Still, they band together. And something must hold them so."

"I believe I have given you the impression that they have called me to their pulpit. No. It's just for a single Sunday. They are inviting clergy from some of the denominations to give 'overviews' of their churches' tenets."

Alenda relaxed, and asked Thomas to bring her a sherry. "Whatever you say. But it will make you sick." And he went into the dining room.

To have heard the closing volumes of my life promise to be the happiest of all my seasons...I'm not able to relinquish it. Unless I have to. And I haven't, not yet, God be thanked.

Thomas, back with her drink, said: "Apparently the first guest speaker was

Father Gavin; do you know Michael? He spoke, apparently at some length, on the Doctrine of the Immaculate Conception of the Blessèd Virgin Mary."

"Hardly an 'overview' of Roman Catholicism, I should think—little as I know about it."

"The Program Chairman made a point of saying to me that they had thought not, themselves. So that I'd be sure to speak generally, I imagine. I can probably undo some of Michael's damage, too, because the two churches were identical until recently. Anyway, the Doctrine of the Immaculate Conception is poorly understood among non-Roman Catholics. And among plenty of themselves!"

"What on earth do you mean by that?"

"The Immaculate Conception?"

"No, no. By identity of the two Churches." The Sherry was a little sickening. That was because it was cream Sherry, which both Bena Lucas and Mary Lou Taliaferro favored. Thomas—Thomas and Alenda—kept it on hand.

"Well, the second Act of Unification was in 1559; Henry had made Parliament declare the Sovereign Head of the Church in, I think, 1534. To the end of his life, though, he thought himself entirely Catholic."

"I realize, Tommy, Darling, that it is not easy to pinpoint the beginning of the Church of England. But the Sixteenth Century can hardly be considered 'recent.'"

"And they're probably not going to get a completely typical version of Anglican doctrine, anyway."

"Certainly not from you, I should say. But if not typical, it will at least be...engrossing."

"Some of my views may go over better with the Universalist-Unitarians— That's what they're called now—than with my former parishioners." He continued to look at the early roses, while Alenda finished drinking her sherry, which seemed to be getting steadily worse.

On the Sunday appointed, Thomas showed up at the Unitarian Church in Wilmington. Dr. Harper, his host, didn't seem to have any particular preparations to make. Thomas put on a cassock and surplice. Then, he produced his purple stole—they were in Lent—kissed it, and placed it about his shoulders. The Roman Catholic priest, with whom, incidentally, Thomas was on terms of pleasant friendship, had worn only clericals, the equivalent of street clothes, he not being in what he thought an authentic place of worship.

The Unitarian Clergyman didn't know what to make of Thomas' vesting; he wondered whether the Program Committee hadn't inadvertently led his own flock from the frying pan into the liturgical fire. Well, the Program was envisaged as a broadening experience; besides, Thomas had been encouraged to believe—as all the Universalist-Unitarians in the County by now already believed—that the topic of the Virgin Mary had been exhausted. All would be well.

When the service was underway and Thomas had been introduced, he did not go up into the pulpit, thinking it the domain of the Denomination's own clergyman, but stood upon the topmost choir-step, if that were what they called it here.

He began: "Dear People of God,

"In thanking you for the opportunity of addressing you, I ask that you forgive me if I say anything which should be to you out-of-the-way, in either form or content. I count upon the breadth of thought for which your Denomination is known and which its name—and here I refer to the recently-formed Unitarian Universalist Association—implies.

"The Church I represent lacks that breadth." And he went on to describe the historical and liturgical likenesses of Anglicanism and Roman Catholicism... and corresponding differences.

"We profess belief in One God, omnipotent, the Creator of all that is.... Of His own Being begat of man a Child, but One already begotten without any other agency or substrate; as we say in the Creed formulated by the Church Councils, from a. d. 325 (Nicæa) until the Sixth Century, 'before all worlds,' *ante omnia sæcula,* taking the Latin *ante* 'before,' in its temporal sense.

"This God-Self—the awkward expression is my own—was sent into the world to be offered to the Father as sacrifice for atonement, man having access to no other sacrifice sufficient for this purpose, and for potential access to everlasting life.

"Christians, when they think to do so, stand in wonderment at God's taking on the flesh of man. What, though, of His exchanging the divine for a human *soul?* I mean, Whole for fragmented. The Councils seem easily to have considered God-with-us Man enough, but worried about His being God enough.

"Be assured that I am aware of the discord between this and others, and the beliefs held by most of you. I am nevertheless aware that Unitarianism originated as a response to Trinitarianism, Universalism as a response to the notion of limited Predestination, so that, historically, your worship of God started out from a background having much in common with my own.

"At this point, I wish I could say to you: 'And that's about it.' However, onto this core have been added so many beliefs, practices, ideas, and variants— though far fewer than in Roman Catholicism—that I must instead tell you that you haven't time, nor I knowledge or stamina, for the cataloguing of them all.

"And nor have I the heart for it."

Thomas, once he had finished these remarks, which he had in a vague way planned, was beset by a sudden anxiety, but it left him as suddenly. For he had no further official duty toward the Episcopal Church, and might say what he would. He removed his stole, touched it briefly to his lips, and folded it. There was a small tabouret near the place where he stood, so he laid the yoke of his priesthood down, and turned back to the congregation.

"My conscience compels me to qualify some of what I have said, because as an individual, although formerly a parish priest, I no longer hold with all of it.

"I cannot think, for the foremost example, that the life of this world should have begun with a bitter conflict between our Creator and ourselves. At that, with a practically Vaudevillian squabble over a snake and a fruit.

"If you leave your child in a comfortably furnished room and, on your way out, say to him: 'Do not look inside the box on the table beside my chair,' then his first act, once alone, will be to open the box and take out whatever is inside.

"But you will not banish him from home because he does this; for you were nearly certain—or ought to have been—that he would behave exactly so. Nor do you cause him to think that, in order to have the ill effect of what he has done set aside, you must have your right arm amputated, that this pain must be endured so that the child may come home. Perhaps my example is distorted and excessive. Perhaps, however, it is not. In any case, this seems a bizarre and arbitrary sequence of acts and outcomes, such as one might believe to have been conceived by a self-hating child who projects his feeling onto the figure of his father.

"Jesus…also taught, probably, that the kingdom of God was already ours, within ourselves.

"Beyond these considerations there is one other: Leaving faith aside (where it belongs, I think, until there is clearer understanding of the very plain and simple Greek word which that word proposes to translate), do we know anything about the Godhead, and, if we do, what do we know, and how do we know it? I shall ask myself these questions every day, until the end of my days.

"Now I shall give you the only thing I have to give; I hope it may not be unpalatable." He took up the violet stole, kissed it a third time, and put it about his shoulders. Then, making the sign of the Cross over the congregation, he blessed them, in the name of the Father, Son, and Holy Ghost.

Then he sat down again in the chair from which he had got up.

"How did it go, Darling?" Alenda asked Thomas. She had arrived before him at the restaurant where they had agreed to meet after the service.

"You would have to ask them that. I did not receive a standing ovation, but everyone was most cordial afterward."

"Did you say anything outrageous?"

"How would I know…not knowing their beliefs?"

"It may be you should have researched all that a bit."

"No. It might have colored what I had to say. That would have defeated the purpose."

The first course arrived (they were both having the *table d'hôte*). About this time there had been introduced a kind of cookery called *nouvelle cuisine*, and this particular restaurant had subscribed to it lock, stock, and barrel. Both Alenda and Thomas could read French fluently, and Alenda could likewise speak it. But the names of the dishes disclosed little, and nor did eating them. Nevertheless, everything was quite delicious.

"I did not say that I no longer held with any Judeo-Christian doctrine." Alenda had known Thomas for a long time. She considered herself proof against anything he might say or claim to believe or deny. But it now appeared she had been wrong. She sought for a reply, but Thomas continued: "I did say, though, that I could no longer accept the notion that the life of man in this world should have begun with a conflict, an act of disobedience by man followed by a terrible retaliation on the part of his Creator."

"That doesn't sound so…heretical."

"Too bad! I meant for it to." Then they spoke about other things.

Early in the evening of the following Thursday, the Strikestraws had been sitting again on the verandah, even though it was drizzling rain. The early roses luxuriated visibly in the gentle shower; Thomas was watching them drink in the moisture and flourish. Alenda seemed abstracted. Presently, she said: "You're still in love with Grace, aren't you?"

"How could I be? She can't mesmerize me with her elegance, nor dazzle me with her wit. Nor make me feel like a king."

"I do those things?"

"Yes, you do."

"You ought to have mentioned it."

"Do people our age speak in those terms?"

"When inspired, yes, they do. All the same, you do still love her."

"Oh, of course I still love her. If I loved her in the first place—nothing has happened to make me not."

Alenda was too kindhearted, and certainly too much in love with Thomas to say anything like: "Well, she did die on you." So she waited.

Thomas watched the raindrops falling from the eaves, mentally tracing their downward paths of retreat from the ridgepole of the house. "But," he said finally, "she did die on me. Death, though, hasn't force enough to interrupt love."

"But I am your favorite wife?"

"At this moment, my absolute favorite out of all of them." They had not taken places at opposite ends of the verandah, but neither were they sitting side by side.

"All right. You're right, and it's quite good enough for me." Then she arose. Walking with the rhythm of a cat stalking a butterfly at rest or a shadow in motion, she came along and—not menacingly—confronted her husband: "Have you filled Edward's head with all this? Mary and I keep in touch, you know. And it wounds her that Edward is unconcerned about her continuing to love Josh."

"Well, she seems to love the Jones boy still. Ashfield-Jones boy. And deeply. But, I trust, not in a...passionate or romantic way. She will become confident of Edward's devotion before long." The rain on the roof was coalescing as it ran downward; now it plumped loudly upon the gravel below the eaves. "Or, perhaps, it is she herself who is concerned about continuing to love the other boy."

They moved into the library, where Alenda brought up again the subject of Thomas's address to the Unitarians.

"You know...or it strikes me so...the whole thing...."

"What whole thing?"

"The Church."

"Oh, that. Yes."

"...deals with bouts of separation of man from God."

"Stories! God and man are quite separate to begin with. Man doesn't need divine wrath and banishment to clarify that issue. The whole thing is a myth—meaning nothing pejorative—that we haven't yet rightly understood." And then the telephone rang; while a far more sophisticated instrument than had been there so long before, it still stood upon Thomas's desk in his study, and it was still the only ugly thing in the room.

When he rejoined Alenda, Thomas's eyes were alight, not, she thought, with the mania of the heretic, but in joyful wonder. He said: "It's almost too good to be true! That was a Unitarian!"

"Darling, I'm sure the town's full of them."

"But guess what he told me!"

"I couldn't in a thousand years. Say."

"That they believe in one God; that He bears no attribute in common with man; and they don't believe in any form of original sin!"

"And they have invited you to come back?"

"Yes, but this time only for an informal discussion, and luncheon, with the Men's Study Group. It's next Wednesday. May I go, do you think?"

The next Wednesday morning, Alenda and Thomas went to the big closet off their bedroom (originally used as a trunk-room) to select an outfit for Thomas's appearance. Alenda began to take out coathangers by turns, examining what each held. "There's nothing suitable. You'll have to wear your clericals."

"No. I'm not going to do that."

"Why not."

"They're unsuitable, too, just as much as you say everything else is."

"We must go shopping for a wardrobe as soon as possible."

"In the meantime, then, I'm going to wear my poplin suit."

"You can't wear a poplin suit, not before Easter!"

"I'm going to, though."

"Thomas, men are basically impossible to deal with. And you needn't think you're an exception, just because you're a priest and have an agreeable manner."

"My own dealings with men have usually been satisfactory."

"That's because they're other men."

"By that kind of reckoning, then, if men are impossible to deal with, shouldn't dealings among men amount to impossibility compounded?"

"That is exactly the kind of remark I'm talking about. It's specious."

Thomas said nothing in reply. Alenda: "Choose your own clothes then." [Thomas had chosen them the day before.] She left the room.

In at least this respect, marriage is like a vaccination: Sometimes, without the occurrence of an acute, somewhat repulsive reaction, in cannot be said to have "taken," that is, been successfully founded.

Once at the Unitarian Church, Thomas was surprised to find so many cars already there. Probably they belonged to staff and presumably to members of some other organization meeting at the same hour as the Men's Study Group. He found the clergyman alone in his study. This was where the "informal discussion" was to have taken place.

"Good morning...day, Canon. We are so glad to have you as our guest, once again. But I must tell you that there has been a change of plan: A good many more signed up for this session than we'd expected."

"Good gracious!"

"I don't quite see how we can have a 'discussion' among so many. Your talk will take place in the Church."

"That is not a misuse of the building?"

"Oh, not at all. I suppose the best explanation I can give you is that our churches are 'dedicated,' rather than 'consecrated.'"

So the two men started the short walk to the Church, and Thomas asked: "If I am to speak rather than discuss, what am I to speak about?"

"Whatever you think best, of course—Are you a good extemporaneous speaker? I am not."

"No, I'm not either. I could begin at the beginning—of the Church, that is. Then see where that leads us. Would that do? Would it be appropriate for me to invite questions?"

"Oh, absolutely."

For the second time, Thomas felt awe upon entering the beautiful, lofty volume of the old sanctuary. He nodded to the congregation, who were numerous, and went again to his same place; but this time one of the members had produced a comfortable chair for his use. However it was standing that he began:

"Ladies and Gentlemen [*How odd it sounded!*]:

"...I shall speak about the beginning—for it has long struck me as a very anomalous beginning—of the Holy Catholic Church. I don't know what result to expect, since I have not fully formulated nor ever before expressed these views, but I am afraid I may seem irreverent, and a reprobate.

"Let me liken the inception of Christianity to the planting of a seed. Not very original, to be sure, but it is to be remembered that there is a time for planting. If the seed be planted too late, then it will not germinate, and nothing will come of it; if too soon, the seed may germinate, producing root and shoot, but the resulting tree (let us say) is likely to lack both vigor and fertility.

"To my way of thinking, the seed of the Christian Church was planted prematurely. I would not say so if I considered this to have been done or directed by the Godhead. The seed of the Church was planted by man.

"...These kinds of [practices of the primitive Church] we might all ourselves, in varying degrees and combinations, undertake in order to commemorate our own departed mentors and other benefactors. A kind of Founder's Day, or series of them.

"...The element of the miraculous had been introduced, and, it appears, it was hard to let it go. In the troubled times of the First Century of our era, magic, prophecy in the sense of foretelling the future—these and many other things of a supernatural cast, in the absence of what we now call knowledge, prevailed in many lands and among peoples of dissimilar cultural extraction....

"...By the First Century of our era, the making-sense of babbling was common, both in the Roman World and in the Greek World, the latter having the illustrious oracular precedents of Dodona and Delphi. But well into later times many persons claimed ability to serve one or the other function (that is to babble prophetically, or, on the other hand, to make sense of the babbling). And the Delphic oracle itself was not finally closed for business until the late Fourth Century a. d.

"Against this background, the tradition of Pentecost, the fiftieth-day arrival of the Holy Spirit, grew up. And I think it grew up to replace an earlier planting that had not waxed sturdily. A further infusion of divinity was needed, although I imagine it originated within a backward glance....

"Well...the seed of the Church was sown, but that too early. The ideas were too volatile, I think, for abrupt inauguration. For the Church is an organization of human beings, no matter to what degree ratified by the Divine, and we do better forming institutions after at least a moderate period of planning, or trial run. Little time seems to have been set aside for studies, presentations, seminars, referenda, and so on.

"There was the further, unique difficulty that Apostles and followers, disciples at every level, believed that Jesus's return, marking the Day of Judgment and the end of Time, was imminent, and certainly expected to occur within their lifetimes.

"So there was understandably no time to be wasted upon planning for the unforeseen, mammoth, world-winding meshwork of doctrines, beliefs, and practices which in our own time make up the Church.

"...After his own conversion, Paul's theology was firm. He ruled that Gentile Christians were, through trust in Christ's sacrifice, equally eligible, with Jewish Christians, to receive a favorable judgment and be counted among the sheep. His achievement is to have brought a Christian core of thought out of the obscurity of Jewish sectary into the light of a preëminent world religion. However, he relied in a necessarily limited way upon the teachings of Jesus, purporting to have been recorded elsewhere, and he never met Jesus. Ending, I think, a period of neglect during which the seedling-Church failed to thrive. The name was carried over this lacuna, but not much more than the name. Practically or administratively, that is.

"Of all the questions, though, that St. Paul must face as a leader, the thorniest by far—though it appears not to have caused much trouble at the time—as it seems to me, was the concern brought by mostly Gentile converts, soon after the middle of the Century, to the attention of St. Timothy, who conveyed it to St. Paul: Some converts had taken to dying; their fellows had been led to think that this ought not to have happened—that, with the end of the world just around the corner, they would be (favorably) judged and forwarded on to their Heavenly reward. St. Paul was able, apparently without difficulty and I think most remarkably, to give assurances that, dead or alive, the trustful, the dead ones having been resurrected for the occasion, would receive their Crowns of Salvation. It should be remembered how far desperation may go toward allowing us to overlook inconsistencies and to cobble together ideas that 'explain away,' as some express it, impalatable realities.

"For my part, I cannot understand how the communities were so readily convinced of this, as they had been converted with entirely different promises. But these came from within the wilting, primitive cult. After a generation or two had died out, still there seemed no Last Day on the horizon. The Gospel of John, in Chapter Six where Jesus speaks of Himself as the Bread of Life, contains several instances of the Lord's saying: 'I will raise you up (using the verb *anístêmi,* typically meaning, "raise from the dead") at the Last Day.' I do not recall very many instances of this offer in the Synoptic Gospels.

"It is interesting, to me, to note that, following this somewhat involved passage in John, verse 66 reads: 'From that time, many of his disciples went back, and walked no more with him.' Can this have been an expression of disaffection, or worse, on the part of some who knew that the first followers had been led to believe that they would not see death, then found that they might in fact have to undergo death, then, at the best, be resurrected, *then* to be taken up into Heaven? Who can say? St. Paul, who died probably in a. d. 67, grappled with the problem during the 50's; the Gospel of John was not written until toward the end of the First Century. Jesus Himself had died, we think, in a. d. 30.

"I have given as my opinion that the seed which grew into the earliest Church was planted too soon, and I think this because it was after the seed had been sown that this seismic anomaly occurred. A young tree is green all through, and supple. And the nascent Church was tugged, possibly twisted, about in many directions."

Here, a gentleman stood up. Thomas saw him, said: "Yes, Sir?"

"You have given us Paul's ruling. But was the notion that Judgment Day was very near taught by Jesus himself."

"I think it was. Look, when there is time, in the Gospel of Luke, the twenty-first chapter. (Thomas was always pleased to be able to cite Scripture; since he bothered himself so little about it, he hadn't many opportunities.) Jesus gives a blood-curdling account of the prelude to the Last Day, then tells his audience (He uses the imperatives; He is commanding those gathered about Him): '*Then* look up, lift up your heads, for your redemption draweth nigh.' No delay for the purpose of raising the qualified dead is stipulated. Whether this were part of His general teaching, or indeed of His teaching at all, we cannot, I think, say. The Gospel of Luke and The Acts (of which Luke is thought the author) were not written until late in the Century, and in the latter work the Evangelist makes a point to Christians, putatively quoting the Master, that it is not for them to know the 'day or the hour' of Christ's return. One way or other, Jesus and St. Luke never met. Not personally, and neither, it seems to me, upon the topic of eschatology." The gentleman had not seen fit to remain standing throughout all this, but afterward rose again, and the two exchanged courtesies.

"By this time, the interval was inexorably lengthening. And still, no End of the World. The 'Any day, now' doctrine had for some reason without disrupting anything—or anything very much—given way to the 'We'll just have to wait and see' approach. The young sapling was, meanwhile, having much—I think, too much—baggage hung upon every new branch as it came forth. I have not always been able to find evidence of what we might term "hardening-off" nor an adequate root-system to stabilize all of it. There were surely shorings-up and guying-out to compensate for this want. And I am very much afraid that a certain amount of grafting, by which I mean specifically allografting, took, has taken, and is still taking place. This seems to represent a decided discontinuity; not that I claim with complete conviction that the Church is a heap of ornament and enigma concealing a withered sapling at its core.

But close.

"Please bear these things in mind; then I shall close: I have cited events and a few dates, I think without giving you incorrect information. I have limited my observations to the First Century, it may seem constasting the first thirty years of it with a twenty-year shadowy transition and then the rest. We are told much *about* that first segment, but only a very small proportion of the accounts in our possession actually dates from that time; that is, the writings were put down mostly in retrospect; none of them even pretends to have been written during Jesus's stint as Man, nor the authors to have known Him.

"Seeing the Last Day arrive prior to one's death, versus dying, then being resurrected for judgment, is to my mind a momentous distinction. Yet nobody else seems to think so now, and in antiquity only a few behaved as though they thought so, as far as we know, notwithstanding that we are told of the disaffection, at one point, of 'many.'

"I hope some of you—and I wish it could be each of you—will write to me with whatever reactions you may have to what I have said. Again, I thank you." There was polite but quite definite and general applause. Thomas was shocked.

And then everyone crossed the grounds to luncheon.

That afternoon, when Thomas arrived back at home, Alenda tried to show genuine interest in what had taken place at the Men's Study Group. She tried and tried. She tried as hard as she could. But she failed, because in fact she had next to no concern with the Primitive Church (and little enough with the Church of her own day; which she almost never attended, "because I cannot bear to see people I like and others whom I love in a setting of such degradation").

After two days had passed, two of the responsive letters which Thomas had solicited arrived in the same mail:

My Dear Canon Strikestraw,

First of all, I want to thank you for a charmingly errant, completely engrossing talk at our Church on Wednesday. I knew about those early expectations, and of course I knew that they had not been fulfilled. But I had never thought of the really savage impact that anomaly, to borrow your term, may very well have had on the early converts, and on more than a few, at that.

I hesitate to propose my explanation of the continued adherence of so many, because my expression does not reflect my own way of speaking, nor does it convey my way of understanding.

Having given those qualifications, I do wonder whether those who "beheld the Savior's face" and listened to His words may not have been uniquely moved, even to the extent of feeling that they had seen the Countenance and heard and Voice of God?

I should imagine that the force of such an experience would be held closely, and so be passed down through many generations. Perhaps I am very foolish in this.

Again with thanks, yours very truly,
[signed] Mary Rose Gelzer Huet
(Mrs. Jonathan J. Huet)

The second was not like unto it:

Dear Mr. Canon Strikestraw,

I am a plain woman, and that's about the best as can be said of me. I left the church I was raised in because I couldn't stand it no longer. When I left, my Pa (God rest the dead) asked me why I was leaving. He was the one to make me go to Church in the first place. When I told him, he said I might as well go off and be a Unitarian, if that was all I believed. So I did. And it suited me fine, because I felt like I had a chance to worship the Almighty without really having to go to Church. Found me a husband, too. Married fifty-eight years. Andrew (God rest the dead).

The reason I'm writing is, I know you young preachers travel a mightily rough road in this day and time. I want you to know I'm praying for you, that you come to a right vision of the Lord, and bring your flock to Him to add into His own flock.

You left me behind a good deal last Wednesday. But I liked what I could tell of what you said, and I knew, when I could follow along, that you were laying your beliefs on the line, and I liked that. The preacher at the church I was raised in did that, too, but I couldn't stomach what it was he laid—telling me what to believe, like I and everybody else didn't know what. *Everybody* knows what. (That don't mean they necessarily *understand* what they know.)

And I also want to say that I'd have smelt a rat a lot sooner than them limpards you spoke of, the ones in the Gospel of John.

I thank you for a right good talk, Son, and I'm praying God will give you increase of understanding, as long as you can hold out, so you can bring the rest of us children of His to seeing things as true.

God bless you, Son. From Elsie Martindale

XI

"…by the god's design two
green eyed serpents tended him, with blameless venom distilled
of bees. The king, riding from rocky Pytho,
questioned all in the house when he came for the child
Euadne had had borne, and called him issue

of Phoibos, to be beyond all men a seer among mortals
pre-eminent, nor his race fail ever thereafter."

Pindar: Olympia VI, ll. 45-51 (tr. Richmond Lattimore)

"There is a kind of superstition, a tribal order which is always respected.
Each year the azalai gather round the Tree before facing the crossing of the
Ténéré. The Acacia has become a living lighthouse…."

Michel Lesourd, *Commandant des A. A. M., Service central des
affaires sahariennes:* Journal Entry of May 21, 1939

"Before [sc., in 1934], this tree was green and with flowers; now [November 26, 1959] it is a colourless thorn tree and naked. I cannot recognize it—it had two very distinct trunks. Now there is only one, with a stump on the side, slashed rather than cut...."

Henri Lhote: *L'épopée du Ténéré*

ONLY A COUPLE of months after his marriage, Edward entered Law School, and after that he and Mary returned to Wilimington, where Edward became associated with the firm that had, or had had, in it all those men who had considered belonging to his Club in college a type of apotheosis, triggering his roommate Sandy Thomas's ever-near sense of having made a wrong choice, and thus running a risk ultimately of not "fitting in." Edward exhibited an unforeseen facility with maritime law and quickly came to be valued by his colleagues.

Josh and Juliana returned to Peell County, and both went to work—a thing Julie had always done, Josh, never. But he, too proved to have a gift, especially where it came to winning motion-hearings. Julie took up nursing at War Memorial Hospital in Ashfield; little scope was available to her ability, but she had several remarkable experiences, as we shall eventually see, before she had to restrict nursing to the sort given at the breast: Laurence des Champs-Locuplétisis Ashfield-Jones was born in 1967 (causing Edward to remember Laurence's recommendation that the latter hyphen eventually be dropped), and the next year twins were born to them.

After considering doing so for some years, Josh bought the ruin of Dodona house, with its lands (the Paget Family cemetery excepted, as through the years) and set about restoring it.

At last after almost ten years, the younger Strikestraws set off upon their long-belated wedding-trip. They had chosen three places to visit in particular, planning to follow their incidental interests and inclinations about what to do and see in between.

Edward, not as the first, had a momentous dream while asleep in the desert: He believed that he awoke just minutes before dawn, that he arose, dressed and lighted a candle; it would not disturb Mary, still sleeping, for light was already increasing all about. When he ventured from their tent, though, and looked back, the glow from the candle seemed a stoutening surety for return, if there should be need. This was, after all, the Desert. He sat down, facing the stark metal symbol of a tree that had been set up where the famous *Arbre du Ténéré* had stood for...actually, nobody knew for how long. "Always" was the consensus among the Tuareg and the other local folk. It had been a way-station on caravan routes through the Sahara in northeast Niger—so well known that it was the only tree to be shown on a map at a scale of 1:4,000,000. The Strikestraws had heard that, while living, or possibly only standing where its seed had anciently found nurture, it had been knocked over by a drunken dwarf of a truck driver from Libya, who had tried to mitigate his culpability by claiming not to have been able to see the Tree over the dash-panel until he was upon it. So his driver's license was revoked, and he was thrown into jail and finally deported, a Thyrsites, who cowered down, and let fall a big tear.

Now Edward sat down, drew up his legs, and, glorying in the gaining suffusion of morning light, examined closely the metal tree. Many, who required of "art"—whatever that might sometime be shown to be—either ornament, or fidelity to things seen or known of before, or some other restrictive covenant, found this staff a useful marker, but nothing else.

He initially saw it glowing red in the first rays to bow toward the earth in flaming gale, then burn to gold, as the sun rose above the dunes and struck it full. It had all a tree really needed to make itself a tree, and beautiful: A *Stamm* and branches. If roots, naturally they'd be underground and out of sight. If there were to be leaves, then they would appear in their season. And in their kind.

All of a sudden, the head, neck, and markedly sloping shoulders of a very large serpent appeared at the brink of a well—the one still open, for another had been sunk nearby but then neglected. Offsetting the cleft tongue, alternately and repetitively cast forth and retrieved, were the creature's large, kindly green eyes. When it saw Edward, it popped down again out of sight.

But soon it was back: "Good morning. I hope I didn't startle you," it said graciously to Edward.

"Good morning. No, I was not at all startled. But I had not expected to see…anyone else."

At this point, Mary came out from their tent, dressed in walking-shorts with cargo pockets, and a silk shirt. Everything about this manly attire was feminine. One might have expected her to have latched up her hair for a day in the desert. But she always wore it falling loose. She did not appear alarmed by the snake, which was quite large, as that order goes, but smiled prettily and said: "Good morning, Edward." And to the snake: "Good morning to you."

"Do the two of you belong to Mankind?"

"Yes," Edward answered. "Both of us do. And can I assume that you are yourself Reptilian?"

"I know I give that impression. However, I am not that." Here a second serpent appeared, and it became clear immediately, through comparison, that she was the mate of the first; she had a lovely, womanly look about her, especially about the soft, dark green eyes (His were paler).

"Oh! Good morning to you all; how delightful to have guests!"

"Hello, Dear. They are men, as you can see. I was trying to explain that I—we—in spite of aspect to the contrary, are not Reptilians."

"Oh, Madame…," the second serpent began.

"Please call me Mary."

"Mary, then," the second serpent said, who later asked to be called 'Sis,' from the acronym, "he is not too careful about verbal nuances. Do forgive him, for I am quite sure that he knows the difference between a man and a woman."

"Yes, indeed," the first serpent interjected. It is a distinction we have had to deal with hereabout for a long time. Now I must admit right away that, though I do use expressions like 'hereabout' and 'a long time,' I do not have a genuine grasp of their meanings. I have a feeble *Sprachgefühl* for them, but it is not reliable."

The first serpent, whom they would call "Sss," at his request ("That comes as close as possible, at least in Tuarick, to the pronunciation of my Ancient Name," he had said, disingenuously), continued: "That brings me back to my explanation of why we are not of the Reptilians. We have no time." He said it conclusively, as though it were an answer.

"Besides," Sis said, "we have no room." She evidently considered this the full explanation of something, for she said no more.

"Well," Mary said standing, "I am hungry. Just let me go inside, prepare a few things, and we can have breakfast together. How would that be?"

Sis asked whether she happened to have "a little box of toads."

Edward excused himself and followed Mary into the tent. He said, in a low voice: "What can they possibly mean by 'not having time' and 'not having room'?"

Mary turned from the low table where she had laid out a tray of flatbreads and was brewing tea from a copper kettle: "Edward, you astound me…as often; of all inexplicable things to wonder about, why those?"

"I think they may be fundamental. Besides, nothing else has struck me as inexplicable."

"What of sitting about chatting with snakes as big as we are?"

"What about chatting with snakes of any caliber, for that matter?" Thomas Strikestraw's own true issue replied.

So they took the breads and tea and went out to join the others. When they had gone into the tent, only the smoothly-blending but intense colors of low light in clear air, sharp shadows etched by cusps of dunes, and bleached carcases of camels were to be seen.

Edward reflected with regret upon their not having any toads to offer the snakes (believing that Sis had meant candied or otherwise preserved ones). And he thought it odd how fully things had commuted in so few minutes. For when he and Mary had come out with the rather bald breakfast, the landscape all around was far other than that so wholly vacated one they had turned their backs upon. But since Sis and Sss seemed oblivious of change, neither Mary nor Edward said anything right away. The sun mounted a few degrees. The tea cooled a little. The flatbreads remained—to the extent that they remained at all—crisp, as though in the atmosphere of a desert.

Yet all around them a mist arose, full of rainbows. Grassy rides meandered away in various directions. Pathways of mosses branched from these. Some of the spaces reminded Mary and Edward of the little gardens and pools embraced behind the Ashfield mansions. There could be no gauging the season: Every plant was at its most splendid, and every plant was there. Mary said something about this plenitude, and Sis replied: "It truly is amazing, isn't it? Do you know, there are more than seventy varieties of cauliflower here!"

Sss had noticed that the pair were glancing about in discreet wonder. He said: "Oh, Dear. We must have changed parallels while you were getting breakfast. And it was very good, too, I must say."

"I'm so glad you enjoyed it," Mary said, creating a clausula, so that the question of "changing parallels" might not have to be gone into. The subject did not recur. Mary was a young lady stout of heart, but she knew her limit, and she knew she was speedily reaching it.

Edward had become absorbed in watching the place where the disused well had been. Now it was uncovered, and all the fountains of the Great Deep had got broken up, and there came up clear water, flowing in a silent stream. Silently and swiftly. And the streambed in which the water flowed was deep, so that the bottom of it could only be suspected. He asked: "Is this pure water?"

And Sss replied: "Do you know of a lake in a place now called Siberia? Some name this lake *Dalai-Nor*; others, *Baykal*."

Mary and Edward looked at each other in astonishment, and together said: "We have just come from there!"

"Then I expect you know, among all the remarkable facts about it...."

Sis interrupted: "All learning is one lesson, of course."

"...That a potter's vessel, taken direct from the kiln, then plunged one hundred times into boiling water, and dried in the heat of a furnace between immersions...."

Sis: "Or just an ordinary flask, autoclaved."

"…When filled with water from that lake will defile it, because its water is entirely pure."

"That is one of the many things we were told," Edward was able to answer, before Sis had a chance to maintain that all those many wonderful things known about Lake Baikal were really just one.

"Yet," Sss continued, "the water of even that lake will defile this fount."

"Perfect in its purity?"

"Perfect in its purity."

Mary had begun to look more objectively at the two serpents, with their heads and shoulders rising from one well, while near beside them poured the pristine, never-failing waters to which defilement was unknown. Really, she thought, they made an imposing pair; Sis was especially entrancing, with her deep, green eyes, set off against the fragile vapor of Covenant-hues, as it floated about her in the air. "Sis," she said, after thinking about it, "You are truly lovely. Enviably so."

"Well, now, that is certainly praise from Cornelia, as they say. It is very kind of you, my Dear."

"Could I ask…do you use anything…perhaps about the eyes?"

Sis laughed, producing an entirely characteristic sound: "No, Dear. Nothing at all. But I must own it's not for want of trying. Of course, through the millennia, we've seen varieties of that sort of thing around here. And, oh yes, I've tried it. The difficulty has always been that nothing will stick. Scales, you know. So I gave it up."

"In any event, I can't imagine anything improving the effect." At this, Sis blushed a little, once more to very specialized effect.

"Thank you again, Mary. I'm sure you flatter me." Then she turned to her consort. "Come along, then, Dear." And to the Strikestraws: "We do best if we sun ourselves a little. The two of you make yourselves at home. Later, I know, Sss is going to want to tell you the story of the trees." And they climbed all the way out of the well and sinuated off into the Garden.

Edward and Mary heard a soughing, like the sound of sand running from a hopper for transportation, and soon Sis and Sss appeared, returning from their sunbath. He asked: "Have you enjoyed your day?"

"We've enjoyed it," Mary said, "but we are exhausted from it. We climbed that dune." She pointed. The wind had already removed the vestiges of their trek.

The two snakes glanced knowingly toward each other. "Walking in sand is next to impossible," Edward said, "harder, even, than trudging through running surf. I have to admire the way you two get about—over the sand, instead of through it.

"There is much to be said for not having limbs."

"That poor Tree, for instance. Such a glorious heritage! And such an ignominious end!"

"The loss of a limb was not what undid the Tree, Dear. Besides, I was speaking of arms, legs...that kind of limbs."

"Yes, then you're not subject to breaking them, having them cut off. And the incidence of arthritis drops off sharply as the absence of them."

The two young people had arthritis, but it would not become symptomatic for many years yet. So they listened with mild amusement. But everyone noticed that Sss was frowning slightly, and this produced again a unique facial expression. "My Dear, I'm going to tell them about Billie Jean." At this, there was a silence. Then the desert wind howled mourning. Sis looked suddenly, as we sometimes hear it put, "down in the dumps." Billie Jean was her niece.

"Snakes aren't entirely without joints—we do have spines, after all, and rather significant ones, at that. From the clinical standpoint. Of course, spending as little time as we do coiled, and the rest more or less stretched out, we bear little weight upon our vertebral columns.

"But there is a form of spinal arthritis—mercifully uncommon—that used to be called 'ankylosing spondylitis.'"

"It still is," Edward said. For in addition to being broadly well-informed, he had, to everyone's surprise who knew them, kept up a close friendship with Sandy Thomas, who had changed his mind again about medical school, but not about Claire Cloudsley Elder. "The spine can fuse, straight as a ramrod in some cases."

"That's what happened to Billie Jean. Not to change the subject, but has either of you heard of a man called Moshe?"

After Edward had murmured a word of explanation to his young wife, both said they had.

"Apparently this man—somewhere up in the Northeast, I think—was conferring, off and on, with God Most High...." At this phrase, both serpents bowed their heads briefly, so from then onward, the Strikestraws joined them in this practice. "...about leading his people from one place, where they were not so well off, to another, where they supposed they would fare better.

"On the way to one of Their meetings, Moshe picked up what he thought was a stick. But it was Billie Jean, who was having an extremely severe attack." Sis's eyes were suddenly flooded with tears, and she turned away. Luckily, she was wearing no eye makeup.

"Moshe expressed doubt that his people would follow him; the escape involved a degree of danger. So God Most High"—all bowed their heads briefly—"Intructed him to throw the 'staff' that he held, which was actually Billie Jean, to the ground. He did, and did so very roughly.

"The impact...." At this, Sis burst into sobs, and made her way, in doleful arcs, to the edge of the well. Then she disappeared inside it. "...Lysed all the vertebral fusions, and the poor child began to writhe in pain, the intensity of which can only be guessed at. Moshe apparently shrank back in terror—for serpents had somehow got a 'bum rap,' as some say, by the era in which this man Moshe lived—but was ordered to take B. J. by the tail. When he touched her, the pain increased, and all her muscles, the poor thing, went into spasm from it, and once again, when she went rigid, Moshe thought her a stick. He reckoned that if he could repeat this apparent magic before various people, then his leadership qualities would stand in no doubt. He assumed he'd be able to do it with any stick, so he went away, leaving Billie Jean behind.

"I don't think I could have brought myself to tell you that part, unless Sis had left. She worries about her constantly."

Edward asked: "How is she doing now?"

"She's in a home."

"Oh."

Edward, awakening, mistook twilight for sunrise. He and Mary had had a nap while Sss was down in the well trying to reassure Sis. Edward awakened Mary and said: "Ordinarily, I don't recount my dreams, but you've got to let me tell you about this one." After he had told her she said to him: "That was not a dream, Edward."

"No? How do you know?"

"I took part in the whole thing."

"Are you saying, then, that we spent a whole day talking to serpents."

"Unless I had the same dream—a complementary one, rather—at the same time."

"Well, then, maybe that's what happened."

"No, Pumpkin. That is not what happened. And it is evening, not morning, now. And they are going to tell us about the Two Trees. You remember that, don't you?"

"Yes. Sss said it was a 'beautiful and gracious' story."

"See? It did happen, all of it." They changed for dinner, although the clothes they changed into were very much the same as the ones they had been wearing all day, but fresh clean.

Edward said: "Look outside and see whether they seem to be ready."

"No, they haven't come up yet."

"Then I think I'll shave again. This could be a very important night."

"Very well. And while you do, I'll start a fire. It's getting dark, and that means it will be getting chilly." The serpents had returned from their day's relaxation with a plenty of faggots curled within their tails, although you can never be quite sure where a snake's tail ends and its torso begins.

"The lighter is on the table."

Mary took the lighter and went outside. It was already darker than when she had put her head out of the tent, just moments before. The Garden was held in sleep. She made a pyramid-shaped fire, and hadn't to wait long before it was crackling jauntily and sending up tongues of white flame, against the blue band of light that hung just above the distant dunes, far beyond the...oasis?

Soon, they were all together. The evening meal was much like the morning one, but more elaborate. There was honey for the flatbreads, wine to drink, dried figs and dates, and some toads, which the serpents ate *au naturel*. However, these creatures got their lives back forthwith. The Strikestraws were by this time past amazing.

Sis was in good spirits, and when they were comfortably ringed about the fire, which had fallen in upon itself and was sending up plumes of sparks shaped like Arabic and Hebrew letters, she said: "Now it's time for you to hear about the Trees."

"We're both eager to hear."

"This one [Sss indicated the Acacia, which was standing unbroken, in full leaf and fruit], the Tree of Knowledge of Good and Not-so-Good, has always been my particular province. You'll notice it's associated with the well we live in."

"Not to boast," Sis said, "but we do have quite a charming little *pied-à-terre* around *trente mètres*. I'd like to invite you down to see it, but...."

"I'd better get on with the story. Beside it stood, at first another Tree."

"The Tree of Life," Mary put in.

"Just so. I see you already know the story. But I wonder whether you know the correct version of it."

"I," Edward said, "don't know of but one. The one in the Bible, in the Book of Genesis. Do you know it? Is it right?"

"I know of it, Young Sir. But I have not read it. It was passed down by some people who were really not very, ah...."

"Happy about things in general." Sis.

"As it was told and retold, and finally written down, some distortion had crept in. However, as we were here all along—I think 'all along' is right—we can give you an accurate version."

"I'm excited about all this," Mary said, and Sis smiled at her benignly. Benignly and knowingly.

With blessing and knowledge!

"I'll bet I'm even more excited," Edward said. "Because my grandfather is a priest—of God Most High, we believe—and he has got so he cannot put up with the version you spoke of. I can say why, later."

"Or I may know why. But let us see. When Man were created, God Most high placed them here, just as the Book says, provided with every kind of delight. But He had a conference with them, during which He explained that, if they wished to remain as they were, and to have everything go on about them as was the case at that...juncture, then they should not eat the fruit borne by this Tree.

"Latterly, as I gather, there has been some confusion about the exact horticultural designation. Some have thought it *Acacia raddiana*, others, *A. tortilus*. In fact it is *A. luminifera*. Eva and Adam could, though, eat some of the fruit of the Tree, if they chose to. But then things would change, they would have problems to solve, challenges to meet, difficulties to overcome, and so on. We were not present at the meeting, but we were told about it later that evening at a little gala—not many were invited. The Children, of course, some from the Orders, Orbs for music. Messengers. It was a solemn celebration, as you can imagine.

"Eva and Adam—they by themselves constituted Mankind—hemmed and hawed over the thing a good deal, mainly because conditions were rather nice for them as it was. Ultimately, Eva came to us here after a few days and said: 'We've gone into it from every angle we can think of; our position is "Nothing risked, nothing gained".'

"So I went up into the tree and brought down some of the fruit, enough for both of them to get the effect they'd decided they wanted. Eva thanked me, and went off munching upon one of the pulpy rinds, naked as a jaybird."

"We were brought up to think that God...Most High warned Adam and Ev...a against eating that fruit under any circumstance whatever," Mary said.

"Yes, and that He got enraged against them, and threw them out of the Garden."

"To lead a life of hardship and misery."

"Nonsense! What Father would deal with His children in that way?"

"Some human fathers do, I think."

"Yes, and that's exactly where that notion came from." Sis was indignant.

Mary replied: "I can tell you that Edward's grandfather couldn't believe that sort of thing of the Creator." The serpents seemed to understand the identity, and bowed their heads.

"And I don't accept it any more than my grandfather does."

Sss and Sis spoke for a moment between themselves. The he said: "It is a relief to find that at least some, even having been told a distorted version of the story, know how the Creator treats His Creation."

"With care," Edward said. "Even the merest sub-contract creators among Mankind do that. Though some high-strung human 'creators' have indeed flown into rages and mutilated or even destroyed their creations."

"That, my Man, is precisely how this kind of thing got projected onto the Godhead!

"The Children did leave the Garden, of course. That was the whole point of their decision. They intended to risk just about any alternate to living on as hothouse-plants. However, God Most High keeps watch above His own, irrespective of who they are or of what they do, but He does it usually from within the shadows, behind the dim unknown."

"And," Sis uttered almost breathlessly, "He didn't let them go off ill-equipped—He made them coats."

"Now, I will say that—I think; Don't you, Mary?—that part is included in our Book."

"But does it give an adequate description of them? Well, Adam's was rather tailored but with raglan sleeves, very straightforward, quite distingué. But *hers!*" Here Sis turned toward Mary in particular. "My Dear, you would have to have seen it to believe it! Calfskin, buffed, and colored like the sand of the desert, near sundown. At the sleeves and neck, fur of the silver fox. Of course, the calf got back replacement-skin instantaneously, as, indeed, the fox, its fur. But let me tell you they left here in *great* style!"

"The Father," Sss said, having now got very grave—though all responded to the Reference, as they were by now learning from each other and "catching on"—"did ask them to leave via the service-entrance (I believe your Book states that the Garden was planted 'eastward,' and that they left from the eastern boundary). Sis and I had to change form, as we must in the Presence, and put on our Court uniforms. When we change form, we look rather like you two, but a little taller, and we, umh...."

"We shine."

"...Shine—You can count on Sis for *le mot juste*—but not with an ordinary light. Ours is a mixture of a lot of what we call 'spans,' 'cubits,' 'reeds,' and determinants of that sort. Can you tell from this what I mean?"

"Yes," Edward said, I think I can."

"I can't," Mary said.

"I think, Sss, that those are obso...are, to us ancient, measurements of length."

"That's right."

"Mary, he is speaking of wavelengths."

"That is exactly what I am speaking of. Sis, I'm surprised you couldn't come up with it. Simple as it is."

"In that case, Dear, I can't see why you didn't come up with it yourself. But I do know a little of what the two of you are talking about. Progenitor-talk, I call it." Edward looked at Mary, startled, joyful. Sis, too, turned again toward he woman: "They are talking about color, and other kinds of 'shining-range.' Our light—when we're in the Presence, or carrying out a divine commission—is of every color, so that all creatures may see us: Birds, pards, insects, amphibians [she licked her chops at this, though instantly reeling in her branched tongue], even bats. Do you know about bats?"

"Well, yes" Mary answered. "I know a little about them."

"Do you like bats, or not?"

"I love them," Edward answered.

"I am not greatly attracted to them," Mary admitted, "but I'm in favor of anything that eats mosquitoes."

"There are a hundred and thirty-nine species of them here," Sis said, with, in the tone of her voice, evident admiration. Sss said he could take or leave them, that he only wanted to point out that he and his consort, when in Court attire and keeping Divine State, were visible even to bats.

"And," he added, "we emit so many differing measures…wavelengths, you said they are called nowadays?…that we can be detected by radio. You do know what 'radio' is, don't you?"

"Yes, we do know what radio is. Do you know exactly what frequencies—wavelengths—you emit in the radio spectrum, at those times? It would be nice if we could tune you in, just in order to stay in touch."

"A lot. But I can see that you're getting at something, and I think I know what it may be."

"What, then?"

"You are wondering, I think, whether we emit those wavelengths that escaped as Primal Light when subatomic particles combined, following the Original Interdistantiation. The Creation. When the Creator struck a spark to the charge of this Universe. A great many people talk a great deal about it. They call it something vulgar. I forget just what. Anyway, they seem to like to bandy this phrase about, whether they know much about what it means, or not."

"Do you know what he's talking about?" Sis whispered to Mary.

"No, but I think Edward does. He keeps up with a lot of things other than his work."

"Well, I leave it gladly to Sss; I have enough to do keeping abreast of the taxonomy of all the plants and animals—a few forms die out, but having existed, they remain in the classification, or what we call the 'Plenitude.'"

"It certainly seems to fit."

"And no sooner has one species died out, than one or two others pop up."

Edward said he was no expert on the subject of Primal Light, "But I do find the little I know tremendously interesting. I mean, that the Light made to shine at the moment of creation should have passed now through the visible spectrum, that's to say ours, with the stretching of space, and entered the zone of microwaves—and I know the term you mean, Sss; I have always been embarrassed to call so great…and holy…a thing by such a foolish name. 'Original Interdistantiation' seems so much better. And for that matter, as scientific designations go, it's really not all that elaborate."

"I'm glad you like it. I think it's appropriate that we are made radiant with that Original Light—and we change its wavelength as we must, to fit the extending universe—since we were…not 'there,' because we haven't room. But, since we *were*. Oh, Dear. Now I've used a tense of 'be' again. And that is misleading." He looked a little forlorn.

So Sis gave him a toad and a little wine. She said: "Try not to worry about it, Dear. You'll get a headache. Remember: 'All shall be well, and all shall be well, and all shall be exceeding well.'"

"Thank you, my little Fig Blossom; you are such a comfort to me. But, the Tree of Life. It stayed just where it was, and by your reckoning, for quite a 'long time.' Just after Eva and Adam left, Sis and I—shining, as I've mentioned, and transformed—stood on either side of their way out, and a sword blazing to white, from any direction unapproachèd Light, appeared to prohibit access to the Tree of Life. That had been stipulated during the conference, when they made their Choice."

"But, do you know what?"

"What?" the Strikestraws asked in a voice.

"The very next thing was that the Children coupled, and she gave birth, brought forth life. Right off the bat. In your Book, it's written in the very next verse, I think. Look it up when you get home."

"So you see," Sis mentioned, "they had vacated any claim to *eternal* life. That is, uninterrupted eternal life. Probably you'd better take that up with Edward's grandfather. But they yet had *transmissible* life, and could see it regenerate, and see the regeneration before their own lives were interrupted. So you can see that they had made no unwise choice."

Sss added that the wisdom came as part of soul, that their souls were part of World Soul, and that….

At this point, there came a crackling flash of lightening, and a bone-splintering thunderburst with no interval between.

"I think," Sss said, trying to appear unshaken, "That we'd better leave it at that.

"They had some trouble with their children, initially, and I'm afraid that set some kind of precedent. But their issue formed a great race—leading one poet to write: 'There are many fearsome wonders, but none more fearsomely wondrous than man.'"

"I know. In college, I read the play those lines come from."

The fire was beginning to burn out; they added fuel. More sparks arose, more light broke forth from among the blackened cinders. "I shall finish the story with the part about the Tree of Life—or, since that was her province—let Sis tell it."

"This part," Sis assured them, "is a bit more solemn. And I find it so... gratifying, My Child, that your name is Mary. Well, here goes:

"I think you are those later People of the Book; for, Mary, I have noticed you wear that little symbol upon a golden neck chain."

"Why, yes we are, Sis. It's among those later people that Edward's grandfather is a priest."

"Good. Then you will be familiar with this passage: 'As Moshe lifted up the serpent in the wilderness, so must the Son of Man be lifted up.'"

Mary said they knew it.

"God Most High decerned to affirm the Creation every now and again. Moshe's lifting up of that serpent had nothing to do with my niece, Billie Jean. Nor, in fact with a serpent of her kind at all. People do—and understandably—get the Mosaic herpetology confused. This is what happened on that other occasion:

"Moshe's people were pressing on across the wilderness, trying to get to a place where they thought they could finally settle down. On their way, they passed through a region infested with serpents. A good many were bitten, and of those many, most died.

"These travellers were a people who tended to drag God most High into everything, and so they took the infestation as punishment from Him for something they thought they had done to offend Him. A very sensitive folk, always inclined to blame themselves. A form of self-importance, of course. So this Moshe asked the Creator what to do. And this is what He commanded: That Moshe wright a serpent in bronze and lift it up on a staff.

"Back here, the Garden was stilled; no living thing throughout its length or breadth moved; every life-force was canceled away. When it had passed, the Tree of Life had been removed. We have never seen it again, although, as you can see, Living Water, still rushes from the font."

Mary and Edward looked. The other well, the one not inhabited by Sss and Sis, was capped, as when they had first seen it, and the Tree of the

Knowledge of Good and Not-so-Good had once more been substituted for by the branching form in metal.

"The Sons of G.... We hear things, and from time to time—although we haven't any of either of our own—we see and sometimes hear the time and room that belong to those who wander the earth. For instance, we saw Moshe take the figure he had made of a serpent, burnished bright, and set it up upon a staff. The staff, though few know it, had been fashioned from the Tree of Life."

Mary asked: "How could you tell?"

"We just could."

"Ah," Edward said, to show he was paying attention.

"Those who'd been stung and bitten by the snakes in the wilderness infestation were brought, by the Father's direction, to look upon the snake on the stick, and they didn't die from the venom. The tree of life undid its potency."

Edward mentioned that that was in their Book, and that, hearing it, he just then remembered. He hadn't known, though, that the pole had been made out of the Tree of Life.

"Well, but I'll bet you don't know *this* part, for I think it was left out. They brought up the bodies of those who'd been bitten and died before Moshe could put the final touches to the serpent of bronze, and *their* lives were restored."

"'Man can heal disease, sometimes, but cannot find a way to turn aside from death.' Edward quoted.

"It's a later line in that same play you mentioned."

"And, as you have heard, he need not try."

They had stayed awake talking all through the night. When the sun rose over what the Strikestraws took for the ridge of a dune, revealed instead were the grassy rides and mossy byways, life abounding in manifold appearances; air clear like desert air, but mists from all the pools and lakes rising, in splendor of their own, but refracting, too, the light again into all its colors. And space herself was crowded with radiation in all wavelengths, some far smaller than grains of fine sand, others as long as the distance Mary and Edward had gone to climb the high dune. Some fixed, or lengthening with the opulent burgeoning of space.

Sis had only a few more words, and then the story of the Tree of Life would be complete. "Remember," Sss mentioned, " Eva and Adam had a little trouble with their children. Just as the two of you are going to, with yours."

Edward asked abruptly: "Sis, several things you've said...are you trying to tell us that Mary is going to have a child?"

"'Trying' to tell you? I am telling you. But you knew, didn't you?"

"I had begun to wonder," Mary said.

"Well, it is a certainty."

"How do you know?" Edward asked.

Sss feigned wounded indignation: "You ask such a question of the Keepress of the Tree of Life!"

"Trouble with children, as I was about to say, or repeat, was one of the things the Choice entailed. It got to be rather dreadful in time. Mankind still possessed transmissible life, could still survive to see his own life recurring in his children. However, things had got to the point that there was uncertainty whether that would be 'all she wrote.' In the mind of man; the Father, of course, knew that this development would arise.

"Therefore, God most high set up upon the post made from the Tree of Life, Death. So that all who were to die the death, and all whose sleep was furled in death, could look upon it or be brought before it—or even who could not—could have a too-great ill abolished. Because, you see—we heard this, too, at the little post-conference gala—that ill had not been included in the Choice. Sent to No-Hell to dwell with No-Evil.

"Now, hurry and pack. I know you are going to Agadez today, and I want you to be there in time for lunch."

Goodbyes had been said, and the young people with their treasure were on their way, bumping along the "road" in their battered Jeep.

"Did you tell them we were going to Agadez today?"

"No. I didn't know we were."

"Neither did I, but it seems we are."

"To think how frightening I've always found snakes; but not these, not at all."

"I don't think these are actually snakes."

Many sights seem more beautiful from afar; Agadez, the ancient Capital of Aïr in Niger, is probably not an exception, although within the city itself you can be lost in the beauty of certain things of a lesser scale, such as the enchanted silver work of the artisans in the marketplace whose tapping rings out a strange and magical melody and seems to be telling you something, something you must know, know urgently. For just beyond is desert.

As Mary and Edward Strikestraw crashed along in their Jeep, they felt they were seeing the sands of the desert forming themselves into the outline of a distant City, the bristling tower of the *grande mosquée*, far lower buildings gathering about its base. And when they had entered the town, and were beginning already, unconsciously, to hear the silverwrights' tinkling, a pressured song, they saw that the other buildings were in degrees like the tower of the mosque in color and fabric.

Mary, when she could focus her gaze during their short journey, had read about the City in a travel guide, and now had her heart set upon staying, during their brief visit, at the Hôtel de l'Aïr, because it stood across a square from the Old Mosque and because it had been a sultan's palace. Upon arrival, they remarked a striking similarity between the Hotel and their Jeep. But they came quickly to like it. For inside there *were* traces of The Palatial, with corbelled arches springing in four opposing directions from pillars, a worn but in places wonderfully patterned marble-and-faïence floor. And it was cool inside. The amenities and service were generally a whimsical desert-city adaptation of what the management conceived to be the European way.

Edward and Mary attempted a little sightseeing, but it was too hot. They rested, then, at sunset, ventured out into the square. They sat down at one of the tables outside a café. Mary ordered a *Pschitt Citron*; Edward ordered the companion product, a *Pschitt Orange*. They were a bit furtive about adding slugs of brandy from Edward's flask, situated as they were literally in the shadow of a mosque. The air had cooled; a light breeze flowed in from a sidestreet, sweeping the paving stones and, striking a high wall, producing an eruption of chaff, pods strewing their ripened content, bits of paper, some with writing, or without.

After dinner, they went through to the courtyard of the Hotel, where they sat looking at the stars and at each other. The *patron*, who had rarely been farther from Agadez than ten or twenty miles, habitually took great pleasure in talking with his guests. Mary and Edward were a winning-looking couple. The *patron*, therefore, having given them what privacy his own eagerness could afford, went up to them, introduced himself, and asked whether they were comfortable, whether he might meet any need of theirs. After they had reassured him, he lingered. Edward asked whether he had a moment to join them. With "A thousand thanks" he sat down, then turned, clapped his hands loudly twice, and presently a waiter, who wore an evening shirt and black tie, no jacket, and a tablecloth wrapped around his waist and reaching almost to the floor, arrived with a jug of wine and three sparkling glasses. When they had thanked him, he bowed profoundly and went away. This was evidently an establishment too cosmopolitan to think of the feelings of Muslims only.

As had happened so many times before, the hotel manager, whose name proved to be Mr. Rasuul, made an evening's entertainment out of entertaining his guests. Willed they or nilled they. After some introductory exchange, Mary said: "We have come from visiting the *Arbre du Ténéré*—or at least the place where it stood, and the sculptural symbol erected to replace it. Can you clarify any of the stories people tell about it? I ask, because we had an extremely interesting stay there, or, at least, nearby."

"Ah, yes, *Madame*, with pleasure; and there is much to tell. Further, there would likely be more to tell, except for that cursèd Libyan midget, whose mother was a camel and whose father, an ass." A remarkable parentage. "I refer to the drunkard who ran into the tree with a lorry, and uprooted it once and for all. It had stood there since the Day of Creation. By the way," Mr. Rasuul said, interrupting himself, as very loquacious people sometimes do, "is either of you by any chance and aficionado—or aficionada…," he added, bowing a little toward Mary, with whom, like most men, he had been instantly taken [*Her eyes in this lamplight are like wells so deep you can just make out the water stirring in their depths.*] "…Of Wagner? *Der Ring*? Yes? For that Tree was like the *Weltesche*; the world has been going to ruin ever since it was felled.

"Oh, My Children, yes. There is much one could recount about the Tree of theTénéré—Ténéré…wasteland within a wasteland, for mile upon mile hereabout far different from what it once was. I'm sure you know that the Sahara was once the sea-bed, still full, if you look for them, of ancient seashells. I'm sure you know of the green glass formations and lodes in what is now Egypt. Egypt, that borders upon Libya!" He proceeded to spit upon the ground.

"What I am going to recount is a legend few know. Or it is truth undiscovered to our times. Forestland used to reach to just twelve miles or so north of the Tree. It was not dense, nor choked by undergrowth, but pleasant to walk through. The wood of many of the trees was fragrant. Balsam, sandalwood. So, they say, was their sap. A Great City stood on the farther side of the forest. Some tell that it was so rich in springs that watercourses ran down the centers of all the streets. It was rich in every other thing, too. Towering walls, terrifyingly splendid portal. And it had never been sacked, or even heavily besieged.

"The Tree stood out even then, although it was surrounded by many others, including a companion tree as great as itself, all set within meadowland. But the desert between was already becoming the Ténéré, wasteland within wasteland. One evening, a woman came to the well beside the tree; sometimes, it overflowed and poured floods of clear water onto the meadow all around. Like the watercourses in the streets of the Great City. But those streamed without ceasing ever.

"She looked out across the desert. She was curious. For her husband had told her that when he had been there at daybreak, he thought he had seen first one, then another light flare up, before directly going out. As the woman gazed there came up to her the figure of a man. She pointed out to him the well and fruit trees, so that he might be refreshed. He thanked her and told her that he was on a quest. She asked what he was seeking, thinking that she, as she dwelt in those parts, might offer him guidance.

"Mine," said the man of the Desert, "is like all other quests. Seeking, you may travel, dig into the earth, rise high above the land, even above the earth; you may study the sun, moon, and stars; you may learn of sightings, measurings, angles, and arcs. In each of these cases you are questing for Good.

"Sometimes, the deeper or higher you seek, the farther you may think yourself from Good. But you are drawing nearer. Whether you have wisdom, or strength, or time to achieve the Goal, you will, questing, draw nearer.

"Or you may travel, and yet not seek."

"'These two trees,'" the woman said, "'are older than anything else in the world. Are they not the Good you seek?'"

"In part, for all is good; except that of The Good, there is no 'part.'"

Under the starry sky, the three sat and drank some of the wine, although not all of it. They were thinking about the story, and Mary and Edward thought also about Sss and Sis. Eventually, Edward asked quietly: "How old do those who know it think this story to be?"

"Well," Mr. Rasuul answered, a little guardedly: "It is certainly before The Prophet. Some say it is older than that Commotion they had in Egypt. And that was, I believe, thousands, yes, thousands of years ago." Then they were quiet again. Finally: "We must drink all of this wine," Mr. Rasuul said, filling all their glasses, as they sat in lamplight between lofty heights and mighty depths.

XII

"Pistyll Rhaeadr and Wrexham steeple,
Snowdon's mountain without its people,
Overton Yew trees, St Winifride wells,
Llangollen bridge and Gresford Bells."

> Doggerel verse (prob. S. xviii) enumerating "The Seven Wonders of Wales"

"—say...//—how far it is
To this same blessèd Milford. And by th' way
Tell me how Wales was made so happy as
T' inherit such a haven...."

> Wm. Shakespeare: *Cymbeline*, III. ii., ll. 58; 60-63

"Across the entrance to Milford Haven the streams run approximately at right angles to the line of approach; within the entrance they run nearly parallel to the channel. There is often a confused sea off the entrance where the streams meet."

Admiralty Sailing Directions.

"…Now lettest thou thy servant depart in peace, according to thy word…."
The Gospel according to St. Luke: II. 29 (AV)

THAT NEITHER MILFORD Haven nor anything in it is counted among the *Seven Wonders of Wales* suggests what is true: That Wales is a Country abounding in wonders. The Town and Harbor of Milford Haven were entirely wonderful to Edward Strikestraw, who was there to have a passion gratified. To others, their appeal is homely and indispensable as the leek's; their grandeur is of lesser roselands looming into an ocean of silver, with the sun burning, burning in the west.

Edward and Mary had put up at a small hotel, which Mary considered a bit "less-than." But it was clean, and it was directly beside the Haven, the guest rooms overlooking the shipping channel. And because this was what Edward had come for, it pleased him. Moreover, "After all," he mentioned grandly to his wife, "I gave you the choice of accommodation when we were in Agadez."

Even then he was on his way to meet the Harbor Master, to whom he had a letter of introduction, of which he had sent a copy in advance. He was going to be allowed with one of the pilots to board a ship and observe the navigating of her through the Haven, then the docking. Mary wondered why men had these eagernesses. She had begun by wondering at Edward's eagerness, but then she thought of Josh's absorption in the complex design and framing of the structure which, once lifted by cranes, would be set down upon the stout walls of the Ruin of Dodona House to form the roof.

"It's skyline will be authentic; the roof will pose only downward pressure on the walls—nothing to splay," Josh had said. Certainly, according to the drawings, it was very beautiful, and Edward, who had gone over the mechanics of it with Josh, had said that, hard as it was to believe, it did appear to him that much of the lateral forces would be internally compensated.

Maybe it was a property not of all men, but only of those bound in marriage; maybe the cached obsession was a place to which they could stray outside that bond. Well, certainly there were worse attachments.

During Edward's absence, Mary had gone down to have tea. The tea-tables, at this season, stood along a narrow balcony, accessible through the main dining room. It overhung rather than overlooked the Harbor. After she had been seated, she noted with abstracted concern the masonry on her right.

It was of brick, pointed flush, with mortar right out to the surface. *Nothing to cling to—not even a toehold, in case the whole arrangement should come loose and crash into the water* [actually, rock] *below.* But this was just another of the misgivings Mary had done battle with all day, objects of a fear that had no legitimate object.

Tea, when brought, was relatively sumptuous, served immaculately, reinforcing Mary's prejudice that almost nothing in Great Britain was ever entirely uncivilized. She began to enjoy herself. She drank tea and looked ahead and to her left toward the entrance to the harbor, at the sea and land-formations that constituted it. She believed she was seeing, among much else, St. Ann's Head, but she knew the corner of the hotel stood between herself and the Light. They could drive out to see it tomorrow…after Edward's voyage was done.

She watched the great ships come and go, pleasure craft dancing and racing among them like a swarm of gnats. The end of teatime had come; the waiters were asking at each table whether anything further were required. Guests began to rise and depart. A portly gentleman, who had been seated back to back with Mary, pushed his chair away and stood, just as Mary was attempting to do the same.

He came around to her, still seated, and said: "I beg your pardon, Miss; let me at least hold your chair for you." When she was alone, Mary's marital status was often mistaken by hopeful men of every age and sort. She was fed up with this, anxious, and now out-of-sorts, so, as she thanked the stranger she simultaneously took her napkin from her lap with her left hand, bearing its rings that read as clear as International Nautical Signal, and placed it with deliberateness upon the table. "Oh! Ah, that is, Madam." They started to move with the others toward the dining room. "I see you are American." Now Mary was somewhat mollified, for most Britons said: "…you are (or 'are you…?') *an* American."

"Yes," she answered, and she suddenly warmed to the man, who was not really extremely portly. At home, in a like situation, anyone would simply have pushed past, saying nothing. "My husband is going to go out with one of the pilots tomorrow and watch a large ship brought into dock."

"I gather you will not be accompanying him?"

"No, and I wish he weren't going, or that I had the courage to go with him and watch over him." By now they had reached the pair of French doors opening into the hotel's interior. They paused, causing a backup of guests waiting to go inside, of waiters trying to get outside to clear the tables.

"My dear Lady…."

"Mary Strikestraw, Mrs. Edward Strikestraw."

"I am William Fitzwilliam, Mrs. Strikestraw." Mary gave him her hand briefly. Then they moved out of the doorways, relieving the congestion. "I am one of the pilots here. I do not think you need worry about your husband. Everything will be done for his safety. And all he will do besides stand on the bridge and watch and listen, or be shown by the navigator how their course is plotted, is climb a rope ladder. Is he fit?"

"He's tryingly fit."

"Then he will have no trouble at all."

"Oh, well, I do thank you. But won't he have to climb up a great distance?"

"Probably no more than thirty feet."

"But that's three stories!"

"Or forty. I do it nearly every day. Unless he is much older than you appear to be, my Dear, I am probably twice his age. And *not* terribly fit." A little silence fell. Mary was taking comfort from the words of a complete stranger. And she was still a little diffident. And now he was inviting her to have a drink with him in the hotel lounge. "It really is necessary to offset the undesirable effects of the tea—which I have only because of the good things that come along with it. I ask in case you think there is time for a tot before your husband returns. Unless you think he would object. Or unless you object."

"Edward wouldn't object at all. And I certainly don't. In fact, a glass of whiskey is probably exactly what I need."

"I think so." He gave her his arm, and the older man and younger woman moved decorously toward the cocktail lounge, taking a table on the periphery. Out of decorum. And in order to be able to see Edward when he should come in.

"From where I was sitting at tea, I couldn't see the open ocean."

"No. We were too far round the bend. A chart would show you that if we'd been a little farther west, we'd have seen the mouth of the Haven, and through it the Atlantic Ocean, just before it runs into the Bristol Channel."

Mary sat bemused, then said: "Thirty feet are a long way, and a rope ladder is so flimsy!"

"What made you think of those things?"

"'Mouth.'"

"Mouth?"

"Yes. You referred to the mouth of the Haven, and it made me think of Edward's being swallowed up. That has set me fretting again. But I hope I can make you believe I am not usually—or ever—like this. It's just this one time. So far."

"I have no trouble in seeing in you a very sensible young woman. I was about to add that that Mouth has been swallowing up ships and men since the time of the Vikings, but now I shan't."

"Thank you. I'm greatly relieved."

"A long time ago," the Pilot said, "I knew an old lady from the East. The East of England. She used to buck us up a bit, whenever the need arose, by telling us that 'Though sin be behovable, yet all shall be well, and all shall be well, and all shall be exceeding well.' Or words to that effect." He paused, frowned. "Behovable. What kind of word is that supposed to be? The verb 'behoove' and all its forms and all their derivatives have mystified me for all these... years. Can't seem to develop a *Sprachgefühl* for it.

"She spoke in that way?"

"Oh, Dear; was I imitating her? Sometimes I do that, when I quote people. Well, yes, she did speak in that way, but she came from just outside Norwich. Perhaps you know what those people sound like? And she was old when I knew her; she held to the olden ways."

About then, the attendant from the reception desk came toward them, stopped a little way off, and waited until Fitzwilliam acknowledged his presence. For he had been trained to behave toward disgusting old men making fools of themselves with younger, beautiful women as though they were just as good as anybody else. "I have telephone messages for you—for both of you." He handed a folded slip of paper to each. As they began reading, the attendant said further: "I could not help noticing that both are from the same number; if you wish, I can bring a telephone to your table." He would save Mary's honour, if by any means he could.

Fitzwilliam's message read: "An early arrival is at The Gates. I'm going for her myself—need the practice—but everybody else is either out or due for home and supper. Somebody's got to mind the shop. Call me. Herrold." And there followed a six-digit telephone number. Fitzwilliam excused himself with every mark of courtesy and left.

Mary's note was from Edward. The same number followed.

Mary went up to her room.

Earlier, about to get into the car to drive to his meeting, Edward had taken Mary into his arms, saying: "I hate to leave you."

"I hate for you to go." They didn't usually feel that way about partings; they normally left each other already looking forward to being together again. Mary told herself it was the rope ladder, which had by now taken on in her mind an antediluvian and reptilian character, but it wasn't that. Edward told himself that, for his part, it was guilt at leaving before he must, because he meant to get pleasantly lost in the town in order to see a bit of it on his way, now that he was oriented, but it wasn't that, either.

Edward arrived on time at the interim offices of the Haven Conservancy Board. Eventually it would be called the Port Authority, housed in up-to-date quarters that would have large windows overlooking a great range of shipping operations. For now, though, it remained the Conservancy Board, and for its interior appearance might have been the headquarters of any small business in Middle America, except for the portrait of the Queen. No one was about. Edward thought of tapping one of those little summoning-bells you see on countertops, but there wasn't one.

From the recesses, someone called out: "Be right along!" And after a moment a man appeared, smiling. He said: "You must be Mr. Strikestraw," putting out his hand. "I'm David Herrold. Let's go back to my office, where we can at least sit down and talk."

"Yes, Sir. I'm Edward Strikestraw. Are you one of the pilots?"

"I am. Another is, I hope, on the way here. A ship is marking time at the harbor mouth, waiting to be docked."

On the door to David Herrold's office was a small sign with his name, and under it, "Harbour Master." They went in and sat down. The Harbor Master was relaxed, but somehow expectant. Edward asked him: "Do I address you as 'Captain'?"

"Sometimes pilots—my duties are administrative, now; but I serve as pilot occasionally—are called that, as a courtesy. But for God's sake don't do it on the bridge, with the ship's master present. Well, then. I'm very happy you want to watch us do what we do—it's agreeable to have someone take an interest in one's work. How did you come by yours? Your interest in pilotage. I know you come from near a seaport."

"That's a part of it, certainly. But the Port is eighteen miles upriver; the mouth of the River is the interesting part, because of the bar—mariners know more-or-less where it lies, but it keeps shifting. Some very interesting beacons and ranges have been installed at different periods. I wanted to see, though, one of the world's great natural harbors."

"It serves."

"But I became fascinated by pilotage in an unlikely port. Patras."

"I've never been there. Of course, I know of it."

"Well, it's a small port, but if you don't want to drive all the way around the Adriatic, the ferry, at least at that time, was the only way to get from Greece to Italy.

"We arrived early for our departure the time I'm speaking of. We went to a movie to pass the time. It was one of the most grueling experiences of that whole year."

"The picture?"

"Yes. It was '*Les parapluies de Cherbourg.*'"

"I thought that was supposed to be light entertainment."

"It was, *light.*"

"Oh. There used to be so many of those."

"This version was dubbed…in Modern Greek. I got more from lip-reading the French. But, at any rate, when it was over, and we went outside, it had got dark. The rain had stopped. Although, come to think of it, the rain may have been just in the film.

"But we went aboard, and the little ship got underway. I had been moving around all the decks, looking at the lights, at the town; I had the impression someone was pulling the whole thing away at once, as on a huge table-cloth."

"How apt an image!"

"Well, then, from the bows, I looked up at the bridge. The light inside was dim, but some instrument threw a glow back onto the pilot's face. He was looking dead ahead, except for quick glances, every once in a while, this side or that. Mostly, though he was looking steadily forward.

"Passage out of the little harbor didn't take long—I saw the Pilot getting aboard the landing craft—but while he was on the bridge, it struck me, he had charge of all of us, and he took his charge seriously. And, always, *he knew what to do.* I imagined that he could see the bottom, reflected from underneath the surface, all the soundings reversed to elevations. And he taught the helmsman to steer among them, clear as a whistle."

"Another striking image. And it says more than merely being underwater and looking upward at a mirror."

"Does it?"

"Mirrors reverse right-to–left."

"Yes. A great difference. I must not have been thinking too clearly. '*Les Parapluies de Cherbourg*' had been an ordeal. But ever since then The Pilot has for me been the epitome of the expert, and guardian."

"That is a very nice story. Really, it is very good indeed, and I shall remember it when next I have to tick off one of my own pilots." They heard the door to the outer office open. Fitwilliam, Captain Fitzwilliam, had read his note at the hotel. He knew what it meant and hadn't bothered to call.

"Lift up your hearts!" he shouted. "Relief is at hand!" He barged into the Harbour Master's office.

"You seem merry enough," Captain Herrold said, as Fitzwilliam nodded to Edward.

"I should be merry. I've just had cocktails with the most beautiful woman I've ever seen!" Then Herrold introduced Edward, and explained why he was there.

"Oh, My God! The lady I mention must be your wife. I do beg your pardon."

"I can see no need to pardon a good eye," Edward said. "And, thank you."

"Well, Son, she really is lovely. I'm sure everybody says so. And she's very charming, and she's...." They thought he'd become tongue-tied with awkwardness. But tying the tongue of William Fitzwilliam took a lot more than that. He had hesitated, but continued: "She's terrified." The others looked surprised. "She's terrified on your account, Mr. Strikestraw. Has she had a tragic, or near-tragic thing happen to her at sea? Or to someone else, but whom she knew?"

"Not that I've heard," Edward answered.

"Tell her we'll take great care with you." And now the telephone rang. It was Mary, answering Edward's message. He went to the outer office, in order to be able to speak privately.

As he went out, Captain Herrold called after him: "Bear in mind: You may, if you wish, go out with me now. Discuss it with your wife."

The two applied themselves to the difficulty at hand. The Harbour Master said: "*Kviedründe* is four miles, by now, from the Entrance. We were expecting her at this hour, but in the morning. It's what comes of using the twelve-hour clock, combined with carelessness in consulting the calendar. But she's here, and I'm willing to fetch her in."

"It's terrifically trying for you; I am quite content to spend the night here."

"You are better-natured than I am. I really can't say I relish bringing her in after dark."

"You've done it a hundred times."

"More like a thousand. It's just that I'm getting old, set in my ways."

"I know more about that than you do." Here, Edward returned.

The others looked up. "She doesn't like it—thinks it's all more dangerous at night. But I think she's glad to be getting it over with. That is, if I really can go out with you, Captain Herrold, now?"

"I shall remain here," Captain Fitwilliam said, with feigned delight, "concocting schedules, reviewing manifests ...all that sort of thing!"

"Come along, Edward."

Mary ordered supper sent up to her. She was halfway through a book she liked. So she supped, went to bed, read for a while, then slept soundly through the night.

Edward and the Harbor Master went outside. Night was fully fallen, and deep mist had rolled off the Haven and onto the quay. They walked along, leaving footprints in the even dampness, vestiges soon lost to the fog, which, though not dense, was gathered into droplets the next step down from the softest of rains. Soon they reached a Jeep, parked as though about to leap into the water. There was a seal painted upon the door, showing that the vehicle belonged to the Conservancy Board of Milford Haven.

They hadn't spoken while walking, nor during the drive until near the end. Herrold said: "We're not going out in one of the sleek pilot boats you see in brochures. I like a bit more boat under me, especially after the sun has gone down. The Haven bought and modified a number of trawlers when the fishing fell off. We'll go out in one of those."

"I noticed we had just begun passing a lot of them. *This Jeep must have a suspension system identical to the one in Niger.* I read that there had been a time when you could walk the length of the Haven on the decks of fishing craft."

"Everyone says that; I think it's true. When I first came here, one could still almost do it."

"I think I noticed the winches left on a lot of them," for the quayside lighting had been dim, yellow, and diffuse.

"On all of them. I wish I had time to tell you how many good uses they've been put to. The winches."

"I'll bet they were made in the United States."

"What makes you say so?"

"There is, or was, a company in Stroudsburg, Pennsylvania, that made an exceptionally good winch…with not so good a name. It used to be claimed that you could find a Stroudsburg winch in every harbor in the world. I think it was nearly literally true, too."

Now they had come abreast of the mooring of a trawler that was lighted: Running-lights and light from inside the wheelhouse. They stopped and got out onto the slippery pavement of the quay. Aboard the boat, the pilot stopped to confer with the skipper, and Edward examined the winch. The Pilot and a deckhand came out and cast off, and they put forth into the splendid dark waters of the Haven. Then Captain Herrold came up to where Edward was waiting. "Look at this." Edward swept a field clear of droplets, and there appeared the identification-mark: "Stroudsburg Machine Works, Stroudsburg, Penna., U.S.A."

"You learn something every day. Now, what about the bad name this good wench has?" Edward was surprised to have caught the double meaning, since he himself had never before heard, since he did not pronounce, the vowel-difference between the two words. He grinned appreciatively.

"You see how the main train is exposed? These large-radius cogwheels...."

"Can move the Earth from her course?"

"And since they're not better encased, if the deck should be slippery, and the sea rough.... There have been gruesome accidents. In my part of the Country the winch is known as 'The Man-eater.'"

"Well, then, I think we'll keep that to ourselves; you can't imagine how superstitious seafaring people are."

"I *know* how superstitious they are." They leant upon the bows. The air seemed to have cleared, once the Haven had got them to herself. And the dark waters disclosed to them all the lights about the place, redoubled in their reflections. "My Grandfather has a large painting hanging in his study. It seems to be some sort of abstraction when you see it at first. In fact, though, it is painted with nearly photographic realism, though it remains 'painterly,' as they say. It shows the deckhouse of a trawler, seen precisely head-on: Mast in center, outriggers off the vertical about eighty degrees each, making a very much *impending* sort of Cross. The Winch is painted in squat majesty, centered in the foreground. The title of the picture is 'Stroudsburg Good Friday.'"

After the Pilot had gone away, back into the deckhouse, Edward wondered about him; he could see a man of wit and energy, probably appearing younger than however old he was, handsome for whatever that age might be, when it didn't do any good. There was an incongruous, tried-on looking rim of moustache continuing into that kind of light beard that encircles the mouth and ends at the chin in a little checkmark. He seemed a happy man. Edward wondered whether he had a family of his own, what his education had been, by what grades he had reached his present position. And he wondered, of course, whether he were himself making a favorable impression. He couldn't think it should matter, so long as they could get on in a civil way until the end of the voyage.

When he returned to the deck, the Pilot went to stand in the starboard bow, alone. He, in his turn, thought about Edward, whom he was coming to like. An improvement over what he had expected. Suppose David should be asked to give an account of his own life up to now, as though he sensed the younger man were wondering about it? Going backward, when he reached himself at the age he guessed Edward to be, there he would have to stop. Or to fabricate, which he was not prepared to do. Would Edward Strikestraw ever wish to press beyond that? Through all those years, though, he had developed a formula for dealing with the thing: "I was a foundling, but, thankfully, I was found by the Right People." Only one person had ever pressed him about it, and that was his wife. She had decided to marry him, and reasonably felt herself entitled to fuller detail. And there had been one other, of no importance....

When it had entered David Herrold's mind to wonder what the young man saw in himself, he, too, wondering why it mattered, concluded, after some thought, that he would be competing as a model with the pilot away off in Patrai [as he knew it], and he wished not to be found wanting—to excel those imagined virtues if he could.

It was disturbing, for the boy had a way of exalting the lowly—the harbor and whole process; not just the pilot. How true was he himself to his own summons?

David walked to where Edward had remained and said to him: "*Kviedründe* has got in to about a mile-and-a-half from the outer light-buoys, making dead slow ahead. We should be alongside her and ready to board in ten minutes. Her Master speaks workable English, it appears. I just got off the radiotelephone with him."

"Is everything as it should be, then?"

"Nearly so. I usually pick up the vessels around four miles out."

"How big a ship is she?"

"About a hundred and seventy-five dead weight tonnes. Long tonnes, and she's roughly three-quarters laded with crude oil.

"It could be worrisome somewhere else. Not here. The '-ford' in Milford is from the Old Norse word for *fjord*. Here it's rocky and wide and steep and clear—with exceptions, especially the Mid Channel Rocks.

"But eventually even they won't matter."

"Why not?"

"Because Bill Fitzwilliam says that when all the valleys are exalted and the mountains and hills made low; the crooked, straight, and the rough places plane, then every shoal and rock will sink away and all the straits will open."

They had come alongside *Kviedünde* upon her starboard side. The tide had ebbed; the flood was beginning, west to east, and the Pilot wished to board in the ship's lee. They could not have been more than ten feet from the immense hull, silent if living. There was no sense of its movement through the water; it might have been rising from the seabed. Edward was gripped, as he looked, by something akin to fear, but deeper. The wavelets between the two craft were writing a sinuous, illegible script in moonshine.

David went into the deckhouse again to give instructions to the trawler's skipper, and to speak briefly over the radiotelephone to *Kviedründe*'s Master.

Meanwhile the skipper turned a powerful white light onto the Tanker's hull, and began to search for some recognizable feature in the welding, something he could use to mark his speed. As he gazed, down came the ensnaring net. No, it was the pilot ladder. But looking as it unfurled like a net. A snare.

David told Edward to begin his climb upward against the black hull. "And I'll come after you."

"You'll be just behind me?"

"No. I'll wait till you're aboard. Two of us on the ladder would be too much weight."

The breeze was blowing the ladder abaft. Motionless, though. The deckhand said: "Your weight will help stabilize the ladder. The higher you get, and the less is left for you to climb, then the more it will feel just like a regular, rigid ladder."

Edward took the ropes and began to climb. All happened exactly according to the deckhand's briefing.

The skipper was having trouble matching speed with the Tanker, which was deliberately making as little way as possible. But he could see Edward upon the ladder, for a time, and then just the ladder, which, not weighted, was at the mercy of the breeze. It was something to go by, nevertheless.

His gnomon was about to fail him. None of them could have predicted the woesome result. The tail of the ladder snagged upon a sprung chain plate, which had gone unnoticed —loosely at first. There was a pause. It hadn't yet made any difference. Then, the skipper noted that the ladder was being drawn rapidly farther astern. A freshening breeze, he thought—or hoped. But now he was left without a reference. He had fallen slightly behind *Kviedründe*, as the ship moved forward, he more slowly; he lagged farther.

The ladder straightened, but well off the vertical. Edward had been climbing with his arms around the ropes, gripping their opposites. He hoped he didn't seem to be clinging in terror. In fact, he felt very much alert, and completely free of fear. When he felt the rungs and ropes stiffen abruptly into what seemed to be a fixedly integrated structure, he assumed this was the phenomenon he had been told to expect—he only wondered why he were being now held askew, leaning, as it were, markedly to his right, that is, head toward the tanker's bow.

David Herrold shouted orders to the skipper; at the same time, he laid hold on a rung of the ladder, placing nearly all of his weight downward upon it. The deckhand patted himself down hurriedly, seeking a knife, looked about the deck for anything that would cut, break, abrade.

The rung splintered at the chain plate and nearly folded the loosened strapping back upon itself. The Pilot's grip was broken; ropes, rungs plunged down onto themselves, into the wash; the Harbour Master lost his footing, stumbled back three short steps, and, falling to the deck, instinctively reaching with his arms, crashed with the right into the Maneater, striking the power-takeoff rod.

The drums turned.

Then the turning stopped, sickeningly. The deckhand thought the man's limb had jammed the machinery; he moved quickly to disengage the apparatus, which had to a great extent milled David's right arm.

At this time, Edward felt a general kind of releasing of things, finding the ladder a little more lax. He swung back toward the bow of the great ship, seemed to stand upright. A flock of white shorebirds—Could it be?—fell flirting all around him. He looked down. They were life-rings, most of them now bobbing about, having fallen into the waters of the Haven, between the gigantic ship and the little trawler at her side, where Edward noted great commotion of things. But he could not see that the ladder had parted, no farther below him than two yards.

He looked up. At the rail were five or six faces, all registering terror. The group of men were shouting at him and straining to hold out their arms toward him. He felt a little indignant, aware of no danger and feeling himself quite up to his task.

As soon as he had been pulled bodily aboard *Kviedründe* by a number of strong hands, a cheer arose, and the men began to cuff him on the shoulder, pat the palms of his hands reassuringly, dust off his clothing as though they wanted only to touch the cloth he wore, which was dry. They wanted to press upon him, to be sure he was real. Safe.

All looked down. The trawler, once Edward was out of danger of falling into the water and possibly of being ground to pulp, pulled away and made all speed ahead and a little to starboard.

The catastrophe was approaching its pole. Almost no one on board spoke English, and those few barely did. The Pilot had overestimated the Master's grasp, which—And this was true of the others on the bridge—turned out to be limited to nautical terminology, command responses, and a few banal phrases from everyday usage. Everybody thought Edward was the pilot, and it took five minutes of emergency French, English, whatever language the crew were speaking, and gesture to convince them that he was not a seaman of any kind.

Where was the Pilot? Probably still on the boarding vessel, which was well away from them by now, for all her speed had been called up. The tanker was still making as little way as possible. Disaster seemed inevitable. No guide, no guard, no one to look unmoving ahead and to teach the helmsman to keep safe. One of the crewmen lost control of himself and had to be confined below. With the Master, the Chief Officer, the Helmsman, and himself left on the bridge, Edward got onto the radiotelephone and contacted the skipper.

After a moment he finished speaking and turned his back to the others but the Master: "The Pilot has been seriously injured; he will lose his right arm."

"Ah?"

This time, using the edge of his left hand as though a knife, Edward sawed mimetically and chopped at the opposite shoulder, shouted "New pilot comes," and then he gave the only non-recreational navigational order of his life: He grasped the Master by the shoulders and pointed him first toward what he believed was St. Ann's light buoy, then to the Mid Channel Rocks light buoy—both coming up fast—then he wrote on a slip of paper the fraction one-half. The Master nodded, and rattled off instructions to the helmsman, who tried to give the correct verbal responses, but couldn't keep up. Then all was quiet.

By and by, the unmistakable sound of a helicopter approaching could be heard. A number of crewmen appeared at the rail of the deck below the bridge, staring into the spangled black. The searchlight blazed again from the mast of the now-distant trawler. The Master of *Kviedründe* ordered light thrown… but intent failed him. The helicopter was making for the *trawler*, while time was running out for the Tanker, by this time no more than three quarters of a mile from the western entrance to the Haven.

Edward took a pair of glasses from around the Master's neck, with every possible courtesy of manner, and focused. A figure swathed in sheets was being hauled up to the hovering aircraft in a kind of litter.

A many-voiced groan, a wail of despair went up from those on the bridge and those at the rail of the deck below. For some reason, however, Edward realized he didn't care about himself or about huge, horrible, hulking *Kviedründe*—just her Designated Pilot. And then he felt shame for his selfishness. The mighty thing couldn't be stopped. There could be extensive property-damage; an oil-spill, about which the end would never be heard; loss of life…of his own life, for a particularly unpleasant example.

But then they heard with jubilation the approach of a second helicopter. Or they thought so. Then the sound of rotor-blades was lost, or possibly could be heard as a fanning of wings unfurled. Low green light sprang up around the vessel's landing-pad. Bill Fitzwilliam appeared beside the others on the bridge.

He greeted Edward and said, "David is badly injured, but will live. Where are we?" He added, having looked ahead: "Ah, better than I had feared." He turned to the helmsman: "Steady as you go."

"Steady as you go, aye. Steady on twenty-seven degrees."

"Very well."

I must have the world's worst luck when it comes to being entombed, the

Dead Man thought. *Is this bloody coffin being borne on a collapsing tumbril drawn by a malnourished goat and a crippled mule?* He was getting a bumpy ride, and he didn't like it. Especially, having no idea how far he was going to have to travel in these circumstances.

No. I won't be fooled again. No, no! I'm not dead. No more than last time. I can hear, and think—that sort of thing—all which contend against my being dead. Yes, and I am breathing. I can tell that. And my heart is beating.

What he could hear outside himself was a muffled roar. He opened his eyes, but immediately closed them. Too-bright light was everywhere. He opened them again. There had been some pupillary adaptation. A man was leaning over him. He closed his eyes again.

The man, who was a medical technician, said: "Sir? Can you hear me?"

"I can."

"Can you tell me the date?"

"What time is it?"

"Half ten."

The living man gave the correct date. The little interrogation continued: "Who's the Queen?"

"Elizabeth the Second." And then: "D.g."

"Can you give me your name?"

This is where things had started to go south last time. But no more John Doe. That...wants to be it, is trying to be. But, no. There's something else. Ha! A second name had come. He spoke that name in a kind of sigh, as of one returning to a place sometime born of searching fire, but long since deep in green. To a resting-place.

The medical technician consulted the top sheet on his clipboard. He said: "All right, Sir. Good." His patient's reflexes and blood-pressure had been stable from the outset. The normal blood-pressure had been puzzling; there ought to have been considerable blood-loss from the subclavian system, one would have thought. The towels that held ice around the shattered arm were splotched with red. But there was no frank hemorrhage.

Well, before coming round, the man had been groaning a great deal. Now the hospital corpsman knew the patient was oriented to place (more or less), to time, and to person. He could safely alleviate his suffering.

So into the intravenous line he introduced a tentative five milligrams of morphine sulphate, and when he saw this well-tolerated, added another ten. Thus, the Harbour Master of Milford Haven hadn't to bear the discomforts of an evacuation-helicopter flight, against a buffeting wind, to London.

"Come right to thirty-two degrees."

"Come right to thirty two degrees, aye."

"Very well." To Edward: "We've cleared the Mid Channel Rocks. Let me show you how we did it. Aside from the navigator's keeping track of us, that is. Right ahead, do you see two very strong white lights?"

Edward was watching them already. "Yes, Sir. I see them. I thought at first they were mounted together. But I've noted watching steadily that one is behind and the other before."

"Good Lad! While David is learning how to be a one-armed pilot he'll also be well advised to watch his job!"

"I'm guessing we're in mid-channel when we see them aligned?"

"Yes. And if we see them open to east or to west, we must keep our heads up and mind our course."

"There are remains of two old ranges that worked the same way—or were supposed to—near the mouth of the River I grew up alongside. I'm afraid they didn't prove as helpful. But they were built about a hundred years ago. I think."

"Steady on thirty-two degrees, Sir."

"Very well."

"Guy's-St Thomas'.....I don't read; say again, please." The weather over the South had grown unexpectedly ferocious. The helicopter pilot rather enjoyed that part of it, but he couldn't hear the dispatcher clearly. He could read Morse Code like a nursery tale and was sorry it had been abandoned. Of course he couldn't send and steer at once. And no co-pilot had been available.

The technician was now immersed in the exercise of "clinical judgment," which exists, to be sure, but it comes down to deciding what to do when What to Do is inapparent. When he had first unwrapped the limb, he had been met with a sight far more benign than he might have expected. It was perhaps true you had to know in advance that the thing was a man's arm. But, given the process through which it had gone, it looked very promising. The hand was intact (the nail-beds pink!). There seemed to have been no injury at all to the shoulder. But between, the tissues were flattened and deformed. No spring of blood. There appeared to be hundreds of small lacerations, hundreds of bone splinters, raising the skin and in most cases piercing it. The aim was alternately to wrap the extremity again in ice, to slow metabolic processes that would lead to tissue-death from compromised blood-supply. Alternately to remove pressure and cold, so that available perfusion by bloodstream could proceed. The trap of disease and injury! Further one process; retard another.

The airman spoke again: "Be ready to receive us in five minutes, though we'll be longer. What? Yes! Reconstruction *and* orthopaedics—yes, both—and vascular, neurological, general. Don't ask me! I'm reading from a list handed me."

"Now, Edward, watch all the lights on shore, in the sky, reflected in the water. Forget the Leading Lights. They and the red ones, farther out to either side, are going to open wide to the west." To the helmsman: "Right full rudder. Come right to forty-five degrees."

"Right full rudder. Come right to forty-five degrees, aye."

"Very well."

Edward looked out. All the lights, all the stars he could see, and their Joseph's-coat reflections upon or within the cursive ripple, swung about them in a majestic strophe to westward.

"Steady on forty-five degrees, Sir."

"Very well. Keep her so."

Inside the operating theater at the renowned if somewhat ghastly teaching hospital, things were not as in days gone by. Around the table upon which the patient lay, the light was dim, though startlingly bright within the surgical field itself. There seemed to those watching from an arena of glass panels canted inward a storey above a great many people in the theater itself. For there were many surgeons, each narrowly specialized, therefore each with an indispensible assistant of his own choosing and usually of his own training. There were the customary professional personnel to swab and irrigate and cauterize and clamp, and to move between the surgical field and the numerous tables at the periphery, over which were spread seemingly thousands of shining instruments, like polished silver forks set in rows upon tablecloths at a large buffet supper. In a sense, that is what, for the medical appetite, it was.

There was the anaesthesiologist, empillared beside the patient's head, manipulating his array of gear, exercising his customary authority over the proceedings, dealing stop-work orders for low blood-pressure, high blood pressure, cardiac arrhythmias, variations in the several blood-gas tensions. He performed tonight with bravura, aware that this historic surgery was being televised for benefit of those in the gallery above, and doubtless recorded, probably to his own eventual benefit. He played to the tiny red lights glowing about the room. Secondarily, he played to the spectators above, so numerous as to be packed into their places, though it was getting on toward three o'clock in the morning.

It didn't occur to the anaesthesiologist that he looked exactly like everybody else—a pair of eyes, all else draped and coiffed—anonymous as a dame of Arabia.

Kviedründe, at the direction of the anointed pilot, was brought to berth at Pembroke Dock. The Pilot, before exchanging the customary courtesies with the Master and Chief Officer, addressed the helmsman in his own language, to this effect: "One last 'Very well.' Shoals to port, rocks to starboard, and by seeking neither, but shunning both, we kept to the deep. And all has been very well." They shook hands.

Fitzwilliam and Edward descended onto the quay. "I will give you a lift to your car. It's back at the Station? Then I'm going to see whether I can obtain some kind of bulletin about Herrold. What was that I said just now?"

"'Do you mean 'Herrold'?"

"'Herrold.' Yes. Of course. I was told that either he would lose the arm, or that the reparative procedure would take all night. Here we are. I've enjoyed having you with me."

"Thank you, Sir. I enjoyed being along. I really can't say enough in thanks, or describe how wonderful an experience it has been. Milford Haven, I know, is the finest natural harbor in the world."

"That claim has been made. The Haven, you know, is port to a far Greater City than Milford."

Edward opened the car door. "When you are in touch with the Harbor Master, please tell him I'll hold him in my thoughts…and prayers, for what that's worth."

"He will consider it worth a great deal."

"And can you…think of any way for me to express my regret." Silence. "I consider myself responsible; everybody else will, too. The bungling fool from America."

"Look here, Edward. You're in no way responsible. And those who hear about the disaster will doubtless hear no mention of any 'bungling fool from America.' You merely happened to be the man on the ladder. Don't play yourself up, remember!"

Edward tried to thank him, but found himself unable.

"Good night, Son."

"Good night, Sir."

Edward returned to the hotel at five o'clock; Mary had slept an untroubled sleep and was awake. She saw upon her husband's face the shadow of some despair. "Good morning, Darling. What's wrong?"

"You can see that something is wrong?"

"I can; even just from the way you're standing."

"The Harbor Master was injured. Injured very seriously. His right arm has to be amputated."

"My God! How horrible! How on earth did it happen?'

"*How* it happened is one thing. Why it happened is another. He was trying to rescue me. It happened on my account."

"Let me give you something to steady you; then tell me exactly what's gone wrong."

"Thank you. I'll try to give you a brief and clear account." *In a judge's chambers, maybe.* "And maybe then we can have breakfast? I haven't had so much as a drink of water since I left here."

"Of course." But by the time the spirit had taken hold, Mary realized that she was going to have the benefit of the whole story. Full details. In truth, she had known all along this would be so. They lay side-by-side upon the bed, Mary under the covers and Edward upon their cool, satiny surface, and they held hands. Edward told his tale while the darkness broke into bits and stole away. He was in tears as he finished.

"It's my fault, isn't it?"

"It is certainly *not* your fault. You may have been the one he was trying to rescue, but you neither willed nor acted in such a way as to have him injured. Order breakfast, then we must see the town. There are so many bits of public park, it seems to have been plunked down into the midst of somebody's garden. Complete with *folies*, which are actually historic ruins. Ones that speak, if you listen. There is much more here than just the Haven."

That afternoon, Edward learned that the Harbor Master had recovered and could have visitors. They turned in their car at Cardiff and travelled by air to London.

There are numerous illustrious teaching-hospitals and hospital trusts in the Capital. The Harbour Master had been taken to St Thomas' Hospital, because that was where the numerous specialists required could at the time be most easily assembled. To Mary and Edward the experience of visiting a patient in such an institution was novel and initially trying.

But when they had cleared the barriers in the van and reached the ward where the fallen Captain lay, all became suddenly simpler. There seemed few formalities and fewer restrictions than in the ordinary hospitals each knew. The nursing sister primarily charged with the Master's care was a middle-aged woman, polite, even friendly. But, above all, self-assured.

"It is one of the most remarkable cases in the whole consortium at the moment; there has been much curiosity. Of course, only *professional* curiosity has been gratified. To think that the Press have tried to get in here! Naturally, they have met with no success. I was myself among the phalanx organized to rebuff them. A few are young and deliberately put on sweet faces. But they get no more from me than the rest. No less, either."

They came to a door. Edward stopped. So did the two women. He said: "May I ask you before we go in? Were they able or unable to save the extremity?" Two factors came into play: One was Edward's choice of words. With 'the extremity,' instead of 'his arm,' through conditioning the nurse assumed he had a medical background of some kind. The other was the expression of doubt that, at St Thomas', the possibility of failure could be imagined.

"Come with me," she ordered. She led them down a narrow corridor, and into a darkened room, along one side of which ran a desk-like shelf. Above this were lighted panels of white glass. Radiograms were strewn all over the desk. Some had been left fixed to the light-boxes. A few had even fallen onto the floor. This was the Work-Only found in teaching-hospitals and, probably, to an extent cultivated. The nurse deftly extracted two films from the jumbled heap. "Now. Look at this." She flicked a square of celluloid into a clip at the top of one of the viewing-boxes. It looked as though a handful of pebbles and sticks, white, had been scattered onto a dark ground. The pattern overall suggested a chevron. Demarcations of soft tissue were detected once pointed out.

"Good God!" Edward said. The nurse registered satisfaction.

Mary achieved some credit by exclaiming: "I hope that isn't as bad as it looks! To the untaught eye, of course."

"My dear, it is *worse* than it looks. But, compare:" And the nurse arranged for their examination the second film. Here the twigs and gravel had been arranged to form an easily recognizable human elbow.

"And they are one and the same?'

"Sir, they are."

"It almost defies believing," Edward said as they trooped out of the room. "What a rich resource this hospital is to Great Britain!"

"Oh, no. A great deal—if not the preponderance—of our work here is done for the sake of cure...purely."

"I meant 'rich' in terms of training and skill."

When they had got back to the door to David's room, they were asked to wait outside, to be announced. "We don't want to wake him if he's asleep, or disturb him in any other way."

"Mr. and Mrs. Edward Strikestraw."

They were admitted at once.

The Dead Man, the Survivor, John Doe, David Herrold had begun in the recovery room to awaken before he gave any sign of it, and he intended to maintain matters in this state as long as he might. For byways within his brain had begun to reopen as the anaesthetic wore away, and many others had further begun to open into each other, making connections between declivities in his mind separate and vacant up to then. It was not so much that his lost memory, along with consciousness, had suddenly begun to return in flood intact; he could now identify an armature, some of its wiry branches in leaf of the modeller's clay, others in bud, others merely beginning to be a little more turgid than before with promise of vitality; others were dormant, and some were quite rusted dead.

But he was aware of remembering things forgotten, and of the potential for remembering others yet. For the man he had been in that bare room at Scapa Flow a quarter-century before, with the clock which had waited for consent from Good King George before ticking over to the ensuing second, had survived all the long years and was with him now, apparently to meet, to guide, to control the man he was becoming, at who knew what behest.

"Remember," the man of 1942 was saying, "that you had put down what you had been until that afternoon. You abandoned your baggage on the concourse and boarded a train forward."

"I don't deny it."

"But you are preparing to deny it, because you have somehow got an inkling of what was inside that baggage."

"Shouldn't you be curious—even covetous—if you were in my situation now?"

"Remember, I *am* in your situation."

"Then why don't you stop talking down to me."

"Why not leave the answer at this: My mind was waking when yours was sleeping?"

"Are you saying you knew then all that had gone before?"

"Yes, in a way I'm saying that; but we are one. You knew everything I knew. But I was able to access it quickly; it has taken you until now, and you're not even yet acquiring data particularly efficiently."

"I can't help that."

"No. That is why I've come to see you while you're rather...'betwixt and between.'"

"Aren't you so?"

"Hmm. Yes. But rather more betwixt than between. If you take my meaning."

"I don't."

"No, I don't really think you ought to. The crisis here comes from our being only...."

"...Being only beasts of burden."

"Yes. We seem all to be beasts of burden, and the heaviest burden is our identities...ourselves. Each one of us is supposed always to be himself, and keep always at it. And it requires effort...Oh, at times nearly superhuman effort!"

"I came to myself one day free of any burden. They wanted to heft it—bit by bit, I should imagine—back onto my shoulders."

"Weren't you due to let them try?"

"I hadn't any trust in them. I thought they were out of their own depth, were charlatans. That I might get somehow bound up with them and their methods for the rest of my life. I hadn't much self-confidence, having no memory. No self, as a matter of fact. Certainly not enough resolve to face *that*.

"I arrogated the choice of leaving the unremembered aside.

"Yes, that is what I did. From overestimation of my ableness—a delusion that's been with me from a child! But I believe a lot of weight was behind the idea of my being myself, envying no one else, not very much interested in anyone else, speaking in a restaurant no louder than so as to be heard only by those at my table, and so on."

"Cut off from the burden, without knowing its value, I think you were unwilling to stoop…to resume. The weight of your identity."

"What makes you so sure you know what moved me, how I felt then, alone."

"We weren't alone. While you've been 'fighting the good fight,' I've been going back over it all."

"Did we know why we did what we did?"

"I've concluded that we did it that way because you could stride out unburdened for a while, freely into whatever we were to become. And we did, and now you have become it. And we haven't the right to grasp greedily at what I had been, just because now it drifts back across our life, a refreshing breeze, its renovating aftertaste the first sweet breath of spring."

"You can start over, if life falls apart. But only from where you stand. You can't go *back* and start over."

"No, you can't."

"Then I must resume none of it—we mustn't. Because, if I should, everyone to whom I might owe allegiance would feel that allegiance had been divided, and in division, diminished."

All that time ago, he had quoted to himself, almost heard the walls whisper to him: "…rather bear those ills we have/ Than fly to others that we know not of." He had not known at that time what heritage he might be due from the past, but he sensed his abilities, and therefore sensed a large part of his chances for the future. He had decided upon that future; it, at least, was actual. He had decided to relinquish a past which in any case might remain forever closed to him. But whether or not, to relinquish it for good and all.

For all that some of that past had now been recovered, he was left no ullage for reversing his decision. He must look at the obverse of it and look it steadily in the eye and squarely in the face.

He must have moved. Or he must have spoken—or more likely groaned. For a nurse was immediately at his side. She spoke, and he answered. She called others to join her. "Sir," she asked, "are you aware of any pain?"

"No."

"Do you feel able to wake up a little more?"

"Yes. But it would take more effort than I wish to make just at the moment."

"Would you like to see your wife?"

"Yes. But it would take more effort than I wish to make just at the moment."

The nurses moved off a distance and conferred. "Is that perseveration?"

"I don't think so. He meant the same answer to both questions, and he had framed it once. I think he repeated it because it was apposite."

The first nurse returned to the patient: "Sir?"

"Yes?"

"Do you know you have been injured?"

"No." Then: "Oh, yes, I had come to that conclusion somewhere by the way. I don't know much about it, though."

"Can you open your eyes?"

"Yes. But it would take more effort...."

"Never you mind. You have been treated successfully. Can you hold this?" She slipped the handle of a call-bell into his left hand; she did not wait for an answer. "If you should need anything, or when you feel a little more alert, then depress this button. The doctor will come in and speak with you about what has happened and what has been done."

"Thank you. But now there are some things I want to think about."

"Don't try to think, Sir. Just rest, for now."

Thinking, to David, required no trying, and being left alone to do it was the most restful thing he could imagine.

He gave himself up, then, and settled back into the lingering cloudlets of anaesthesia and, he hoped, into the simultaneous anamnesis it was producing as in vapor it departed. After a little while he roused himself and said aloud: "No. I may not." And he depressed the little red button beneath his finger, not so forcibly as if he could have done it right-handed.

The nurse, coming out of the hospital room, added: "He's extraordinarily eager to see you; please go inside. Lady Frances and the children are with him." She closed the door behind them. David was looking well. He was clean-shaven, and his hair had been parted and combed. The hospital gown had been untied and the right side folded away from his chest. An intravenous line was in place for administration of an antibiotic and other medication, in the back of the left hand. Everything seemed hospital-normal, with the conspicuous exception of a pneumatic apparatus that encased the right arm. This was divided axially and circumferentially into a large number of separate compartments, which were being variously pressurized and depressurized automatically, in inapparent sequence.

"Edward," he said, extending his left hand, "I am so grateful you've come." He was understandably emotional, eyes brimming a little. Edward offered his own left hand. The man looked long at the boy. Then: "This must be your wife; I thought Fitzwilliam was exaggerating. He often does, by way of compensating for his own bachelor state. But he was speaking the simple truth."

Mary extended her hand; impulsively, David kissed her on the cheek.

"That should buck you up a good deal, Darling!" David's wife said, as she came forward to greet the couple. She was a small, fine-looking woman in a black dress, unadorned.

David said: "This is my wife, Frances, and these are our children." Frances mustered the brood for introductions: The eldest was a girl ten years of age, named Grace. Another two years and there was a boy, evidently ready to take on all comers, called David. The next step down brought an ethereal-looking child named Arabel.

Their mother then announced: "I'm sure Mr. Strikestraw and your Father would like to take up where they left off. Mary, shall we take them down to tea and have a little visit of our own?" The children formed up once more to kiss their father goodbye, and then the two men were left together.

"You're looking very well indeed, Sir. And I've been shown the radiogram of the injury. I can't think you're not in terrific pain."

"No. Really, very little. If it seems to be fleeting, I ignore it, of course. But if it sets in, then I've been told in terms very plain—you've met Nurse Sutton—to tap this little pad, and I get a jolt of morphine. I don't think it's much. I don't want to end as a derelict living in the Underground. Come to that, there is no underground in Milford.

"By the way, I hope any erratic behavior of mine will be put down to the drug." Here there occurred another fractional loss of voice. Our lives are full of them, if one notices.

"Well," Edward said, "the 'before' picture looked like porcupine's quills...."

"'Porcupine,' yes.... That's the woodland creature we call a hedgehog, isn't it? I have seen that picture; by comparison, what I have now seems to have been modeled by Michelangelo."

"Yes. I saw the other picture, too."

Then there came an awkward pause, for which each of them wrongly thought himself accountable. Edward took the first plunge: "I have a little speech I have to make you; I'm sorry, but I don't think I'm clever enough simply to weave it into conversation."

"Then let's have it as a speech."

"During passage up the Haven I didn't think about the accident aboard the trawler any more than I had to, and there was plenty to distract me. But as soon as it was all over, I felt oppressed by grief—mainly because we thought you'd lose your arm. And I thought it was my fault."

"Your fault? No!" David said, genuinely surprised.

"Captain Fitzwilliam said to me: 'Don't play yourself up.' That shamed me into taking myself out of the picture, so to say. Then Mary told me that any part I had in it was conditional."

"Do you know what she meant?"

"She was using grammar as a means of explanation, I believe. Any part I played was an 'If.' For example, if I hadn't had to go up first...; if I hadn't asked for this privilege in the first place...; and so on."

"And she's quite right. It's more useless to put If's to the past than it is to put them to the future: If I fall down the elevator-shaft when leaving the hospital; if I'm killed in a car crash on the way back to Wales. Please don't blame yourself. It will only make me, for one, feel worse."

"No, Sir. I will not blame myself. But I want to say to you that I am nevertheless otherwise very much distressed about it."

"Thank you, Edward."

"I must go, then."

"Please stay a little longer." Edward sat down.

"My dear girl, do leave it at 'Frances.' I thought I had made it clear to my husband that he should not introduce me the other way."

"He didn't. But the nurse said 'Lady Frances.'"

"Well, but she's the nurse; you and I met as friends."

"Thank you."

"Please! I did ask him to mention that my Grandmother died two days ago, and he left that off. I loved her a great deal. I love her still. But what must your husband think of my wearing *black* at half past two in the afternoon!"

"Edward doesn't know about things like that. But I will tell him, and explain.

"And I must tell you, English children are justly famous; yours are absolutely charming."

"Thank you. Yes, they can be sometimes. Have the two of you any?"

"We are expecting one…a boy I think. You won't believe this, but a snake told me." *Why on earth did I mention that? And to a complete stranger!*

"I say! That's not something you run across every day! Did the snake tell it you in words?"

Mary was stricken with shame, but she said: "Yes, in words."

"Well, there you are! I've always maintained that eventually you will encounter an actual instance of anything you can imagine."

"I'm relieved you don't think me insane. If in fact you don't."

"My dear Mary, if that were the strangest thing I'd heard this week, then I'd be a much less perplexed woman than you see before you.

"Speaking of seeming insane, I can't imagine what you must think of David's state of mind."

"I think, in part, it reflected his fondness for Edward, which is charming. If unexplained."

"Yes. Well. On we go! My husband insisted we name our son David, not after himself, but because he is so much attached to Wales and to everything Welsh."

"Is your husband Welsh by origin?"

"Nobody knows. He was involved in an explosion of some kind during the war. He remembers virtually nothing from before." She had been pouring, but now banged the teapot onto the table. "That was the trouble with my Mother and Father. When I told them I had found the man I meant to marry, they wanted, naturally, to know Who he Was—I suppose you know what that means in England."

"I do know. Where I grew up, it means the same."

"Well, they were perfect stinkers about it."

"I don't have to ask how it ended. But what did you do?"

"I brought him to them. They never uttered another word of dissatisfaction. I think Father was afraid, in addition to everything else, that somehow I was bringing in a kind of replacement. I had an elder brother, you see, but he was lost at sea during the War."

Fifteen months before, "Sir," David Herrold had said to his father-in-law, "I want to propose a thing to you. I have tried to think through it carefully, but I may blunder in spite of that. If I do, can we just set it aside? And continue our relationship…which for my part is very cordial?"

"Of course, David. You mustn't wound me again with this kind of mistrust." The old man was gazing out through leaded panes of misfiguring glass at the water garden, all that remained open of the original moat.

"Well, Sir, I wonder whether you might gain any solace from adopting young David?" The elder gentleman continued to look onto the water garden.

There was a variety of *Nymphaea* that opened in late afternoon—now— and remained open through nighttime, closing a few hours before dawn. He had seen it swell, betraying striae of white among the encapsulating green. Since he watched so long on this afternoon, he saw it open, and float upon the surface like a star fallen into his demesne. It would later be borne upward upon its stem.

The son-in-law resumed: "I realize we don't know anything about my lineage, and that presumably we can never know. Discounting me, however, as at least educable and in health, with Frances's genetic contribution, if you should wish to take this step, David could unite the blood, the name, and the honor." Silence. The water lily had become a phosphorescing lamp in the deepening dusk.

The Harbour Master had concluded that he had given offense and was about to see himself out.

"What does Frances say?"

"I wanted to speak with you first."

"You would give me your son?"

"Not as Abraham gave his son."

"No. Not to slay, but to keep, and to teach to keep."

"Yes, I will give you my son, to be yours under the law, so that he may give up my name and have yours."

The elder man turned to look out through the glass panes again, to be sure the water lily was burning in the darkness, then he came about and said: "What you offer me is beyond my setting a value upon.

"As to yourself, no one could find sounder breeding-stock in Town or County. And the great-heartedness of your offer makes me feel...exalted... and humbled...to know...."

"Sir?"

"I came within a hairbreadth of wounding with mistrust in my turn, in case I ventured where I ought not. But you and I do not deal in that way. I was about to say, given that you...ah...have lost so much of your past, it is immeasurably generous of you to offer your...to-come. Anybody else in your circumstance might exhibit desperate covetousness."

"There is no point my clinging to my name...to its being handed on. It is not even mine in the first instance."

"David, you are better than other men. I am not in a position—in the position you envisage—to accept your generosity. Peers can sometimes bequeath their titles, but I cannot do so in this case. It is complicated. One must go back to the Letters Patent. Usually such a bequest is made to one who might have inherited the title directly, under conceivable circumstances, which excludes Little David. I went into all that after we lost John.

"So instead, you must agree to be my son—indeed Audrey and I both think of you in that way.

"The Ridel Stones [the surname pronounced "Riddleston," as if a single word] have had a long run. We can have another of a different sort. The estates are no longer entailed. The National Trust can be surprisingly malleable. Depending upon ones's leverage, of course.

Frances continued her account: "My dear grandmother—And do please be sure to explain about the black—was the Dowager Countess of Fleatring, and my father is the present Earl. That's why I'm called 'Lady,' and very probably it is the only reason." And she went on to explain about the offer of adoption.

"But how did you feel about it, when you heard? I mean, if you don't mind my asking."

"Of course not. Feel? Cross as Hell, to tell you the truth. And I didn't recover overnight, either. But only because I resented not having been brought into it from the first."

"So all is well."

"Yes. And I'll give you an excerpt from their negotiations, to illustrate: They were in the writing room at Father's House. He drew David over to a window through which he had been serially watching a white, night-blooming water lily open, and he said, "Do you see that, David, how it seems to burn? You have made one of those open within my heart."

So both ladies burst into restrained tears.

In St Thomas', Edward had begun to feel he was making the patient weary.

"No. No, it's just the pain."

"Shall I depress the tab for you?"

"I have it, thanks." A few pale orange-colored drops passed into the intravenous line. After a moment the Harbor Master relaxed visibly, exhaling in a sigh breath he hadn't realized he had been holding.

"When it's time for me to leave, you say."

"I shall, but this is a great deal better. Please sit down again, if you have the time. I want to tell you about something, then I should like to have your view of it. My Father-in-law is *fin de ligne* .

"Lady Frances is his only child?"

"Now. But he had a son. John. Older than Frances. He was lost in the War. Anyway, Pater was naturally grief-stricken. But it was more painful and distressing even than it would have been otherwise, because he seemed determined to accuse himself of grieving for the lack of an 'heir male' in part, and in part grieving for a lost son. He thought all his sorrow should be for John his son and none for John his heir.

"What, though, do you think of that kind of grief?"

"I don't know yet. What I can tell you is that every married man in America, though, so far as I can tell, wants a son, to 'carry on the name.' And there are cases where the names they want carried on can make you wonder. I can understand the widespread desire in Colonial and Federal times, when there were only few of us. I suppose it simply endured, even though now we are bursting at the seams, and the Government is urging 'zero population growth.'

"Did you know you brother-in-law?"

"No. He was gone by the time I entered the family."

"How was he killed? I mean, if you don't mind my asking."

"He may have died near where you live, speaking broadly. He was in the Royal Navy. The Americans were suffering immense losses in sunk merchant tonnage—U-boats all up and down your Eastern seaboard, even before America came into the War. Of course, Britain had a big stake in it; if supplies couldn't be got up to the Northern ports in North America, then they couldn't be convoyed over here...and that in itself had got to be rather a desperate enterprise.

"We had been sinking German submarines already for a couple of years, so some of our sailors went across in specially-equipped trawlers, but with any weaponry concealed—they were supposed to be taken for fishermen—to try to help with the Hun pestilence over there. My brother-in-law was one of them. Nobody ever discovered exactly what took place, nor precisely when. Sometime in March of 1942.

"Remind me, what is the name of the eminence upon your coastline, the one where ships have been sinking for three...the 'Graveyard of the Atlantic'?"

"Cape Hatteras. It's shallows are called Diamond Shoals."

"Cape Hatteras. Well, southward of there, but in that region of the Ocean. It's believed John's boat engaged a submarine. Probably they were sent down by the deck-cannon. Though they may have been torpedoed. There were vague reports of an explosion. Fuel tanks, I expect. No wreckage was ever seen, no bodies were recovered."

"It's a very sad story. They all are, when you hear about particular instances like that one. Or when you know the people involved." Edward developed a lump in his throat and decided to gaze out through the window. The view did not have much to recommend it. But there were planes: Vertical ones, horizontal ones, ones aslant. Openings, stacks, flues; a flag waved among them. There was color. Photographic film would have registered it. To the sorrowing eye, it was all *en grisaille*.

"It reminds me of something, probably quite far-fetched. I grew up near Cape Fear. But you know that already. That's conceivably within the quadrants you've mentioned. In that year, and at that time of year, I think I remember hearing, the body of a seaman—not in uniform, without any sort of identification about him—was washed ashore nearby and was retrieved. It became a coroner's case of course, and my Grandfather Strikestraw was the Vicar, I think you'd say. Both of them recorded that the body had been in very deep water at some point, because it remained quite cold to the touch for many hours. The immediate coastal waters were warm. Grandfather was consulted regarding burial. He saw the body, and felt that the subject, perfectly preserved and appearing only to sleep, ought to be photographed for eventual identification, possibly, and this was done. I was only a few months old, then, and not yet living there, but I remember much later rummaging through papers one evening. I found the photograph and asked my Grandfather about it."

"Do you mean to say you think the man could have been a crewmember... even John himself?"

"I don't have any specific reason for thinking so. It's only that the circumstances you told me of suggest it as not impossible. Would you recognize him from the picture, do you think?"

"Oh, without a doubt. There's a portrait, some photographs of a formal sort, and dozens of snapshots. Do you think you could send me the picture, or a copy of it?"

"Yes, I can do that easily. I'll telephone ahead so that Grandfather can have copies made. I can put one in the mail to you—to your headquarters?"

"Yes. I won't mention it to any of the family."

Edward rose to leave. He hesitated, and then he said: "Captain?"

"Yes?"

"If the occasion arises, and if you think it fit—Well, I have obviously not experienced this myself, but I have grown up rather close to it—you might tell your father-in-law that if any father, of whatever station, is bereft of a son, then the father will mourn—and rightly mourn—all that the child was to himself and all that the child might have become to the world."

"Do you think the converse situation true? If my meaning is clear."

"Entirely clear, and, yes, I do believe it to be true, too. At least if the orphan knew the parent. If not, then, No."

A few more drops of the orange-colored fluid passed into the intravenous line. A crimson few millimeters of blood flowed retrograde into the fine tubing at the back of David's hand, then was washed clear. Edward waited for a moment. Then: "Goodbye, Sir."

"Goodbye, Son."

Their several remarkable experiences now receding from them as the lands where these had taken place fell back, the New World hastening up to the horizon, Mary sleeping in order not to be on hand for the flight, Edward took stock of the life of home. In the first place, that meant Alenda and Thomas, for when he had telephoned from London to ask that the photograph be found and reproduced, Alenda had given the impression that Edward's grandfather was in no condition to fulfill such an obligation. Not just then. That he would see for himself upon his return.

Accordingly, nothing had been accomplished in that direction, although the Harbor Master was already eagerly awaiting the copy, as well as word from Edward of a general sort.

They ran into turbulence; Mary awoke. "Oh, is it tomorrow morning?"

"It is," Edward answered. For the sun, as if astride a Lion swifter than any pard in his eagerness to reach his Virgin consort, had now overtaken them, speeding ahead, leaving the ink-blue darkness suffused with light. The leading edges of the wings of the aircraft glinted silver. "I've ordered you a glass of orange juice." But Mary had gone back to sleep, her head on Edward's shoulder.

Once at home, as soon as they had got settled, Mary and Edward went to New Brunswick to have dinner with Alenda and Thomas. The conversation, which they all had assumed would be about the adventures in Siberia and Niger and Wales, was not. Nothing the travellers felt they could relate seemed of any interest. Besides, Alenda seemed distracted, and this was clearly because of Thomas's condition, which was altered. He had by now lived for eighty-five years.

He was amiable; he seemed comfortable. He didn't blurt out batty things in the middle of talk. But his purposiveness seemed relinquished.

When dinner was over, and the table cleared by a still fully purposive Rhodë, Thomas asked that his and Edward's coffee be served them in his study. "I want to give Alenda an opportunity to tell Mary, who can tell you, how 'poorly' I'm doing."

"Are you doing poorly, Grandfather?"

"No, I don't think so. I think I'm doing rather well to be drawing breath upon the wheat-bearing land at all. The rest are almost all dead, and so shall I be, soon."

"Drawing breath upon the wheat-bearing land, but your knees not quick beneath you?"

"Exactly so."

"Well, then. I can't see the problem. But if there is one, or are some, that you'd rather describe to me than to Alenda, be sure to, and I'll come and help in any way. And, if I can brighten your days, tell me how."

"Just be my buddy."

"From start to finish. Now, though, I have something in particular to ask you about: I met a lady in London whose brother was lost at sea during the War. She is the wife of the Harbor Master of Milford Haven, where I had the opportunity of being aboard an oil-tanker as she was brought into the Haven and through, to be docked. He was able to tell me a good deal of what was known of the circumstances surrounding the brother's death. It all brought to mind the drowned sailor whom you buried—wasn't it in March of 1942?"

"Yes. That's right. It was. I remember it clearly. Alenda's son was involved in that business from the first, and he can refine my account, but this is what I recall." And Thomas went on to tell the story, to his grandson's mind apparently in complete detail. He mentioned how the body had been uncorrupted and spoke of the photographs he had had made. "I remember that, at the last minute, I interrupted the photographer in order to open the eyes and instill a drop of glycerine into each, hoping that the reflected light would not allow the camera to record the cloudiness of the corneas. I didn't know what the effect might be, so of course I got the man to make the picture we had originally planned, with the eyes closed. And when I closed the lids, the glycerine was expressed onto his cheeks, and ran down, I thought, like tears."

"Do you remember where the pictures are?"

"Certainly. I'll get them." Thomas got up from his chair; Edward sought to stop him.

"Stay where you are, Grandfather; tell me, and I'll look."

"No, no. I can put my hand on them right off." Indeed, there was no blunting nor retardation in his speech or movement. But there was a sense that his impulse to do what he was doing came not from within, but entirely from outside himself, that is, from prevailing circumstances. "Here they are," he said, as he withdrew from the 'relegation drawer' in his desk, as Alenda had called it ten years before, a thin sheaf of papers. He sorted through them for a moment, handed two to Edward, and returned to his chair.

Edward was startled by the image of the drowned man with the eyes open, the globes glistening with what seemed to be the normal film of tears. This man seemed, on the evidence given, quite alive. The other picture—the one he had come across in childhood—as he had expected, seemed to show a man asleep. Edward was therefore undecided about which to mail to Milford Haven; the 'alive' one would surprise David Herrold, but it could not, in case it should prove to represent his brother-in-law, be shown to the parents, and, he thought, should not be shown to Lady Frances, either. "The open-eyed one is remarkable, Grandfather. Your genius crops up everywhere! But it could give the family in Britain a jolt. If it's of the right man. I'm going to leave both of them here..." He replaced the pictures upon the desk, shuffled through the others cursorily, recognizing the larger, brighter figures as relations he knew, had known, or had known of; failing to see anything familial in the smaller-drawn persons, deeper shadowed in sepia. "...Think over it, and make a decision, and bring an addressed folder for mailing—they'd crack, I think, if rolled into a tube. I'll telephone first, of course."

"There is no need for you to call ahead; in this house you must come and go as freely as you and Bobby McCallum did as lads in summertime. I'll leave all this out until you've decided."

Edward kissed his Grandfather Goodnight, for he was growing fearful of Goodbye, and soon he and Mary were back at their house in Wilmington, attempting to calculate Mary's estimated date of confinement. Mary was unable to offer with certainty any information they might use in this effort, and both of them realized they ought to have asked Sis about it.

"Alenda?"

"Hello, Edward."

"We enjoyed our evening with you."

"Do you see what I mean about Thomas?"

"Yes, but I don't think anything's particularly wrong; I think his life here is just drawing to a close. He thinks that, I believe."

"Yes." And she did not continue for a moment, following which she asked: "How is Mary getting along?"

"Getting along?"

"With the pregnancy."

"Oh. She told you."

"No. She didn't. I heard it over the radio. Additionally, men treat their wives in a specific way when the wives are *enceintes*. And of course I noticed that. But I assure you, I did first learn of it over the radio. I'll tell you about it, next time you are free to come over the river and through the housing-developments to 'build' us a pitcher of martinis."

"Alenda, are you…is anything the matter? I don't think I've understood you correctly."

"Oh yes you have. But it can wait. If you can."

"Well. Did Grandfather tell you about the photographs?"

"He did. What an extraordinary thing!"

"It is. Although I can't see how you can regard *that* as extraordinary, if you've heard on the radio that Mary's going to have a baby.

"Anyhow, I had meant to come there today, but I'll be tied up in Court. A courier is coming for the photograph I want to send. If you could give it to him, he'll slip it into an addressed envelope and bring it back to the offices. I'll add a note to Captain Herrold, then it can go out in the office-mail tomorrow."

"Or the next day, and so on, and by the time it reaches Wales, no one there will know what to make of it. I'll post it as soon as I have the envelope. You can write your letter during the session and send it separately."

"Thanks. Give my love to Grandfather. Thanks, again."

As he was hanging up, "Edward!"

"Alenda? Did you still need me?"

"Which picture have you decided to send? Or, both?"

"Thank God you asked! No, not both. The second one from the top."

But Rhodë, while seeing to the study that morning, had noticed the little stack of papers on the Canon's desk, which was not usual. She bent over and squinted at them, with, of course no plan to put them away. That was not her business. She had been as shocked as Edward at the portrait of a dead man with his eyes open, so she had rearranged the stack a little.

William Fitzwilliam, as he munched a bit of *pâte à chou* in the form of a swan, *crème pâtissière* jetting satisfyingly all about, realized that the life of time and change had a lot to recommend it. He had staged for his own enjoyment a fantasy, a reliving, with every sensible thing or circumstance woven into the fabric of a daydream. He sat, now, upon the perilous balcony of the hotel in Milford Haven, amid billows of crisp white table-linens, having the most sumptuous tea the establishment could muster. He reveled in the sweetmeats, and pretended that Mary Strikestraw was seated, back-to-back with him, at the next table. He pretended to anticipate the delightful collision.

You never knew what autumn—or another season, for that matter—would bring to the Haven, to her headlands and shining waters, but today all was blue and sparkling; a fragile pane, a flake as of carnelian, though, seemed to filter the sunlight. He had arranged this, as well. Perfection!

A little later, in the hotel bar, in deeper recesses of it this time, where he resorted for an antidote to the tea itself, for he was extremely susceptible to theism, he reviewed the memories of summer he had in reserve—Mary, Edward, David Herrold as he'd been then, the excitement of the catastrophe, which he had not been accorded an opportunity to prevent, *Kviedr ünde,* her Master, her Helmsman, crew, the opening of the leading lights at just the expected moment, the reeling of the heavens, sprinkling their light among the wavelets. He must admit there had been a magic in it, and he felt for those moments and days a wistful recall.

It is not impossible that I am becoming human.

David Herrold had recovered, the only sequelae being that he now wore long-sleeved shirts exclusively of other kinds, and had become slightly ambidextrous . Well, two large whiskies down the hatch. Time now to get to work.

At last the photograph from America arrived; the envelope lay upon the Harbour Master's desk. There would certainly be a letter from Edward included. David Herrold sat down, took up a paper knife, slit the envelope carefully across the top, for, unless a copy, the picture would, after three decades, be fragile.

He drew out the contents: There was no letter, and the photograph was of Edward.

Yet he had not thought of Edward Strikestraw as a young man to be in the habit of sending round likenesses of himself. But David knew this man; it was Edward. Edward, yes. The features, the mildly quizzical look straight into the camera-lens, the lips parted a little. About to protest something? To interrogate the photographer?

But there were obstacles: The subject looked to be about twenty-five years old. The hair seemed far too tidy for the late 1960's, when Edward would have been that age. Neither did the cut of the collar to the open sports shirt square with the style of those times. The photographic print itself seemed much older than ten or twelve years.

Fitzwilliam's reverie continued for a while, failing gradually. When he reached the quay at Pembroke Dock, the sun still shone. The paving-stones were dry, but damp leaves clung closely to them, seeming skillfully painted there; maple-leaves, glistening yellow against the grey rock, smooth at once and edgy as sand of the desert.

He removed three cardboard boxes from the boot of his car, stacked them for awkward portage, and set off down the way to Conservancy Headquarters. The parcels, a "lazy man's load," swayed, threatening to fall, and bumped against the door as Fitzwilliam scrabbled at it, seeking the handle. The Harbour Master, when he heard the noise, came to help.

But a squall of dawn-and-twilight uncertainty had gusted up within him.

"Hold tight," Fitzwilliam said, "while I go and set these down." He disappeared into the recesses of the place. And then his voice was heard, raised: "Gosh, David!" He returned; David was standing, just where he had been, quite still. "You were a fine looking young fellow!"

"What do you mean?"

"The photograph on your desk. How old were you then?"

"The picture! What were you doing in my office?"

"Setting down the new forms you ordered, Captain, Sir."

"Oh. Of course."

"I didn't rifle your desk—the thing was lying out in full view. Was I not supposed to see it?"

"Oh, no. Of course."

"Someone sent it to you? It was on top of an opened envelope."

"Yes. It was taken a long time ago."

"You could see that. It's a very good likeness, though. You must be gratified to find you were once so well to be seen as that."

"And, now?"

"For your years, you still cut a very good figure."

"Wonderful."

No accompanying letter. No word from Edward. No key to what he'd got in the mail. Besides, he didn't know the wards of the lock.

Admiring the photograph her husband had silently handed her, Lady Frances asked: "How old were you?" But her husband made no answer. "Around twenty-five, I should say. If we'd met then, they'd never have let me marry you. As I'd have been only twelve or thirteen. But I should gladly have run away with you!"

"What of the suggestion that it is a photograph of someone else?"

"If you are claiming that, then either you are lying or have a twin brother."

"I may have one, for all I know."

"Then how did the two of you come by exactly similar scars at the right upper corners of your foreheads?"

David abruptly withdrew from consciousness. His wife did not notice, since he did not fall or give any other outward sign. While absented, he saw himself entering a classroom, one used for instructing "non-college-bound" boys in automobile mechanics. Opposite, a row of shelves; above, a row of steel-casement "awning" windows. A cage of ball-bearings was hurtling toward him, struck him upon the forehead. Copious blood trickled down. He could see who had thrown the object. He could see through and beyond the windows. Then, his usual state of mind held him once more.

This was the first of three days during which David might have continued in perplexity. But he did not do so, mainly because he held that particular state of mind in low water. He brought a gin-and-tonic onto the terrace of their house, which overlooked the inner Haven. The sun had dipped below the farther bank and headland, but the sky was bright.

It's really quite simple, now I come to look calmly upon it. A photograph has arrived in the mail. I was expecting one. Only not this one. I thought it was of Edward Strikestraw; I had not been expecting that. Everybody else has taken it for a likeness of me as a young man. There are reasons for thinking they are right, and I, wrong. It's too early to allow confusion in. Lapse of time will bring the explanation for it.

No great lapse, at that. The next day, a letter arrived at the Coservancy, addressed by hand to the Harbor Master, the envelope made of white stock, at once sturdy and slightly translucent. The return address in the upper left hand corner was engraved; black ink: A law firm in Wilmington, in America.

This letter would cast all into the light.

Not all. But it did contribute additional information:

Dear Captain,

I hope you are as well as Fitz claims you are; he says you have—or appear to him to have—no trouble climbing. If you can do that, then you can do anything. Well, to be honest, I rather thought from the first you could do anything, anyway.

I want to explain about the picture. Grandfather (He, also, can do anything, or could. He seems now to be about to finish up) had not just the one I saw, but two photographs made of the drowned seaman you and I spoke about. The one I hadn't seen had been made with the subject's eyes open, and artificial tears added. It was a little alarming, actually. I did think of sending it for just you to look at.

If it came to it, then you could have shown the other one to your wife's mother and father. I consulted Mary, and she advised me to send only the one with the sailor's eyes closed. She considered it respectful.

Whether you see your brother-in-law in this, I hope all will be for the best. But I usually hope all will be for the best in everything. Even in the American system of "justice," for God's sake!

I hope you won't think this perverse or offensive, but I had a wonderful time there with all of you this summer. And I miss it, somehow.

[Not knowing how to close, wanting the closing to convey some sort of acknowledgement of nostalgia he unaccountably felt, Edward nevertheless in the end simply put:]

Yours,
Edward

All that David, now in a mode of assessing discovery, which allowed him to suppress other ways of thinking and feeling, gleaned from Edward's letter was that the picture he had got had been sent through error. He could let thought of that picture die away, keeping it to himself, without, of course, knowing what it was he would be keeping. Or he could question Edward about it. But for now, he forfeited his move.

On the day after that, a transatlantic telephone call came into Conservancy Headquarters.

"Captain? This is Edward Strikestraw."

"Oh, Edward; I'm glad to hear from you."

"Did you get my letter?"

"I did. I think you made a quite reasonable decision about the photographs, even though I should have been interested to compare the two."

"Well, I'm afraid you aren't even halfway to doing that, not yet." He hastened on, which was as well. "I had left the pictures on my Grandfather's desk. I got tied up, so I sent a courier from my office over to New Brunswick with the addressed envelope. Then I called my stepmother—step-grandmother...."

"How is your Grandfather?"

There was a little halt in the barrage of speech. Then: "He is well, given that he is nearing the end of his life."

"You feel that he is?"

"I do. And it makes me sorrowful. But nothing seems imminent."

"Good. You were saying, about the envelope...?"

"Yes. Alenda—That's my step-grandmother; but she was a close friend long before she became that—must have misunderstood. I can't think how. But she posted the envelope without either photograph. I found them both still in Grandfather's study. So I wanted to alert you about the confusion. Before you looked into an empty envelope."

So David discovered a further thing...that Edward had not himself and deliberately forwarded the by now less-than-mysterious image. All that was mysterious was who had done so, and, if there were a reason, then why.

The post-mortem photograph of John had been identified and recognized. His mother, father, and sister were coming to visit his last—or, anyway, latest—resting-place. The dates for the journey had been decided upon, and the family were beginning to prepare themselves. Their son and brother had vanished away from them thirty years before.

"I hope, Audrey," the old Nobleman said to his Lady, "that you have not got to the point of believing that we are going to be reunited with Johnny. We always knew we should be parted from him, supposing ourselves to be going first. And it has fallen out the contrary way."

"No, I am not expecting to be reunited with our son." She was, though. Her own earthly remains, which in any case, she felt, were wearing rather thin, were going to be physically closer to those of her adored boy than for many and many a long year. Long. Did longing come from "long," length of time, extent of distantiation?

"But I do wonder why people visit tombs, other than to draw closer to those they've lost. Physically, I mean. Of course we, and everyone else, go about claiming that '*They* aren't really there; only what is left of their *bodies*.'" But there will have been an especially close link between the child's and the mother's bodies.

"Custom."

"I feel awfully creaky to be making such a voyage. On the other hand, what else ought I to be expending my strength upon?"

"That is my view. I mean, regarding myself. I do wish David could go along. For Frances's sake. We shall have each other."

"Were you high-and-mighty as a little boy?"

"I suppose so," David Herrold answered his wife. "They all seem to be."

"Oh, Dear. It was heartless of me to ask. I'd forgotten: You don't know."

"It isn't heartless, in fact." At this, she wondered whether she didn't suspect he did know.

"Well, *our* little boy *is* high-and-mighty. Much as I wish it could be so, in another way I'm glad we don't have to endure his being 'Viscount Duffield.'"

As his natural parents sat talking together, presently the boy came into the room. "Mummy," he asked, "do all classes of people in America go about fully clothed? Or do some, for instance, possibly, descendants of the Red Indians, wear practically nothing. Particularly the women. Most especially the rather youngish women?"

"I've no idea. Why not ask your father?"

"What has driven you to this thirst for knowledge of foreign custom?"

"This." He handed his father a page taken from a magazine article about American celebrities having a festive gathering around a swimming-pool.

"I think, Son, that this sort of thing is played up a good deal. But that doesn't mean it's usual. Just as here the Queen doesn't ride about Town in the State coach all the time, wearing a crown and holding the Orb and Scepter. Yet to leaf through some of the rubbish published here, one might think she did."

"Ah," plain David Herrold said, apparently satisfied with the explanation.

"But surely your mother knows as much about the ways of the New World as I do.

I wonder; yes, I wonder, rather.

"Ask her view, and by all means show her the...illustrations." Which the lad crossed the room and did.

"Heavenly Father! Where on earth did you get this?"

By now plain David Herrold had started out of the drawing room and down the passageway. But he could be heard saying, his voice growing distant: "From Grandfather."

"Good Lord!" the Harbour Master said.

"I really feel he shouldn't go to America. He's too young to derive any benefit from the voyage."

"No, I must insist you take him along; it's the opportunity of a lifetime.

"And I may not go."

"You mean, you *may* go, then?"

"Not 'may' like that; I may not. I'm not allowed."

Thomas and Alenda were discussing the impending visit of the Fleatrings and their daughter. Alenda said: "You really are to be congratulated, Darling, upon having the foresight you did when the body was found. When thousands are being killed, identifying one body doesn't spring to the mind as excessively important. Then, it's someone you know; everything changes."

"Thank you, my Girl. But I was thinking only that if Robert should be lost in that way, meaning generally, then I should certainly want to...."

"Find the lost?"

"Exactly. And here was this dead boy—We keep calling him the drowned sailor, but he didn't drown, as a matter of fact—whole and sound, not at all hard to look upon for a family member waiting in a morgue, when the sheet is drawn back from the face. I just thought...."

"He didn't drown?"

"No. There was no water in the lungs. The coroner found the chest resonant on physical examination. His report was very clear, even to a layman;

I think the man's family might like to see a copy, since the findings so strongly suggest that their son was killed instantly…and not in a savage way. I shall telephone to the police station. May be they still have the original."

They had. Thomas drove the short distance himself. Alenda did not express any objection to his driving. As he was going into the station, he noted that the Living Fountain Assembly of the Saved, which had once stood next door, had been demolished. The space it had occupied had been given to the Town for conversion to a small park, and this had been nicely arranged: The area had been made into a lawn, with crosswalks of gravel. Tall shrubs, varied, but mostly Cape Jessamine, grew against the exposed walls of the buildings on either side. At the back, which was open, the grade fell away, down one of the crazy Confederate earthworks. Where the paths would have simply crossed there had been placed a rather handsome old fountain, which had been owned by the grantor of the land. It was made of zinc, with pastoral scenes in low-relief on each of its four faces. Water rose abundantly to spill from four lips in the shallow rim, one in the center of each side.

Thomas paused for a while to watch the streams fall into a surrounding gutter at the base, sunk into the ground just within the deflected paths, just out of sight. The falling streams drove up mists, and these, in the mid-morning sunlight, seemed full of rainbows.

I must hurry and get this done.

At home, Alenda was sitting at Thomas's desk. The telephone rang. She had been inclined to expect a call to come in.

"This is the Police Station, Mrs. Strikestraw; Chief Arnon would like to speak with you." She simply held the receiver, listening in silence to the transfer-noises at the other end of the line.

"Mrs. Strikestraw?"

"Hello, Iakov. I'm glad you were with him."

"Ma'am?"

"My husband is dead, isn't he? Isn't that why you're calling?"

"He's not dead, but he's not well. We want to take him to the hospital, and we have an ambulance right here, of course. But he won't go."

"What, exactly, is the matter? I mean, so far as those of you there can tell."

"He seemed very quiet—slow, without being slow. Does that make sense? It doesn't. I realize it doesn't. We handed him the copy we'd made for him. He seemed all right. Pleasant. He still does. He's alert, in a far-off way."

"One of my men counted his pulse. He said it's slow. He said it's *very* slow."

"Don't be worried. Don't take him to the hospital. I'll come and get him, and bring him back here."

"Whatever you say, Mrs. Strikestraw. I just want to be sure to do the right thing."

"Thank you; thank you for everything, Iakov—Chief! You're doing exactly the right thing."

There is no use pretending that an old man whose heart is beating only forty times a minute will be able to do anything quite normally. Not think. Not speak. Thomas, nevertheless, had lain down upon the sofa in the library and was going to try his best.

"Dear Girl, I've something upon my conscience: Since in the practical event—And I have often maintained this, including publicly—all any of us can do, short of self-delusion, is wait and trust, why did I feel I had to rile all those poor people, those poor good people, with suppositions nearly impossible to grasp?"

Alenda, who had pulled a straight chair close to her husband, now took his hand and said: "You felt you must batter their hearts, and thereby help them fend off self-delusion."

"I once thought that."

"I can think of no other reason."

"There is none, for me. But why not allow delusion to those who need it? I have delusions."

"I can't think what they may be."

"Well, I can't, either. If I could identify them, then they wouldn't be delusions." The heartbeat slowed a little further. Thomas's cerebral cells were not reaping a very rich supply of oxygen from the circulation. However, they weren't employing much oxygen, either. Alenda had begun to weep; she had known it would overtake her along this path, eventually. She bent over her husband and kissed him.

Rhodë tapped at the door jamb. Alenda beckoned. She entered cautiously, and, as Alenda held out her free hand and drew her near, the dying priest looked up and said, brightly if softly: "Rhododactylë, I am earnestly relieved you're here. I don't think I could have lived with myself if I had left without saying Goodbye."

Now! Now, Miss Grace. He's coming home to you. God be thanked and praised!

"I'm out of time, now. Nearly outside time." The present Rector of Christ Church arrived with the Holy Sacrament. Once having made sure Alenda knew he was there, he sat down in the hallway to wait until called.

"Let me see whether I can say what is in my heart.

"When our life on earth has ended, we look back and, following the

Psalmist, and many others, suppose ourselves to have been creatures of a day. Only of a day.

"Yet in the last years everyone has considered us so old, to have lived so long. And, taking particular things into account, we think the same, ourselves. But, no." Edward and Mary arrived. Edward jostled a table and lamp, and bodily drew the end of the sofa away from the wall, so that he could take his grandfather's other hand, which he kissed, from respect. Then he kissed his cheek, for he loved him.

Then the Lucases came in. Alenda summoned the Priest from the hallway. "He may like, now, to have Communion."

Thomas then said, upon seeing the Priest: "'O spare me a little, that I may recover my strength, before I go hence, and be no more seen.'" Everyone withdrew, except Alenda and Edward, who would receive the Sacrament with Thomas. Rhodë started out with the others, but Edward called her back, and Thomas said to her: "You stay with me, too, my dear old Friend."

It was raining in the West; the mountains wept.

After Communion, Alenda and Edward saw the priest to the door and Alenda said to the others that Thomas seemed to be asleep, that she would be glad if they would all return to the library. Thomas bestirred himself and continued as though there had been no interruption: "Green like the grass, we spring up in the morning; at evening we grow sere and are rept. Morning and evening, only a day. I don't mean I have recovered youth…but acquired it for the first time.

"We expend little here; there is much before us.

"I saw a vision in my blindness; I see it now: Indistinct and distant. High gates of a Great City. When I saw it first, I thought I was outside, perhaps approaching. But now, I see that here we are inside, enfranchised townsmen already."

He looked at each of them. Those closest could see without ambiguity beacon-fire reflected in his eyes, before he closed them and sighed softly, as their tone abandoned the diaphragms.